THE DAPHNE JONES MYSTERIES

WEDDINGS. FUNERALS. SLEUTHING.

PHILLIPA NEFRI CLARK

The Daphne Jones Mysteries

Editing by Nas Dean

A QUICK NOTE...

This series is set in Australia and written in Aussie/British English for an authentic experience.

CONTENTS

TILL DAPH DO US PART
Book One

THE SHADOW OF DAPH
Book Two

TALES OF LIFE AND DAPH
Book Three

TILL DAPH DO US PART

BOOK ONE

Till Daph Do Us Part

A PERFECT LITTLE TOWN

The township of Little Bridges was pretty at any time of the year with century old oak trees lining the main street and shopfronts colourfully painted to give a sense of olde-worlde charm.

On this spring afternoon people wandered about enjoying the warmth after a long, cold winter. In a small park, families shared fish and chips and locals stopped for a chat with each other. A peaceful, happy place.

Until a chilling screech filled the air.

Daphne Jones didn't have time to admire the scenery as she pursued a hooded figure across one of the 'little' bridges which was actually quite long, arching high above a slow moving, wide river.

"Uh...ah," She puffed and panted, and as she ran, attempted to remove her jacket, giving up when the gold buttons which had looked so smart in the dress shop refused to budge.

Legs pumping at the ground and much as she wanted to

believe she was breaking a sprinting record she suspected it was for slowest not fastest runner.

It was far too hot to be doing this in business clothes and shoes with heels. Even low ones.

Reaching the highest point of the bridge, she saw the hooded figure dash onto the path along the river, glancing over their shoulder.

"Staap!"

Daph, you sound like a banshee.

If she didn't hurry up she'd lose any chance of catching the criminal.

Why was nobody else around to help? John hadn't answered her rushed phone call.

She flew past a group of women, squeaking a plea to call the police but all she heard in return was a comment about how tight her clothes were. Followed by laughter.

Well, at this rate she'd be as skinny as they were in minutes. She forced down the hurt feelings. No time for self-pity.

On the flatter surface of the path, Daphne sped up. Every step squeezed her toes and jarred her ankles but she wasn't letting them get away. Not away from her and most certainly not away with murder!

As the path wound under the trees the shade brought immediate relief from the heat. But the further she went, the denser the undergrowth.

"No, no, no!" She was going to lose the hooded figure.

Heart pounding, she rounded a curve and with a sickening thud ran straight into the person she'd pursued, knocking them both to the ground.

Daphne got to her knees and then to her feet just before the other person, who pulled the hood back.

Daphne's mouth dropped open. "You."

"Me. And now you know who I am."

A few days earlier...

"I have the great pleasure of announcing our newlyweds—Mr and Mrs Tanning! Please put your hands together to congratulate them." Daphne Jones frowned and crossed out the line she'd quoted in a notebook on her lap. "Needs more oomph. Not quite right, is it, love?"

When she got no response, Daphne glanced at her husband, John, who was driving. His focused expression was familiar as the car slowed. New town ahead. He needed to concentrate.

Daphne was terrible with navigation so didn't offer to find the road to the caravan park. Instead, she closed the notebook and put that and her pen into a large floral patterned handbag on the floor near her feet. She'd fix up the speech in no time once she'd met with the bride and groom this afternoon.

John checked the side mirrors and flicked on the indicator as they approached a large sign pointing down a side street with the words 'Little Bridges Caravan and Camping Ground'.

A tingle of excitement fluttered in Daphne's stomach and she couldn't help smiling as the car, towing their caravan, turned the corner. This was a dream come true. Travelling with their own caravan. Her new career helping people celebrate the happiest and saddest times in their lives. And watching John relax as he unwound from a lifetime of running a busy real estate agency.

John drove through a wide entry and soon was pulling the car over to one side of a long driveway. He turned off the motor and grinned.

"Made it, doll!"

"Of course we did! Another wonderful place to discover."

"I'll pop into the office over there and find out where our site is."

Daphne gazed around after he left. It was a quiet time of the year for tourists in between school holidays which made booking their sites easier than during busy season. With her new line of work, she had a well-planned itinerary right through to next autumn, and even managed to factor in a couple of breaks when they'd go home to River's End for a week or two.

Once John returned with hand drawn directions, they followed a dirt road past the office until they reached an open area not far from a long row of trees. He deftly backed the caravan into the allotted space.

Out of the car, Daphne stretched and breathed deeply of the country air. "Is that the river?" She didn't wait for an answer. John was already unshackling the car and would be busy for a while setting things up the way he liked, so she headed in the direction where she'd caught a glimpse of water.

There were no other sites between theirs and a buffer of gum trees. Beyond the gums, a row of willows dipped their branches into a wide, slow moving river. The town peeked through trees and bushes on the other side and Daphne couldn't wait to explore. She hurried back to John.

"Do you think we should drive to town? Or walk?"

John had backed their large sedan next to the caravan and was working on connecting the power. "Bit busy at the moment."

"Yes, but when we've settled in. It looks so pretty!"

He got the plug in at last and finally gave his attention to Daphne. "You are so pretty, doll. Look at you. All excited about being here." He kissed her forehead. "Let's sort Bluebell out and then we'll go for a drive."

From the first moment Daphne set eyes on their caravan, Bluebell was its name. It might be older in style and not as flashy as some of the new ones they came across, but every inch of Bluebell had been lovingly restored and improved. The interior was as modern as one would wish for with every convenience that could be fitted into the small space. But it was the outside, with its vibrant blue colour and touches of white in contrast which drew attention wherever they went.

'Sorting' Bluebell out took an hour. John was particular about his routine after settling at a new ground. Inspect the exterior including the tyres for any sign of wear or damage. Ensure the caravan was secure and properly plugged to power and water. Unravel the matching awning so they had an outdoor area ready to use.

Meanwhile, Daphne checked inside for anything which might have come loose. From a drawer she took out a handful of special things she always put away when driving. One of these was a snow globe and she turned it upside down then placed it onto the windowsill in the kitchen. The globe was a gift from their dear friends, Christie and Martin, and depicted their own little town of River's End.

She made up a shopping list. They'd used up the

remainder of their food before leaving the last town and she needed to find a supermarket.

"Can't have John hungry after such a big drive." She added the ingredients for chocolate chip cookies as an afterthought. Nothing like them to go with a cuppa.

"Ready, love?"

Daphne ran a loving hand over the door as she closed and locked it after climbing out. "We'll be right back."

Little Bridges was a delightful town. Daphne longed to take a leisurely stroll around the shops but John reminded her she had an appointment. She'd come back tomorrow, after the wedding. They located a supermarket and as they wandered, John added a few items to the list. Daphne made sure he didn't notice her put the packet of biscuits back on the shelf. He loved her homemade ones much more and she'd bake them after meeting with the happy couple-to-be.

"I'll unpack, love." Daphne piled bags onto the small counter in the caravan. "Then I'll make us a quick sandwich before getting changed."

"No, you get changed and I'll do this." John opened the first bag. "I thought I might cook outside tonight on the grill. Maybe take a picnic blanket down near the river to eat."

"You are so romantic." Daphne kissed his cheek. "I might be a bit distracted though, depending on this meeting." She squeezed past him to go to the bedroom. "You know I do like to practice a bit before the ceremony."

"You can practice all you want. Have you seen the chocolate biscuits?"

He'd noticed. Of course he would.

"All that processed stuff isn't good for you, John Jones. And not nearly as nice as the ones I make." She peeked back to the kitchen. He was holding up the packet of chocolate chips in one hand and flour in the other with something which surely wasn't a grimace on his face. He must be imagining how delicious they were. "Keep those out, love. I'll make a batch once I'm back."

"Um, no need, Daph. You have enough to do today."

How sweet of him. "I always have time for you. You and homemade cookies."

A NOT SO PERFECT FAMILY

At exactly three minutes to two, Daphne waved to John as he drove away. He'd dropped her outside the home of the bride-to-be, Lisa Brooker. And a monster of a house it was with multi-levels, columns and balconies. Almost something out of a glamour magazine. It took up the full width of the end of a dead-end road.

She straightened her jacket. "Deep breath, Daph." Meeting her clients always got her heart beating a bit faster. Bookings for her officiant services were usually done through the fancy internet portal on her website so she rarely met a couple more than a couple of days before their wedding. There were always phone and often video calls between first contact and first meeting, but still, she never ceased to be amazed by how different some people were in person than she'd expected. She tightened her grip on the soft-sided briefcase John bought her as a Christmas gift last year and lifted her head. Time to get to work.

Stained glass double doors swung open before she'd climbed the half dozen stairs and a man stepped out.

"Mrs Jones?"

"Why, yes. But its Daphne. Please, call me Daphne, or Daph." She reached the man, who was about her age and dressed in a sombre black suit. As if in mourning. She pushed the silly thought away as he extended his hand to shake.

"Lisa and her mother are in the garden if you'd like to come with me." He closed the door behind her as she stepped into a foyer with a sweeping staircase to the next level. "I'm Lisa's father. Bob."

The house was perfect. It might have been a display home with movie stars being photographed on its deep sofas. A wide hallway led past open rooms, all in white with timber floorboards and cowhides scattered around. She sniffed. Fresh paint smell.

"This is a lovely house."

"Not looking forward to it being overrun with guests tomorrow." He walked faster than Daphne and she had to hurry to keep up, her heels tapping on the boards. They cut through a huge country kitchen where two women stopped talking to stare at her. She smiled and offered a small wave which was met with frowns. Oh, dear. This wasn't giving off the vibe of a happy home.

After crossing a casual living room complete with an enormous television, pool table, and pinball machine, they stepped through a sliding door onto a vast timber deck. It wrapped around the back of the house, disappearing beneath a roof where a built in spa bubbled away near a tropical themed bar area. Steps led to a path around a resort style and sized swimming pool behind clear fencing. A shirt-less man in his thirties was polishing the tiles around the pool on his hands and knees.

Beyond this, the path split, one way leading to a beautiful, rose-bordered garden where a handful of people worked on creating a reception space.

"It isn't good enough, Mother!" A wail filtered through a trimmed thick hedge along the other part of the path. "I wanted lilac. Not purple. Not pink. Lilac!"

Bob shook his head and muttered. "I want. I want."

An open wrought iron gate split the hedge in two. On the other side, more wedding preparations were underway. About one hundred white chairs, half on each side of a purple carpet, faced a partly-built, circular podium large enough for Daphne, and the bride and groom. Behind it, an elderly man attempted to connect parts of a mesh backdrop together. Covered with artificial flowers, it looked more awkward than heavy but it towered over the poor man who barely kept it upright.

"Excuse me. Always something to fix." Bob sprinted to help the other man. "Dad, really? Told you to wait."

One thing Daphne had learned from her few months as a celebrant was that weddings really did bring out the best and worst in people. Most of her clients so far were lovely. Nervous sometimes. But always polite and respectful of her role. A role they'd asked her to fill and paid her quite well to do.

As she stood on the path, alone, gazing at the scene before her, an odd sensation fluttered in her stomach. One that had nothing to do with how quickly she'd eaten her lunch earlier.

An inkling of unease.

A box of ribbons and bows sat open on one of the chairs and this was where the bride and presumably her mother stood. Lisa Brooker had her hands on her hips. For some reason Daphne had expected a woman in her early twenties but Lisa was perhaps ten years older than that. Her face, although pretty, was red with rage as she glared at the older woman holding up a bow.

"But, dear, this is a pleasant colour and will look nice on the chairs."

"Are you quite insane?" There was the wail again. "This is almost the same colour as my previous wedding. I cannot be married again using the same colours!"

"Then don't get married again! Stop putting your dad and I through this!" her mother snapped.

Lisa put a hand on her chest, her voice sad. "I thought you wanted me happy. Maybe I'll just elope."

"But Lisa—"

"No but anything. If you want this wedding to go ahead, send them away and find me the right ones. Oh. Hello." Lisa spotted Daphne. "Who are you?"

"I'm Daphne Jones, your wedding celebrant."

The change in Lisa was immediate. She smiled and hurried to shake Daphne's hand. "As you can see, things are a mess. People don't listen to instructions."

"I'm sure it will all come together."

Lisa's mother stared into the box and Daphne's heart sank. The older lady was crying. She found the spare clean handkerchief kept for such emergencies and skirted around more chairs, not brave enough to step on the purple carpet.

"Hello, dear. I'm Daphne." She used her calm and supportive voice as she held the handkerchief out. "Weddings are such emotional times."

"This is my mother, Margaret. She cries a lot."

Daphne hadn't noticed Lisa follow her. The younger woman grabbed a handful of bows from the box.

"Well, what do you think, Daphne? A girl can't possibly use the same colours for consecutive weddings? Can she?"

Great. Asking the opinion of the one person who had to be all things to all people on these occasions. Daphne considered her response. If she agreed with Margaret, who wasn't her client, then the bride might have more of a meltdown. On the other hand, Lisa had already made her mother cry and in Daphne's opinion, the mother of the bride should only cry happy tears on the day of the wedding. For that matter, how many weddings had there been already?

The eyes of both women drilled into her. Tears dripped down Margaret's cheeks. Lisa had a steely expression. There really was no way to win this one.

"Sorry I'm late! The boys at work wanted to give me a send-off and I couldn't say no."

Phew. Disaster averted.

A young man wearing shorts and a sleeveless checked shirt ambled down the purple carpet. Saved by the groom... perhaps? He looked barely out of school.

"What on earth are you wearing, Steve?"

With a lopsided grin, Steve Tanning put an arm around Lisa and kissed her. She put both hands against his chest and pushed him away, her nose wrinkled in disgust.

"How much have you had to drink?"

"Couple of beers. Can't blame a man for letting his mates buy him a drink the day before he gets hitched." Steve wasn't the least bit put out by his fiancée's response and wiped his hand on his shorts before shoving it at Daphne. "I'm Steve and you must be the wedding photographer. Except where are your cameras?"

"I told you we don't need one! Don't you listen either?"

"Best not to let me loose with a camera," Daphne said. "I'm Daphne Jones, your celebrant."

"Really? Thought you'd be younger."

Margaret gasped and covered her mouth with a hand. Bob's head shot up with a glare that would frighten most people, and Lisa turned even redder than before. Bob's father, who was weaving fine wire around two pieces of background, did nothing. Except grin to himself.

Daphne lifted her chin. "We're only as old as we feel."

Steve laughed. "Well, I feel twenty three and am twenty three so what does that say about me?"

A few replies came to mind but none of them mattered. Forcing down a sudden urge to turn and walk away and not return, Daphne stared straight at Steve without a word. He shuffled his feet and looked away.

The silence dragged until Daphne remembered she was here to help them get to their happiest day. Sometimes stress made people do and say things they normally wouldn't. These were nice people underneath.

"Shall we get started?"

A HAPPY MARRIAGE

"Now, doll, you make yourself comfortable and I'll pour you a nice glass of wine and let you relax a bit." True to his word, John had laid out a picnic blanket close to the river and made several trips back and forth to Bluebell to bring their dinner over. He'd taken one look at Daphne's set face when he'd picked her up from the Brooker house and decided to make her feel extra special tonight.

Not that it was hard to spoil his wife. Since their days as high-school sweethearts, he'd loved Daphne with his whole heart. She made him smile, gave him her full support in any endeavour, and knew when he needed space. Daphne was one of those rare humans who truly did care about other people's feelings and put their needs before her own.

"I didn't mean for you to do all the work." John helped Daphne down onto the blanket. Some days her knees weren't as good as they once were and she'd been on her feet all afternoon. "Thanks. This is a lovely spot."

John opened the cooler he'd carried across. Inside on a bed of ice was a bottle of wine, dessert, and glasses. He poured the wine and handed a glass to Daphne before raising his in a toast.

"To Daphne Jones. Celebrant extraordinaire."

She touched her glass to his but didn't take a sip and to his dismay, began blinking rapidly. Since she'd got into the car, she'd said little and when she had spoken, her voice was strained. He reached for her hand and squeezed it until she looked at him.

"Tough day at the office?"

Her lips were pressed tight against each other. John took both glasses and set them on the lid of the cooler, then held his arms open. In an instant she'd shuffled close enough to lean against his shoulder and he closed the hug.

"I don't want to cry." Her words were muffled and he loosened his arms a little to better hear her. "Not worth crying over rude people."

"True. But sometimes a good cry makes you feel better."

They stayed like that for a few minutes until Daphne's heart stopped pounding against his chest and was once again a normal beat. She hadn't cried but the rims of her eyes were red when she straightened. He handed her back her glass and this time she took a sip.

"Why don't you fill me in while I serve dinner?"

"Shall I help?"

"Nope." He opened the picnic basket and drew out a foil wrapped platter. "Went fishing in the river. Thought you'd like some of my world-famous fish tacos."

"You made all of this?" Daphne sniffed the air as he unwrapped the platter. "Why do you look after me so well?"

"Hey. No tears now!" John leaned over and kissed Daphne's cheek. "Tell me what happened."

"You know I don't take offence easily but the groom was

not pleasant. Nor the bride nor her father and even her grandfather. No lilac and past weddings and my age." The words tumbled over each other.

John shot her a look. "Your age? What has that got to do with anything. Or anyone?"

"The groom said he didn't expect me to be so old. That's after he mistook me for the wedding photographer. And nobody told him off."

"Wait on, love. The groom said that?" His chest tightened. Why would anyone say such a thing?

"He did. He's so young, John. Twenty three but he acts a lot younger. Turned up after going to the pub with his mates. In shorts and old boots."

"Age is no excuse for rudeness. So, they're a very young couple?"

Daphne took a minute to answer, enjoying a mouthful of the white wine before shaking her head. "Lisa, the bride, is thirty two. Now I'm not one to judge, and that age difference might not matter when both people are sensible, but the way they behaved today was immature. Lisa yelled at her mother a few times over silly things like the wrong colour bows for the chairs."

After filling a plate for Daphne, he started piling food onto his. "Maybe you've been lucky so far. Every wedding has been wonderful and you've come away thrilled to bits. Do you think they're just nervous?"

"Him, I can understand although he didn't even act as though tomorrow is his big day. But Lisa knows what to expect. This is her third wedding."

"I beg your pardon?"

"Only time I felt a bit sorry was when her mother told

me she'd lost two husbands." Daphne put down her wine glass and picked up her plate.

John had it on the tip of his tongue to point out that if Lisa Brooker was really so unpleasant her previous husbands may have had reason to divorce her.

"Nobody should be a widow so young." Daphne lifted a taco. "You're so clever, love. I'm starving." She took a bite and closed her eyes with a moan and then a smile.

Twice widowed and now about to marry again. John couldn't imagine marrying three times in a few years. With a bit of luck the Tannings would enjoy a long life together. Lots of time for them to annoy each other rather than ganging up on his wife or any other unsuspecting folk.

SAM, SHANE AND STEVE

A wonderful evening by the river, listening to the birds settle for the night, watching the sun set with the man she loved was enough to leave Daphne in a calm state of mind. Ready to begin again. She'd slept well after deciding not to work on the ceremony while upset. After breakfast and a nice cup of tea, Daphne had taken her notebook and gone for a walk where it was quiet beneath the willows.

She spent an hour tinkering with the words and then rehearsed until everything clicked into place in her mind. Despite their behaviour, Lisa and Steve had helped her out by having their vows typed and ready. She'd had them practice a few times so the whole event wasn't a complete shock, but whether Steve would remember was another thing. He'd definitely had a few beers and by the time they'd finished, he looked more interested in sprawling on the grass than standing in position.

Her last job before dressing for the event was to transcribe her most important notes into the ceremony book. Here she kept every service she did and she loved the look and feel of the bound and engraved book. When she'd been little, her mother had a diary with her name engraved on the front. It was forbidden to touch, which made it all the more mysterious. Mind you, it had a combination lock so was quite safe from the prying eyes of small children.

When John drove up the street to the Brooker house, Daphne's stomach churned and her hands shook so she held them tight within each other on her lap. This wasn't good, this feeling of dread in her gut.

Marry them and leave. It is only an hour until the ceremony. You can do this.

Daphne's life growing up was tough and she'd learned to talk herself into a better mindset when the old feelings of anxiety emerged. One day she'd talk to someone professional but most of the time she could talk reason to herself.

"Daph? You okay, love?" John stopped the car a short walk from the driveway, which overflowed with cars. "Would you like me to hang around?"

Yes! Except, no.

"You're so sweet. But I'm fine. And in exactly," she checked her watch, "two hours, I'll be waiting here and there will be a newly married couple in town."

A kiss or two and a check in the mirror later and Daphne was forcing her feet forward. The sense of dread hadn't lessened but at least she could concentrate on action rather than worrying.

She decided to go around the house first and take a look at the final set up in the garden. Then she would find the bride and go over any last minute questions. People were mingling in the reception area. It was bright and beautiful with lots of lilac and white decorated tables and chairs. There was a spot for the band who were going to play for the afternoon and white aproned catering staff busied themselves unpacking plates and glasses.

Half a dozen or so young men in suits took turns drinking champagne directly from a bottle. One of them was Steve. Daphne raised her eyebrows but kept going. It was none of her business.

A handful of guests were already seated for the wedding. It was quiet here apart from soft piped music and hushed conversation. Daphne smiled at those who glanced at her and inspected the podium. The purple carpet was gone, replaced by one closer to lilac. Each chair was covered with white fabric decorated with lilac bows. Lisa had got her way. The podium itself had a couple of large vases of flowers. The backdrop of greenery was wound with lilac coloured artificial flowers, and although it looked ready to fall with a gust of wind, it did provide a pretty background. She stepped onto the podium and faced the audience. This was a nice sized area so no need for a microphone. Her voice would carry to the back.

As more people trickled in through the gate, Daphne returned to the house.

"Mrs Jones." Margaret carried a tray of champagne glasses out of the kitchen. "Would you like a glass?"

"Daphne. Thank you but no. Best I keep a clear head."

"Someone should. I apologise for everyone's behaviour yesterday. You were spoken to quite rudely."

"Weddings sometimes put people on edge. No need to worry."

"The problem is Lisa's choice of husbands."

Daphne didn't know how to answer, so kept her mouth shut.

Margaret handed the tray to someone going past and

looked over her shoulder before continuing in a hushed tone. "Steve is nice enough, of course. But I keep thinking Lisa is trying to find someone just like her first husband. She loved him so much."

"How awful for her to lose two husbands. Is Steve like her first one, then?"

"Like him? They were cousins. Same as her second husband. Lots of big families around here and all three men she's chosen to marry were related to each other."

Daphne clambered for an appropriate response, but only came up with, "Did they both have a genetic disease? I mean, to die so young? And related."

Stop babbling, Daph.

Margaret didn't blink an eye. "No. Actually, they both had accidents. Sam was electrocuted and Shane fell off a ladder. Terrible accidents. Steve's family won't even attend the wedding because they somehow blame my Lisa."

"Oh goodness. What a shame. Best to keep Steve in bubble wrap!"

Aware she was at risk of going from bad to worse with her words, Daphne excused herself and found a bathroom where she locked herself in and fanned her face. She grabbed her phone from her bag and dialled John.

"Love? You okay?"

She whispered. "Yes. But Steve is the third in his family to marry Lisa."

"Unusual."

"Sam, Shane, and now Steve. Electrocution and a bad fall."

"Must have been bad. I mean if the poor bloke died."

"Yes! Exactly. And his family don't approve. Do you

think she's one of those black widows, John? What if Steve is next? Should I refuse to marry them?"

Even as she said the words, Daphne knew she was over-reacting. The upset from yesterday must have clouded her judgement. Good thing she'd not accepted the glass of champagne, although perhaps she should. It might calm her nerves a bit.

"Daph? Take a deep breath and pull yourself together. It won't be long and then I'll be there to pick you up. What if we go into town for dinner tonight?"

She gazed at her reflection. Her eyes were too wide open. Startled. John was right. Take a breath and stop seeing things that weren't there.

"Sounds lovely. Dinner with my husband."

"Are you feeling a bit happier?"

"I am. Thank you, love."

"Only ever a call away. See you in a bit."

Daphne switched her phone to the silent setting and pushed it to the bottom of her bag. A glance at her watch made her heart jump. Time to check on the bride.

"You can do this, Daph." She smiled at her reflection. "Everyone is counting on you to make this a perfect ceremony and you can. You are special, and have a good heart."

With no further ado, Daphne opened the door and strode out.

A SHORT MARRIAGE

Fifteen minutes past schedule, the bride emerged through the open gate and walked down the aisle. Lisa gripped her father's arm and took care with her footing. If she'd had too much champagne then she was a good match for the groom. Short of doing a breathalyser test, Daphne couldn't judge their exact state and decided if they couldn't manage their vows then she'd call for a postponement. People had to be of sound mind when taking such a big step and she was the one who had to make these moments flawless.

Her job was to ensure their ceremony was perfect.

As perfect as a wedding with only one side of the family present, plus the groom's large group of semi-inebriated friends, and a demanding third time bride could be.

What could possibly go wrong?

Her concerns were unfounded and the ceremony, including the vows, went as planned.

As the final words were spoken, Daphne crossed her fingers beneath the ceremony book. Lisa had made her declaration first, a mix of old and new they'd chosen themselves. Now, Steve finished his part of the vow.

"Forever together, sick or well, rich or poor, until death do us part!" he finished with a flourish. And should have stopped there but as he slipped a wedding band onto Lisa's finger, he leaned closer with a grin and in a loud whisper, "You before me, darl. Given the age difference."

Lisa stepped back and the colour drained from her face as she snatched her hand away.

A stunned silence from the guests at the front was followed by queries of "What happened?" "What did he say?" from further back. Bob's mouth had dropped open and the expression of fury on Margaret's face was enough to scare anyone.

This could turn ugly fast. Daphne closed her book with a loud, "I pronounce you husband and wife. Steve, you may kiss Lisa."

For a moment it was more likely Lisa would storm off the platform. Steve gave her a lopsided smile. "Sorry, darl. I'm so nervous. Love you to the moon and back."

The anger in Lisa's eyes drained away and then she threw herself at Steve and they kissed.

"Let me introduce the happy couple, Steve and Lisa Tanning!"

Daphne raised her hands and the guests stood, clapping. And some whistling from Steve's friends. The newlyweds stopped kissing and joined hands and moved into the audience, leaving Daphne alone on the platform to pack away her things.

"Bet you're pleased that's over."

She jumped. Lisa's grandfather glowered at the backs of the happy couple.

"Always nice to see a couple married." She said in the cheeriest tone she could summon.

He turned his gaze onto her. "You have no morals marrying them two. No conscience. Shame on you."

The book slipped from Daphne's fingers, hitting the floor with a thump, notes falling here and there. Her mouth formed a question which couldn't come out, so tight was her throat. What did he mean? Why was he angry with her? Did he hate Steve so much he thought the world should conspire to stop the marriage of two grown adults?

"There you are, Dad." Bob appeared through the crowd. "Time for photographs."

"Not with me." The older man shook his head and pushed past his son, disappearing in a moment behind the backdrop he'd helped build.

"Dad, wait on!" Bob sighed. "Sorry about that. Dad is losing his faculties and can't remember his own name half the time."

Daphne didn't know his name but didn't care to ask.

"Nice ceremony, Mrs Jones. Will you stay for a glass of champagne?"

Her voice returned with a bit of a squeak. "I need the couple to sign their marriage certificate."

Bob nodded. "Of course. I'll go and find them. And thanks for being such a good sport. Can't imagine anyone else putting up with the behaviour of my family yesterday. And that little rat's comments at the end of the vows."

It took Daphne a minute or two to compose herself once he left. She collected the fallen notes and her book, packed everything back into her briefcase and then stepped off the podium. The dread was back in her stomach and she had to remind herself this was almost over. Sign the certificate and other papers and then walk away and never return.

Nothing was that simple.

The signing table had been forgotten about, so space was hastily made in the middle of the gifts table. Daphne stood back as gifts were moved to one side by Margaret and staff. Quite a number were already open. A set of crystal glasses, placemats, toasters. Photo frames. Cutlery. And lots of envelopes, probably containing cash or gifts cards. If this was the third wedding in a few years, some guests might have run out of ideas.

Daphne handed her phone to Margaret and asked her to take a few images of herself with the couple she could add to her officiant website. Once the table was dressed with some flowers, the happy couple sat and signed, stopping often for photos and kisses while their bridal party drifted away to a bar.

Once finished, Steve joined his friends for another drink and Lisa's bridesmaids returned with a bottle of champagne. Hopefully, none of them were driving later. Not that this was her concern.

Daphne made it as far as the back of the deck when Margaret caught her.

"Have you seen Bertie?"

"Bertie?"

"Bob's father."

Bertie Brooker, Bob Brooker. Steve, Shane, Sam. Did every family in Little Bridges keep to an alphabetic theme naming their children?

"Last I saw him was right after the ceremony. He went in the other direction from the guests. Behind the backdrop."

"Oh dear. He's been known to try and cross the river at the back of the property. We'll have to search for him."

By 'we', Daphne sincerely hoped Margaret meant 'they'. Finding a rude and grumpy man was not on her to-do list.

"Marg? Still can't find Dad so we're heading to the river." Bob called from near the gate. He had a group of guests with him, some carrying full glasses as though they were going on an excursion. "Can you search closer to the house?"

Margaret waved in response.

Steve and his friends followed Bob. Just before the gate, Steve stopped, reached into a pocket and removed a phone. He answered the call as the others went on ahead.

"My husband will be here to pick me up soon. I can look around out the front if you like." Daphne said.

"Yes please. I have to help the others." Margaret hurried off in the direction of the reception area and Daphne breathed a sigh of relief.

She wasn't waiting to be stopped again and took a short cut through the house, diverting to use the restroom. The place was deserted and her heels echoed on the floorboards in the long hallway. There were family photos all the way along, some on the wall and others in frames on side tables. Lisa's previous weddings to two men who resembled Steve. Bob and Margaret's wedding which made them look as though they'd not aged a lot. Bob as a young man holding a trophy aloft. No, that wasn't Bob but Bertie. The next photo showed him crossing a finishing line in a running race.

"Probably ran to the river to get away from the wedding." She grumbled. Outside again, Daphne glanced around. "Bertie? Are you out here?" He didn't answer and there was no sign of movement.

The driveway and the street was like a carpark with cars and flatbed utes parked at angles on verges. Four-wheel-drives lined up in rows. Half the town must be attending. Except the Tanning family.

A large white van was parked on the lawn. Its back doors were wide open and a young man, carrying a crisp white apron, emerged from its depths just as Daphne went around it, startling them both.

"Oh my! Sorry." Daphne laughed. He glowered at her and slammed the doors, then swiftly pulled the apron over his head before striding away. Poor thing must have spilled something over himself and was embarrassed. His shirt, now covered with the top of the apron, had wet splashes on it.

Daphne took a minute to send a text message to John, then found herself a spot where she'd see him drive down the street. Time to think about dinner tonight. Somewhere nice with a glass of wine and a laugh about the events of the day.

When John appeared in the distance she was well and truly over standing around. The car was almost close enough to see his face when a cry from the house made her turn and look. It sounded like a woman in pain. And again, this time the voice was recognisable.

Lisa.

And she shrieked one word over and over.

Steve.

THREE TIMES A WIDOW

Daphne's head shot back towards the street where John was searching for a place to stop.

"Steeeeeve!"

John waved.

She couldn't wait.

Daphne turned and ran towards the sound of shrieking.

"Daph? What's wrong?" John called.

"Emergency!" She managed to call over her shoulder as she wound her way around and between cars.

The screaming stopped. Daphne puffed her way past the house, her eyes darting to the reception area and then...to the pool area.

Lisa slumped on her knees near the swimming pool with her mother, staring into it. But at what? Daphne pushed on and went through the open gate.

Bob and a waiter were in the pool, fully dressed and drenched from head to toe as they paddled either side of someone floating in the water. Someone wearing the exact wedding suit Steve had been in. Sobs wracked Lisa and as Daphne stepped to the edge of the pool she saw why.

Her heart almost stopped. It was Steve in the pool.

Face down.

"Turn him over!" Margaret cried.

A third man jumped in, stirring up the water. Between the three, they managed to rotate Steve onto his back.

Daphne rummaged in her bag for her phone and rang John. She didn't wait to explain. "You need to phone an ambulance and let them know there is a drowning victim here. Give them my number if they want a contact." She hung up and shoved the phone into her pants pocket.

The men got Steve to the side of the pool. Daphne tossed her bag to one side and dropped to her knees, leaning over the edge to hold his arm as Bob and the waiter climbed out. Steve's eyes were open and staring straight at her. Lifeless. Beneath him, a cloud of red panned out, seeping into the shirt of the third man, who remained at his side. It was the man who'd been polishing the tiles yesterday.

Bob virtually pushed Daphne aside in his haste to grab Steve and she plonked onto her behind. She shuffled out of the way as the men lifted Steve onto the tiles. On the far side of the pool, a small red mark marred the pristine white edge above the water.

"Doll, are you okay?" John was there, his hands strong under her arms as he helped her get to her feet. "Are you hurt?"

She shook her head, words unable to find their way out.

"There's an ambulance coming." Arm around her shoulders, John guided her a few feet away, scooping up her bag. Daphne looked at the hand she'd held Steve's arm with. It was red with his blood. She yanked her jacket off.

More people piled into the area and a woman announced she was a nurse and would everyone step back. She began to work on Steve, snapping orders at Bob and the other men to help her position him.

"We need an ambulance!" Margaret screamed.

"On its way." John answered. "Perhaps people could move their cars to make a way through for it."

A few guests took off in the direction of the street.

"Daph? I need to move ours as well. Do you want to come with me?"

She shook her head again.

"I've got your bag and jacket. You'll be here?"

How could she leave? Less than an hour ago she'd pronounced Steve married to Lisa. He'd been rude and stupid but nonetheless was a living, breathing person. How on earth had he ended up in the pool of all places?

Lisa collapsed in a heap, letting out loud, heaving sobs. Margaret patted her back but gazed at Steve with a vacant stare. Three times a widow. Something snapped Daphne out of her shock. Surely this wasn't possible. Three men from the same family all meeting with lethal accidents when married to the same woman. Something was terribly off. She narrowed her eyes to memorise the scene.

A large swimming pool surrounded by tiled flooring. A handful of sunchairs. Two buildings on the opposite side with their doors facing each other. The first had a sign 'change room'. The other was smaller and closed up. This building had a tap at the front with a short hose snaking off to one side. Clear pool fencing and gate surrounded the area. There were a lot of people standing outside the fence, while inside, the attempt to resuscitate Steve continued.

Bob joined his wife and daughter, water streaming

down his clothes. The waiter stood apart, his hands clenching and unclenching and his teeth chattering.

Daphne hurried for the change room. She pushed the door open. A shelf against the far wall held a variety of folded towels and Daphne collected a selection, hugging them against her chest as she closed the door behind herself. The door to the other building suddenly opened, revealing a glimpse of pool cleaning equipment and tins of paint before a man stepped out and shut then locked the door.

He slid keys into his shorts pocket as he saw her and what she carried.

"Good idea." He held out his hands and Daphne noticed he was also drenched. It was the other man who'd been in the pool. The one polishing the tiles yesterday. "I'll hand these out."

She let him take them. At least he had a shirt on if sopping wet with streaks of Steve's blood. He tossed one of the towels over his shoulder and took the others to Bob and then the waiter. The latter he spoke to and patted on the back and after a minute, the waiter nodded and left the pool area.

Some of Lisa's friends got her back on her feet and led her away. Margaret still stared at Steve. At the people working on him. All for nothing for he was gone.

"I have to find Bertie." Margaret announced to nobody.

"Let me help." Daphne touched Margaret's shoulder. "He wasn't at the river?"

"River? I don't know. Everyone came running when Lisa..."

"Come on, there's nothing we can do here. We'll find your father-in-law."

No sooner had they left the pool area they found him. He sat alone at a table in the reception area, back to the pool, drinking a beer.

"Dad! We looked everywhere for you."

Bertie stared at his beer. "Didn't look hard enough."

Margaret began to cry.

"What's wrong now, Mags?"

With a gulp, Margaret sat at the table. "Steve. In the pool."

Daphne hurried away to the bar and poured two glasses of water. All the catering staff had vanished. Perhaps still looking for Bertie or else curious about Steve. She swallowed one glassful and took the other back for Margaret. "Here, sip slowly."

Bertie suddenly looked straight at Daphne. "You're still here."

She wished she wasn't. If John had arrived a moment sooner she'd be back at Bluebell. If this mean old man said one more nasty thing...

"Wanted to apologise. My head gets muddled sometimes when there's too much going on." He held out his hand to shake. "Will you accept my apology?"

A bit of Daphne's hurt drained away. "Oh, of course I will." She reached her hand out and gasped. She'd forgotten about the blood on it, now dried around her nails.

All three of them stared at her hand. "I need to wash this off."

She dashed off to the house and locked herself in the bathroom again. After scrubbing both hands as clean as she could, she dried them, talking to herself all the time.

"None of this is your problem, Daph. Take a deep breath

and soon John will be back for you. We can go to Bluebell and I'll have a long shower and a cup of tea."

A siren wailed as she made her way outside. Guests congregated in the reception area, some seated, others walking aimlessly around. Some of the waiters stood at the bar not knowing what to do. One was the young man Daphne had startled at the van. He stared at her and a chill crept up her spine.

His shirt had been wet. He'd been getting a fresh apron.

"There you are, love." John put his arm around her shoulders. "Thought you were staying by the pool."

"There was blood on my hand. From holding his arm. Steve's."

"Do you want to go?"

"I don't think I can. Police might need a statement."

"But it was an accident."

They walked towards the pool area. The siren had stopped. The nurse still worked on Steve, her movements as precise as at the beginning, but her face lined with exhaustion. Blood formed a puddle around him which trickled across the tiles and dripped into the water.

"I don't believe it was accidental, John. And I think I know who is responsible."

"You're wrong!"

Daphne and John turned. Lisa swayed behind them, one of her friends keeping her from collapsing with an arm around her waist. Black trails of mascara cut through her makeup, all the way down her neck to the top of her white dress, leaving dark smudges along the lace.

"It was an accident. The tiles were polished for the wedding when the pool area was spruced up. Dad insisted everything look new again. He just slipped." Her voice broke. "Slipped. My poor boy." She had no more tears and there was an emptiness in her eyes which tugged at Daphne's heart. "All my poor boys."

With that, her eyes fluttered and she fainted.

SUSPECTS GALORE

Two paramedics wheeled past with a stretcher loaded with medical equipment. As Lisa fell to the ground, they stopped, confused.

Daphne pointed to the pool. "She's just fainted, we'll look after her. You need to go there."

John, with the help of Lisa's friend, managed to get her onto her side and she came around almost immediately.

"Just rest a minute. We'll get you some water." John said.

Margaret and Bertie hurried over and Bertie sank to the ground next to Lisa, patting her shoulder with soothing sounds. His eyes though flicked to the paramedics and the scene around the pool.

"What's going on?"

"I told you earlier, Bertie." Margaret said.

"I've lost my Steve, Gramps." Lisa lifted her head. "I'll never keep a husband, just like Dad used to say."

Daphne's ear pricked up. Who would say such a thing to their own child?

"He never meant it, sweetie," Margaret said. "You always got bored so fast. New toys lasted a day before you'd break them. You'd make a friend then decide they weren't good enough. But that was a long time ago."

John's mouth had dropped open and Daphne took his arm. "We might go and sit for a bit. If you are all okay here?"

Nobody answered.

Daphne was happy to find a table away from the pool and from the lines of worry on her husband's face, so was John. He reached for her hand.

"Are you doing okay? This must have been a shock."

"I'm fine now you're here, love." She drew in a deep breath and exhaled. "So much happened today and when I saw you driving down the street all I longed for was to have a shower and cup of tea and tell you all about it."

"Surely there's no need to stay though?"

"I know things."

"O...kay." He said.

"Suspects."

"But we don't even know if a crime's been committed. The poor young man may very well have slipped as the bride suggested."

Another siren sounded.

"I guess we'll find out." Daphne said.

John leaned closer. "Before, you said you knew who is responsible. Daph...what do you know?"

Daphne looked over her shoulder. Most people now stood in a semi-circle around the pool as the paramedics did their job, but a few guests and a couple of waiters remained in the reception area.

"Quick rundown, love. Not everyone approved of the wedding. For a start, there's none of Steve's family here."

Daphne's eyes widened. "Oh goodness. Has anyone contacted his family?"

"Quite a few people are on their phones."

"This is terrible. Can you imagine not attending your loved one's wedding and then they die?" She heard her voice rising and put a hand over her mouth.

"Stay here, doll." John went to the unattended bar and overfilled a glass of champagne. He returned and put it in front of her. "I know this is highly inappropriate given the circumstances, but there's only that or beer and I feel a little drink might settle your nerves."

Not one to drink during the day, Daphne wasted no time to sip the bubbly alcohol. It warmed her stomach. She'd not noticed how upset she was until hearing her tone change. Once she'd had a couple more sips—and didn't the champagne go down easily—she was ready to continue.

"Since stepping onto the property yesterday, I've observed a lot of strange behaviour, and honestly, some quite disturbing attitudes." She put down the glass and counted with her fingers. "Three men from one family all marrying the same woman within a few short years. And all three now deceased."

John nodded. "That is unusual."

"Quite. None of the groom's family in attendance."

"Families can be difficult."

"The groom himself was very rude to his bride during the vows."

"Not a good start to a marriage." John said.

"The bride's grandfather told me I was...immoral marrying them."

"Oh, love." John frowned. "What a dreadful comment."

"He did apologise later. Poor old soul seems to have dementia so I can't hold a grudge."

"You are the sweetest woman I know."

His words helped. They always did.

"Mind you, there was a lot of drinking going on before and after the ceremony. Which might have led to Steve slipping and falling into the pool." Daphne pressed her lips together.

"But you don't think it was an accident."

She didn't.

Police officers made their way to the pool, where paramedics were zipping Steve's body into a bag. Lisa was sobbing again, surrounded by her friends. Bob and Margaret stood back, silent. Bertie was nowhere to be seen again. Hopefully not another disappearance.

"Something strange happened. I was on my way to the street to wait for you and went past the caterer's van, surprising a waiter." Daphne said.

"Go on."

"He had wet patches on his shirt. And sleeves. And he was putting on a fresh apron."

"You think he got wet pushing Steve into the pool?" John asked.

She finished the glass of bubbles, surprised it was gone already.

"Should I get another?"

"Goodness, no thanks, John, you'd have to carry me out of here."

The paramedics pushed the stretcher out of the pool area, followed at a distance by Lisa and her friends. Her parents were with the police but Bob, arms folded and face set, watched the body of his ten-minute son-in-law wheel away.

"And that's another thing. According to Lisa, her father used to tell her she'd never keep a husband. Apparently as a child she became bored with friends and toys easily."

John looked in the direction Daphne discretely pointed. "That's her father and mother?"

"It is."

"Do you think he'd kill his daughter's new husband?"

"He needs to be on the list."

"List?"

"Suspects, John. I am keeping track up here," she tapped the side of her head. "Although it might pay to write it all down."

He gave her a slight smile. "Anyone else?"

"At least two more. Her mother didn't like Steve and she really wasn't happy yesterday about hosting another wedding."

"Not really a motive to kill someone."

"Tip of the iceberg, love. Tip of the iceberg. There's always more lurking beneath the snippets they let slip. And of course the obvious suspect is Lisa although I don't believe she did it."

"Bit odd to kill her new husband off only minutes after saying 'I do'." John glanced over Daphne's shoulder. "Think the police are heading our way."

Daphne scanned the reception area. The waiter was missing. He might be simply helping pack things away. Or he might have done a runner. She should have taken a photo of him the instant he became a suspect.

SUSPICIONS IGNORED

John didn't know what to do. Not knowing what to do was a worry. In a lifetime as owner and principal of River's End Real Estate, he'd encountered all kinds of folk and a myriad of situations. In the past couple of years, he and Daphne even had to deal with their house being broken into and treasured items destroyed by a fiend who was part of a conspiracy by a shady land developer. Despite all the turmoil, he'd always been able to keep a handle on his emotions, keep a cool head, and be there for Daphne.

This was different. As he sat at the table in a beautiful garden on a warm spring afternoon with his wife and a police officer, the situation was surreal. Daphne had been uncharacteristically nervous when he'd dropped her here. Perhaps nervous wasn't the right word. Uneasy. She had good instincts and was an excellent judge of character and today she'd been uneasy.

With good cause, so it turned out. Everywhere in view, people were in a daze. Some stood in small groups, others sat at tables or on the grass. Few spoke. The laughter and happiness expected at a wedding reception was non-existent. A second ambulance had arrived and one paramedic was checking Lisa while the other spoke to each guest to see if any of them needed assistance. What a dreadful way to end a wedding.

"Mrs Jones, we wanted a word, given your unique position as an outside observer." The young constable opposite John kept an eye on those around them, some who'd moved closer as though to listen in when he'd joined them.

"Of course, Constable McIntyre. And I have some information."

He took out a notepad. "Information?"

Now it was Daphne who gazed from group to group as if judging whether it was safe to speak. "I saw someone acting suspiciously earlier. A waiter."

"Suspiciously?"

She nodded. "He was in the catering van changing aprons. I noticed his shirt was wet in places, and his sleeves."

Constable McIntyre didn't write anything down. He stared at Daphne as she continued.

"This was a few minutes before Steve was found. He'd have had time to push Steve in and get changed. I assume poor Steve hit his head on the way in."

"The coroner will determine the cause of death in due course. This may well have been an unfortunate accident. Did you observe any odd behaviour from Mr Tanning prior to his death?"

"I've only met him twice. Both times he was unpleasant in the regard that he spoke before thinking. Whether that is true of him always, you'd need to ask someone better acquainted with him, but you tell me...is it odd to make a comment during your vows that you expect your wife to die before you due to her age?"

"Can't say."

"Going back to the waiter, I really think—"

"I'll look into it. What other observations do you have of the events of today?"

Daphne wasn't happy. The way she pressed her lips together was a giveaway to anyone who knew her. And John did. He reached a hand under the table and squeezed her leg and the corners of her mouth softened.

"There were a number of people unhappy with the couple getting married. Lots of people drinking too much before and right after the ceremony. And at least five suspects. Likely more once I've had a chance to catch my breath."

"I'd rather you don't look for suspects. That's our job. May I have your contact details?"

Through almost gritted teeth, Daphne told them where they were staying and exchanged her business card for one with his details.

The constable stood. "We'll be in touch if there is a need for a statement. How long do you plan on staying in Little Bridges?" He directed this to John, who also stood.

"For as long as Daphne wants to be here."

"Right. Well, thanks."

With that, the constable headed for Margaret and Bob. The latter had changed into dry clothes but his hair was still damp and sticking up at odd angles.

"John?"

Daphne's voice was strained and he immediately held his hand out.

"Can we leave now?"

"We certainly can." John helped her to her feet. Her face was pale and when they made their way to the front of the house, her arm in his, her steps were slow. He'd make sure she had a rest and some tea and even some of the packaged biscuits he'd bought on his way back to Bluebell earlier. She wouldn't mind for once.

The caterers were packing up, the back doors of the van open. Daphne tugged at John's arm.

"Let's wait a minute." They were a few metres away, between a row of bigger vehicles.

"Why, love?"

Two of the staff loaded glasses, plates and the like into the van. They finished and headed back towards the house, leaving the doors open.

In an instant, Daphne was off, scrambling into the back of the van. She was rummaging around before John knew what was happening. "Daph!"

She didn't listen and was in the depths of the van by the time he caught up. "What are you doing? You'll get caught."

"Then be a lookout."

A sudden bubble of laughter rose in his chest and he had to force it down. This was his girl at her finest. Following her instincts.

John turned to face the house. He'd give her time to do whatever it was she needed to do. After the couple of days she'd had, she deserved this chance. Daphne always did the right thing and he would back her one hundred percent.

"Anything?" He whispered over his shoulder.

"Hmm."

A procession of vehicles turned into the street. Four or five cars, one after another. Over at the house the paramedics were packing up their ambulances.

"My, oh my!"

"What?"

Silence again.

The cars slowed and one by one, pulled over to park. From the first car, four people emerged. A man and woman about his and Daphne's age, plus two young men. All wore an air of disbelief, of panic, and moved quickly towards the house.

"Um, Daph?"

"Almost done."

"Think Steve's family are here."

The catering staff headed directly towards them.

"Daph, get out. They're coming back."

"Almost done."

"I'm serious. You have to get out."

John took matters into his own hands. He made a beeline for the caterers, who between them were carrying a couple of tables. They squeezed through the cars and he blocked the way.

"Excuse me. Do you happen to know...um, where a nice place is in town for dinner?"

They stopped and stared at him as if looking at a crazy person.

"We're just passing through...for the wedding. Thought we'd go out tonight."

The first one went to push past and John stepped in front of him. "Whoops, sorry. Meant to go the other way. So, no suggestions?"

"Oh, there you are, John. Shall we go?"

Thank goodness.

John let them pass. The second person grinned and said, "Bell's Bistro. Most of us work there. Just off the main street."

Daphne appeared from around the end of a car and grabbed John's arm.

"Let's go." She whispered, tugging at him. He got the message. She'd found something important. They hurried away from the van, from the house, passing a long procession of people from the newly arrived cars.

"I need to speak to the constable again." She whispered.

"Looks like he'll have his hands full for a bit."

John ushered Daphne into the car just as Bob and Margaret and some of the other guests came around the side of the house to meet the newcomers head on. Everyone stopped for a second. Two seconds. And then the yelling and pushing began.

"What's happening?"

John closed her door and ran for his. Throwing himself in, he locked the car and started the engine.

"The other side have arrived and there's going to be a fight."

"Should we help?" Daphne craned her neck to catch a glimpse as John turned the car.

"Police are there."

"But I think we—"

"We, my love, are leaving. Enough of these people and this madness. I need you safe."

BLUEBELL'S BLESSINGS

Daphne didn't say a word all the way home. Her mind raced and a little bit of her heart broke. She'd wed those two and they'd not even enjoyed one day of married life. Her throat was tight and she knew if she spoke about them she would cry. John had been wonderful during the brief discussion with the constable who'd not believed a word she'd said. And he'd had her back when she'd got in the van.

"Here we are, love," John parked the car beside the caravan. "Time for you to have a shower while I make a nice cup of tea."

With a quick nod, Daphne climbed out and when John unlocked the door, was quick to climb the couple of steps to the cool and inviting interior of Bluebell. For a minute she paused in the kitchen, hands on the counter and eyes closed. Quiet. She could breathe again.

The boot of the car closed. John must be bringing her jacket and bag. Not ready to talk, Daphne closed herself in the cosy bathroom and stripped off. First stop tomorrow would be to locate a dry cleaner. She needed her clothes fresh again. No lingering smell of chlorine or...death.

The young constable didn't want her involved and he was right. She shouldn't interfere in police work. What she thought she'd seen was in her imagination, over-active from the shock.

She gulped.

Shower on, Daphne stepped under the water. The caravan carried its own supply so showers were normally short, but here, being hooked up at the site, she could afford the extra time to wash her hair and clean off the makeup and dirt and any trace of blood on her hand.

It isn't fair.

Not the way she'd been treated.

Or how Steve spoke to his bride during the vows.

The family arguing beforehand.

A young man's life cut short.

The perfect ceremony forever ruined.

Tears poured down her cheeks and she let out a sob. None of it was fair.

Twenty minutes later, Daphne emerged from the bedroom in a short sleeved, floral blouse and soft, half-length pants. Pretty, cool, and comfortable to wear. She'd partly dried her hair then stopped to peer in the mirror.

"Are those greys?"

Holding up a strand, she almost bumped her nose on the glass trying to see.

"Time for a new highlight colour. What about bright blue?"

She'd normally straighten her curls but was in no mood to bother. Let them curl. There was no sign of her earlier tears under a light application of makeup.

"There you are, doll." John was in the kitchen. "Shall we have tea in here? I've got it ready."

"Let's. Nice and cool inside." Daphne slid behind the table.

The table was booth-style, big enough for four diners. There was a plate of packaged chocolate biscuits in the centre and although Daphne disapproved of John's love of them, for once she didn't care to mention it. In fact, for once she was going to enjoy eating one. Or three.

They chatted over the first cup of tea about everything other than today. The weather, how pleasant the location was, and whether to go out for dinner or get take away.

"I'd really like to go out, if you feel like it." Daphne eyed off another biscuit. "Being somewhere happy, where people are laughing and happy would be nice."

"Agree. Did you want to try the bistro the waiter mentioned?"

"Didn't he say that's where most of them work? Maybe another night, John. Less reminder of what happened today."

"We'll go for a walk around town then and see what appeals. Do you care to share what you were doing in the catering van?"

"Oh! I almost forgot about it. I'll get my phone." She wiggled out. "I must have left it in my pants pocket."

Sure enough, it was in the laundry hamper.

"Sorry I dived into the catering van without a word." Back in her seat, Daphne tapped on the gallery. "Had to take the chance while nobody was there."

"Chance to do what?"

"Look for evidence, of course."

"Of course."

"I know Constable McDon't-get-involved wasn't going to believe me so I got some proof." She handed the phone to John. "There's about ten photos. Tell me what you see."

The third chocolate biscuit made it to her mouth as John inspected the images, zooming in and scrolling from one to another.

"This one looks like a rolled up piece of cloth. Tablecloth?"

"Negatory. If you look closer you'll see a name tag."

John opened the case of his reading glasses and put them on, then enlarged the image. "I see it. Lloyd? So, an apron, not a tablecloth."

Daphne couldn't help smiling. "Yes! And it looks wet to me. See how part of it is darker than the rest?"

"You think this belonged to the waiter you surprised."

"I do indeed."

John grinned across the table. "Clever cookie. What about this photo?" He turned the camera. "What's that tub?"

In the corner of the van, almost hidden behind folded table and chairs, a white tub about the size of a large paint tin was pushed to the back.

"No idea. Cleaning stuff? Anyway, I thought it worth recording. The police officer thought I was a nosy old woman."

"Doll, no." John took her hand and squeezed. "He would have had a hundred things to worry about. Arriving to what looked like an accident but all those guests and family standing around and perhaps a homicide. Probably didn't know where to start."

Unconvinced, Daphne nodded. She knew what she knew. She just didn't know how to help. But the police had to see these photos.

"I'll quickly call the constable and let him know."

"Good idea. Then, how about we shelve all of this for now? Would you like to know what I got up to while you were at the wedding?"

The way John's eyes lit up warmed Daphne's heart. He was so sweet, trying to distract her and excited about his news. She squeezed his hand back.

"I can't wait to hear!"

John had a couple of projects on the go. Accustomed to working long hours and being active for his adult working years, the caravan life—as he called it—left him wanting more. He loved being on the road with Daphne, exploring Victoria and seeing her happy in her new career, but he couldn't fish all the time and needed his mind busy. Genealogy was a growing passion but what he had to show Daphne was something for them both.

He opened his laptop on the table. "I've been dabbling with this for a few weeks, mainly to keep our friends in River's End up to date with our travels."

Daphne shuffled closer, resting her head on his shoulder as he connected to the internet and then typed in an address. The screen changed and she sat bolt upright with a gasp.

"But...that's Bluebell!"

"Sure is."

"Is this a blog? Called Bluebell's Blessings?"

"Yup."

"You clever man! I love it."

For the first time today, John's spirits lifted. His girl was happy and he found himself grinning. "As I mentioned, the original idea was to keep our friends up to date. I've taken lots of photos of Bluebell," he moved to the 'gallery' page. "Inside and out."

Daphne squealed. "How did you make the living area look so big?"

"Found a neat little trick with my phone. Now here, on this next page, is our itinerary on the map of the state. At least, a rough outline, based on your commitments. And if you like, I can link this to your website. Gives potential customers a bit of insight into who you are as well as allows them to look here and see if you are already booked on a certain day."

Before John knew what was happening, Daphne threw her arms around him and planted a kiss on his cheek.

He laughed when she released him. "Take that as a yes."

"Yes. I'm so glad you're doing this. Not just for our friends or as something to look back on, but so you have something to do. I've worried a bit whether you would get too bored traipsing the countryside for me."

"Bored is not a state I could ever be in when you are involved. If there's one thing I've learned from being married to you for some forty years, Daph, it's that life always has a twist."

TWISTS INDEED

Those words of John's rattled around in Daphne's mind for a while. Life always had a twist. When she'd married her high-school sweetheart after they graduated, she'd relished the idea of raising a large family with him. The twist was trying to start a family for ten years before discovering it could never happen.

A cruel twist.

Daphne believed in silver linings though. They moved to the seaside town of River's End where John opened his business. For a long time they were foster parents and loved welcoming young ones into their hearts and home until more permanent arrangements were made. As a teen, local lad Martin Blake, who'd lost his own parents young and lived with his granddad, made it his business to help the Jones' out and befriend often troubled and confused kids who needed a new path. And even now, Martin spent time each year teaching at a camp for troubled teens.

A good twist.

Some of those foster children kept in touch while others

stayed with the Jones's only long enough to tiptoe into Daphne's heart before they were moved to their permanent homes. One in particular lingered in her memories and perhaps one day, they'd meet again.

Daphne was unsure yet how to view today's events. A twist indeed. Tragic. Unexpected. But was it murder? With the arrival of evening and having spent a couple of hours talking with John about Bluebell's Blessings, her earlier contention of foul play was a bit dented.

"What about this one?" John asked.

They wandered arm in arm after walking into town, following a path to the river and a bridge not far from the caravan which offered a short cut.

"This one is Mexican. Oh, but we had tacos last night." John said. "Looks like Italian up on the corner."

"Italian sounds ideal."

For a country town in the middle of Victoria, Little Bridges had a wonderful selection of eateries. They had planned to stay another two days, but that might change if the police needed them to be available for interviews. As long as they left by Thursday, they'd cover the distance to the next wedding with time to spare.

Once settled at a window table made cheery with a red and white checked tablecloth and matching candles, they choose from a small menu and John ordered a bottle of local red wine.

Daphne sighed and reached across the table for both of John's hands. "This is lovely. Thank you, love."

"I'm happy to see you smiling."

"Well, I feel much better. And seeing all the work you've put into Bluebell's Blessings filled my heart up."

John's face reddened but his eyes sparkled. He wasn't a

man to expect compliments but deserved every one ever given. Over their lifetime together, he'd helped more people than Daphne could remember. The real estate agency sponsored local kids sports as well as making a hefty donation each year to different local charities. He was a good man.

Two waiters moved a couple of tables to form a large one beside Daphne and John. They set it up for eight patrons and chatted the whole time.

"Didn't think they'd still come out tonight."

"Boss says they never cancelled but yeah, who'd go to a restaurant almost straight after what happened."

"Did you know him?"

"Steve Tanning? Went to school with him."

Daphne smothered a gasp as the waiters continued.

"Sorry, man. Are you okay?"

"Oh, we weren't friends. He and his cousins were part of the cool group. You know, the ones who think they're better than anyone else and push everyone else around. Can't say he'll be missed."

The conversation ended as they returned to the kitchen. Daphne leaned closer to John. "You heard that?"

"Would you like me to see if they can move us further away, love?"

"Further? Oh goodness, no. Right here is perfect."

Perfect to listen in and perhaps get some updates on the events after they'd left.

"Daphne, what are you thinking?" There was a touch of lament in John's voice.

She smiled as widely as she could. "Nothing at all. Here comes our wine."

By the time their wine was poured, the diners on the other table were settling in. Daphne decided to focus on her evening with John. They chatted about plans for the next day, which included a nice long walk around town and a visit to the local bookshop.

From the corner of her eye, it was impossible not to recognise some of the faces from the wedding. Most were around the age of Bob and Margaret.

Daphne moved her chair a bit so she couldn't see them. A plate of garlic bread arrived and that gave her something yummy to concentrate on. More people arrived and before long, the restaurant was filled with laughter and talk. Exactly what she'd hoped for.

"They should have been arrested."

She wasn't going to listen. Daphne shuffled again, as close to the window as her chair would allow. But the man's voice carried and she couldn't very well put her fingers in her ears.

"Coming onto Bob's property and starting a fight."

"I suppose the police took their grief into account." A woman suggested.

"What about Bob and Margaret's grief?"

Nobody could have expected what came next.

Laughter.

Daphne and John turned as one. All but two of those at the next table were laughing. The ones who weren't amused were the oldest couple, a man and woman in their seventies.

"Come on, Pat and Gina. You know it's true." It was the first man. "They were horrified that silly girl of theirs wanted another go with a Tanning. Best thing for everyone if you ask me."

Gina frowned. "Be careful nobody outside this group hears you say so. A family feud is still no reason to wish harm on another. And he was only a boy."

Before they were caught listening, Daphne and John each grabbed another slice of bread. Their eyes met across the plate.

The first man continued. “Bertie will be happy. I reckon Lisa marrying into the family of his arch enemy started him going downhill. Nothing like a couple of good accidents to set things right.”

Daphne shoved the bread in her mouth. She was getting tired of having to suppress gasps and really shouldn’t be listening.

More laughter.

A waitress attended the other table and talk turned to selecting food and drinks. Seemed as though at least one of them already had quite a bit to drink from his loud-mouthed comments. Did he actually know something about the deaths of Sam and Shane?

What if he’s the killer?

Oh dear. There she went again, thinking of Steve’s death as murder. It wasn’t her business and she wasn’t about to make it her concern.

“John, I’m staying out of it. Promise.”

“I know.”

Their mains arrived and the table near them stopped discussing the wedding. The food was a delight and Daphne wasted no time enjoying it rather than worrying.

Before dessert arrived, she visited the restroom. As she washed her hands, the woman who’d been referred to as ‘Gina’ came in. She was a thin woman, heavy makeup covering deep wrinkles, wearing pearls and a fitted black dress. Their eyes met in the mirror.

“Don’t believe everything you hear, dear.”

Daphne tilted her head. “What do you mean?”

"I know you are at the next table. Saw you the minute we arrived. One of our party had a few drinks earlier from the shock of the events at the wedding, so don't think for one minute he is making sense."

There was nothing to say. Daphne dried her hands with paper towel.

"You'll be leaving soon. On your way to the next town. No reason to dig around in our family history. Or in my family's town. So move on and forget about us." Gina said as if making small talk. "You were in such a rush to speak to the police at the wedding. Not a good look."

Well, well, well! Somebody wanted to hide something.

"I'm sure I have no idea what you are talking about. My husband and I are simply having dinner—"

"At the same restaurant half of Lisa's family are attending. Did my great-niece tell you we'd be here?"

"Lisa? Of course not. We just walked—"

"Either way, you aren't welcome. You played your part and now is the time to toddle along." Gina looked Daphne up and down, her eyes stopping on her stomach. "After your dessert of course."

It took a moment for Daphne to get the message but then ice filled her veins. She couldn't answer because Gina had left. Obviously, her visit to the restroom was designed to speak with Daphne. To insult Daphne. And warn her off.

Daphne lifted her chin. She might not wear pearls and a tiny little dress but she had heart.

"And courage." Half-tempted to follow Gina and tell her some truths, instead, she straightened her top. "And manners."

CHANGE OF HEART

Dawn was John's favourite time of the day and since they'd embraced the travelling life, he'd managed to photograph some glorious sunrises. One day, he might put all of them into a book and publish it. For now it was a hobby to enjoy.

He wandered down to the river, a steaming cup of coffee in one hand and phone in the other. Daphne was still asleep, exhausted from the previous day. Once she woke, he'd make them a nice breakfast. Being able to spoil her a bit more these days was long overdue after her dedication to his needs for so long. His and their foster family over the years.

The sun peeked through the gums near the town. The river turned to gold.

John put his cup onto the grass and took lots of photos. Phone cameras today were every bit as good as a high quality camera and he loved the little tricks he was experimenting with to get the most out of every shot.

Birdsong filled the air. Magpies warbled. A family of kookaburras launched a cacophony of chuckles quickly elevating to their characteristic laughter. A flock of sulphur crested cockatoos screeched overhead as they swooped to see if John had anything interesting on offer.

"Come to the country, they said." John picked up his coffee. "It'll be quiet, they said."

He turned back. There was movement in Bluebell, a shadow crossing the kitchen window. He must have disturbed Daphne. For a moment he stopped, nursing the cup and sipping the coffee.

Their dinner last night was meant to help her unwind and move on from the trauma of the wedding. Instead, something happened to upset her more. He'd seen that woman called Gina follow Daphne to the restroom and leave first. Daph came back to the table a few minutes later, her eyes down. She forced a cheeriness he recognised as covering up hurt. On the walk back she'd said little and once in the caravan, headed to bed.

This mess with the accident yesterday, compounded by comments from the next table at the restaurant, all stirred Daphne up. Back when they were still in River's End, her friendships and sense of adventure dragged her into a few unusual situations. Mysteries she'd helped solve. She'd always been one to jump in. And more than once, John had asked her to stay out of other people's business. Just when she got too enthusiastic. But she had a way of seeing through lies and deception and if she really believed Steve was murdered, then John would back her all the way. Even if it meant getting a bit more involved than he was comfortable with.

"There you are!" Daphne opened Bluebell's door. "Kettle's on if you'd like another."

"Good morning. Yes, please."

She stepped back to let him in and he gave her a kiss on the cheek.

"John, do you mind if we go to the police station this morning? I'd like to see if they can take my statement." Her voice was flat.

"If you'd like. Or we can wait for them to call."

With a shake of her head, she took John's cup and turned to the kitchen. "I thought if I can do the statement, then perhaps we can get going. To our next destination."

"Today?"

"I think it's best."

"Daph—"

"So, would you like eggs for breakfast?"

When John let himself out of the caravan earlier, Daphne was awake. She'd heard the kettle boil and considered getting up to join him. But the thoughts in her head weren't ready for sharing and she had to find a way to deal with all of this without getting worked up and teary.

Gina had hurt her last night. Not only by insinuating Daphne was there to snoop around but the swipe at her weight.

Daphne turned on her back to stare at the ceiling. Her hands moved to her stomach. Where Gina had stared. It might be a bit more round than a few years ago, and she'd never fit into the figurative 'little black dress', but what business was it of anyone other than Daphne? And perhaps John, who was too sweet to ever comment on her growing waistline. Sliding her hands from under the blankets, she held them up. Her fingers were a bit thicker than they used to be although her long nails gave an illusion of length. But those hands were used for good.

In all the years she'd lived, Daphne had never concerned herself with fitness or being trim. Long ago, she'd decided her body would be what it wanted and she'd care for it to her best ability without obsessing. Enjoy her cookies sometimes but also love a good long walk. It all balanced up in the end.

Speaking of ends, she'd noticed her suit pants were a fraction tight when she'd donned them yesterday. Either they were shrinking with the regular dry cleaning, or she was spreading thanks to all the good food they enjoyed. A bit more walking might be the go. And walking away from this place was something high on her new list of priorities. There was no point staying where she wasn't welcome. John deserved better than the flow-on effect of nasty people. No, it was time to go.

Once dressed, Daphne put the kettle on in anticipation of John's return. Well accustomed to his pre-dawn wanders to take photos, it always gave her a few more minutes in bed and she appreciated how he tiptoed around so not to disturb her. She'd cook some eggs for them both then once the police station was open, she'd ask if she could do a statement today.

Don't run away, Daph. You're an adult now.

She held back a sob. No more tears. It was best they left now. More time to spend along the way to the next town. And get away from the upsetting events in Little Bridges.

NOT GOING ANYWHERE

Constable McIntyre was apologetic but firm. "We're understaffed and working at capacity to investigate yesterday's incident. That and dealing with almost constant interruptions from...well, other parties, means we can't get to all the interviews just yet."

Daphne and John were at the counter in the police station. Behind the constable were three other police officers. Two spoke on the phone and one covered a whiteboard with notes. Sadly, a bit too far away for Daphne's eyes.

"If you really need to get to your next town, we can arrange an interview at another police station."

"I understand. It's just that I have some information you might find useful."

"Is it about the photos from the catering van we discussed on the phone? The photos you should not have taken?"

"Well, yes. And last night we overheard what sounded like inside knowledge of the deaths of Lisa's previous husbands." Daphne said.

"Didn't we talk about not getting involved?" There was no malice in his tone, only a touch of defeat. The young man was obviously tired. His eyes were a bit bloodshot and he looked as though he'd been up half the night.

Her initial assessment of him changed. There was nothing offensive or dismissive about him. He was right. They didn't need her help or her getting under their feet.

"Let me check I have your details. One minute, please." He headed towards a desk.

"Daph? Why don't we stay a day or so. Have that walk around town and enjoy the river. Would love to get some photos of the bridges." John rubbed her back. "Check out some of those boutiques you like browsing."

"Hmm."

"We'll get a coffee somewhere nice and have a talk if you like."

"A coffee sounds good."

Constable McIntyre returned with his notepad. "You are staying at the caravan park in lot seventeen?"

"In Bluebell."

He glanced up with a question in his eyes.

"Bright blue caravan with white highlights. You won't miss her."

Now, he smiled. "Great name."

Daphne smiled back.

He checked the phone numbers for both of them were correct and shut his notepad. "Mrs Jones, your willingness to help is appreciated but please don't do your own investigation. One of us will be in touch." With a nod, he returned to his desk.

At the front door, John reached for the handle just as it burst open. Three people pushed past without as much as an excuse me, or sorry. They crowded into the area, forcing John and Daphne to squish up against the wall to avoid contact. John put an arm in front of Daphne.

"Where's the sergeant?" The speaker was a woman in her late forties. She wore pink tracksuit pants, orange sheepskin boots, and a red sleeveless top, half tucked in. Her hair was a mix of grey and light brown and needed a good brush. "I demand to speak to him."

Two people were with her. A man about her age, balding, dressed in shorts and singlet with mud-caked leather boots. The other was an older teen and by his expression, he didn't want to be there.

Constable McIntyre returned to the counter. "Sorry Mrs Tanning, he's out."

"Out where? Why hasn't he arrested the serial killer?"

"Come on, love." John whispered and gently tugged Daphne's arm.

She pretended not to hear, her eyes on the scene at the counter.

"I'm not at liberty to say where."

She slammed her fists onto the top of the counter.

"That's quite enough, Mrs Tanning."

"No, you lot haven't done enough." That was the older man. "We want answers about our nephew's murder."

"We have no evidence of the cause of death as yet and—"

Mrs Tanning threw her head back and laughed. Everyone looked at her, including her husband and son. She stopped abruptly.

"Lisa Brooker married three men from one family over the course of five years and each one died within months of the wedding. Steve within hours."

Minutes, even.

"I am sorry for your loss. We are gathering information and will be in touch with any questions." The young constable's face had reddened but his manner was calm and steady. If the Tanning family were all like this, no wonder the police had their hands full.

The man spoke again, more under his breath than out loud. "Feud is killing us off."

"I'm not moving until someone in authority presents themselves to me." Mrs Tanning crossed her arms and leaned against the wall and her husband followed suit. The teen rolled his eyes and got his phone out.

John tugged a bit more on Daphne's arm and this time she let him lead her outside. A large flatbed ute was parked half on the footpath and they went around it.

"Well, that was different." Daphne said. "Are we having a coffee?"

"You sound cheerful for someone who wanted to be back on the road in a couple of hours."

"There's something to be said for not being too hasty. I may have allowed my emotions to run a way a bit."

John glanced at her. "So, we're staying?"

"Let's start with the coffee and see what happens."

What happened was a text message that shocked them both.

Sitting outside in the morning sun was pleasant and they elected to sit in the fresh air with their coffees. The café they sat outside was small and quite crowded as people hurried in and out.

Daphne was in two minds about what to do thanks to the visit to the police station. It was clear how hard the small team was working to investigate Steve's death. If there was one thing she was familiar with, it was understaffed police stations. Back in their home town it was a one-officer set up. When Trev Sibbritt was the leading constable there, he'd managed. Just. Since he'd left to move to a new post in Kingfisher Falls, there'd been a quick succession of appointees who'd decided not to stay. Hard work for one person when there's a large region to cover.

Little Bridges was bigger than River's End, but still a small town. It appeared they had four police officers in attendance which was probably sufficient for most situations.

"Doll? You are deep in thought."

Daphne smiled at John. "I was thinking about home."

"Anything in particular?"

"The police situation and how different it is from here. Lots more officers but my observation is they also have more trouble to contend with." Daphne picked up her cup. "Did you hear what Mr Tanning said under his breath?"

"Something about a feud."

"Yes. Feud is killing us off. I wonder..." she took a sip.

John leaned back in his chair with a small smile.

"What?" she asked.

"I can see your mind ticking over, Daph. But it isn't up to you to fix their problems."

"Oh, I wasn't considering that. Mrs Tanning is quite scary. But it does raise some questions about the history of the Brookers and Tannings. What is this family feud about? Are there more suspicious deaths on either side, I wonder."

"I would imagine the police have it under control, love."

He was right, of course.

Daphne gazed around as she sipped her delicious coffee. Many towns they'd stayed in recently had quiet Sundays with few or no shops open apart from the obligatory café or bakery. But Little Bridges was different. In either direction from where they sat, shops were open and people wandered. The atmosphere was almost festive and invited her to explore.

The strangest sensation gripped the back of Daphne's head and the hairs rose on the back of her neck. Someone was watching her. She always knew.

With a casual movement, she let her eyes drift until she found the source.

It was the waiter.

Her heart skipped a beat.

Across and down the road, on the footpath, he stared at her.

Hoping he didn't know she'd seen him, she moved her eyes away. "John, don't be obvious about it, but if you look over my left shoulder to the other side of the road, can you see a young man?"

John took a moment to find him. "The one who is walking away?"

Daphne's head shot around. He had stalked off, glancing at her with a scowl before turning onto a path leading to one of the bridges.

"He's the one you saw coming out of the caterer's van? Possibly Lloyd?"

"He is. I could feel him staring at me."

"But why? If he's guilty of something, it doesn't make sense for him to draw attention to himself."

"Perhaps he wants to scare me."

"What?" John half-stood then dropped back in his seat. "Sorry. I think we need to finish our coffee, go back to Bluebell, and head to our next town."

The waiter's odd behaviour didn't frighten Daphne. It made her curious.

Her phone beeped as a text message arrived.

"Hold that thought, love."

Her eyes read the message but her brain didn't understand.

"Who is it?"

"Um...the mother of the bride of the wedding I'm officiating in two weeks. But why?"

"Can you read it to me?"

She would if she could find her voice. Her mouth was dry. She licked her lips, stumbling over the words. "Daphne, I'm letting you know we've decided to use another celebrant. Considering what is being reported on the news I prefer not to bring bad vibes to an otherwise positive day. Will send you some money to cover your expenses."

"Huh?" John sounded as confused as she felt.

Tears prickled at the back of her eyes but only for an instant. Her heart thumped an uncomfortable beat and she dropped the phone onto the table to clench her hands.

John scooped up the phone and read the message to himself, his forehead creased. "I don't understand. News has already travelled about Steve? And even so, what does his probably accidental death have to do with their wedding two hundred kilometres away?"

"Bad vibes."

"Doll, it isn't your fault."

"Do they think I pushed Steve into the pool?" her voice

rose and a passer-by turned to look at her with a horrified expression. Daphne clamped her lips together.

"Come on. Let's go back to Bluebell and make some plans." John stood and offered his hand.

They walked arm in arm, following the direction the waiter took. When they were at the middle of the bridge, Daphne stopped. "I've made a decision, love. We're not going anywhere."

A MATTER OF WHO

John had to sprint to catch up with Daphne after her bombshell on the bridge. He'd frozen in surprise as his fired-up wife took off at a cracking pace towards the caravan park.

"Hang on a min, Daph!" he puffed as he reached her side. "Can't talk if...if you go so fast."

"Oh. Sorry, love." She slowed right down and slipped her arm through his. "Thought you were right behind me."

It took a minute to catch his breath. At least Daphne didn't look upset now about the text message. But what she'd just announced...

"Can you repeat what you said before you took off?"

She glanced at him with half a smile. "Which bit? That we have to stay in Little Bridges for a bit longer? Or the part about finding out what really happened to Steve Tanning?"

"The second part." He said. "You're serious."

"Of course I am. The poor police department is overworked and it can't help them having the Tanning clan fronting up and wasting valuable time."

"But it's their job, Daphne, not yours. No matter how much your desire to help comes from a place of kindness."

Daphne stopped abruptly and turned to John. "I don't feel very kind. I've lost a client. What if I lose more?" Tears glistened in her eyes and John put his hands on her shoulders. "Being a celebrant means the world to me and all because of something happening which had nothing to do with my ceremony, I'm seen as...well, I don't know what. A bad omen?"

"Oh, doll." John dug around for a handkerchief as a tear rolled down her cheek. "Here, this is clean." He tapped at the tear and then wrapped Daphne's fingers around the cloth. "You are not a bad anything. There'll be a silver lining somewhere in there once you get past the shock."

"Lisa and Steve chose me. I promised them a perfect day and somebody stole that away from them. And from me."

"That's the point, love. Somebody else did this. Either by accident or design."

To his relief, she nodded. "You're right, John. But it hurts and from a practical, business perspective, I need to make sure my other clients understand how serious I am about my role in their important moments. They have to trust I will always put them first, even if I have to solve a murder to do so."

"Daphne?"

They continued on, following the path towards the camping ground.

"Daph, I know you have suspicions but what makes you believe the groom was murdered? You said he'd been drinking before and after the ceremony, so maybe he really did fall in."

"A definite maybe."

He had to grin. Her mind was ticking over and who was he to stand in her way? If there was one thing he knew about Daphne Agatha Jones, it was that she didn't give up. Once she set her mind to something, she was going to get answers.

John was the wisest person Daphne knew. And if he told her it was a mistake to pursue this new direction then she would listen.

Most likely.

There'd been the odd time in the recent past when she'd carried out her own investigations without his approval. Well, without his knowledge because that way he didn't have the chance to say no. Not that he'd ever try to boss her around. Their marriage was one of equality and true love. She'd seen his smile earlier and it warmed her heart.

"First things first." She announced as they climbed into Bluebell. "I think a pot of tea is in order and some more of those commercially prepared, overly sugary but somehow delicious biscuits of yours."

Daphne collected her large notebook, the one she used to scribble ideas for ceremonies. After finding a fresh page, she sat at the table while John made tea. "I'm going to write down everything I remember from the last two days. Every person I met or saw. All the incidents like people arguing and words spoken."

"Good idea. After our tea, do you mind if I do a spot of fishing? Let you have some quiet and I can find us something for dinner."

He needed some time to himself. Daphne understood.

He'd want to process all the ups and downs of the past day or so.

"Sounds delicious! Well, once we cook what you catch."

She pushed the notebook away until they'd enjoyed their tea and gave John her full attention. By the time he changed into shorts and polo top and headed outside to collect his fishing gear, he was smiling and relaxed again. The way it should be.

You've got to be careful not to worry him, Daph.

Easier said than done, given how well he knew her.

An hour or so later, she stretched and got to her feet. She'd covered several pages of her notebook in writing and she'd clarified some things in her mind. What she needed to do was go back to the Brooker house and try to get some photos of the grounds. But how? She discarded the thought about sneaking around in the middle of the night. How would it look if she was caught? No, she needed a reason to visit them and then find a way to access the grounds.

A tap on the door interrupted her musings. "Forget your keys, love?" She swung the door open.

"G'day."

"Oh. Mr Brooker."

"Bertie. Nobody calls me mister anymore."

This was a surprise. Bertie stood a few feet back from the door, gazing at Bluebell. "She's a beauty. Did you fix her up yourself?"

Daphne climbed down. "We consulted on the work and I decorated inside. But we both were working full time so left the actual rebuild to professionals. Do you like caravans?"

"Used to build them. Had a big company. Once." He frowned. Moving closer to the side, he ran a hand over the join where a line of white cut through the blue. "Clever use of colour. Beautiful job."

This was a different Bertie from the one Daphne had met the last two times. The earlier disdain was gone, as was the sense that his mind was a long way away. Dementia was such a dreadful disease.

"Thank you. John and I are very happy with Bluebell... that's her name."

"And it suits her." He stepped back and crossed his arms. "Things aren't good at home."

"I'm very sorry for your loss."

His eyes didn't move and the longer he stared, the more Daphne got a sense he was sizing her up. She didn't think he meant any harm but his visit was unexpected.

"I didn't lose anything. But the place is like a mad house. Lisa weeping and throwing herself onto any comfortable surface whenever anyone looks her way. Bob and Margaret arguing all the time. House staff keeping out of the way."

"Grief affects everyone differently."

"Yeah. Hoping you'd come to the house."

"Me?"

"Say a few words. Don't celebrants do deaths as well?"

Daphne opened her mouth and closed it again as her mind raced. She'd wanted the chance to take photos. But the idea of another ceremony for those people had her blood pressure shooting for the stars.

"Nothing formal. Just the family gathered around. Thought Lisa might feel she has some closure. She likes ceremonies. All the pomp and glamour." He continued. "Not like a funeral. Just something to make her happy."

"Well, I guess I could."

"Good." He turned to go.

"But when? And I'd need some details."

"I'll talk to them. Want me to call you?"

"Please. Just give me enough notice."

Bertie waved as he walked away. He moved fast and with purpose in the direction of the river, but further north than where John fished. Daphne estimated the Brooker property backed onto it about two kilometres away. Bit of a hike for a man in his late seventies if her guess was right.

Back inside, Daphne added to her notes.

Under 'Lisa' she wrote:

Appears more upset when being watched.

Loves ceremonies.

The idea that Lisa killed Steve didn't sit right with Daphne. She might be a bit of an attention seeker but her shock at seeing her new husband dead was genuine. She was sure.

Beneath 'Bertie' she added:

Used to own a big company building caravans

Physically fit

The elderly man was at the bottom of her list of suspects but it paid to keep a record of her thoughts. One never really knew another person so how could anyone be above suspicion?

A FAMILY AT ODDS

Here she was, back at the Brooker residence as if it was two days ago. This afternoon there were fewer vehicles around, only a couple of cars in fact. The expansive front garden was empty of people and the place might have been deserted if not for Lisa's now-familiar raised voice coming from somewhere inside the house. Her words were muffled but her anger was clear.

Daphne sighed and glanced down the road. John was right at the end. Too late to turn back. He'd dropped her there after voicing his concerns.

"What if they treat you badly, love?"

"Bertie assured me everyone wants me there to discuss his idea."

"So, it isn't an actual ceremony yet."

Bertie had phoned just after John arrived back with a couple of fish in his bucket and a smile on his face. They'd had a nice salad for lunch before Daphne changed into tailored pants and a button up blouse. It would have to do until she could dry clean her jacket.

"No. Apparently Lisa wants to ask a few questions first." Daphne had kissed John's cheek. "I'll be fine."

Once John turned the corner and the car disappeared from view, Daphne adjusted the strap of her handbag on her shoulder. If nothing else, she might get the opportunity to go into the back garden. Take a few secret photographs.

At the front door she knocked twice before footsteps approached. Rapid footsteps. The door swung open and a woman—tears streaking her face—hurried past, gripping a suitcase.

"Are you alright, dear?"

At the top step, the other woman stopped. "That terrible woman...how could she?"

"I don't understand."

"She wanted them all dead."

Other footsteps approached and the woman started down the steps.

"Wait." Daphne followed. "Lisa?"

"Margaret." The word was hissed and then, the woman was off again.

"Mrs Jones?"

Bob was again the person to greet her at the front door and as before, he wore a black suit. Perhaps he was an undertaker. Which would be useful with the amount of dead sons-in-law he had.

Daphne Jones! Too soon.

Afraid she might giggle from her nervous humour, Daphne kept her eyes down as she turned around.

"Are you alright?"

"Me?" she raised her head. "Um...yes, just admiring the mosaic tiles."

He screwed his face up. "Another one of Margaret's

fancy ideas. Me, I'd be happier with a cabin in the woods. Please, come in."

All was quiet inside.

"I hope the cook didn't startle you."

"The cook? Oh. She was a bit upset."

"Happens all the time. This was because we got caterers in for the wedding."

A snippet of a memory popped into Daphne's mind. Walking past the kitchen where two women glared at her the other day. Yes, she'd seen her before.

"The others are outside on the deck." Bob led them outside.

Lisa, Margaret, and Bertie sat around a glass top table on a corner of the large deck in an area covered by clear roofing. A ceiling fan pumped warm air down, which didn't really help. Daphne was glad her jacket wasn't cleaned yet because even in the past hour, the temperature had risen.

Although it was early spring, this part of the country was considerably warmer than coastal towns. Little Bridges was surrounded by flat plains and known for its hot summers and cold winters. And now, as all eyes turned her way, at least one set were as icy as the season just gone.

"Daphne. Oh, I'm sorry..." Lisa burst into tears. She covered her face with what looked like a silk handkerchief and sobbed.

Bertie patted her back from the next seat. Bob pulled out a chair for Daphne and once she sat, he plonked himself down with a scowl, ignoring his daughter. Margaret smiled at Daphne. It was as forced and artificial smile as Daphne remembered seeing, and she'd seen a few over the years. And those cold, cold eyes of hers sent a short chill up Daphne's spine.

A young woman wearing an apron placed a tray with a jug of lemonade and glasses on the table and almost tripped over her own feet in her hurry to leave.

The sense of dread Daphne experienced leading up to the wedding was back in force. The Brookers were as dysfunctional a family as any in her experience. Mum and Dad at odds. Adult daughter who lived at home and lost her temper a lot. Grandfather on a decline but possibly manipulating them all. And staff frightened to do or say the wrong thing.

Why are you here, Daph?

Telling them to get counselling was an appealing idea. But leaving wasn't going to help uncover the killer. Assuming it was one of them. And now Margaret was top of the list thanks to the throwaway comment by the cook.

"I'm terribly sorry for your loss. All of you." Daphne began. "My heart goes out to you and Steve's friends and family."

Lisa dropped her handkerchief. Her eyes were suspiciously dry. "His family? Do you not know anything about them?"

Daphne shook her head.

"They are awful. Dreadful people who prey on others." Lisa glanced at Bertie. "Steal their hard work and dreams."

Interesting.

Bertie pulled a silver flask from a top pocket and took a swig.

"Dad, it isn't even mid-afternoon." Bob admonished.

"Isn't it? My bad." Bertie had another drink.

"My *bad*?" Margaret shook her head. "Really, Bertie. Time to stop being on the internet so much."

"Nothing else to do."

He exchanged a look with Lisa. A strange look which Daphne couldn't decipher.

Bob poured glasses of lemonade and passed them around. "We thought Dad's idea was a good one. Having a small ceremony to say goodbye to Steve."

"Except that is what a funeral is for." Margaret grabbed her glass.

"But Mum, we don't know when it will be. The police said they won't have any news until at least tomorrow from the coroner and you must remember how long these things can take. I imagine Mrs Jones needs to leave sometime soon for her next appointment and then who will we get to say nice things about my husband. My...poor...husband." Lisa touched the handkerchief to her eyes.

Nobody in her family took any notice of her action but Daphne kept an eye on her. After a moment, Lisa dropped the fabric away and sniffed, then picked up her glass and drank. The silence dragged and only the distant mooing of cattle cut through the quiet.

"This is such a lovely spot you have. The house, gardens. How big is your property?"

Bob grinned. It was the first time Daphne had seen him look remotely happy.

"Almost a hundred hectares. Two hundred and fifty acres old school."

"I hear cows. Is that what you do here? Breed cattle?"

"We have half a dozen bovine grass mowers. And a couple of retired racehorses and a few sheep. Bit of a menagerie. No, we just like our space." Bob laughed.

"Besides," Margaret added. "We might live in the middle of nowhere, but showing the locals what a proper lifestyle is matters a great deal."

"It is a grand house." Daphne said.

"Isn't it? I had an award-winning architect come from the city to draw up plans."

"Good thing I love you, Mags. Spending all that money on the place."

"Well someone had to do something. Bertie would still be living in the last of his caravans near the river if I'd not intervened."

"Loved my caravan."

"It was a dump, Bertie. You were holding onto the past."

"Mum. How about facts?"

But Margaret had an audience and was on a roll.

"Mrs Jones doesn't understand what we've had to contend with. You see, Bertie once ran this town. Owned the biggest business and employed almost everyone. But he needed a partner and—"

"Mum! Stop it." Lisa stood so fast that her seat fell over. "Mrs Jones came to discuss a farewell ceremony, not hear about the worst of my husband's family."

"Isn't it three husbands?"

"Dad!"

With that, Lisa flounced away.

Bertie swigged from his flask, but he didn't seem bothered. If anything, he looked amused.

As interesting as these insights were, Daphne wanted to go after the younger woman and offer some comfort. Even if she was seeking attention with her exaggerated sighs and crocodile tears, losing her husband minutes after saying 'I do' was a dreadful tragedy. Daphne couldn't even imagine what she must be feeling. And she never wanted to know.

"Sorry about Lisa," Bob said. "She's an emotional girl at the best of times."

Margaret hadn't taken any notice of Lisa's exit. She'd sipped her lemonade and stared into the distance but when the conversation stopped, she glanced around the table, then to the chair on the ground.

"Tell us more about this farewell ceremony, Mrs Jones."

A HISTORY LESSON

"Did I mention what Bertie said about our Bluebell?" Daphne and John sat under the awning in twilight. Their dinner of grilled fish, potatoes baked in foil, and fresh bread rolls from the Little Bridges bakery, was now a delicious memory. John was doing far too much of the work, which did tend to happen around the times Daphne officiated ceremonies, but tonight a twinge of guilt reminded her it was time to give him a break. Tomorrow she'd manage all the meals and even find time to make cookies.

"What is that little smile for, love?" John leaned over and topped up her glass of apple cider.

"You look after me so well."

"Easy to do. Now we don't need to be involved in the day to day running of the real estate business, I am enjoying doing a bit for you."

John's original plan for retirement was to sell the business, but an offer from a young realtor changed his mind. Gavin wasn't in the position to buy but was managing the business with the view to buying in a few years. It suited Gavin. And them.

"And no, you didn't tell me what Bertie said."

"He said she's a beauty and the use of colour is good. He asked if we'd fixed her up ourselves."

John chuckled. "Much as I'd love to be that clever, it was a bit outside my skillset."

"You can turn your hand to anything."

It was pleasant sitting here as the sun set. The air carried the ruckus of native birds settling for the night, squabbling over perches and finding their spot. Little else moved close to their site. Only a handful of other caravans were in residence and none of them close by.

"You've not told me much about the meeting with the Brookers. Only up to the point of Lisa upturning her chair and leaving the conversation."

"She came back after a few minutes. Either she'd walked off her upset or..."

"Or?"

"I'm going to sound cynical and unkind. But it strikes me Lisa thrives on attention. Nobody followed her into the house."

"So the impact of storming off was quickly lost." John said.

"Her mother didn't even seem to notice Lisa had gone. She stared off in the distance the whole time. Oh. Not the distance." Daphne tapped her glass with her fingers. "It was at the pool."

"I would imagine that pool will give the whole family sad memories for a long time. How awful to have someone die on your property under such circumstances." John sighed and leaned back in his seat.

"I wonder where the others died?"

"Others?"

"Sam and Shane. Electrocution and falling off a ladder." Daphne reached behind her chair to a table beside the caravan and collected her notebook. "Might be worth finding out a few details of their respective demises." She scribbled some words. "Depending upon the coroner's findings about poor Steve, one would think Lisa would be a suspect."

"Love, don't you think you're speculating? For all you know, Sam and Shane might have had their accidents at work and anyway, they would have been investigated at the time."

Daphne grinned. "Which is why I need to find out!"

A magpie landed nearby and elegantly tiptoed towards the awning without a care in the world. The stately black and white bird stopped a few feet away and tilted his head.

"Feeding a baby?" John got to his feet and uncovered some uncooked fish pieces. He took one piece and tossed it close to the magpie, who wasted no time spearing it with a sharp beak before gliding away. "I heard a young one calling for food up in a tree near the river. Guess we're right in hatching time. I'll wash my hands and be right back."

As John disappeared into the caravan, Daphne added another note.

Why did Lisa choose three men from one family to marry?

It was a puzzle indeed. She gathered the Tannings were a large extended family but even so, Little Bridges wasn't so small that there wouldn't be other men to meet, let alone any further afield.

"Here I am."

"Where would you go to look for a husband?" Daphne

said.

His eyes widened. "Sorry?"

She giggled. "If you were a woman living in a small community, where would potential husbands hang out? I never had to go looking, thanks to my high-school sweetheart." She smiled at John. "Market research."

With a slightly pained expression, John shook his head. "I'm struggling with it. But what if we turn it around and ask where would a young man be likely to find a potential wife?"

"I'm all ears."

"My interest in genealogy might help us on this occasion."

"Oh. Research on marriages."

"Yes, along with other things. Some of the websites have interesting snippets about people's backgrounds, even where they met. Or where they were employed. So a shopkeeper might meet a customer. Church is a popular place for many reasons, not the least being the common ground of sharing a faith."

Daphne grabbed her pen. "Keep talking, love."

"A young man might be in a trade. A carpenter, possibly at a home to build an extension and meets the daughter of the house."

"An electrician who gets zapped at his new wife's house." Daphne was writing and only glanced up when there was no response. "Bad taste?"

"Daph."

"Sorry. Please keep going."

"Some things have changed over the years but people would still meet at school or college. They might work together." John said.

"What about socially?"

"Also shared interest in sports. Or hobbies."

After putting down her pen, Daphne swallowed some of the sweet apple cider as she thought about it. At the restaurant, they'd overheard the waiters say the Tanning boys were part of the cool set. Lisa came across as belonging to that crowd but would have left high school before Steve started.

"I wonder who Lisa went to school with? How would we find out when her previous husbands died? Or lived?"

"Best way to get a look at when they died is a quick walk through a cemetery, assuming they were buried locally." John said.

Daphne clapped her hands, scaring away the magpie which had returned. "Oh, sorry, birdie. But you are so clever, John. Can we go now?"

"In the dark?" John shook his head. "You go. Not me."

"There's no such thing as ghosts."

"Still not going. Why not finish telling me about the meeting?"

He was right. She'd see more in daylight than with a flashlight in an unfamiliar graveyard. "The long and the short of it is they've asked me to do a farewell ceremony of sorts on Wednesday. Lisa is going to email some ideas across and Margaret will invite the bridal party to join the family. Keep it very small and quiet."

"Shall we plan on leaving on Wednesday afterwards? Gives us time for the drive to your next wedding location and to settle in."

"Excellent plan, love. As long as the coroner finds no evidence of a murder, there's no reason to believe we need to be here any longer."

HEARING AND SEEING STRANGE THINGS

Daphne finally got the chance to have a proper look at the shops in Little Bridges. John was content to go wherever she wanted. He didn't mind browsing with her, or waiting if she wanted to look at something he didn't find interesting. Which wasn't often as they had similar tastes and interests most of the time. Today they planned to be tourists. No talk of the wedding. Not even any writing up of the farewell ceremony.

While she was cooking breakfast for them earlier, Daphne announced it was time they enjoyed their visit to the area and forgot about everything else. She'd already spent an hour on the laptop checking her website. Thankfully no more cancellations but no new bookings either.

The first place they headed was the dry cleaners. Daphne handed over her jacket and pants with a smile and was promised it would be done by the next afternoon. Outside, he gazed around.

"Which way, love?" he asked.

"If you don't mind, I may need to buy another suit. With

everything that happened...well it made me take a good look at my wardrobe. I have plenty of casual wear but not a lot for the ceremonies."

They spent the next hour or so visiting the half dozen ladies' boutiques. Daphne told John he didn't need to wait around for her but he was doing a bit of research on his phone and was happy enough to find a bench along the footpath.

John's interest in genealogy began years ago. Daphne came from a troubled background which he suspected was why she'd opened her heart and their home to foster children. And then, in midlife she'd found out about some discrepancies between her birth certificate and what she'd grown up believing.

Although she'd refused to look into startling revelations about her father, John made some quiet enquiries which led nowhere. There was no immediate family to consult. With the busy business they ran, he put it on the back burner and they'd rarely mentioned it since then. Now he had a little project of his own to make Daphne happy. He had no intention of telling her until sufficient facts came to light, and their current itinerary around Victoria was perfect for his research.

"Here I am!" Daphne sat beside him, both hands filled with clothing bags. "What are you up to?"

He slid the phone away. "Taking a look at a map of the area. I take it you found some clothes?"

"I've got two new jackets and then some pants which go with either." Then the other hand. "And some cooler tops seeing how warm the weather already is. I hope you don't mind."

John kissed her cheek and took all the bags. "Why would

I ever mind? I love seeing you doing something nice for yourself."

Their next stop was an ice cream shop. Cones in hand, they crossed the road to the shade along the river. A long path meandered between the water and the main street, old trees offering respite from the growing heat of the day.

"What would you like to do next?" Daphne asked. "Didn't we see a fishing and tackle shop a bit further along?"

"I wouldn't mind a browse. I won't be long." Although Daphne enjoyed eating what he caught, she had zero interest in fishing.

"Take all the time you want and then come and find me in the bookshop over there once you're finished."

Sounded perfect. And a bookshop was about the safest place he could think of leaving Daphne on her own in this somewhat strange town.

Stepping into the bookshop just off the main street in Little Bridges, Daphne sniffed the air to capture the unique and beloved smell of books. Delightful. Every wall was covered in bookcases and used books were piled up on the floor in the middle. Chaotic, but ideal for those who enjoyed rummaging. Behind a small desk covered with food wrappings, a woman in her thirties ignored Daphne as she tapped on a phone.

"Good morning!" Daphne smiled.

The younger woman grunted and didn't look up.

Well. You're a friendly soul. Not.

Customer service mattered to Daphne. She and John treated every person who stepped through the door of their real estate agency as a welcome visitor. When she visited shops and was ignored, she never knew if it was because the staff weren't trained properly, or that they weren't paid well, so didn't love what they did. Loving what you did mattered. No point doing a job year in, year out, and not finding pleasure in it.

She pushed aside her feelings of being snubbed and browsed the shelves. There wasn't any order, with non-fiction sharing space with children's books. Gardening books with romance. Somehow, it made it more interesting. It took no time at all to lose track of the minutes. With carpet underfoot there was hardly a sound as she selected a couple of mysteries to buy. When a phone rang, she jumped.

"Friendly Books. This is Tiffany."

The woman didn't even sound welcoming. Much less 'friendly'. Until she heard the voice on the other end and brightened up.

"I am so glad you called! Bored out of my head."

Perhaps talking to customers would help.

"Wednesday? Like, what time? And do I have to wear the stupid bridesmaid's dress?"

Daphne took a step back so she was out of direct sight of the woman but could see her through a gap in the bookshelves.

"No? Good. I know Lisa wanted yet another colour for this wedding but lilac did nothing for me. You looked good in it though." She listened and then giggled. "Next time we'll tell her we want black dresses. Perfect to wear at the wedding then straight to the funeral." She gave a shriek of laughter.

Hand over her mouth to stop herself speaking her mind, Daphne almost dropped the books. What a terrible thing to say. She peered at the woman and recognised her as one of the bridesmaids.

"Yeah, count me in. I'll tell the boss I'm sick. Probably enough leftover champagne at Lisa's to make it true anyway. Gotta go, babe, can see the boss heading in."

Off the phone, Tiffany threw the mess on the desk into a bin and jumped to her feet, reaching a bookcase as the door swung open. An older woman with a walking stick shuffled in, muttered at Tiffany, and made her way to a door between bookcases which Daphne hadn't noticed.

"Bring me the orders book."

As Tiffany disappeared into the room with her boss, Daphne didn't waste a minute. Sending up a quick 'sorry' to the tidy bookstore gods, she shoved the paperbacks she'd chosen onto the nearest shelf and was outside before either woman returned.

"Whoa, Daph, slow down!"

She'd exited without looking and almost ran into John, who had both hands full between her shopping bags and a new fishing pole.

"Thank goodness it's you. We have to go."

Not waiting for a response, she hurried off.

"Daph, wrong way."

She needed to put a bit of distance between herself and Tiffany. Most likely she'd see her tomorrow at the ceremony and had no desire to be viewed as an eavesdropper. Again.

"Okay, we'll go the scenic route." John sounded amused from somewhere behind her.

At the next corner, she waited for him to catch up and for her to take a deep breath. There were less shops along here, apart from a large, modern supermarket beyond a carpark over the road. A white van was parked facing the street, its driver obscured by sun glare.

"Would you like to tell me what got under your skin?" John put the bags down to free a hand and put his arm around Daphne. "You ran out of the bookshop like you'd seen a ghost."

"Sorry. Accidentally overheard a disturbing conversation and didn't want anyone seeing me."

"What? Are you okay, love?"

A car drew up next to the van and when its driver climbed out, Daphne moved behind John. "Let me hide for a minute. She's less likely to recognise you."

"Who?" John followed the direction Daphne was looking in. "The woman?"

"It's Lisa."

Lisa was dressed in jeans and T-shirt, her hair in a ponytail and sunglasses covering her eyes. She went around her own car to stand at the driver's side of the van.

"Do you think they're talking?" Daphne whispered.

"Hard to tell from this distance. But why does it matter?"

"I know the van."

"Actually, now you mention it...looks a bit like the caterer's van. But, doll, it's a common brand. Lots of businesses use them and it isn't badged up."

"We need Charlotte Dean right now." Daphne said.

"Charlotte?"

"She takes photos of everything. What a good idea. I have my phone in my bag."

Doctor Charlotte Dean was a friend from River's End who'd moved to a new town where they'd recently visited so Daphne could perform a wedding ceremony.

"Do you think you should be taking photos of people

without their permission? What if she sees you?" John asked.

"True. How about you take a photo. You're better at it."

John faced Daphne. "Neither of us are taking photos. Lisa is allowed to talk to people in her own town, and we aren't here to follow her around."

Over his shoulder, the van moved and Daphne peered around him. Lisa was getting back into her car and she raised a hand to wave as the van passed her.

"I wonder who the driver is?"

With an audible sigh, John picked up the bags. "I hear lunch calling. Time to go home before it gets too hot."

"Let me carry something." Daphne said.

"I've got everything but you are welcome to push the button on the traffic lights on the main street."

She giggled.

"Come on, young lady. You can tell me about the bookshop on the way home."

UNEXPECTED SUSPECT

John elected to have a shower to cool down when they reached Bluebell and Daphne was quick to take the opportunity to make some notes while events were fresh in her mind. By the time he emerged she'd put the notebook away and made lunch.

Determined to keep her earlier promise about staying away from anything to do with the Brookers, Daphne encouraged John to tell her about his new fishing rod and some accessories he'd bought. Most of it went over her head but his enthusiasm kept her interested. Then, she showed him her new clothes as she sorted them to wash or send to the dry cleaners in the next town.

"One can't be too careful with new things."

They decided to spend the afternoon playing board games. Outside, the sun was beating down in what was an uncharacteristically hot afternoon, according to John's internet search of temperature averages.

"Reckon there'll be a storm tonight." He opened the box of games they stored under a seat. "Getting a bit humid."

"You know, we've not had a storm since we've been travelling." Daphne poured icy water into glasses. "What if we're hit by lightning?"

"Not likely, love. Not with those tall gums all over the place."

"Oh my. What if one of them is hit by lightning and falls on top of Bluebell?"

"Think we're far enough away. Stop stressing before anything even happens."

Storms weren't Daphne's favourite event. And she should be well and truly accustomed to them after decades living in River's End. Being on the edge of the Great Southern Ocean, storms were common. She carried the glasses to the table, where John was setting up a game of scrabble.

"Good choice. You know you can't win."

"Fighting words!"

A tap on the door stopped the banter and John and Daphne glanced at each other.

"Mr and Mrs Jones? It is Constable McIntyre."

"My, oh, my." Daphne breathed. She slid out of her seat and opened the door. "Please, come in out of the heat."

The young constable took off his hat and climbed in. He was quite tall and seemed uncomfortable in the small space.

"Please, take a seat. Would you like some water?"

"That would be nice. Thank you." He perched on the edge of the spot she'd vacated. "I'm very sorry to intrude. Looks like you're getting ready for a game."

"You might have saved me." John said. "Daphne tends to win these ones."

"There you go. Iced water."

"Thanks. Mrs Jones, Mr Jones, I have some news."

"Please, it is Daphne and John, Constable."

"Matty. Call me Matty."

Daphne sat beside John, who moved across to make space.

"We received the coroner's initial report. It isn't complete yet. There's tox screening, bloodwork, all kinds of other findings yet to come. Anyway, without getting into the details, it would appear Steve Tanning was indeed murdered."

The hairs stood up on the back of Daphne's arms and her stomach clenched. She'd *known* it wasn't an accident.

"That is sad to hear. A young man at the beginning of his married life cut down like that." John said.

"The purpose of my visit is to ask you to come into the station and make a formal statement."

"Of course I will." Daphne asked, reaching under the counter for John's hand. "Are we allowed to know the cause of death?"

"Not at liberty to say. Not until further information comes to light." Matty drank the glass of water in a few gulps and set it down. "That hit the spot. Would now be convenient?"

"We'll drive over right away. Is it just Daphne you need to interview?"

Matty stood and opened the door. "At this stage, yes." He stepped down and gazed at the outdoor kitchen set up beneath the annexe. "Doing some fishing in the river?"

John joined him with Daphne close behind. "I am. Just purchased a new rod in town today."

On the side of the sink, the utensils John used for the fish were in a plastic container. Matty took a look and glanced at John.

"Mind if I borrow your filleting knife?" From his tone of voice, it wasn't a request, and he felt in his pocket and pulled out a glove.

"I guess so. Why?"

Matty lifted the knife by the tip of the handle and inspected it. "Probably no reason. I'll get you to make a statement as well, Mr Jones."

Daphne had no intention of correcting the constable to 'call him John'. Her hackles were up. Why would the police have an interest in the filleting knife belonging to the husband of the celebrant from the wedding where a man was murdered?

Unless...

"Steve was killed with a knife." She crossed her arms and stared at Matty. "And you think we had something to do with it."

"I'd really like to know, please." Half an hour later, Daphne sat opposite a different police officer in the open plan station room. John was at another desk with Matty, his back to Daphne. It all reminded her of a bad television show from the last century.

Senior Constable Barber tapped on her keyboard for a minute before leaning back in her chair. "There's not a lot to tell."

"I understand you are waiting on more results from the coroner's office. And under normal circumstances—not that a murder at a wedding is normal—I wouldn't pry. But taking my husband's filleting knife for forensic profiling casts a different light on this. Do you believe he had anything to do with Steve's murder?"

As much as she was proud of how steady and calm her voice sounded, it was all a front for the panic coursing through Daphne. She wasn't good with uncertainty. Her hands twisted around each other in her lap.

"Assuming John wasn't present at the wedding as you've told us, then no, he isn't a person of interest."

"Then what? Do you think someone stole his knife, stabbed poor Steve, then returned it?"

The officer didn't respond but her eyes never left Daphne's face.

"Oh! You think I did it."

Nothing.

Unsure whether to laugh or cry, Daphne licked her lips as she considered her next words. The police might be guarded about the cause of Steve's death, but their action of confiscating a filleting knife gave it away. Somehow, it hadn't been obvious at the pool that he'd been stabbed but there'd been blood in the pool, on Steve and the man who'd helped. Even on her hands. She glanced at them.

"Care to comment?"

"Yes." Daphne lifted her chin. "I'm not a killer and I have no motive to murder a stranger, so let's get that out of the way first. What I can help you with is my observations of people and events from before the wedding right through until this morning. Some of which I have tried to tell Matty about in the past."

"Mrs Jones, isn't it true that Steve Tanning was rude to you the day prior to his death? That he was insulting in front of other people?"

"It is true. He said he thought I'd be younger. But if that

was sufficient reason to harm him, why didn't I go after Bertie Brooker? He told me I was immoral for marrying Lisa and Steve. And then there's Gina, who is Lisa's great-aunt. She implied I am overweight, among other things."

Senior Constable Barber pulled her chair closer and rested her hands on the keyboard. Her expression had softened.

"What an unkind thing to say."

"It was. But the point I'm trying to make is that insults are never a reason to hurt someone. People say nasty things all the time and it is a reflection on them. Not the recipient."

With a nod, the officer typed a few lines, giving Daphne a chance to settle her racing heart. But John must be stressed about his interview. A sudden burst of laughter from him put that thought to bed. Her muscles relaxed.

"You said you have some observations to share. Where would you like to start?"

THE FALLOUT

Senior Constable Barber guided Daphne through the interview with no further mention of suspecting Daphne of wrong doing. Partway through, John joined her. The officer excused herself for a moment.

"Sounds as though you and Matty hit it off." Daphne said.

"He's a nice young man. Does a spot of fishing himself."

"Does he have a filleting knife?" Daphne muttered under her breath. She wasn't quite ready to be forgiving. John patted her hand.

The officer returned with some bottles of water and offered them to John and Daphne. "Warm day. Best to stay hydrated."

"Thank you." Daphne needed the water and drank quickly.

"So, we've covered the day before the wedding and the day of the wedding as far as the signing of the marriage certificate. Do you recall who else was there?"

"Lisa and Steve were seated in the middle of a long table otherwise filled with gifts. I stood to one side and their witnesses watched on. I have their names in my ceremonies book, sorry, I should have brought that along."

"We can check who they were."

"Some were from the bridal party. Not Tiffany though."

Senior Constable Barber tilted her head and Daphne explained.

"This morning I was in the bookshop and overheard a telephone conversation with the sales assistant. She answered the phone as Tiffany. And talked about being one of the bridesmaids."

"I know her. We'll come back to the telephone conversation shortly. What happened once the signing was completed?"

"There were photos taken as they signed and afterwards. Once I was no longer needed, I made my way to the house, but Mrs Brooker—Margaret—stopped me. She asked if I'd seen her father-in-law, Bertie." Daphne said.

Where was Bertie all that time?

"And had you seen him?"

Daphne shook her head. "Last I saw, he was walking in the opposite direction of the house. Margaret was worried he'd end up in the river based on previous incidents. She and Bob rounded up a search party."

"So the reception was delayed while people searched? It was quite an early wedding." Senior Constable Barber opened her own bottle of water and sipped.

"Apparently Lisa and Steve had a plane to catch that evening for their honeymoon and the reception was to wind down around six. But Lisa didn't search. She sat down with her bridesmaids." And a bottle of champagne. "Steve and his groomsmen followed Bob. Actually, Steve stopped to answer his phone."

"He had his phone on him?"

"A few things were different than most ceremonies I officiate for. But I'm there to marry folk, not judge their choices. The others all went ahead. I'm afraid I didn't see what Steve did."

"We can check who phoned and the time. Might help."

Daphne smiled to herself. Something she'd seen might be the key to finding the murderer. Who had phoned Steve? Surely it was someone asking him to go to the pool. The waiter?

"Mrs Jones?"

"Oh, sorry. Lost in thought. I got as far as the street when Lisa began to scream and I ran back to help. Steve was face down in the swimming pool. Bob and one of the waiters were in there, pushing him towards the side and then another man jumped in and between them, they turned him over." Her heart raced as she remembered. Poor Steve's vacant eyes. The blood on her hand. Lisa sobbing. "He was gone."

"Take a break if you like. This must be upsetting for you."

"I'm fine to keep going, Senior Constable. Finding the murderer is all that matters."

"Daphne was a strength to those around her." John chimed in. "She helped at the pool and then offered comfort to others. And from the start she believed it was a suspicious death."

"Why is that, Mrs Jones?"

So many people with something to gain. Or for revenge.

"Weddings are interesting events. At least for an outsider, like me. Many are filled with genuine love and happiness. Some also have an element of disapproval, or having some guests along who would be better left at home. But this wedding—or at least the time around it—had an adversarial feel."

"You've mentioned, to Matty and to me, some comments directed towards you that weren't pleasant. I take it this isn't your normal experience?"

Daphne shook her head. "Far from it. I'm so lucky as a celebrant to be the one person most people treat well. Even at funerals. But it wasn't about how I was treated. Everyone was at each other, one way or another. Lisa was upset at her mother. Bertie was upset at everyone. Bob as well. Steve might have been one of those people who speaks without thinking or maybe he liked to stir the pot."

Matty wandered over. "Sorry to interrupt. Barbs, she's been picked up for questioning. They reckon they'll be here in twenty."

Barbs? Short for Barber. Nobody would call their child Barbara Barber. Unless she'd married a Barber. Stifling a giggle, Daphne realised everyone's eyes were on her. She was sensitive to being watched, much like this morning at the café.

"I just remembered something."

"About the wedding?"

"About this morning. The waiter was watching me from over the road while we had coffee."

"Which waiter?"

"Well, I did phone Matty about it... How fast can you type?"

"Sorry?"

"There's a lot to fill you in on."

As the interview continued, John's eyes wandered around the station. Desks. A couple of whiteboards. Posters on walls, some for wanted criminals and others with motivational quotes. A small kitchen was through one door, a second one led outside, while another had a sign 'Interrogation and Cells'. Gave him a small shiver.

Daphne and the senior constable were in deep discussion. Matty had gone through the door to the cells and now emerged. Who was coming in? Assuming it was to do with the murder, was it Lisa or Margaret? What if one of the bridesmaids was a suspect Daphne hadn't pick up on?

He honed in on Daphne's words.

"I don't know the lady's name, but Bob referred to her as the cook. And she told me Margaret wants 'them' all dead."

"She left with a suitcase? Matty?"

Matty hurried over.

"Look into a staff member of the Brooker's, please. The cook, perhaps. She left their employ yesterday in an upset state and may have some useful information."

"Yes, ma'am." He headed for his desk.

"Mrs Jones, you've been most co-operative. And there is a lot of information here so I'd like to go through it and then make up a report for you to sign. You mentioned you'll be staying until Wednesday afternoon?"

"Yes. Once I do the farewell ceremony, we're leaving for my next appointment."

"Lovely. Either Matty or I will be in touch before then."

Everyone stood and shook hands.

The back door opened and a police officer entered, followed by Lisa. A second officer closed the door as he came in behind them. Lisa's eyes were red and puffy as she glanced around.

The minute she spotted Daphne, she ran towards her. John instinctively moved to cut her off, as did the senior constable, but she got to Daphne first. And flung her arms around her.

"Daphne. Thank goodness you're here. Telling them the truth."

"Of course, dear. Telling the truth is all that matters." Daphne looked surprised, of course, but there was her genuine kindness shining through. She patted Lisa's back as she disentangled herself.

"They think," Lisa stopped, sobbed aloud, and put her hands over her eyes. "They think I killed my Steve."

"I would imagine these lovely officers are just getting statements from anyone involved. Witnesses."

"This isn't the first time I've been wrongly accused. But Dad will get our lawyer here and then they'll have to release me."

Behind her, Senior Constable Barber rolled her eyes, then nodded to the other officers. One stepped forward and gently took Lisa's arm.

"You're not under arrest, Ms Brooker—"

"Tanning! Mrs Tanning."

"Sorry, Mrs Tanning. Let's go have a chat and your father's lawyer is free to join us."

Lisa went with him, her sobs getting louder until she was out of sight and the door closed.

"Do you think she did it?" Daphne asked.

"Lisa is just one of several people of interest. And again,

thanks for coming in and we'll be in touch."

John took Daphne's hand and nodded to Matty. They'd been dismissed and he, for one, was happy to leave this behind and step out into the sunshine.

A CHANCE MEETING

"Do you mind if we stop at the supermarket, John? In this heat, I'm thinking of taking some ice cream home." Daphne wiped her forehead. Clouds gathered in the far distance. "And some sedatives."

John laughed aloud and Daphne joined in. She'd never taken a sedative in her life but always joked about them when it was stormy. Laughing was every bit as therapeutic and by the time they reached the supermarket, some of the stress from the police station was gone. John parked not far from the door.

The air conditioning was ramped up high inside and Daphne considered staying there for a while. But there were only a few items to select and they lined up at the one open checkout. The sales assistant chatted to each customer at length and it took a few minutes until they were next. It didn't bother Daphne. Not when she'd had plenty of chats at the supermarket in River's End over the years. But the sales assistant interested her and she whispered to John. "Steve's aunt."

This time her hair was neat in a bun and she wore the supermarket uniform. But her voice carried as she regaled every customer with the sad news of Steve's death and the curse of Lisa Brooker. Either the customers weren't friends with the Brookers or they were too polite to say anything. With a bit of luck she wouldn't recognise Daphne or John, particularly as she'd barely glanced at them in the police station.

No such luck.

"You're that celebrant person." She crossed her arms and stared at Daphne.

John unpacked the basket without a word and from his body language, he was ready to intervene if it got nasty.

"I'm Daphne." Forcing a friendly smile, Daphne put her reusable bag on top of the shopping.

"A little bird told me you are doing something for those evil people. Some kind of ceremony."

Daphne was unsure how to respond. Her arrangement with the Brookers wasn't something she would talk about, at least, not with a person who made it clear they were enemies. Her heart sunk. Was Mrs Tanning about to do as Bertie did. Call her names. Or worse?

Dropping her arms, the other woman began scanning the shopping. "I'm Marlene. Steve meant the world to us all. His parents are inconsolable." She stopped and leaned across the counter. "Would you come and do a ceremony for us?"

"A ceremony?" Talk about unexpected. Daphne's mind worked overtime. This might be a gift of sorts. A chance to evaluate for herself if anyone from Steve's family might be responsible for his murder. "Of course."

John turned to her with his eyes wide. Daphne winked at him.

"Good. What about tonight?" Marlene said.

A gust of wind rattled the long glass windows.

"I need a little more notice. The best I can do is tomorrow." Daphne said.

Shopping scanned and packed, Marlene nodded. "Pretty sure everyone is around mid-morning. I start here at lunch time. Can I get your phone number to confirm?"

Daphne found a card in her handbag. "Email is best. Let me know the time and the address. Oh, and anything special you want said. And I will send you a return email with any questions and my fee."

A few minutes later Daphne and John were back in the car.

"Are you sure?" John turned the engine on. "All we know about the Tannings is what we've seen. People quick to anger and not afraid to get into a brawl."

"True, but there were extenuating circumstances, love. Fancy losing someone you love under such conditions."

"Even so."

"Let's see what the email says and make a decision then."

Daphne had already made her decision.

"I'm sure the Tanning family are nice people."

John's silence indicated he didn't share her optimism.

The sky was darkening as they drove towards Bluebell. Storm clouds loomed over the town, heavy with rain. The wind scattered small branches across the driveway.

"I might lock the awning down. Make sure nothing is loose in this weather." John pulled into their parking spot. "Let's get the shopping inside and I'll get started."

"And I'll help."

"You sure, love? Storm's close."

"Four hands will get it done faster."

As it was, they only just managed to pack the outdoor kitchen away, roll the awning into its travelling position, and secure the caravan before the first rain drops fell. John insisted Daphne go in as he did a final check and then, a minute after he joined her, a streak of lightning tore through the sky.

A STORY OF SUSPECTS

While Daphne busied herself making a pot of tea, John did a quick tour to make sure there were no leaks. The rain was heavy and relentless but Bluebell was rock solid. Not a sign of water where it shouldn't be. Daphne set their cups and the teapot on the table and sat, staring out of the window and jumping with every lightning strike.

"You're going to exhaust yourself doing that." John put her notebook and a pen on the table. "I know you have a million thoughts running through your mind, so what about you pretend I know nothing of this week's events?"

"You mean, tell you the story?"

"I was listening to you talk to the officer earlier and it had me thinking."

It was obvious John wanted to distract her from the storm, give her something else to consider. And he was the sweetest man because he must be bored silly with hearing about the murder.

"Thinking about what?"

"The cook. There has to be a story there. So why don't you run through your suspects—for want of a better word?"

She didn't need a second invitation. There was a lot she hadn't added to her notes. Daphne picked up her pen.

"Where shall I start?"

"Who and why?"

"I can do that." She flicked back through the pages and glanced at John with a smile. "There's a few of them."

"Perfect. We can pretend we're working on a game. Like Cluedo." He picked up the teapot. "I'll do this and you work through your list. Who is the chief suspect?"

Good question. It changed. And the more information that came out, the more often it changed. Much as her gut said the woman was innocent of murder, there was a stand out.

"The obvious one is Lisa."

"Why?"

"History. She married three men from one family group, all cousins. Each one is dead following what appeared to be an accident." Daphne made a note, reading aloud as she wrote. "Find out how Sam and Shane died. And how long the marriages were."

"Doesn't mean Lisa is responsible though."

"True. But she has a flair for the dramatic. As if any kind of attention is good attention. The wedding, for example. She made a big deal out of the wrong colour ribbons and carpet. And a lot of her crying produces nothing but big sobs. Now I sound cynical."

John put a cup near Daphne. "Not cynical. Looking with a critical eye. The way a detective would."

"Fair enough. In that case, I'm curious why she kept marrying Tannings." Daphne tapped her pen against her fingers. "The Brookers and Tannings appear to have some feud going on—Gina said as much the other night—so why would she bring the enemy of her family into their home?"

"Good point. Does she think it will stop the feud? Bring everyone closer? Or is it to rebel against her own family?"

Thunder boomed overhead and the rain intensified. Daphne's heart pitter-patted faster and she bit her lip. It was just weather. She forced herself back to the notebook.

"I feel I'm missing something. There are a lot of odd connections and I can't work out where they lead. Not yet."

"If nothing else, you'll end up with a lot of stories to tell. You should write a memoir." John said.

"Only if you take photos for me to include. Something else bothers me about Lisa—those close to her have little in the way of nice words to say. One example is her own father telling her she would never keep a husband."

"Which is coming true."

I wonder if he's making it come true. No, that's plain silly.

"Quite. Then there is her own bridesmaid joking about wearing black next time so they use the same dress for the funeral. The other strange comment was from Gina, Lisa's great-aunt. She asked me if Lisa had told me where the group was having dinner. Either Gina is paranoid, or Lisa has a history of bizarre behaviour."

"Or both."

He was right. The whole Brooker family might be a den of irrational fears and dark secrets.

Daphne started a new page and titled it 'Margaret'.

"She isn't high on my suspect radar, but Margaret has made the list."

John tried to hide a smile and Daphne kicked him gently under the table.

"More tea?" He asked.

"Thank you. And you don't have to sit with me, love. I'm really alright."

Before John could reply, thunder cracked overhead and the lights flicked off. Daphne squealed. Water poured down the outside of the windows in a sheet as if the sky had unleashed the ocean on them and the earlier heat of the day was well and truly gone.

The lights came back on.

"We have plenty of candles, doll, should the power go out."

"Sorry. Didn't mean to scream like that!" Time for this storm to be on its way. Daphne took a few deep breaths. "Actually, I take it back. I would like you to stay right here with me."

"I have no plans to be anywhere else. What if I take something from the freezer for tonight and we can have an early dinner."

It did sound good. At least if the storm continued, Daphne could cuddle under the blankets and hope the sound of the rain would send her to sleep.

MORE SUSPECTS

With the oven warming, John returned to the table. "On to Margaret."

"Yes. And she is of special interest."

"I'm curious, Daph. Lisa is in her thirties, married three times, but still lives with her parents?"

"I know. Unusual."

"Money? Security? But why if she's marrying someone? Wouldn't she move out?"

"Good questions. More to add to my future queries." Daphne scribbled the question down. "When I first met Margaret, I saw a mother who believed she was disappointing her daughter. She was crying and I thought it was because she couldn't please Lisa over the colour of the ribbons and so on. But what if she genuinely didn't want her daughter marrying Steve. She didn't like him."

"Because of how he spoke to people?" John asked.

"Probably didn't help. But I feel in my bones that something sinister happened between the two families in the past. She began to tell me about Bertie's caravan business and how he'd needed a partner, which was when Lisa stormed off. I have to wonder if this partner was a Tanning and it all went bad."

John opened his phone. "Happy to do a bit of research, love."

This was nice. The two of them working together to solve a terrible crime. Even if they were holed up inside with a savage storm rattling Bluebell's windows.

"The other thing about Margaret is her background. From what I've gathered, she moved from the city to marry Bob and was accustomed to a different lifestyle. Insisted on the design of the house being so—is ostentatious an unkind description?"

"With our lifetime in real estate we've seen every kind of home. But hers is out of keeping with the area and my first thought was if it is a way of showing off their wealth."

"Just going to the restroom. Be right back." As Daphne washed her hands a few minutes later, she stared in the mirror. Something was off about this whole family feud thing. She couldn't make sense of it yet, but it had to do with Bertie, and money, and him living in his old caravan by the river. "You'll figure it out, Daph. Let it simmer away."

"Think your phone just made the email arriving sound." John had got a piece of paper for himself and was copying information from his phone. "Anything else about Margaret?"

"Only the comment by the cook that Margaret wants everyone dead. Sounded as if it was straight out of the Lisa Brooker/Tanning book of how to dramatise events."

For a while, the only sound was the rain and thunder, as John wrote and Daphne read the email. From Marlene Tanning, it was surprisingly long and detailed, including a brief story to use about Steve as a child. Daphne found herself wiping a tear away. These people loved Steve and were no less entitled to a beautiful eulogy than the Brookers. More, if anything.

"Okay, love?"

"I'm going to write a lovely farewell ceremony for each family in the morning. For now though, we haven't discussed Bob yet."

"What makes him a suspect?" John put his phone down. "There's no big red flags around him that I've seen."

"No, just lots of little ones. He might very well have just been over the whole wedding thing, but Bob wasn't happy about having the event at the house. Said he'd rather have, and I quote, 'a cabin in the woods' than their mansion. Lisa annoyed him with her demands and even his father made him impatient." The hairs stood up on Daphne's arm and she held it up for John to see. "I have an odd feeling."

"About Bob?"

She shook her head. "Eyes on me. You know I can always tell."

"Not mine?"

"Never yours." Daphne slid closer to the window and peered through. "Surely nobody is out there."

John was on his feet and grabbed a torch. "I'll go and look."

"I'd rather you don't. You'll be drenched in seconds and all for a feeling. Which is gone now." Daphne stretched the muscles in her back, forcing the sensation away. It almost worked. "Too much thunder!"

After checking the door was locked, John sat again. "You sure? I can wear my wet weather gear and carry a fishing pole in a menacing fashion."

"Yes. But thank you." A giggle rose in her throat.

"Don't want you worrying."

"All this talk of murders. It was like when Bertie arrived. I was surprised to see him here."

"Speaking of Bertie, at least he can be omitted from your list." John stared through the window with his eyes narrowed.

"Negatory. I thought the same but despite his age and health concerns, Bertie Brooker is on the list. Aged he might be, but did you know he was once an elite athlete? A runner. His disappearance that day sent lots of guests on a wild goose chase and I, for one, have no idea where he was. Only that it gave somebody the opportunity to murder Steve without witnesses. If our speculation is right about bad blood over Bertie's business, then he might harbour a grudge strong enough to kill at least one Tanning. Or three."

John returned to his seat and lifted the piece of paper he'd been writing on. "I can shed a bit of light."

"All ears."

"I found an old newspaper article which I can't fully read, thanks to a paywall. But a visit to the local library might get the information. A decade or so ago there was a fight over Bertie's business and it did involve a Toby Tanning. Went to court but that is all I could access."

"Interesting. What if Bertie is killing off every Tanning who marries his granddaughter. For revenge?"

"Mustn't care about Lisa then." John said.

"Or cares more about revenge than about Lisa."

"Not a nice thought."

"Not at all. Mind you, if he does have dementia, as some of his family have suggested, how would he be able to plan and implement a murder which didn't even look like one?"

The next roll of thunder was further away. Overhead, the rain wasn't as insistent and no longer fell in sheets around Bluebell. John put their dinner in the oven. A casserole. Daphne tried to have a cooking day every fortnight where she'd prepare meals for freezing. They had chosen to allocate more than usual space for a combination fridge/freezer to make the most of fresh produce they came across in different areas. Soon they'd head towards Shepparton, known for its canneries where excess or second grade, but perfectly fine, fruit and vegetable products were heavily discounted.

"Earth to Daphne."

She laughed. "I can't wait for us to go to Shepparton."

John's expression of confusion made her laugh again.

"Sorry, love. For some reason, my mind was planning our future meals and I do love a bargain."

"And you can make the best meals from bargain purchases. I've watched you with a sense of pride and amazement over the years. And particularly when we had the kids."

A ridiculous tickle behind Daphne's eyes made her blink fast. Those were wonderful times, but hard times. The real estate agency wasn't always bringing in a lot of money and making sure every foster child was properly clothed and fed meant being creative. But Daphne grew up having to make do to get by and she used that to her advantage to create a better life for the wonderful youngsters who came into their lives.

As though he could read her mind, John reached across and squeezed her hand. "You did good. And look at us now with a blue caravan and the freedom to follow the road. I think there's a special bottle of sherry we've not opened, so I'm proposing a glass before dinner."

"I second your proposal."

John dug around in one of the cupboards and found a bottle and two glasses. "Think we were given this one by Christie and Martin."

Christie and Martin were dear friends living in River's End.

"I wonder what Christie would make of all this." Daphne tapped her notebook. "She'd most likely already have worked out who killed Steve, why they killed him, and where they are."

"You're not doing such a bad job, love." John returned to his seat and handed Daphne a glass filled with golden liqueur. "To solving crimes."

They clinked the glasses together.

"Last suspect and then dinner. It is beginning to smell quite delightful!" Daphne's tummy rumbled, which made a change from the thunder. "And although I said Lisa is top suspect, I really don't believe she is responsible. But this one..."

"The mysterious Lloyd."

"You read my mind. There is something about him which makes my skin crawl. The way he stares at me. And how he didn't respond when I apologised for almost running into him as he alighted from the catering van. Not so much as a smile. And the staring at the reception and near the café."

"It made you uncomfortable."

"Yes. It may be he simply doesn't deal with people well. But the damp shirt and fresh apron...something else is going on. I wonder if it was him in the van meeting Lisa this morning."

"And I'm curious about the interview at the police station. She was pretty upset when she arrived. It doesn't make sense why she would kill her own husband the very day of their wedding." John said. "They were about to go away on their honeymoon as well."

Daphne agreed. This town had something ominous going on—or at least, the Tanning and Brooker families did.

"What I just said about Christie—if we can work out the 'why', then the 'who' should be obvious. So why would someone kill a young man on the day of his wedding?"

AN ODD FIND AND A NEW PUZZLE

The morning sky was crystal clear and the air was free of humidity as Daphne strolled along the river to work on her two ceremonies. She'd slept much better than expected and was woken by the enticing aroma of fresh coffee. Daphne slipped her feet into a pair of sensible shoes, shoved her phone in a pocket, and with her notebook in hand, gave John a quick kiss. He had his hands full putting the outdoor area back up.

There was a narrow track alongside the water and it made for easy walking, although the ground was still a bit soft underfoot. The river was higher than usual and swept fallen branches and other debris along in a hurry but otherwise there was little to remind her of the ferocity of the storm.

Talking to John last night about the death of Steve Tanning helped her mind focus on the facts rather than feelings.

"Although feelings matter."

She glanced around. Whew. Nobody overhead her. Not even a squawk from the pair of magpies hunting for worms in the soft ground.

For a while Daphne dawdled along the track as she whispered ideas to herself. It wasn't only which words to use, but when and how to use them. Two grieving families. Two different approaches. Her intention with the Brookers was to tread lightly. As she already had a good idea of where each of them stood regarding Steve—unless one was the murderer—their ceremony offered some challenges. Best not to fuel Lisa's need for attention nor Margaret and Bob's dislike of the young man.

Daphne found a tree stump between the track and river and sat there to write her ideas down while fresh in her mind. For the Tannings, she formulated a celebration of Steve's life. Thanks to the email from Marlene, she had snippets to include. Writing about the good memories was easy. But how to broach what should have been the happiest day of his life without making it about the worst one?

"Can't really reminisce about how happy he was to marry his beautiful bride, only to end up face down in her pool."

She sighed and closed the notebook. His family hadn't even attended his wedding so mentioning it was bound to stir some distress. If they had been there, he might still be alive. Whoever was responsible for his death would have been forced to change their tactics with more people around. People who probably would not have joined the search for Bertie.

Daphne sat bold upright. Was Steve's death planned, based on knowing his family wouldn't attend, or was it opportunistic? The answer to this question would narrow down the list of suspects. Presumably, the medical examiner would know the cause of death at some point, and speaking of points, if it was a knife then Matty must have information about the type of knife after his reaction to seeing John's filleting knife. Weddings have knives. The cake knife—had anyone checked it? And caterers have knives.

Finding a blank page, Daphne noted her thoughts to come back to later. Perhaps she could pop around to the police station and see if there was any new information.

She got to her feet and her hands went straight to her behind. Damp, thanks to the soggy tree trunk.

"It rained all night, Daph. Now look at you!" Thank goodness there was nobody around to see her undignified wet bottom. She turned to go back but a movement across the river caught her eye.

Surrounded by thick bushes was an old caravan, perhaps a couple of hundred metres away. The only reason Daphne noticed was thanks to a person moving about near it. Her eyesight wasn't good enough to see much detail but she thought it to be a man. He wore a heavy, long jacket and hat pulled down over his head. In one hand he carried a bucket similar to the one John used for fishing and in the other, a short fishing rod. In a moment he was gone, behind the bushes.

How interesting. She scanned the area around the caravan. No sign of a car or other vehicle. No houses in sight. But this might be the back of the Brooker property in which case, the caravan would be the one Bertie once lived in.

Had it been Bertie? Hard to tell under the big coat and hat and the distance. If he lived in the house now, why would he bother with the caravan?

The alarm on her watch reminded her to get going. When she could see Bluebell in the distance, she took a short cut through the trees. And regretted it the minute she stepped into mud. Back on the grass she stopped to wipe the worst of the wet dirt off her shoes, glaring back at where she'd stood. By the look of the ground she wasn't the first person to misjudge the ground. There was another set of footprints. Much larger than hers.

How odd. Daphne took a closer look. The indentation was deep and faced Bluebell. Almost as if somebody stood here for a while. And just like that moment last night, the hairs stood up on the back of her arms.

John dropped Daphne at the meet up point for the Tanning's farewell ceremony and nosed back onto the road. He'd been relieved it was at a park—rather than a home—just out of town in the opposite direction from the Brooker's. When Marlene welcomed Daphne with a smile, the tension left his shoulders.

But after the chaos of the Brooker wedding...Shaking his head, John slowed the car.

Just up from the park was an old stone church, its wooden doors open. He found a parking spot under some trees and locked the car. Quite apart from how interesting he found country churches was the benefit of what usually accompanied them.

Sure enough, an old iron gate between overgrown hedges announced this was 'St Peters of Little Bridges Graveyard'.

The town's public cemetery was closer to the caravan

park, the place for modern burials. Thanks to Daphne's celebrant status and his interest in genealogy, he often visited both public cemeteries and parish graveyards when staying in a new town. And seeing as he was going to wait for Daphne, he might as well use the time to indulge his hobby.

This graveyard was small and old with few fresh flowers and a lack of tending. Many of the headstones had crumbling corners and some inscriptions were hard to read.

"That belongs to one of the town's founders, Richard Brooker."

John jumped at the voice close behind.

"Sorry, son. Didn't mean to startle you." The speaker was a tall, elderly man wearing a dog collar. "I'm Father McIntyre."

They shook hands.

"I'm John Jones. McIntyre. Related to the young constable?"

"My late sister's grandson. A good boy."

"I hope it is alright for me to wander around? I'm a keen student of genealogy and I find beautiful small churches such as yours are often accompanied by local history."

"Spend as long as you wish. Is there a particular family of interest?"

With a gesture towards the headstone in front of them, John nodded. "You mentioned Richard Brooker as a town founder. What is his relationship to the current Brooker family?"

"Robert senior is his great-great-grandson. I think there are sufficient greats in there. Richard, from all accounts, was an upstanding man of faith. A hard worker who was fair in his business and private life."

"Robert senior is Bertie?"

"Yes. Bertie. And Robert junior is Bob Brooker." He led John to another headstone. "This belongs to Richard's one-time close friend and fellow town founder, Joseph Tanning."

"One-time?"

"Quite a history there. Do you have a few minutes?"

"My wife is at the park for a while so I'd love to hear anything about the families. What stopped their friendship?"

The priest glanced up at the sun and moved them both to a shadier spot. "Doctor says I have to reduce my time outside. Had some of those pesky skin growths removed."

"Not good."

"No. I rather love the sun, but there it is. Where was I?"

"The story of Richard and Joseph."

"Ah yes. Richard had several children in his middle years with his first wife before she sadly succumbed to a snake bite one summer. With youngsters to raise and his position in town requiring his full attention, he took a young woman on as a nanny. Before long, he'd married her."

"Giving his children stability again."

"Or so he thought." Father McIntyre said. "Joseph Tanning, who was almost the age of Richard, was also a widower and took a liking to the young lady."

Oh dear. John had a feeling he was about to be given shocking information.

"He enticed the new wife away from his friend and moved her into his...dwellings. Outrageous in any era but a terrible scandal back then. It was reported Richard flew into a rage, perhaps rightly so, and demanded her return. At gun point. A dreadful fight ensued and both men were mortally wounded. The wife disappeared, never to return. Within days, the Brooker children had no parents and the Tannings lost their patriarch."

A light breeze carried music from the direction of the park.

"Is your wife the visiting celebrant?"

"She is." John smiled. "At the moment she's helping the Tanning family with their recent loss."

"Difficult times. But a Tanning will never be anything to a Brooker than a thief. Sad, really." The priest gazed at John. "Are you interested in the graveyard for genealogy, or to help your wife find the killer?"

His surprise must have shown on his face for Father McIntyre burst into laughter and slapped John on the shoulder.

"You must remember who my great nephew is. He thinks highly of your Daphne."

And the young constable shouldn't be sharing confidential information, even with a priest. But John just smiled. "She was deeply shaken by the events at the wedding and wants to be certain the murderer is brought to justice. And she also knows the police have the investigation in hand, so would never intrude."

"Their resources are stretched. Always are when it comes to those families." Father McIntyre sighed heavily. "It has been a pleasure chatting but I have to close up the church and make my way to the back room at Bell's Bistro. Tuesday is bingo night and the older set—as well as some younger ones—will take me to task if I don't have everything ready."

He began to walk away then turned. "You and Daphne are most welcome to join us. If you care for a spot of bingo, of course."

"I'll ask Daphne. You've been most helpful, Father."

John got his phone out and spent a few minutes taking photos and writing notes. The details of these events were too important to forget. Events which just might still impact on the present.

ONE LESS SUSPECT

As Daphne and John drove away from the park, she dabbed her eyes. She'd only done a few ceremonies such as this one and the experience had proved more emotional for her than any of the funerals she'd officiated.

"The Tannings weren't like I expected, love."

"How so, Daph?"

"Despite their grief, every one of them thanked me for making Steve's last day a happy one. And for trying to help him at the end. As tough and blustery as Marlene came across at the police station, she is simply someone at the end of their tether and something of a spokesperson for the entire clan."

They passed the church, where a priest was locking the front doors.

"Father McIntyre." John said. "And before you ask, he is Matty's great uncle."

Of course John would have come to the graveyard. He did enjoy the history of these old towns and made friends so easily it was no wonder he'd chatted to the priest.

"Did you find anything interesting?" Daphne asked, putting her handkerchief away as her emotions settled. Being back with her darling husband made everything right again.

"I did. But it can wait until we go out for dinner."

"Dinner?"

"Thought it time we visited Bell's Bistro."

Whatever have you been up to?

"Why do I get the sneaky suspicion this has something to do with the priest?"

"And the graveyard."

Daphne turned in her seat to take a better look at John. He glanced at her with a wink, then put his attention back onto the road.

"All will be revealed. Tell me about the ceremony."

Although she'd much rather find out what he was keeping for later, she knew John wasn't going to budge until he was ready to talk. He liked to think things through and be sure of his facts.

"Well, it was sad and sweet. Steve's parents said little. His poor mother barely let go of her husband's arm and both are clearly still in a state of shock. The rest of the guests were his extended family, of which there are many. Lots of cousins, aunts and uncles, two brothers. And friends, some I recognised from the bridal party. Someone bought a generator and they plugged in a screen with images of him and some videos from different ages."

"I heard some music."

"Yes. He played in a local band and they sang his favourite song. Everyone joined in which was kind of surreal."

"How so?"

Daphne smiled. "They're a heavy metal band so it was more like screaming rather than singing. But at the end of it, there was applause and hugging."

The car turned onto the main street of the town.

"John, would you mind stopping at the police station? I just want to ask if they need anything else from us before we leave tomorrow." Daphne said.

"I'm sure they'd call."

"This might sound odd, but I'd rather know so I can stop thinking about it."

"Worrying about it, I imagine. Of course we can stop."

The police station was quiet, with only Senior Constable Barber present. "You are on my list of people to phone this afternoon, Mrs Jones. Couple of things to cross off if you have a few minutes?"

Daphne explained they only had another day here. "Just one more ceremony and then we have another wedding to attend some distance away."

"I have your report typed up if you'd like to sign it."

"Perfect."

The senior constable stepped away from the counter to collect the paperwork. "Sorry I haven't rung earlier."

"No trouble at all, but can I ask, if anything needs to be added, should I sign it now?"

"What might need to be added?"

Daphne shrugged. "With the Brooker farewell ceremony tomorrow there's always a chance I'd hear or observe something of potential interest."

"If so, we'll make a new report. But don't put yourself in a difficult position with them."

"I won't." Daphne signed where indicated. "Not likely to

find me snooping around or peering through windows. But people do say things in front of me."

Senior Constable Barber made a copy of the report and gave to Daphne. "You've been helpful and we appreciate your co-operation." She glanced around. "In case you were wondering about our interview with Lisa, seeing as you will be at her home again, we've excluded her as a person of interest. There are too many witnesses to all of her movements for her to have committed the murder."

"What if someone helped her?"

"We haven't ruled out an accomplice but can find no motive for Lisa to kill her new husband."

"Except a history of her husbands dying young."

"Not under suspicious circumstances though." Senior Constable Barber picked up her copy of the report. "Our enquiries are continuing and we'll have homicide detectives arriving to assist us in a few hours. As yet we haven't located a weapon nor been able to track the phone used to call Steve. That lead is one we are appreciative of, Mrs Jones."

They took her seriously. "So you think whoever phoned him was behind his death? Persuaded him to go to the pool and killed him there. Stabbed him in the back and pushed him in."

"Daphne." John put a hand on her arm. "Speculation."

"Not far from the truth though, Mr Jones. He wasn't stabbed in the back but it appears he was lured to the pool. But whether the caller was the killer is unknown. Thanks to accessing Steve's phone's SD card we know the number of the phone that called him. Finding it would help but the owner filed a report more than a week ago of its theft." The senior constable raised a hand as Daphne opened her mouth. "Before you ask, no, I am not at liberty to disclose the name of the owner." Little lines formed around her eyes as she smiled.

"Fair enough. Just one more question and I understand if it is off limits. I wondered if you knew where Bertie Brooker was when he wandered off?" Daphne asked.

"One of the staff found him not far from the house. He was sitting under a tree waiting for things to quieten down."

"Catering staff?"

"No. It was the Brooker's groundsman. Dempster. Before you go, I'll fetch your knife." It was in a bag on her desk. "Matty, as a fisherman, should have excluded this on the spot. Too flexible."

John took it from her. "Appreciate having it back. Old favourite."

"Thanks again for your co-operation."

Outside, John took Daphne's hand and they returned to the car in silence. Once they both climbed in, he grinned at her.

"What?" she asked.

"Are you certain being a celebrant is the right choice? Back in River's End, Trev always talked about the fact Charlotte should join the police force and now I'm wondering if you also missed your calling."

She couldn't help but laugh at the idea of squeezing herself into a police uniform and wearing a badge. Much as Daphne respected those who kept the peace, it wasn't for her. More likely she'd make a good private detective. One of those old-fashioned ones with a hat and coat and magnifying glass.

"Does that sound okay?" John asked.

Daphne suddenly noticed they were back in traffic. "Does what sound okay?"

"Dinner about seven. Unless you have other plans."

"Nope. No plans other than dinner with my husband." She patted his leg. "And it is my treat because you've run me around all over the place this week." Best way to enjoy the extra money the Tannings had insisted she accept for the beautiful ceremony. "It feels nice to spoil you for once."

BELL'S BISTRO, BINGO, AND BAD WOMEN

It was just as well John booked ahead as the bistro was busy when they arrived a little before seven. Attached to one of several pubs in Little Bridges, Bell's Bistro was a large family friendly restaurant on two levels, plus outside tables. And it was noisy, but in a good way with conversation and music trying to outdo each other.

"I had no idea I was so hungry!" Daphne gazed around after they were shown to a table. It was a bit quieter here where a row of tables for two lined a long window. Up a couple of steps was a larger area with an indoor children's play area surrounded by bigger tables. The atmosphere was friendly and happy. "This was such a good choice, love."

"Although I did have an ulterior motive for suggesting it."

John still hadn't enlightened Daphne on why, nor shared even a word about his visit to the graveyard.

"You look very pretty. I like the new top." He said.

Even after all these years married, the sweet compliment

made her smile. She reached out for John's hand and when he took hers, she held tight. "I love you very much."

"Are you ready to order drinks?" A voice interrupted. "Or shall I come back?

They released each other's hands. "What would you like, Daph?"

"You choose."

John asked for a bottle of local white wine and the young woman disappeared towards the bar. By the time she returned, they'd selected their meals. After ordering, John lifted his glass. "To discoveries."

"Oh. I like that. To discoveries!"

They clinked their glasses.

A waiter hurried past and Daphne craned her neck to see his face. Not Lloyd. If Lloyd was indeed the person from the wedding.

"I wonder if he does work here."

"Not sure he needs to be part of your list anymore." John said.

"But he acted suspiciously. And had a wet shirt. And stared at me."

"Yes. All of the above. But he might have spilled something on his shirt. And been surprised when you appeared out of nowhere. And looked at you wondering if you'd report him for being away from his post. There's always another point of view to consider."

True. He might not be guilty of anything other than being in the wrong place at the wrong time. And as far as she knew the police hadn't been interested in her information about him.

"Okay. Let's say he had no part in..." Daphne glanced

around, not wanting to be overheard. "the situation. What makes you think he isn't?"

"Not sure at all. But you've been looking for a motive and I may have one which so far, nobody seems to have considered."

"You do?"

John told Daphne about his chat with the priest and the story of two men, once close friends, killing each other over the woman they both wanted.

"Let me make sure I understand. This was a young woman employed by Richard Brooker to look after his motherless children. And he married her. After a bit, his best friend decides he is prepared to destroy a lifetime of friendship by luring her away." Daphne said.

"Pretty much."

"What happened to her?"

"Disappeared. I'm planning on digging around a bit to see if there is any record of her after leaving the area." He picked up his glass. "Would you like to accompany me to the library in the morning and see if there are old records?"

"Maybe. Still need to finish the Brooker ceremony. But, love, what happened between those men was decades ago. Generations. Surely it would be forgotten and everyone moved on. Bertie even had a business relationship with one of the Tannings."

"Father McIntyre was specific about the feud. A Tanning will never be anything than a thief. That is how the Brookers view the Tannings." John said.

"I guess if Bertie and Toby also had a falling out, old feelings might have emerged. I wonder if Bertie would discuss it?" He'd been nice enough when he visited Bluebell. "Maybe I can speak with him away from the rest of his family."

"Not certain that's a good idea. Dredging up a terrible history on top of Steve's death might upset him. What if we get onto the laptop after dinner and see what we can uncover?"

The arrival of entrees stopped the conversation for a while. This was their last night in Little Bridges and Daphne had mixed feelings about the town. Too many sad and distressing incidents came close to outweighing the good ones. Like now. Best to live in the moment instead of the past.

"This soup is delicious." John put his empty spoon into the bowl with a look of regret. "Do you find the food in small towns rivals anything in the city?"

"I do. Not that we've been to a city for...well, how long?"

Neither could put a year on it. Their life in River's End was busy and fulfilling so visits to Melbourne—the closest city but still several hours by road—were few and far between. There was a wedding coming up which would mean driving to the Mornington Peninsula and the best way was through Melbourne. And about the closest they'd get for a while.

At the end of the row where they sat, a glass door led to other parts of the building, including a room Daphne could see. Its door opened and closed regularly as people came and went, offering glimpses inside of long tables.

"Bingo night." The waitress cleared their bowls. "Popular with the oldies."

At that point, Gina and Pat passed the glass door and went into the room.

As soon as the waitress left, Daphne leaned closer to John. "I just saw Gina and Pat go in there."

He looked around.

"Into bingo?"

"I had got the feeling they didn't live here."

"What made you think that?" John topped up their wine glasses.

"At the other restaurant in the restroom, she said something about me not getting involved in her family's town. As in, their town opposed to hers. I took it that she was warning me off Bob and Margaret. Maybe also because she reminds me of Margaret, more than the Brookers. The way she dresses and speaks is more city than country and I assumed she'd travelled here for the wedding, if that makes any sense?"

John nodded. "It does. We're safe to believe she's Bertie's sister, given she referred to Lisa as her great-niece when she spoke to you. No doubt she is well aware of the Brooker and Tanning history."

Staring at the closed door to the bingo room, Daphne wished she was brave enough to go and ask Gina exactly what she'd meant the other night. But the woman had made it abundantly clear Daphne wasn't welcome. She'd even tried to quell the conversation around her table, telling the rest of the party a family feud was no reason to kill Steve.

"John!"

Her voice was louder than she'd planned but there was enough noise in the restaurant to stop anyone looking at her.

"Doll?"

"What if—and I'm assuming a lot here—what if the family feud is not the one about Bertie and Toby, but the old one. About Richard and Joseph? In which case, Gina and Bertie may very well have known their grandparents."

"And one of their grandparents would have been one of Richards's children!"

"Yes. What if the resentment towards the Tannings was so ingrained from a young age that Bertie made it his business to treat every Tanning as a thief?" Her mind raced. "But why would he then have one as a business partner?"

"Necessity. Didn't Margaret start to tell you he'd needed a partner?"

"Yes. I need to talk to Margaret. She might be a bit odd at times but she's the outsider, as it were and seems to want to chat to me. Do you really think I've been wrong all this time and the killer might be—"

"You're still in town."

Where did she come from?

Gina sneered at Daphne. She'd left her little black dress at home and wore satin pants and a blouse with a plunging neckline. Around her neck were more pearls. Different to those she wore the other night.

"We are." John stood. "I'm John Jones, Daphne's husband." He didn't extend his hand.

The waitress appeared with their mains and worked around Gina to put them on the table.

"When do you leave?" Gina eyed the plates.

"Would you like to join us for a chat? I can arrange another chair." Daphne offered with a wide smile.

"Why would I?"

"We're history buffs and it would be wonderful to get some local information from a member of one of the founding families."

"The. The founding family?"

"Of course. So I understand there was a falling out between the Brooker and Tanning families some time ago."

"Which is none of your business."

"True. But how interesting that three Tanning men have died and the connection, outside their relationship as cousins, is their choice of bride." Daphne said.

John hadn't moved and now, he crossed his arms, his eyes on Gina.

"More fool them." Gina said. "It would serve you well to stay out of our business."

"Are you threatening my wife?"

A sinister smile flickered across Gina's lips. "Take it as you wish. And Daphne? Why not order more potatoes? Or are you saving room for later?"

With that, the woman stalked away, almost running into a waiter who stopped dead in his tracks to avoid the collision.

John sat, his brow creased. "Daphne, what a dreadful person she is."

"She hasn't improved since we last spoke."

"Did you take her comment as threatening? I'm happy to call Matty."

Daphne's stomach churned. "Let's finish dinner and go home. It won't be long until we leave." But when Daphne lifted her fork, her appetite was gone. Mean words would do that to a person.

A MISSING KNIFE

John Jones was not a man to anger without good cause. Nor to wish harm on another. But he wouldn't have minded seeing Gina fall flat on her face. The warning shot was one thing, but to make it personal and bring Daphne's choice of meal into it was appalling. How dare she attempt to make Daphne feel bad with such a low blow. And it had hurt his wife. She'd finished her meal but without the normal enjoyment and critique of the food, and when he offered dessert she shook her head and asked to go home.

They walked back to the camping ground the same route as usual, stopping at the highest point of the bridge without a word. In comparison to the previous night, the sky was cloud-free. The river's level had dropped from this morning and it flowed slowly again, its dark surface reflecting the lights on either end of the bridge.

"This is such a nice town." Daphne turned her back on the river and leaned against the railing, her eyes on the shops peeking through the buffer of trees and bushes. "From a landscape perspective it is. I adore the old buildings and these bridges are worthy of their own picture book. Pity about the residents." Her voice was monotone and her face set.

"I'm so proud of you, love." John joined Daphne against the rail and put an arm around her shoulders. "The way you carry yourself, with dignity and kindness. It sets an example to those who use words to hurt and think so little of themselves that they seek to upset others." She didn't reply but her muscles relaxed and Daphne dropped her head onto John's shoulder. "When people resort to low blows it says a lot about them."

"I know. But I came here on invitation. To celebrate a wedding. There is no need for such rudeness." Daphne straightened and held a hand out to use her fingers to count on. "First was Steve. Saying he expected me to be younger. Then Bertie with his disapproval of my morals for officiating. And Gina. Not once, but twice she has sought me out to have a go at my weight."

"Nothing wrong with your weight. I love your curves."

Daphne kissed his cheek. "Anyway, I think she is just trying to be nasty any way she can. If it wasn't how I look it would be my profession. Or something else. Which leads me to ask if she is hiding something." She took one of John's hands. "I'd love another glass of the lovely sherry we had."

Good girl.

Nobody bounced back from a bad moment more than his Daphne. "Sherry and another search of the Bertie and Toby saga."

"Also, can you help me update my website? I have a few photos from the wedding. Unless you think it best not to include them?"

"Let's take a look first. And while we're at it, let's go over the ones you took in the caterer's van." All of a sudden, Daphne's hand slipped out of his as she picked up the pace.

"What a good idea! Coming?"

A sip of sherry was the perfect remedy for hurt feelings. Let Gina say what she would. Daphne had no intention of allowing the woman to get into her head again. She was probably perpetually cranky from being hungry.

"What would you like to do first, love?" John opened the laptop. "Shall I load your photos onto here and we can take a look on the bigger screen?"

While John did that, Daphne wrote down the latest information, thanks to his visit to the graveyard. "Just confirming it is Richard Brooker and Joseph Tanning?"

"Correct. I have images of the dates from the headstones on my phone."

Daphne found the photos in question and recorded the dates. This notebook was filling up fast.

"Here you go."

Daphne shuffled around to sit beside John as he clicked on each of her photos to make them fit the screen. There were quite a few from the signing.

"Margaret must have snapped away at anything. How strange to see Lisa and Steve together knowing it must be one of the last photos of him. Do you think I should offer these to Lisa...or even to the Tannings?"

"Might be a nice gesture. Did they open their wedding gifts even before the reception began?"

"Lisa unwrapped some before the wedding. Nobody

thought to make a little table up for signing the wedding certificate so it was a last minute rearrangement to create a pretty spot. The flowers look really festive there."

John peered at the screen. "Are those steak knives?"

"Your eyesight is better than mine! I remember seeing a couple of knife sets and hoped the bride and groom weren't superstitious—not that many people believe it is bad luck these days, but still, not something I'd give."

"Maybe they'd be right to be concerned."

"Why?"

John zoomed in and then out a bit when it was too fuzzy. The steak knives were in a boxset, nestled in black silk.

"Is one missing?" Daphne asked.

"Think so. Now perhaps it fell out when space was being made. But look how pointed their ends are."

"Oh my. Almost as thin as your filleting knife!" Daphne fanned her face with her hand. "Have we just found the murder weapon?"

"Or where it came from."

"We should phone the police. Send the photo across so they can investigate."

John checked the time. "After nine. Not likely to be anyone there."

Daphne had already reached for her phone. "Can't hurt to try." She got Matty's card from her wallet and dialled. "If someone took the knife at the wedding, it might very well have been an act of opportunity. Oh darn. Voicemail." Daphne cleared her throat. "Good evening, this is Daphne Jones. John and I have some new information. About steak knives. Oh. At the wedding reception there were steak knives as a gift and one was missing. Anyway I have photos. Goodnight."

After hanging up she looked at John. He smiled. "Never know what to say to a machine."

"I'm wondering if I should dial triple zero."

"Emergency? That's for life threatening calls." John said.

"Well, what if the knife is used on someone else? Or thrown into the river? Actually, maybe that is what happened. Someone took the knife from the set, phoned Steve, met him at the pool and stabbed him. And pushed him in to make it look like an accident. Then they threw it into the river to avoid capture."

"Or the knife fell out on the table and is now safely back with the remaining set."

"John Jones, you are being far too sensible."

"Sorry."

She put a hand over his. "Sensible is good, love. But this is a murder and we have to think like a killer."

"We do?"

Daphne pulled her notebook closer and picked up her pen. "I'll draw the Brooker property. Here is the house." Her lines were angled. "Wrong shape but you get the drift. And the deck at the back and the pool off a bit to one side. This is where the garden splits in two."

She scribbled a row of x's.

"That's the hedge. On this side is where the wedding was held. And over here is the reception. You can't tell from my drawing but if you are in the wedding area you cannot see into the reception area. And vice versa. Hedges are too thick and high."

"Are you thinking someone took a knife during the wedding?" John said.

"If they did, it must be Lloyd or another of the catering staff. Everyone else was seated at the wedding."

"What about the cook?"

This was something Daphne hadn't considered. She nibbled on her bottom lip, playing with her pen.

John looked through the remainder of the wedding photos. "We need some from the actual wedding. Do you know who did the photography?"

Daphne shook her head. "There were a couple of people filming on their phones but Lisa said something to Steve about them not needing an official photographer. Going back to the cook...I saw her briefly with another woman in the kitchen. But that was the day before the wedding. Whether she was there on the day we'd need to find out. Bob said she was upset over them hiring a caterer so possibly she wasn't even on the property."

The phone rang. "That's the number I called Matty on." Daphne answered. "This is Daphne, may I put you on speaker as John is here?"

"Good evening, and yes, please do." It was Senior Constable Barber. "I just picked up the message you left. Can you elaborate?"

Daphne ran through the information about the knife set. "We were just discussing who might have had access. Do you know if the Brooker's cook was there that day?"

"Mrs Jones—"

"Daphne, please."

"Daphne. We appreciate you helping with this, but there's really no need for you to spend your time worrying about this case."

"Oh. Um, well it was just a passing thought. Because of the cook saying Margaret was trying to kill everyone."

There was a chuckle on the other end of the phone. John

and Daphne exchanged a glance. "We've spoken to the person in question and she explained her comment. She's a woman who takes pride in her cooking and was offended by Margaret's insistence on using a caterer. In her opinion, they were likely to give the guests food poisoning which was on Margaret's head."

Plausible excuse.

"Good to rule her out then. But what about Lloyd? He was one of the waiters and acted strangely and—"

"Okay, okay. Just to give you peace of mind, we have taken a look at the van and there was nothing unusual."

"But I have a photo of his name badge on the wet apron."

"We have spoken to him as well as his team mates. He'd spilled water on himself carrying a full tray of jugs and was seen doing so—in fact, some of the other staff made fun of him which he was upset about. All he did was throw off one apron and grab another and before you ask, we have sent the first apron to be tested for pool chemicals."

"What about the white tub in the corner?" Daphne pressed.

"Used for food scraps. Bit of a dead-end, I'm afraid. The detectives who I mentioned are here and running the investigation so while you are welcome to contact me with anything you think of, they'll be the ones to follow it up. Do you mind sending me a copy of the photo of the knife set?"

John leaned closer to the phone. "John here. Shall I send to the email on Matty's business card?"

"Yes. And thank you both."

The connection terminated.

"I'll send this now."

"Running out of suspects, love." Disappointment filled her voice. "Not Lloyd, although it doesn't explain him glaring at me those times. Too many people have alibis. Is it a sign that I should leave well enough alone?"

WORRIES AND PLANS

How was anyone meant to sleep with so many thoughts going on? Daphne willed herself to not toss and turn. John was out cold and needed his sleep, so why couldn't she relax and fall into the arms of slumber?

Counting backwards from one hundred was worth a try. One hundred, ninety nine, ninety eight...

Who is the killer?

There it was again, just as her mind drifted off. Worrying about it at night was pointless. If she imagined a golden beach with a hammock and a nice book...

And who did Lisa meet in the carpark?

This wasn't working. Daphne turned over, an inch at a time, sliding without pulling on the covers so not to disturb John. He mumbled and she froze. Pretending she was on a raft on a gentle sea, she squeezed her eyes shut.

Breathe in. And out.

What happened to the missing knife?

Bit by bit, Daphne slipped out of bed. Her dressing gown had fallen onto the floor and she grabbed it and her slippers.

As quietly as she could, Daphne made her way to the tiny living area beyond the kitchen after collecting the laptop. If she sat facing the end of the caravan, the light from the laptop wouldn't reach John.

She checked her website. John had been busy after the phone call from Senior Constable Barber, cropping photos and uploading them with some captions. They'd decided not to include any with Lisa and Steve until the investigation and the funeral was over. As it was, Daphne was uneasy about sharing much about this particular wedding.

He'd done such a good job. There were three photos of Daphne. In two she appeared solemn and official but in the third she was laughing. Her eyes crinkled around the corners. There were a few images of floral arrangements, the cake, and the signing book open and laid across its pages, the beautiful pen Daphne provided for this purpose. All tasteful and appealing without giving away the bride and groom's identity.

She went back to the one of herself laughing. There'd been little to laugh at before, during, or after the ceremony and she couldn't recall the moment. John had imported all of her photos into a file so she opened it and searched for the uncropped image. Everyone in the photo was laughing. Steve was tickling Lisa and the pen had flown from her hand. Bob, the bridal party, and various guests in frame all laughed. But one face stood out with its grim expression. Daphne zoomed in.

Gina.

Daphne clamped both hands over her mouth.

She'd not noticed the woman on the day, which wasn't surprising given how many people attended the wedding.

The creepiest part of this was not her lack of humour but the hatred in her eyes. Hatred directed at Steve.

One by one, Daphne inspected each photograph taken by Margaret. Gina appeared in a few more but her attention was on something or someone further away.

Daphne attached the image of Gina to an email but even as she typed out the address to send it to the police, she changed her mind. How on earth could anyone consider the woman a suspect? Unkind, yes. Over-protective of her family, definitely. But in the photos she was dressed in a body-hugging cream dress, very high heels, and pearls. Not the attire of someone who would stab a man—one much taller than herself—then push them into the pool without a sound or becoming covered with their blood. And although not one to judge a person on appearance, Gina did not give the impression she'd have the physical strength to kill a fit young man.

Daphne yawned. Going around and around with the few clues available made her tired. She closed the laptop and tiptoed back to bed.

Of course she overslept, thanks to too little quality sleep. Daphne woke with a start to an empty caravan, reaching for her glasses to read the clock.

"Dandelions and ducks!" She swung her feet out of bed.

John had left a note on the table.

Gone to pick up brunch. Noticed you were awake in the night so let you sleep.

Daphne dashed into the shower. John was the sweetest man she'd ever met, but just this once she wished he'd woken her. With the Brooker ceremony this afternoon, she would be pushing it to finalise the words, and visit the bistro.

Or perhaps it was best to stop digging around.

She turned off the water and grabbed a towel.

There were homicide detectives in town who had the resources and knowledge to track down the killer. Daphne was—at most—an amateur sleuth. One with a keen mind and way of getting people to talk to her, but amateur, nonetheless. If she'd not been asked to perform the farewell ceremony today, she and John would already be at their next location. It wasn't her job or her place to uncover the face of a killer.

"Daphne, I'm letting you know we've decided to use another celebrant. Considering what is being reported on the news I prefer not to bring bad vibes to an otherwise positive day."

It was those words in a text message the other evening that set her on this path. Losing one client was awful. The bride and groom in question had already felt like friends yet they'd made the decision to cancel her appointment thanks to the murder of Steve Tanning.

"You could never bring bad vibes, Daph." She rubbed the mirror to clear the condensation. "They were scared."

But if more clients got scared and cancelled, not only would her budding career be over, but her heart broken. Before her eyes had the chance to mist over, she made herself a silent promise to be the best celebrant she could, including help solve the murder of one of her own clients. It was the only way she could prove her integrity. The only way she could stay proud of herself.

"I'm back, love." John's voice was a welcome interruption.

She stuck her head out of the bathroom door. "Morning! Be there in five."

It was closer to ten minutes later that she joined John and gave him a kiss on the cheek.

"Take a seat and I'll bring coffee. There's savoury muffins and sweet croissants. Closest I could find for brunch to takeaway."

"Smells wonderful. And thanks for the sleep in. I was a bit restless last night."

John delivered two fresh coffees and sat opposite. "Too much on your mind?"

Daphne gave him the short version of what she'd seen on the laptop and the thoughts bothering her the most.

"I agree it is unlikely Gina was responsible for Steve's attack. Anyway, the police would have interviewed the family and if Gina had been missing for any length of time, it would have been noticed." John said.

"But what if she relies on her age and appearance of frailty to hide a lethal killing machine." Daphne nibbled on a muffin. "I wish I could work out who took Steve's life."

"Not a lot of time left, love. By the time you've finished with the Brooker's, I'll have Bluebell all but ready to go. You'll have time to change for travel and then we can be on our way."

"Well, whatever I can't find out between now and leaving town, I'm sure I can continue to puzzle over." Or else she could simply get more clues before they drove away. "Are you still planning on going to the library?"

"I am. Care to join me?"

"There's still a bit to write for the ceremony but if I can get it done quickly I did have a thought. The local newspaper has its office not far from where we ate last night. I noticed it when we were coming back."

"You're thinking it might be worth dropping in there?"

"Never know what one might find in old papers. If you don't mind doing the library on your own, I might walk across and see what I can find."

With a quick glance at his watch, John nodded. "Four hours until you need to be at the Brookers. What if we meet back here for a quick lunch at one and then I'll take you there."

Daphne leaned over and kissed his lips. "I love the way you think. And then we'll be on our way again. Back on the open road."

A MAN NAMED MAURICE

It took Daphne less time than she'd expected to finish writing the ceremony. Her fingers flew over the paper and once she was happy, she transcribed the words into her ceremony book. This took longer as she was meticulous about writing neatly but when it was complete, she tucked the book into her briefcase and put on a pair of walking shoes.

Handbag over her shoulder, she locked Bluebell and donned a wide-brimmed hat to deflect the sun. It was a pleasant day without too much sting in the air. Perfect for a walk.

The route to town was familiar. Funny how fast one becomes accustomed to a place. She even knew where there were a couple of loose boards in the bridge over the river. From caravan to main street was ten minutes at a reasonable pace and Daphne didn't stop today at the high point of the bridge. Under any other circumstances this would be a town she'd spend more time exploring. Even returning to stay here again. But the upsetting memories would take a long time to fade.

"Enough of that." She muttered as she crossed the main street. There was only one purpose in her mind and a list of question.

The 'Little Bridges Chronicle' was housed in a dark and narrow shop squeezed between a barber and a bank. Daphne had to peer through the window to be certain it was open, but the door was unlocked and she stepped inside.

It took a minute for her eyes to adjust to the dimness. A small counter was set a few feet back and beyond it were several desks. And not a soul in sight. Every wall was lined with framed copies of newspapers highlighting important headlines and interesting people. At the back, a rickety staircase disappeared to another floor and beneath it was a room with a closed door.

It suddenly opened.

Daphne jumped. She'd thought nobody was in the building with her.

A man in his sixties, dressed exactly as Daphne imagined a newspaper boss would be—pants held up with suspenders over a striped shirt with the sleeves rolled up—emerged, a paper held in front of his eyes as he approached the counter. It was clear he had no idea she was there and when their eyes met, he uttered a swear word and dropped the paper.

"I am so sorry. Please forgive my dreadful language. I didn't know anyone was here." He swept the paper up off the floor.

"Don't apologise. I should have spoken."

"There's a bell on the counter." He looked. "Okay, there

isn't a bell. I must find out where it is. Anyhow, I am Maurice." Hand extended, he smiled widely.

Daphne shook his hand. "Hello, Maurice. I'm Daphne Jones and I wondered if—"

"You are?"

I am...what?

"Mrs Jones, I am so happy to meet you. Please, please come and sit at my desk and I'll make you a coffee. Or tea? Or would you like water?"

"Water would be nice." She followed him to the desk at the very back. It was covered with files and so was the chair he gestured to before he disappeared into the back room again.

Despite the disorder, the feel in the room was welcoming.

"Oh dear. Here, you take the water and I," he grabbed the files from the chair, "will make space for you."

She sat with some amusement as he looked here and there and finally placed the files onto a neighbouring desk. Then he dropped into the chair opposite and smiled again.

"Now, where were we?"

"Is this your newspaper?"

"It is. I took over from my father almost half a century ago. He started The Chronicle after the previous paper slid into bankruptcy and I like to believe I honour his work." He waved a hand at the walls. "We've won awards for our reporting. Small, yes. But more than our share of articles have been picked up by national newspapers, even in recent years, which is incredible considering how much is online these days."

"Technology might advance us in many ways, but in my opinion, there is nothing like a real newspaper."

Maurice beamed.

What a lovely man. There was something so sweet and delightful about him. Perhaps his passion for the work that obviously filled his heart.

"So, Maurice, how do you know my name?"

"My dear Mrs Jones. Everyone in Little Bridges knows of you."

"Oh, my. I'm not sure if that is a good thing."

"I'd hoped to visit and ask for some comments from you but as you can see," he gestured at the room, "no staff. All three of them off this week. Of all weeks."

Because who can plan ahead for a murder?

"Two of them are my son and his wife. How wonderful it is to see our family tradition continue and expand through marriage, but it takes two people away from the paper when they have a holiday. The third staff member went to Melbourne on Monday to be close to the coroner's court for any news and he's still down there."

"So...has he heard much?"

Tread softly, Daph.

"Pretty much what the police know, which I'm sure they've discussed with you." He leaned back in his seat. "Steve was stabbed in the neck and pushed into the pool, hitting his head on the way in. He was still alive but unconscious when he entered the water. Took next to no time for him to pass away. Darned shame for such a young man."

"You knew him. I imagine you must, having lived here for a long time."

"Know the family of course but Steve only from his sport and music. And occasional run-ins with the law. He's been mentioned a few times in The Chronicle for all three reasons." He laughed shortly. "Paper comes out Friday so hoping we get some leads to include."

"Leads?"

Maurice rummaged through the papers on his desk until he found a large notepad. "Keeping track of what I hear. Not that I'm about to do the work of our local police but I want our stories authentic. And as close to the source helps with that. So are you happy to answer some questions?"

"I am. But may I ask you some questions as well?"

Already turning to a new page, Maurice glanced up. "Ask, but whether I can answer depends on keeping confidentiality. Quite serious about protecting my sources."

"As you should. I'm curious about the arrangement between Bertie Brooker and Toby Tanning. The business arrangement."

As if to give himself time to think, Maurice inserted a perfectly pointed pencil into a sharpener.

Daphne continued. "The reason I ask is to get some context for a comment I overheard at a restaurant the night of the murder."

He stopped turning the pencil. "I'm listening."

Daphne smiled. "I may need to protect my sources."

With a big grin, Maurice tossed the notepad and pencil onto the desk. "We'll swap stories then. Bertie created a local caravan industry. Not only his business, which built them from the ground up, but complimentary businesses popped up. A parts manufacturer. A tourism shop based on places to camp. Even the caravan and camping park grew thanks to Bertie. But things changed over time. Bertie made some poor decisions and money was tight. Against Bob's advice, instead of retiring he went into partnership with Toby."

"I heard the families never got on."

Maurice waved his hand in the air dismissively. "A long time ago, perhaps. But generations change and although Bertie and Toby weren't close mates, they liked doing business together. All was well for a couple of years and then Bob started nosing around in the accounts—well, that's his job—and reckoned there'd been some...misappropriation of funds."

Bob was an accountant. Suited him.

"There were accusations and bad feelings and before you knew it, Toby wanted out which forced Bertie close to bankruptcy. Went to court. Got sorted, but after everyone was paid out, all that was left for Bertie was the land the Brookers now live on and a couple of caravans."

Daphne let out a breath she hadn't noticed she was holding. "How devastating for Bertie. I'm a bit confused though. Bob mentioned he had spent all his money on building the house."

"Bob's money?"

When Daphne nodded, Maurice threw back his head to laugh long and loudly. When he stopped, he found a tissue and wiped his eyes.

"Sorry. Did Bob really give you the idea he paid for the place?"

"He did. Was quite clear about the investment. Why?"

"The money came from Lisa. She had a huge inheritance when she was a kid. The second she turned eighteen she threw the money around like it was confetti and some landed with her mother, who had the house built. Bob was an onlooker."

The phone rang and Maurice apologised and answered, taking it with him for privacy.

This changed everything. If Lisa controlled the money then her reluctance to move out was understandable. As was her demanding behaviour. Bob and Margaret might live there but Lisa held the purse strings. It was time to take a closer look at Lisa's parents. Would they be fearful of losing their home and lifestyle when Lisa married?

"Apologies for the interruption. May I ask you some questions now?" Maurice asked.

"Of course, but about Lisa...who did she inherit the money from?"

"Her father when he died."

"Her...what?"

Maurice picked up his notepad. "Ah. I see that you thought Bob was her father. No. He's Margaret's second husband. And those ladies never let him forget it."

ANOTHER TWIST

If it wasn't old graveyards, library reference rooms were right up there for John as enjoyable places to visit. Little Bridges Library was housed in an old, converted courthouse, complete with echoing hallways. Quite appropriate a setting for uncovering past crimes.

Seated in front of a microfiche reader loaded with copies of historical records from the region filled John with a sense of discovery. The librarian was most happy to assist, telling John few people even knew such devices existed today. She'd located records from the earliest days of the town and ensured he knew how to handle them properly. He did.

After setting the alarm on his watch to vibrate in one hour—knowing how he would lose track of time with research—he began his search. The records ranged from births, deaths, and marriages on public record, through to newspaper clippings. All the documents he'd requested focused on the two families who had shaped the early years of this town.

And still do.

Father McIntyre's story came to life as he read accounts from a fledgling newspaper, Little Bridges Bugle. Richard Brooker was mayor of the town and owner of several businesses. Joseph Tanner ran livestock. Both contributed to building the town including the church John had visited. Joseph was a widower with one son when Richard's new wife took his eye.

The newspaper article was heavily slanted in favour of Richard, with the loss of his first wife mentioned several times along with his generosity to the young woman who was employed as a nanny but wanted her own family. Their marriage, according to the paper, was his way of giving her what she longed for.

It was less than six months later when she left Richard. There was a report of her disappearance being suspicious. And a week on, her appearance in town on the arm of Joseph. The next story was on the front page of the newspaper with the headline 'Scandalous woman destroys two families'. Images of a younger Richard and Joseph together in front of a timber and stone house. A rehash of the story of the death of Richard's first wife. And then inside, the account of the night Richard and Joseph shot each other.

John made notes from time to time. Daphne would be intrigued by this saga which continued for weeks with each story outdoing the previous in speculation of why and how this happened. Much was said about the orphaned Brooker children but only one mention of the Tanning boy, said to be living with his aunt.

Buried at the bottom of a long obituary for Richard was mention of his second wife. Mary Smith. "Had to be a common name!" Not one to let a small obstacle stop him, John finished up with the newspapers, and moved onto births, deaths, and marriages records. A glance at his watch gave him a hurry on.

The marriage of Mary and Richard was recorded but not another mention of her. Certainly not in this region.

His watch vibrated and with a sigh, John returned the microfiche to its box and turned off the reader. If he could ready Bluebell to leave early, then he'd drop Daphne at the Brookers and settle down with his favourite genealogy app. One never knew what might result from a good browse.

"I cannot wait to update you on everything I discovered!" Daphne had arrived back at Bluebell minutes before John and was readying lunch to put into a sandwich press. "Can you pass me the mustard?"

"Have a bit of news myself, but nothing which is going to change the direction of the investigation." He rummaged in the fridge. "There you are."

"Wish I'd visited Maurice earlier."

"Maurice?"

"Owns the newspaper."

"The Bugle?"

"No. That was the first newspaper. Maurice's father restarted it decades ago as The Chronicle. While I was there, he had a call from his reporter who is in Melbourne staying close to the coroner's office." Daphne closed the sandwich press. "Almost ready."

"Is there new information?"

"I have no idea how the reporter even found this out but apparently talk is that the steak knife idea has legs. The type of wound fitted a knife not unlike those in the photo. And the angle indicated whoever wielded the knife was a little taller than Steve."

"Rules out Gina, Bertie, Lisa, Margaret. Not Bob though." John collected plates. "How did the reporter find out? Sounds like information the police would keep to themselves."

Daphne shrugged. "Not up to speed on procedures. And the paper isn't printing any of that yet. But Maurice asked me a lot of questions about the day."

"You were careful what you said?"

"Yes, dear."

John smiled. "Sorry, doll."

"I was very careful. What you and I discuss is for our ears. But it didn't hurt to tell him about the wonderful nurse who worked so hard on Steve, or the paramedics who really did their best. He already knew something about a missing phone so I mentioned seeing Steve take the call. Can't see that it changes anything."

After lifting the golden toasted cheese sandwiches onto plates and slicing them, Daphne joined John at the table. "I've got enough time to do a quick read through of the ceremony and get changed."

"And I'll get Bluebell all but ready to travel while you do."

"Not once you drop me off?"

"To use your word? Negatory. I'll wait outside and do a spot of genealogy research. Leaving you alone with those people is not an option, Daphne."

She smiled. It was nice to be cared for so much. "I'm sure they will all behave. But it is good to know you won't be far if any of them show the slightest sign of being unkind. With a bit of luck, this farewell ceremony will go as smoothly as the Tanning's did."

Beneath the table, Daphne crossed her fingers.

SOMETHING TO HIDE

There were half a dozen cars parked in the driveway and along the street near the Brooker's house. John kissed Daphne's cheek and promised to park where he could see her come out of the house, and made her promise to call or text him if she needed his help. She watched him drive fifty or so metres down the road, do a U-turn, and park beneath a tree. He flashed the headlights and she waved.

Rather than going through the house, Daphne followed the sound of soft music, which led her to the pool.

At the corner of the deck she abruptly halted, almost dropping her briefcase.

This was the last place she'd expected to hold a farewell ceremony, yet a small group was gathered inside the pool area. The fence itself was decorated with white lilies, white roses, and lilac ribbons. The music was from a string trio seated in the furthest corner. Hanging from the eaves of the change room was a long, white dress and Daphne gasped in recognition.

Lisa's wedding dress.

It swung back and forth, the mascara-stained top part of the lace visible even from the distance. Daphne shuddered. What kind of macabre event was she walking into.

"Daphne!"

Lisa's squeal got everyone's attention and all heads turned as she rushed through the gate. Margaret, Bob, Bertie. The bridesmaids. The groomsmen. And two more. Pat and Gina.

Daphne's stomach turned. If that woman said one thing...

"We've made it so beautiful for my Steve." Lisa slipped an arm through Daphne's. "We have music, flowers, champagne, and you. What could be a better way to farewell my husband than this?"

They went through the gate and Daphne stopped again. The pool was white. It looked as though milk had replaced water and she couldn't see the bottom.

"Isn't this nice? As if he is a ghost swimming around in there and when my wedding dress is lowered into the water, it will become one with it and him. And with your beautiful words to send him off, Steve will be smiling. Somewhere."

If Lisa wasn't holding onto her arm, Daphne would have turned and run. Heeled shoes and all. Her flight response was in full swing and it took several calming breaths to push down the panic. Margaret joined them, her face more solemn.

"Daphne, dear. Thank you for staying in town to do this. It means so much to our Lisa."

Daphne blinked. Words weren't coming but the other women didn't seem to notice. She found herself swept along to the same podium she'd stood upon only a few days ago. This was creepy.

Get a grip, Daph. It isn't about you.

Bob came forward to shake Daphne's hand. Released by Lisa, who returned to her bridesmaids, Daphne forced a smile. Not very successfully. Bob rolled his eyes as if to say he shared her sentiments. Or was he enjoying an inside joke only he knew? Another of his step-daughter's husbands out of the way. Revenge for forcing him into a lifestyle he detested, or a way to prove he held the upper hand—either were reasons a murderer might rationalise.

Nobody was above suspicion and only those with water-tight alibis were off the hook. Assuming they didn't have a partner in crime.

"Mrs Jones?"

She blinked. Bob had his hand on her shoulder.

"You look pale. Let's get you out of the sun for a few minutes."

About to say she was fine, Daphne clamped her lips together as he led her to the buildings. The change room door was wide open, as was the one opposite which housed the cleaning equipment. Bob pulled a chair from the change room and placed it against the wall between the two facing doors.

"I'll get you some water."

Bob disappeared towards the house and Daphne sank onto the seat. Everyone else was occupied and she leaned forward to better see inside the other room. No sign of the groundsman...Dempster? Shelves on the far wall stored all manner of cleaning products. A series of white tubs, one with the word 'Poison' on the side. Chlorine and other water treatments, cleaning equipment, lots of tins of paint. Perhaps he'd been the one who repainted the inside of the house before the wedding.

"Sorry, it's a bit messy in there."

Daphne almost fell off the chair. She touched her chest over the heart.

"Didn't mean to startle you." Carrying a long pole with a net on the end, Dempster stepped past. "Tend to keep the door closed so guests aren't put off by the chemicals and stuff but Lisa wanted access in case she decides to change the colour of the pool at the last minute."

After pushing herself to her feet, Daphne followed him in. "How would she do that?"

He leaned the pole in a corner and reached for a solid plastic container with a spout. "Pool dye. Well, it also has some other ingredients to make sure it stays opaque and it'll play havoc on the filters, but it does the job." Replacing it, he gestured to a row of smaller bottles. "Lisa initially wanted everything black but there was no way to make it happen in time. And not a lot of black flowers to match."

"And Lisa likes to match colours."

Dempster grinned. "She does. At least with white she's made everything look nice for the wake. I guess it is like a wake?"

Bob stuck his head through the door. "Got you a bottle of water. Demps, can you find Bertie?"

"Wasn't he just here?" Daphne followed Bob outside and accepted the chilled water. "Thanks for this."

"He'll be in the other garden. Probably thinks the ceremony is there because the wedding was." Dempster jogged out of the gate, turning in the direction of the area through the hedge.

Bob muttered something about Bertie needing to go to an old folk's home.

"Once he's here, shall we start?" Daphne asked nobody

and everybody. It was more a public service announcement to remind people there was a purpose for her presence. She opened her bag to get the ceremony book, readying herself to take centre stage on the podium when everyone was in place.

"Actually, I want to voice my objection to this entire circus."

Hand on the book, Daphne let it slide back into her bag as Gina stepped onto the podium as if she was the celebrant.

"The poor boy died in this pool." Gina pointed at it. "In there, Lisa. Yet you glorify this as though he was a prince instead of one of the thieving Tanning family."

"Now, Gina, let's not go there—" Margaret began.

"Go there? Should have gone there before the first wedding. Stopped the nonsense before it began. You should have raised your daughter better." Gina directed this at Margaret, who shrank back, almost stepping into the pool had Bob not steadied her. "And you should have stood up for your family. Your real family." This was to Bob.

A riot of angry voices broke out. Lisa burst into tears. What a surprise. The bridesmaids and groomsmen snuck off to a table near the string trio where champagne and glasses were set out for later. The music stopped.

Daphne stalked away, through the gate and up the path. Her heart pounded in her ears and if she didn't get away from this toxic situation she'd fall over in a faint. Just as Lisa had the other day. No. This was where she drew the line. This was enough.

A PARTING SHOT

"Should never have come back here." Daphne stomped her way towards the front of the house. The arguing continued behind her and she had no intention of ever looking at one of this particular family again. She'd find John and they could exit this town early.

"Daphne. Daphne, please wait!"

If that was Lisa following her then she could stop and go back to her quarrelling relatives.

"I might as well die as well!"

With a glance to the heavens, Daphne came to a halt.

"What does any of it matter? My husband is dead. All my husbands are dead. And I can't even say a proper goodbye because I have the worst family in the world." Lisa managed to add a sob at the end.

"I'm sorry, Lisa. I just can't be around this kind of nastiness anymore." Against her better judgement, Daphne turned around.

The sad figure in front of her tugged at something deep

inside. It shouldn't, knowing many of Lisa's reactions were a performance, but there was a hollowness in the younger woman's eyes. No tears. No more sobs. But a deep sadness which might have been genuine. And there was something about the way Lisa wrapped her arms around herself which reminded Daphne of another woman. Much younger and long ago.

"Wouldn't it be best if you abandon the ceremony until people are prepared to respect your grief?" Daphne asked as gently as she could.

"But then you'll be gone."

Daphne crossed the distance between them and gave Lisa a hug. "I can leave my words for someone else to read. But I don't think I'm able to do this, not when people are yelling and pointing fingers. And your great-aunt Gina really doesn't like me."

"Gina dislikes everyone. Well, everyone who isn't a real Brooker. She never welcomed me. Or Mum." Lisa gazed back at the pool where a calm had fallen, at least for the moment. "Even though I made sure Granddad had a nice place to live and no more debt, his own sister reminds me constantly how outsiders took everything from him. But he thought Dad was wrong about Toby stealing from his company and it was all a misunderstanding, so when Sam asked me out on a date I figured marrying a Tanning man would help heal things."

Not the selfish person everyone painted her as. Not entirely.

Margaret was watching from near the gate. Her shoulders were slumped and all Daphne could do was take pity on the two of them. They weren't killers. Just outsiders trying to fit in with a difficult family whose past controlled their present.

"If you really want me to do this, let's go and do it."

"You mean it?" Lisa grabbed Daphne's hand. "I will never forget this."

Walking back to the pool with all eyes on her, Daphne had a feeling that she would also never forget today.

Without doubt this was the strangest ceremony Daphne had attended, either as a participant or celebrant. Nobody spoke, which was a relief, allowing Daphne to finish reading her prepared words, albeit faster than normal.

The milk-white swimming pool barely rippled as Lisa lowered her wedding gown into the water. It didn't sink immediately, but floated for a while creating a bizarre imprint on the surface. Everyone carried a wreath with white flowers and lilac ribbons and these were slipped into the pool as well. All the time, Daphne stood upon the podium clasping her book against her chest. And all the time, Gina's eyes bored into her.

When all the wreaths were in the pool and the dress was little more than a layer of lace and all of Daphne's words were done, the string trio began to play. In an odd turn of events, it was the same song Steve's band played at the Tanning ceremony although without the words, screaming, and tempo. The families had more in common than any of them would admit and it was sad they couldn't come together to share their grief and memories. At least Lisa had extended an olive branch. Several times.

Daphne dabbed her forehead with a handkerchief. The reflection from the tiles and pool accentuated the heat of the afternoon. Her bottle of water lay unopened on the chair she'd briefly used earlier so when the mourners drifted into small groups, Daphne abandoned the podium for the shaded alcove between the two buildings.

Both doors were closed. Dempster was outside the pool fencing as though keeping an eye on Bertie. The latter gave little away. He'd not got involved in the earlier argument as far as Daphne had seen. Did he even understand what was happening today?

"You can leave now."

Although her heart sank, Daphne didn't look at Gina as she returned her book to the briefcase. Was it even worth responding? If there was another crack about her weight or eating habits, there might be an unfortunate addition to the swimming pool. Almost made her smile.

"Take our money and go off to wherever you want to cause mayhem next."

"I believe Lisa is paying for the ceremony." Daphne straightened and removed the lid of the bottle to sip some water.

Gina opened her mouth but was cut off by Bertie's arrival. He pushed in front of his sister and put his hands on Daphne's shoulders, staring her straight in the eyes.

"You're a good woman, Mrs Jones. Thanks for helping Lisa say goodbye."

"That's very sweet of you to say."

"And a load of crock. Robert, why don't you do one of your famous disappearing acts? Your little helper over there can go with you."

Bertie winked at Daphne and released her. "Ignore Regina. She doesn't have a kind bone in her body and has a problem with anyone she's not related to and many she is."

Behind Bertie, Gina's eyes widened and her faced turned a peculiar shade of red. This was about to become an ugly situation fast. Daphne collected her handbag and briefcase.

"If you'll excuse—"

"Perhaps you need to reconsider how you speak to me, big brother." Gina hissed. "Remember I know all the torrid secrets this family tries so hard to conceal."

With her back to the change room door, Daphne stepped sideways like a crab but Bertie closed the gap between his body and the corner of the building, his attention on his furious sibling. Then, Daphne aimed for a narrow opening around Gina but just as she moved forward, Gina put her hands on her hips, making it impossible to go around her without touching the woman.

Other people turned to look. Bob threw his hands in the air and walked off. One of the bridesmaids got a phone out and held it up as though videoing the pair. Being seen in the background was the last thing Daphne wanted so she opened the door to the maintenance room and stepped inside. She sent a text message to John.

Can you come around to the pool area? Might need an escort out.

Her phone went in her handbag, which she put on the floor so she could replace the lid back on the water bottle before it spurted all over her, thanks to shaky hands.

"The only thing you know is how to offend people." Bertie said.

More voices chimed in. Margaret. Lisa. Pat. Even Dempster, although all he did was ask them to both stop fighting which drew Gina's ire.

"How dare you speak to me! What are you? The groundsman. No, that overstates your purpose. You are a glorified cleaner and babysitter of an old man."

"At least Dempster cares enough to look for me. Like at the wedding. Nobody else came looking."

"Stop it!" Lisa forced her way between them. "Bertie, if you hadn't wandered off, Steve wouldn't have come to the pool. Gina, if you didn't make it so hard for his family, they would have been at the wedding and he would be alive now. You are both to blame and I'll never forgive either of you!"

Well, good for you. Tell them what you think, Lisa.

She did have some spirit after all.

There was a long silence and Daphne peeked around the doorframe. Gina still had her hands on her hips and her face was now as white as the swimming pool. Bertie grinned. He was enjoying this more than anyone should.

"I see." Gina lifted her chin. "Not that I need your forgiveness, Lisa. But you have all made it quite clear my contribution to this family is unwanted."

"Sure is, sis."

Gina leaned close to Bertie. Daphne had to strain to hear the words she spat.

"When the police come calling just remember you forced me to do it."

Bertie didn't flinch as Gina stormed away, out of the pool area and towards the front of the house. She passed John who was almost running in the opposite direction. He glanced at Gina and sped up. Daphne stepped out of the room. The way cleared around her as she ploughed through to meet her husband at the gate.

"Doll?" John panted.

"How about we go somewhere far, far away."

He put his arm around her and they turned their backs on the pool, the Brookers, the wedding dress sinking beneath the surface, and the dysfunction of the past few days.

BEGINNING OF THE END

"Dye in the swimming pool?"

"Yup. And her wedding dress, complete with mascara stains. Flowers. Wreaths. Oh my goodness, John. It was...different."

They were sitting in the car which was still parked under the tree. John took Daphne's hand and they looked at each other. Her lips quivered. How horrible this must have been for his wife. If this was the kind of experience to expect from her new career then perhaps it was time to reconsider it.

"Don't cry, love. It isn't worth it." He squeezed her hand.

"Wreaths with lilac ribbons. In a pool filled with dye which will wreck the filters."

"It's okay. You're safe." He almost held his breath. He should have gone with her. Insisted she have a helper, or something. How distressing this must be.

Then Daphne laughed. She closed her eyes and laughed until she cried, tears pouring down her cheeks. "The dress... it was like a horror movie...and Lisa said it would be...as though his ghost was there."

"Steve's ghost?"

"Yup. Her dress would be at one with him. And there was a lovely string trio playing Steve's favourite heavy metal song. And Dempster had to find Bertie again because he wandered off."

John found a small box of tissues in the centre console and handed them to Daphne. She took a few and wiped at her eyes. As much as she was laughing, he saw through it. There was pain there. And dismay that people would behave so badly.

"Let's get back to Bluebell." John started the motor. "Where was Gina going at such speed?"

Daphne didn't answer and he glanced across. She stared ahead, biting her bottom lip.

John pulled onto the road and accelerated.

"Gina was called out by her brother."

"Bertie? What did he say?" John asked.

"There was a lot of insults hurled between them and then Lisa told them both off. For once I actually liked her."

"Did Gina have another go at you?"

"She tried. But I was prepared and didn't let her get to me. Although I did consider pushing her in the pool at one point, but upsetting Lisa wouldn't have been worth it." Daphne leaned back in her seat. "I cannot wait until this town is in the rear vision mirror."

John agreed. He'd have them ready to go within half an hour. "Bluebell is almost ready. Get yourself into some comfortable travelling clothes and we'll be on our way."

Daphne reached over and patted his leg. "Thanks, love. You've been my rock through all of this and I'm so relieved we're not spending another night here." She settled in her seat again. "Sorry for all the emotion. I'm fine now."

If Daphne had needed to scream or cry he'd have understood. What a strong woman she was. John turned into the driveway of the camping grounds. A day or two away from here and both of them would be a lot happier. Nothing could stop that.

He backed the car ready to hook Bluebell up. Everything else was done. Awning and outdoor kitchen packed away. Power and water unplugged.

"Here we are, love." They climbed out. "Have you got your key?"

Daphne was ahead of him and she'd come to a halt. He thought it was to find her key until she turned with her hand over her mouth.

"What's wrong, Daph?"

She pointed back to Bluebell. The tyres were flat. Slashed, with visible cuts across them. They weren't going anywhere.

Daphne locked herself in the bathroom.

She'd told John she'd gone to freshen up but she was there to cry. Except no tears would come.

This was her fault. The cost of replacing those tyres was more than she'd made for the two goodbye ceremonies which had kept them there. John wouldn't care, but he didn't need to be putting his hand in his pocket for something she'd made happen. If only she'd stayed out of it. Not nosed around and in such a way that other people noticed her interest. Other people who had things to hide and would stop at nothing to keep their secrets.

Secrets about families. About her family. Her parents kept secrets. Terrible lies.

Daphne's throat tightened and she gripped the sides of the sink, her eyes on the basin.

Yelling in the night. Words from behind closed doors which made no sense to ten-year-old Daphne as she cuddled her little sister to help her go back to sleep. Only years later did she understand what unfaithful meant. Let alone a much nastier word her father screamed at her mother.

Count your blessings, Daph.

She raised her eyes to the mirror. Those were memories. Not her life today. Not her life for a long time.

"You're a good person. You have a big heart." She whispered.

John loved her.

"A bad person slashed the tyres, Daph. Not you."

Eyes on her face, she forced herself to smile. Her muscles relaxed.

"You are perfect as you are."

Deep down she knew she didn't quite believe it. One day she would.

"Daphne Agnes Jones, you have a gift of seeing the truth and right now, there are people who need your help. Believe in yourself."

This time her smile was for real and endorphins flooded every inch of her body. Somebody had to solve this mystery and she might as well be the one to do it.

John got off the phone, frowning even more than when Daphne had found the tyres. "Not the news I'd hoped for, love. Nobody has four of the right tyres in stock in town. Best they can do is order them which means waiting until the morning."

"And there's no way to repair them."

"None." He leaned down to run a hand over a gash. "Not a case of putting an inner tube in and patching the hole. These tyres are only suitable for the scrap heap."

A police car pulled up and Matty climbed out. "Thought you'd be well on your way by now."

"That was our intention. Thanks for coming to take a look." John shook Matty's hand. "These tyres didn't slash themselves."

Daphne left the men to inspect the damage and moved to the back of the caravan, her eyes on the trees near the river. Had the vandal waited there for them to leave earlier? This felt personal.

"Any idea who might be responsible? Noticed anyone hanging around?" Matty and John joined Daphne.

"Area is so quiet. Barely see any of the other campers let alone strangers." John said.

"Except somebody was watching us the other night." Daphne pointed at the trees. "From there, I think."

"What makes you say that?" Matty asked, holding his hand up to shade his eyes.

"During the storm the other night, I had the strongest sensation of being watched. And I know it was only a feeling, but when I was walking the next morning there were deep footprints around those trees."

John touched her arm. "You didn't tell me."

"Thought I was imagining things."

"What if we take a look?" Matty headed in the direction she'd indicated and the others followed, catching him up just before the trees, where he stopped. "Can you still see the imprints, Mrs Jones?"

I'll look silly if I can't.

Daphne was careful where she stepped as she circled the largest of the trees, glancing back to Bluebell. This was the spot. And the footprints?

"There. Just before the grass line. Facing our caravan."

Matty took out his phone and took a series of photos before getting close enough to inspect the area. "Looks like boots, large ones so most likely a man. And deep. Might have stood here for a bit. During the storm, you say?"

Daphne nodded. Someone had stood here watching them then returned and slashed their tyres. Quite apart from the cost of replacing the tyres was the knowledge someone wanted to harm them. She blinked rapidly and swallowed. No time for tears. Whoever the someone was, they were sending a message.

"At least you can rule out Gina!"

Both men turned to her with confused expressions.

"She has been telling me to leave town since Monday. Slashing our tyres means we have to stay longer."

Matty smiled. "We'll exclude Gina from our enquiries."

"But only for this. I just performed the farewell ceremony for Steve Tanning at the Brooker residence. Gina referred to his family as 'the thieving Tannings' and made a number of nasty comments of how other members of the family should have stopped Lisa marrying the three men. Her parting words to her brother were along the lines that he shouldn't be surprised if the police come calling and she'd been forced to do it." Daphne stared at Matty. "I wonder if she meant she'd felt forced to do something about Steve and had decided to confess."

Matty put his phone away. A long silence followed, broken only by birdsong. As if he'd made a decision, Matty nodded. "If Gina had anything to do with it, it was from a distance. She didn't stab Steve. Height is wrong and besides, she has an alibi. Everyone does."

"Everyone?" John asked. "What about Bertie when he disappeared?"

"Except he didn't disappear. He went to sit under a tree near the caravan waiting for Dempster to finish feeding stock or something. For some reason, the younger man can calm him when he gets worked up or confused. They came back together. And before you ask how we know, they were seen on the other side of the property at Steve's time of death."

Another suspect to cross off.

"Who saw them?"

"Shall we go back? I want to check for matching footprints around the caravan." Matty headed off without waiting.

Daphne hurried after him. "Please, may we know? It isn't like I'm going to go and accuse anyone!"

She was sure she saw a grin on Matty's face but he said nothing until they were back at Bluebell.

"Okay, it was Gina who saw them both. She was pretty angry about it because in her opinion Steve would still be alive if Bertie hadn't vanished and caused everyone to go searching."

"But she didn't want Lisa to marry Steve."

"A lot of people didn't but it doesn't make them murderers. You need to trust me that we've spoken to her at length about this and the missing phone and at this point, it is up to homicide to pursue any other angles."

"Missing phone? Was it Gina's phone that called Steve?"

Matty rolled his eyes and clamped his lips shut. It was fine with Daphne. He'd said enough to fill in some blanks. She couldn't wait to find her notebook.

NIGHT NOTES

"We finally have neighbours." John stuck his head through the door. "Apparently the people who were further up the river heard what happened and arranged to move closer. Strength in numbers."

"Were they concerned they might be next?"

"Nope. Didn't want us feeling alone."

Daphne shook flour off her hands. "What a lovely gesture. I should go and thank them."

"We will once they finish setting up. Thought I'd pop into town and pick up a bottle of wine to give them. Happy to wait until you can come with me."

"No, no. You go. I'm about to slide these cookies into the oven and thank goodness I've made a big batch so we can give some to those nice people. Do you mind if I give you a small shopping list? I fancy making lasagne for dinner."

A few minutes later the cookies were in the oven, John was on his way to town, and Daphne had her notebook on the table. After Matty left, John had climbed under Bluebell with a torch to make sure there was no damage he'd missed.

Four wrecked tyres was bad enough. Nothing else was out of place and some of John's expression of worry eased a bit.

Making cookies for him was the best way Daphne could think of helping. It was only a little thing but making something nice which he loved surely would provide some much needed comfort.

As the delectable smell of the baking filled Bluebell, Daphne added to her notes about the death of Steve Tanning. The police might have discarded Gina as a suspect but there were too many unanswered questions about her for Daphne's liking. For example, what did Gina mean about the police? Perhaps she had an idea of how to pin it all on someone else in the family. Like Bertie.

Daphne wrote down her thoughts until the oven timer buzzed. The cookies were choc chip and looked as good as they smelled. Perfect for a quick snack once John returned, before she started on dinner. Then, they could finally do a proper catch up on the events of the day.

After dinner, John did one final walk around outside, flashing his torch at the trees for good measure. Daphne closed the last of the blinds as he turned to come inside. The new neighbours were a couple of camp sites over and had their outside lights on as well. Best to keep everything illuminated overnight. Just in case.

"Matty said he'll arrange for the patrol car to drive through a couple of times tonight." John climbed inside and locked the door. "For all we know this might have been nothing more than a random act of vandalism."

Daphne disagreed.

"Would you like another cookie?"

"Um. Thanks but I'm still full. Dinner was delicious."

"In that case, I'd love to hear more about your visit to the library." Daphne dropped onto her seat.

John collected the laptop and his phone. "The library didn't give me a lot of new information but I was on one of the genealogy apps earlier, digging around to find Mary Brooker. Mary Smith. Let me go back to where I was because there were queries about her."

"So a person can join up and add their details to see if anyone is related to them?"

"Kind of. There are DNA tests people take—often just to get an idea of where their ancestors came from—and they can lead to discovering an arm of a family or a lost cousin. That kind of thing. Ah, here we go." John turned the screen so Daphne was able to see. "About twelve years ago there was a query about Mary Brooker of Little Bridges. An anonymous responder provided information including that she died in Melbourne aged sixty leaving behind a daughter. Well, well." He glanced up. "The child was born seven months after the deaths of Richard and Joseph."

"I wonder who the father was?"

"Excellent question."

"What if..." Daphne trailed off as she tried to connect her thoughts. "What if the query twelve years ago was from someone thinking they might be related to her, and therefore the Brookers? They find out about the Brooker wealth and come to claim their share. But the money is Lisa's inheritance. She's only a Brooker because her mother married into the family. So there would be no claim to stake."

"You think the Tanning deaths might be payback? Lisa

didn't pay out so her husbands all get to die? Dunno. Seems extreme."

He was right. Sounded like a B-grade television show rather than real life.

"Here's another theory. This person descended from Joseph Tanning and came to join the family but was rejected. Actually, scrap that. Why only kill off those who marry Lisa?"

The lights flickered and Daphne jumped. John patted her hand. The lights settled and she told herself to get a grip.

"Right. Well, according to my notes, we are running out of suspects. Assuming we believe Matty that Gina is not one of them."

"Which you don't believe. Do you?" John stood. "Care for a glass of wine?"

"Great idea. I'd like to exclude the woman but really, how can I?" Daphne turned to the page headlined as *'Gina. Not a nice person'*. "Let's recap as if you'd never met her or heard any of this and tell me what you think."

John poured two glasses of red wine and returned to the table. "Might be hard to pretend given how mean she's been to you, but let's give it a whirl."

They raised and tapped their glasses together with a 'cheers'.

Daphne put down the glass after a lovely long sip. "I do like the local wines here. Anyway, let me introduce you to Regina...don't know her married name. But a Brooker through and through."

"Nice to meet you, Regina."

"Funny. Although I'd like to mention that Gina takes herself very seriously, to the point of wearing pearls for any occasion and putting down other people to make herself feel better, I won't."

"Very charitable of you." John grinned.

"I thought so. Moving on to the facts as known. She is the younger sister of Robert Brooker, better known as Bertie, Dad, Granddad or Gramps. She has been known to say—on multiple occasions—that Steve Tanning didn't deserve to die."

"Which makes her a good person."

"On the other hand, she hates the Tanning family with a vengeance and has been overheard by a creditable source telling other members of her family they should have stopped any marriages between the clans."

"A creditable source. Well, that is reassuring."

Daphne giggled and drank some more wine.

"Why is this beacon of light even considered a suspect?" John asked, his eyes bright with mirth.

"Well," Daphne leaned a bit closer, "there are some things you may need to consider. Did you know she owns a phone which she claims was stolen before it was used to phone Steve on his wedding day? A phone call which lured him to his death?"

"Intriguing."

"Methinks she made herself sound sympathetic to Steve to draw attention away from her real purpose."

"Which is?"

Daphne leaned forward and whispered loudly, "Murder any of those thieving Tannings before they get another chance to steal."

John went back to the laptop, typing into the search bar. "Did you get more information about the deaths of Lisa's other husbands? Sam and Shane?"

"Some. Maurice from The Chronicle told me there had been investigations into both deaths but there was no evidence of foul play. Sam was an electrician working for himself. He was rewiring an old house and made a mistake. Was alone at the time and there was nothing to indicate anything other than a tragic accident. He was Lisa's first husband and they were together for seven months."

"Not long at all. And what about Shane?"

Daphne went back through her notes. "Fall from a high ladder. This was at the Brooker house and he was helping with a broken branch of a gum tree. Overbalanced and fell. Despite attempts to resuscitate he was pronounced dead at the scene. Married for three months."

"I'm on The Chronicle's website," John read from the computer screen. "This old article mentions Shane falling during an attempt by two men working alone to remove a dangerous branch. He was at the top of an eleven metre ladder with no safety gear and according to this, misjudged his footing and fell straight down."

"Nasty. And stupid. Why on earth take such a risk!" Daphne fanned her face with her hand. "Does it say who the other man was? Presumably, a professional tree lopper, although why they wouldn't bring their own people—"

"Love? The person with him was Dempster. And get this. His name is Dempster Smith."

"I can't find my phone, John. It definitely isn't in the car?" Daphne turned her handbag upside down on the bed, lipstick, purse, and other small items spilling everywhere. But no phone.

"Even looked under all the seats and in the glove box. What is the last time you remember it in your hand?"

Daphne sat on the edge of the bed, concentration wrinkling her face. They'd spent the past ten minutes searching in the usual places. After the bombshell of finding Dempster's surname, she'd wanted to let the police know there might be a connection to Mary Smith and the original feud between the families.

"I sent you the text message. Yes, I'm certain I've not used it since."

"You were at the ceremony."

"I was in the room where they keep the cleaning stuff. I'd put my handbag down to replace the lid on my water. Then I sent the message and dropped the phone back into my bag. Except I was also listening to the argument so I must have missed my bag." She put her hand over her heart. "I have to get it back."

"We will, love. But not at night-time. Even if the family is still awake, it would be best to go there in daylight. And after speaking to the police. Don't you think?" John helped Daphne toss everything back in her handbag. "I'll give Matty a call now."

Daphne was quiet and followed John back to the table. He dialled the now-familiar number and got the voicemail. He kept half an eye on Daphne as he left a brief message and then hung up. He held his arms out and Daphne came straight in for a hug. Her heart raced against his chest and she was shaking. Wrapped up in his arms she gradually relaxed and dropped her head onto his shoulder with a sigh.

The phone rang.

"Sorry." John released her and kissed the tip of her nose before answering. "John here. Hello, Senior Constable, and thanks for calling back." He sat at the table and Daphne joined him as he outlined their latest information before disconnecting the call.

"What did she say?"

"Not to go to the Brookers tonight. Sorry, I know you want your phone back and we'll drive over first thing. She said she'll pass the information to the homicide detectives. She also said it is best if we stop nosing around." He smiled.

"We're not nosing around. We're contributing relevant details which the police may not have had access to. I can't imagine they have time to look at genealogy sites and why would they connect a dispute that happened a hundred or more years ago to a series of recent murders?" Daphne's voice broke a bit. "I think...I am pretty sure Dempster and Gina are behind the murders. All three murders."

A TRAGIC TWIST

The approach of dawn was a relief after a night which had passed slowly, with a head full of worries and fitful sleep. At least for Daphne, for John was a good sleeper and kept her thoughts company with his soft snoring. For once he wasn't up before her and she let him sleep until the sun lifted above the horizon. If she'd had her way, she'd have gone to collect her phone last night. It wasn't just not having it which upset her, but the knowledge a murderer might have found it. If she called her own number would Dempster answer?

Pushing aside the thought, Daphne put the kettle on then began opening the blinds. Everything outside appeared normal. The car looked fine, which was one of her overnight fears. Replacing four caravan tyres was bad enough.

"Morning, love." John disappeared into the bathroom.

By the time coffee was poured, he'd emerged and dressed. As he reached the table, his phone rang.

"Bit early." He peered at the number. "Don't recognise it."

"It looks like Lisa's number."

John tapped 'accept' and put the call onto speaker. "This is John Jones."

There was a long sobbing noise. Definitely Lisa.

Daphne and John exchanged a 'what now' glance.

"Is Daphne there?"

"I'm here, dear."

"Can you...can you both come here?"

"To the house?"

"Yes. And please hurry."

"Lisa, what's happened?" John asked.

More sobs, followed by a faint, "She's dead. Please come."

Then the connection ended.

"What on earth?" Daphne hurried to collect her handbag. "Margaret?"

"Or the cook? Don't even know if she came back."

"We have to go."

John gazed sadly at his coffee, but gathered his keys, wallet, and phone. "I guess we were going there anyway."

The blaring siren and flashing lights of a patrol car loomed behind them as John drove towards the Brooker house. It overtook in seconds.

"At least we know they've called for more help than just us." John said. "I'm not entirely happy about Lisa wanting you there."

"As you said before, we were coming here anyway. We'll see what happened, get my phone, and be out of here. What time are the tyres arriving?"

"Late morning and they'll give me a call before they

bring them. Decent of them to fit them for me and to be honest, I was concerned I'd be trying to change them on my own." John parked a little way from the Brooker's driveway. "We might leave the car here in case it becomes hard to leave later."

On cue, another siren approached and as they got out of the car, Daphne and John turned to look. An ambulance.

"I'm wondering if we should go in, love." John watched the ambulance go into the driveway.

"If the authorities tell us to leave we will. But Lisa sounded distraught. And my phone."

As they walked to the house, people emerged from other homes and came to their front gates, all heads towards the Brooker property. With every step, the sense of déjà vu intensified. Another day, another dead body. What else would be repeated? Bertie disappearing? Gina having another go at her?

"Once I have my phone I am never leaving it anywhere ever again." Daphne muttered.

Police and paramedics crowded through the front door. Lisa appeared from the side of the house and frantically gestured for Daphne and John to come to her. Once they reached her, she hugged them both like long lost friends.

"We have to hurry."

She took off and they followed her past the house, deck and pool. Then through the gate to where the wedding had been held.

"Lisa, you didn't say who died. What happened?" Daphne puffed as she half-ran to keep up the cracking pace Lisa had set. John grabbed her arm to help her along. Not that he was breathing quietly either.

"The most dreadful thing has happened."

There were voices not far behind and Lisa sped up, skirting behind the still-erected backdrop from the wedding and through a space between more hedges. Daphne scraped her arm going through but what she saw on the other side made her forget it on the spot.

This was a large paddock with a few sheep huddled at its far end beneath some trees. Past them the caravan sat by the river.

Face down in the middle of the paddock was a woman. Her body fitting dress and pearls were a giveaway before Daphne was close enough to see her face which was turned in their direction with her eyes closed. A steak knife was in her back.

"My, oh my. Gina?"

"Yes. Didn't I say that on the phone?"

"No. Lisa, we shouldn't be here." John stopped a few metres away and held Daphne's hand to stop her going further. "Careful where you step, doll. Evidence and all that."

He was right. But Lisa was kneeling beside Gina. "This must be the same knife that killed my Steve. It came from the set we were given for our wedding and one was missing, but you know that because the police said they saw one of your photos."

"Lisa, you should step away. What if you accidentally destroy evidence?"

"Too late, Daphne. I found her here when I was going to check the sheep. They were carrying on and now I know why. After she stormed off yesterday we didn't see her again. Pat phoned last night to see if we knew where she was."

The police and paramedics made their way through the

hedge, lifting the stretcher through. Bob was followed by Margaret and Bertie. The latter pushed past and ran towards Gina's body. Lisa leaped up and met him partway.

"Don't look, Granddad. She's gone."

"No. No, not my sister." He skirted around Lisa and dropped to his knees near Gina. "Not my sister. What has he done?"

"Bertie? What has who done?" Daphne asked.

He shook his head as though he didn't understand, his hands wringing each other.

"You said what has he done? Can you tell me who 'he' is?"

The police were closing in and Bertie glanced at them, his mouth opening and closing before he managed, "The killer. That's who. It's gone too far."

In a moment, the area was swamped by police and the paramedics. Daphne took John's hand and tugged. They retreated to the hedge and watched from there as paramedics declared Gina was gone. The officers were ones they'd seen at the station but not spoken with. Bertie was on his feet with Bob supporting him.

"Bertie knows something." Daphne said.

"Got that feeling. Do you think he suspected Gina was behind Steve's death? That she got on the wrong side of whoever she was working with?"

"Let's get my phone before the police stop anyone moving about."

They were almost at the pool when Lisa chased them down. "You can't leave yet!"

"My phone is in the maintenance room. I accidentally left it there yesterday."

Lisa sprinted ahead and was unlocking the door when

they reached her. "That's why your number went to voicemail. I hope it's still there."

So do I!

Door open, Daphne hurried in. The phone was on the floor. She swept it up, checking it but the battery was flat. "Thank goodness. And thank you, Lisa. But why did you need us here?" She gripped the phone against her chest.

"They'll think it was me." Her voice was steady as she gazed at Daphne. "After the things Gina said yesterday about Steve, I'll be blamed. At least until they do their forensics tests and find I'm innocent. Somebody has to find the real killer, Daphne."

Her mind already turning over possibilities, Daphne was confident Lisa was not involved in any of the deaths. Which left just a handful of known suspects.

"Lisa, where's Dempster? I wonder if he heard something from the caravan."

"No idea. But he comes and goes as he pleases as long as he does his job. I phoned him when the sheep were carrying on earlier and he didn't pick up. And now I know why the sheep were upset."

"Should we get the police to check the caravan?" Daphne zipped her phone inside her handbag. No more risk taking.

"He's probably sleeping off one of his nights of binge drinking." Lisa relocked the door after Daphne exited. "Gina was nasty to him yesterday and it doesn't take much to send him on a bender. That's why he never finished his medical degree. Too stressful."

Medical training?

Outside the pool fence, Lisa stopped and ran a hand over her eyes. "Once this is all over, I think I'm done."

"Done, how?" Daphne asked.

"I've tried to fit into this family but nothing works out. I don't remember much about my real father but he left me a lot of money and it made a difference to Mum having the kind of home she had always wanted. And gave Bertie a safe place instead of slumming it in the old caravan. But nobody is grateful. And I've lost three husbands thanks to a family feud my mother married into."

One of the police officers emerged through the gate between the hedges, glancing around and spotting the three talking. He spoke into his radio and began walking towards them.

"I'll head him off so you two can leave. And thanks for everything, Daphne. Maybe one day when I live a long way from here I'll get married again and give you a call to do the ceremony." With that, Lisa straightened her shoulders and made a beeline for the police officer.

"If the police need to speak to us, they know how to find us." John looped his arm around Daphne's waist. "Best we make sure we're back at Bluebell when the tyres arrive."

Daphne couldn't help looking back. Lisa and the police officer had disappeared and only the still-milky coloured swimming pool indicated anything unusual had ever taken place here. Two murders. A family as dysfunctional as Daphne had ever met. And a mystery still unsolved.

DAPHNE'S DECISION

John had rarely been so happy to pull up near Bluebell. All he needed was four tyres and a helping hand to replace those damaged ones and they'd be on their way out of Little Bridges. No more murders. No more difficult and even nasty people. No more worrying when the phone rang. Back on the road with his wife and the wind at their back.

"I feel I should have stayed."

Surely he'd misheard her? John climbed out of the car. "Might put the kettle on before the tyres arrive. For that matter, we didn't get to have breakfast."

Over the roof of the car, Daphne gave him a puzzled look.

"Need to eat before we head off on the next adventure." He said.

"We've not quite finished this one."

"This, my bride, is not an adventure." John locked the car. "Nightmare, yes. And one we need to escape from before the next instalment drops into our laps."

Daphne followed him into the caravan. He started the

coffee while she plugged her phone in, giving him little glances from time to time. Going back to running a real estate agency held a certain appeal at this moment. He'd seen two dead bodies in the space of a few days and now Daphne wanted to go back to where they'd been. Where one still was.

Two arms encircled his waist as Daphne suddenly hugged him. She must need some emotional support after this morning. And he could do that. He could look after her and make sure nothing bad ever happened...John gulped.

"Shh. It's okay, love. We'll get through this." Daphne whispered as she squeezed him. "Not nice seeing Gina, was it? But we are outsiders and can be helpful and that makes me feel useful."

He held on to her until he could trust himself to speak. Whatever had come over him was back under control. The kettle boiled and he gave her a quick kiss on her lips as her arms dropped to let him go.

"What would you like to eat?" she asked.

"Cookies."

"For breakfast?"

John grinned. "Why not. Coffee and cookies. Not like it is early now. More like morning tea."

Even though Daphne raised her eyebrows, she was quick to collect the container storing the rest of the cookies from yesterday and leave it open on the table. He brought the cups across and they sat.

"Why do you think you should have stayed, love?"

"Oh. I thought you hadn't heard me say that, but it occurred to me somebody needs to keep an eye on Bertie."

"An eye?"

"He might be distraught about his sister, but what if he does suspect who the killer is and confronts him?"

John knew he'd regret asking but did so. "Confronts him? Which 'him' is the killer?"

Daphne helped herself to a cookie and nibbled on it for a minute. Her expression was thoughtful and John waited patiently. All of a sudden her eyes met his and his heart sank before she spoke.

"Do you mind showing me something on the genealogy site?"

"Just leave me here and go back to Bluebell."

"Nope. If you are going to insist on this then you're stuck with me."

They stood at the front door of the Brooker house. Neither had knocked because this debate had gone on for the past three minutes. It was surprising nobody had come to the door to demand an explanation for their presence. Daphne had changed into her new pants and jacket. A professional look made a difference. At least to her confidence because it wasn't helping her stay cool. She stepped further into the shade.

She'd put the pieces together and the best opportunity to test her theory was back where it all began. But John was getting more and more concerned and she was second guessing the wisdom of dragging him back here. There were now more cars in the driveway including another patrol car and one she imagined belonged to the homicide detectives.

Let it go. Leave it to the experts.

She took John's hand. "On reflection, the authorities are capable of solving this without me."

The front door swung open and Bertie blocked the doorway. He'd aged, if that was possible, since they'd last seen him. No wonder.

"You might as well come in instead of standing out here arguing."

"Oh, we weren't arguing. Just debating whether we are even needed." Daphne said.

"They're gonna arrest Lisa so come and join the party." He shuffled down the hallway.

"We can go." Daphne whispered, but John shook his head and led the way inside.

They followed Bertie to the living room, where Matty nodded to them from beside two plainclothes officers who were speaking with Bob. Lisa perched on the arm of a sofa and grinned at Daphne. For someone about to be arrested she was calm. But Margaret was not, pacing the floor with tears rolling down her cheeks.

Wherever Dempster had been earlier, he was here now, bleary eyes barely flicking to the newcomers from his seat in the furthest corner of the room. He sipped from a bottle of water.

The detectives stepped away from Bob to speak with Matty. All three glanced at Daphne and John and then to Lisa. Matty said something and younger of the detectives nodded then directed his attention to Lisa.

"Ms Brooker—"

"Mrs Tanning."

"Sorry. Mrs Tanning, if you have nothing more to say at this time, we intend to take you into custody for further questioning. An attorney may be present and—"

"Sorry to interrupt again, but maybe you should ask Mrs Jones if she thinks I did it?" Lisa tilted her head and softened her voice as she leaned forward a fraction. "Another moment or two won't change anything, will it...Captain?"

Matty smirked as the 'captain' glanced at the other detective but didn't bother to correct Lisa's obvious attempt at flattery or flirting. Or both.

"Mrs Jones was here when Steve died and she helped us all. She also came here this morning at my request when I was...flustered and upset by finding my great-aunt, and she has a lot of experience solving crimes."

What? I do?

The eyes of every person in the room shot to Daphne and her legs shook. Just a little.

"I...er, um, no I have helped with a crime investigation back in our home town but I'm not any kind of expert."

"You've been most helpful so far, Mrs Jones." Matty said. "We may need an interview about the events from yesterday by the pool as well as what you observed earlier today in the paddock."

"And I'm happy to assist. But if you want to arrest somebody why not the killer?"

Margaret, who'd stopped pacing and was drying her eyes with tissues, grabbed Bob's arm.

"Do you know who the killer is, Mrs Jones?" This was the older of the detectives. "Or is it speculation?"

Daphne drew in a long breath as her eyes darted from face to face until back on the detective. "That's for you to decide, but I do believe I know. And the person might well be in this very room with us."

A KILLER REVEALED?

The silence dragged until the older detective crossed to the living room door and closed it, before leaning against the timber with his arms folded. This simple action stirred the occupants and Daphne was well aware all three police officers were taking mental notes.

Bob stood to his full height and pushed his chest out. Not a word passed his lips, but his defensive appeared to startle Margaret, who released his arm as if burned. She sank onto the sofa near her daughter.

"The killer is in this room?" Her eyes moved from person to person.

Lisa made herself more comfortable on her perch and drew in air through pursed lips. Margaret reached for her hand but Lisa brushed it away a bit impatiently.

With a grin, Bertie wandered to the window and pushed aside the lacy curtain to look outside. Hopefully, he wasn't losing himself at this important time but at least he wasn't trying to take himself off for a walk.

Still in his seat in the corner, Dempster put the lid on the bottle of water and stared at Daphne. Unwavering. Curious even.

"So, Mrs Jones, when you say the killer may be in this room, can you specify whose killer?" Matty asked. He took his notepad out. "We may have more than one."

What have you got yourself into, Daph?

She touched her lips with the tip of her tongue. A dry mouth would stop the words and for once, she needed them to come out in a way which made sense to every person in the room. Especially the police officers. They'd granted her a rare opportunity to speak her mind and if she messed up, the killer would have valuable information and potentially be free to cover their tracks. Beside her, John smiled in encouragement.

"I believe the killer of Steve and the killer of Gina are one and the same person. Since the day of poor Steve's tragedy, I've made extensive notes based upon my observations. The past few days have exposed me to a number of interesting pieces of information. Overheard conversations, local history, legal records. And watching how people interact and how they speak to each other."

"Sounds like spying. We invited you into our home and you spy on us." Bob ran a finger around the neckline of the business shirt beneath his black suit. Did he ever wear anything else?

"Although spying sounds awfully interesting, I did nothing of the sort. Every person in here has volunteered snippets of gossip, opinion, and outright statements. And almost all were unsolicited."

"Rubbish. What have I said to you that would make me a suspect?" Bob demanded.

"Let me see. You called Steve 'a little rat' in front of me. Sorry, Lisa."

"I've heard him say it enough." Lisa said.

Daphne continued. "You told me you were unhappy about the wedding and having all the guests in your home."

He snorted. "*That* is your evidence?"

"I understand you insisted the pool tiles be polished the day before the wedding which would have made the footing slippery. Easier to push someone into the pool."

"True. You did insist I redo them." Dempster piped up. "They didn't need it."

Bob glared at him.

"There's more but I can't see you as either the killer or the brains behind it."

Daphne changed her focus to Margaret, whose fingers worked overtime on a tissue, shredding it into tiny strips.

"Margaret, you told me you didn't like Steve. I heard you say you wished Lisa would stop putting you through all the weddings. And that the problem was Lisa's taste in husbands. Again, sorry Lisa."

This time Lisa didn't respond. Her body stiffened and her mouth was clamped shut.

"But like with Bob, you are not the killer or the brains behind it."

"Who has brains?" Bertie left the window and sat beside Margaret on the sofa. "Not Lisa. I love her, but she lets people walk all over her. Not real smart if you ask me."

"Thanks, Gramps."

He didn't seem to care, smiling to himself as he played with the buttons on his shirt.

Matty cleared his throat to get the attention back on himself. "Mrs Jones, this is very enlightening, but so far you're excluding people rather than telling us who you think is behind the deaths of Steve and Gina. Lisa had blood on her hands when we arrived. She'd interfered with the crime scene. Yet you implied Lisa is not responsible."

"I can understand Lisa being a suspect. And in both deaths." Daphne decided she'd apologised to Lisa enough and instead kept her eyes on Matty. "Not only were her two previous husbands in the grave, but now a third one was dead. All related by blood to each other and there is a feud between both families which might offer motive. Steve was quite rude to her during the ceremony which for some people might tip them over the edge."

"My daughter is not a killer!" Margaret burst into tears.

"Oh, for goodness sake, Mum. You're sounding like me now." Lisa reached for a box of tissues on a coffee table and dropped them in her mother's lap.

"At the farewell ceremony yesterday, Gina was horrible to Lisa. Horrible to a few people. And Lisa? You gave back as good as you got. I recall you said you'd never forgive her for making sure Steve's family didn't attend the wedding. How better to reinforce your feelings than with a steak knife in her back?"

Oh my. You are on a roll!

"But...but I didn't kill anyone." There it was. The waver in the voice.

Before this turned into a Lisa pity party, Daphne moved on. Two left.

A SHOCK CONFESSION

"I've known the family for a long time, Mrs Jones. Do any of them even look like killers?" Dempster asked.

"But what does a killer look like? Young or older? Quick to anger..." Daphne glanced at Lisa, who averted her eyes. "or quick to disappear?" This was directed at Bertie, who nodded with a somewhat vacant expression. He was clearly off somewhere in his mind. "For many reasons I excluded Lisa, not the least being her visibility at the wedding. She simply had no chance to kill Steve. And, in my humble opinion, she had no motive strong enough to drive her to do so."

Dempster remained still apart from the fingers of one hand tapping on the arm of the chair.

After a quick breath, Daphne continued. "Time for me to be honest. I thought Gina was behind this all. That she was the brains. And I still do."

"My sister? No brains there." Bertie offered with a small chuckle. "Where is Gina?" Margaret patted his arm.

"Gina was a proud woman and an even prouder Brooker, in my estimation." Daphne said.

Everyone nodded, even Matty.

"She had no time for the Tanning family. More than that, she was old enough to remember handed down stories of the original family feud. Two men who fought over a woman, both losing their lives in the process. Friends who left behind their children with no parents. Gina may have heard the story from her own grandparents and parents. Do you remember the story, Bertie?"

He nodded. "I grew up knowing no Tanning is a good one. Wasn't true though."

"You had a business deal with Toby Tanning."

"Good partner. Good friend. Until Bob started nosing around and making accusations." Bertie sighed deeply and returned to his buttons.

Bob spluttered. "Nosing around! I acted on advice from your own sister."

All heads—apart from Bertie's—swung to Bob. This was a new detail.

"Gina told me to take a look. You weren't even using a bookkeeper and money was disappearing with no record. She was worried when she heard you and Tanning discuss buying out the parts shop and she was right. That was once a thriving little business and went under thanks to you and Tanning."

Bertie didn't respond. In fact, he hummed beneath his breath.

Bob clenched his hands then strode to a liquor cabinet and poured himself a glass of something. After swallowing the contents, he leaned against the wall and glared at everyone.

"This reinforces Gina's track record of anti-Tanning activities. I have a whole list of them in my notebook. Obviously, this is for the police to investigate, but my belief is that Gina is responsible for the deaths of Steve, and quite possibly Sam and Shane."

Lisa jumped to her feet. "She what?"

Matty shook his head. "Those deaths were ruled accidental. And Gina wasn't even in the country when Shane died."

Sink or swim, Daph.

Daphne gestured to the corner. "But Dempster was."

"Huh?" Dempster's mouth dropped open.

"But he's been with us for years!" Margaret squealed.

"Hired him myself. What a load of rubbish." Bob helped himself to more liquor.

The detective near Matty opened his phone and tapped away.

Dempster got to his feet. "If you're talking about when the branch fell then yeah, I was there. Worst day ever."

Lisa stalked across the room to stand in front of Dempster. "For Shane!"

"Yeah. And me. Was an accident."

Daphne took control back. "You may have noticed that Gina was stabbed in the back. Quite literally. No way she did that to herself but it doesn't mean she wasn't behind the other murders. I've been mentioning the killer and the brains behind the killer. Two different people. Yesterday Gina stated she was going to speak to the police. Nobody knew what about...or did they? I think Gina had an accomplice. Someone to do the dirty work."

"Not me. I'm clean as a whistle." Dempster attempted to slide past Lisa, but she grabbed his arms and screamed at him.

"What did you do to my husbands? Did you kill my boys?"

All three police reacted as one and surrounded Lisa and Dempster. A minute later Lisa was escorted back to the sofa by Matty, while Dempster stood with the detectives on either side of him.

Daphne fanned her face with her hand. John put his hand on the middle of her back and his support, his gentle reminder he was close, let her push away the little voice in her head telling her she was being cruel. Upsetting innocent people. Making a scene.

You've come a long way, Daph.

What she was doing was standing up for what was right.

"Why would I kill anyone?" Dempster whined. "I just work here."

The older detective watched Daphne, his face unreadable. She'd better get a hurry on.

"Dempster, I think you want more than just to work here. I think you believe you have a claim on the Brooker name and any wealth that comes with. Is it true you descend from Mary Smith?"

The man's eyes widened.

"Just who is Mary Smith and how is this relevant?" Bob sounded a bit slurred and from the look of it was onto his third drink.

"She was the wife of your own ancestor, Richard Brooker. The woman who left him to live with Joseph Tanning. The person the men fought over. And she was carrying a child when she vanished. Probably Richard's. Genealogy records point to Dempster being her descendant."

"But I—" Dempster started.

"It is all true." Margaret got to her feet and faced Daphne. "Clever, aren't you? Dempster came here years ago demanding he be acknowledged as a Brooker. With his hand out. He wanted what wasn't his and when I told him some truths he didn't take kindly to it. Thought I'd need to call the police. Thank goodness Bertie arrived and sorted him out."

"Mum? You never said anything to me."

"Or to me." Bob put down his drink as the colour drained from his face. "Is Dempster my relative?"

"Hello. I'm right here." Dempster waved. "But your wife is nuts. I'm not violent. I was disappointed when she said the Brooker estate was virtually gone and any money was from her side of the family."

Bob stumbled his way across the room to the other man. The older detective held up a hand to stop him getting any closer so he planted his feet and peered at Dempster. "You look a bit like a Brooker. Never saw it before."

"Bob! You're missing the point. He wanted to waltz in here and take our property. Become part of our family. Steal from us the way you say the Tannings do." Margaret wrung her hands together. "Bertie stopped him from pursuing his ridiculous claim."

"Perhaps, Bertie can shed some light...where's Bertie?" Daphne asked. She gazed around the room. His spot on the sofa was empty. He wasn't back at the window. And when she glanced behind herself, the door was ajar.

MORE THAN MISSING

"I'll go and find him." Dempster took a step but the hand of one of the detectives stopped him.

"Not just yet. We'll hear out Mrs Jones and then locate Mr Brooker."

Bob returned to the liquor cabinet. "Silly old man won't be far. Trust him to wander off when we need answers."

"Margaret, what did Bertie do to placate Dempster all those years ago?" Daphne asked. "And why not tell the family about his true identity?"

The other woman turned bright red and hung her head. "I didn't want him here. I'm ashamed of myself for not extending a welcome but Lisa had spent a lot of money on building the house and our lives were going so well." She raised her eyes in Dempster's direction. "I am sorry, Dempster. I treated you unfairly."

Dempster shrugged. His usual friendly manner was gone. His eyes had narrowed and there was a wariness about him Daphne had never noticed before. Funny how people show themselves when under pressure.

"As for what Bertie did? Well, he offered him a job. Said we needed someone to help around the garden and pool. At first it was a couple of days a week and then Bertie and Dempster started going fishing together and before I knew it, Bertie wanted him living in the old caravan."

"And you were okay with that?"

"Not at all. But Dempster gave me a choice. Give in to Bertie's idea or else Dempster would tell everyone he was related and start legal action. He didn't care if he only got a small piece of the pie, as I recall him putting it." Shoulders down, Margaret returned to the sofa and plonked down.

The younger detective checked his phone and showed it to his partner. Dempster craned his neck to see but they stepped away from him. His eyes darted to the door as if judging how fast he could reach it. The muscle in his cheek twitched. John must have noticed for he casually closed the door again and as the detective had, leaned against it. Dempster shot him a look of such malice that Daphne shivered. Thank goodness there were three police officers in the room.

The older detective spoke. "We've had an officer walk down to the caravan. He has observed the trace of a blood-like substance on one of the steps."

Everyone looked at Dempster's feet, which wore socks, but no footwear.

Margaret pointed to the back of the house. "He knows to take his boots off before entering."

"We'll collect them on our way to the caravan. Dempster Smith, we would appreciate your co-operation in the investigation of the death of—"

Dempster made a dash for the door and Matty flew

across the room, stopping him a foot or two away from John ,who hadn't moved an inch and smiled at Daphne.

She'd had about enough now. This was too nerve-wracking for words.

A couple of minutes later, Dempster was in handcuffs being escorted down the hallway. Matty lingered.

"Mrs Jones, you have great insight. But what made you believe Dempster and Gina had an arrangement?"

"Gina hated the Tannings. She believed the old adage of them always stealing from the Brookers. Dempster was someone she could manipulate based on his disappointment at being an outcast thanks to the action of Joseph Tanning all those decades ago. At least, that's my theory, for what it's worth."

Bob was sitting beside Margaret, holding her hand. "You should have said something, Mags. Not put up with being bullied into silence."

A tear rolled down Margaret's face.

Lisa collected the tissue box again and kneeled in front of her mother. "We'll get through this. You did nothing wrong, Mamma."

Matty stepped into the hallway and Daphne could see no reason to stay with the Brookers. She and John closed the door behind themselves.

"What happens now?"

"There's a lot to investigate. Crime scene is still on its way so the body is staying where it is for now. Dempster will be questioned at the station and I imagine formally charged for Gina's murder. And I'm going to ask the detectives if it is worth looking at the deaths of Shane and Sam again."

A pleasant warmth spread through Daphne. If some good came of her efforts—hers and John's—then it balanced out the worry and upset. The ruin of the wedding might be redeemed a little.

John's phone rang. "Looks like the number from the tyre people. I'll go answer it."

"Matty, are we able to leave? Town, I mean?"

"I think we've kept you here long enough." He smiled. "We will need a statement but you can make it in your next town. Just let me know once you are there and I'll arrange it."

"Do you need us to help look for Bertie?"

"Can't imagine he's gone too far. Looks like John's waving to you."

"Then I'll say goodbye. And thank you for allowing me to speak."

"You've been persistent," he grinned. "From the beginning you told me you had suspicions and it turns out you were right."

NOT QUITE DONE

"I don't know if being a celebrant is right for you, doll."

Daphne had gazed out of the window since they'd driven away from the Brooker residence. She'd not spoken once but her body language reassured John she was simply processing and no longer stressing.

"You may be right." She said, without looking at him. "Not certain I can perform another wedding without expecting a tragedy."

"Hm. Not what I meant."

"I wouldn't be surprised if more clients cancelled."

"Doubt it. If anything you should increase your fee."

Now she did turn her head.

"You've done something amazing today, Daph. Solved a crime and with a bit of luck, put a criminal behind bars. Not every bride and groom can say they were married by a celebrant sleuth."

The corners of Daphne's mouth lifted and her eyes twinkled. "Celebrant sleuth. Has a nice ring to it."

"That's my girl. You did good. And now we're getting

new tyres and can finally get back on the road. Time to begin planning the next ceremony. And what we'll have for dinner tonight."

On cue, his stomach rumbled and they both laughed.

"You didn't even get to have cookies for breakfast, let alone a real one. I'll make us a nice lunch while the tyres are being done. What do you fancy?"

He fancied being by a river fishing, but not in this town. Somewhere far from criminals and vandals.

"John?"

"Sorry, love. Anything at all. As long as we eat lunch together and without interruptions, I'll be a happy man."

She smiled. "I'm not about to let anyone or anything interrupt our time together for quite a while."

The intention was good but there was almost no food left in the caravan and it would take ages to defrost anything. Grabbing her handbag and a shopping bag, she went to find John.

He was getting Bluebell ready to be lifted enough to change her tyres. "They'll be along in the next few minutes." He held chocks in either hand.

"I'm going to walk to town and find us some lunch, love. How about some pies from the bakery?"

John dropped an absent-minded kiss on her forehead. "Take the car."

"I think a short walk will do me good. Back soon."

In the distance a work truck approached. Daphne estimated she'd be back before they finished if she got a move on. Ten minutes either way and a bit of time to shop. She might drop in and say goodbye to Maurice at the newspaper. And thank him for his part in helping her reach the conclusion of Gina and Dempster being responsible for at least Steve's murder.

Something didn't sit right with Daphne. As much as Dempster denied it, she was confident he was the brawn behind the brains. With his medical background, hatred of the Tannings, and physical match, it all fitted. But there was more to this and it had to tie in with the deaths of Shane and Sam. Yet Gina had been out of the picture for at least one of those deaths.

At the first clump of trees, where the boot prints were still visible in the dried dirt, Daphne looked back to Bluebell. John chatted to one of the tyre fitters while a second man rolled the new tyres off the back of their truck. Had it been Dempster standing here the other night? Plotting to damage Bluebell? Why though? At the time, Daphne didn't recall even speaking to him, letting alone suspecting him. What reason would he have to watch her?

With a shudder, she got going. No point worrying over what might have happened. Dempster was in custody and with Gina dead, the killings would stop.

Or will they?

"If the police come calling just remember you forced me to do this." Those were Gina's last words to Bertie, overheard by their family, friends, Dempster, and Daphne. A threat to anyone who had something to hide, after she'd reminded them earlier of her knowledge of 'torrid family secrets'. She might be one of those people who stored information on people in order to blackmail them.

"But why would you bring the police into it?" Daphne

stopped again. "If you were the brains then you'd go to jail as well."

Her gut was churning. What had she missed? Was there a chance Gina was not Dempster's accomplice? She needed her notes. A fresh look at them based on the new information from this morning. But first she had to buy lunch and then she could have another read.

The bridge was up ahead and as she closed in on it, Daphne jumped as a large thicket of reeds rustled and a tall, thin figure emerged from its centre. The person wore a hoodie and wiped their hands down their front, leaving white streaks, then sauntered onto the bridge as if that was normal behaviour.

Daphne hurried to the spot the person had stood. A trail of white liquid which looked like paint, led towards the river and Daphne forced her way through the reeds.

Too far into the river for her to reach, a white tub slowly submerged. An open tub with the word 'Poison' on its side. Thick white liquid seeped into the river and just before it sank, a small black object floated out. A phone.

Gina's phone?

Where was the person who'd done this? Daphne's eyes shot back to the bridge and there, heading towards town, the person strolled along. Not a care in the world. She climbed back through the reeds, her fingers in her handbag grasping for her phone. Stopping long enough to dial, Daphne held the phone to her ear and snuck onto the bridge.

"John. It's me. Daphne. I'm following the real brains. Not Gina. But someone else. Get the police. They threw the missing phone in the river. Bluebell's side of the bridge to town. Hurry." She hung up. He had to get the message. She risked taking a photo of the tub which was visible under the surface. The white cloud around it should help the police locate it. That done, she began to dial the police and started up the bridge. Nobody was in sight.

She shoved the phone away and began to run.

At the crest of the bridge she spotted the person almost at the far end. They glanced back and stopped. The face was impossible to see from this distance but she knew they recognised her when they turned and sprinted away.

"Staaap!"

What was meant to be an authoritative command sounded like the screech of an angry bird. And did nothing other than draw the attention of a group of woman—all dressed in fitness wear—doing star jumps partway down the bridge. As Daphne puffed her way past them, she sang out, "Call the police. I'm in pursuit!"

"You're going to pop those buttons, honey." One woman said.

"Or have a coronary." Another added.

Laughter followed Daphne. Her head dropped for an instant and her legs faltered. But there was no time for being sorry for herself.

She reached the bottom of the bridge, grabbing a post to help her around the corner and onto the path. "There you are!"

The figure was still too far ahead to identify.

Sweat poured down Daphne's neck.

It was getting hotter with every painful step.

The path weaved through trees. offering a welcome respite from the sun.

But the hooded figure was out of sight.

Faster, Daph. Don't let them escape.

She might have been in the wilderness with not a soul around between the dense undergrowth on either side and the canopy above the winding track. It suddenly split in two around a large gum tree.

Daphne took the left path and ran straight into another body.

Her feet slid from beneath her.

The ground rose.

With a sickening 'thud' she hit the path.

Silence.

A breath. Hers.

And a moan. Not hers.

Daphne turned over onto all fours and used the trunk of the tree to help her up. The hooded figure was a bit further away and took a moment to stand, straightening with another moan. A male moan. Blood seeped through the fabric of the hoodie down his left arm, which hung at his side.

For a moment they got their respective breaths back.

They were alone.

She was alone with the killer.

The person pushed back the hood with their good arm.

"You." Daphne gasped.

"Me. And now you know who I am."

Bertie grinned at Daphne. It might have been a chance meeting on a spring day in a peaceful country town.

Between a killer and their pursuer.

THE ARRANGEMENT

"Why, Bertie?"

"Interesting question, Mrs Jones. Why run? Why dispose of the evidence? Or why dispatch people who try to harm my family?"

The man standing before Daphne was a far cry from the elderly person whose memory led him astray. His eyes were sharp. His body strong, apart from his damaged arm. Old, yes, but strong. What an odd thing to remember but his photographs and trophies had been in front of Daphne every time she'd entered the Brooking house. He'd been a runner. A champion runner.

"You don't have dementia."

He chuckled. "They all think I do. Made it easy to do what I wanted."

Daphne shifted her weight. The impact of the fall left her ankle throbbing. The earlier churning in her stomach was replaced by a cold and heavy stone. Was she the next victim?

How had she missed the clues?

As if reading her mind, Bertie's smile vanished and he took a step forward. And a second. Daphne's back was against the tree trunk and her eyes darted around. Why wasn't anyone around to help?

"Gina wasn't meant to die. Silly woman talking about going to the police must have freaked out Dempster but she was my sister. He had no right."

With only a few feet between them, the grief in Bertie's eyes was real and in spite of her fear, Daphne felt for him. But more for Gina.

"I'm sorry I accused her. But I don't understand how Dempster got to Steve that day. Gina said she'd seen you both on the other side of the property."

"She lied. Never had anything to do with the arrangement, but she knew enough and we always protected each other. Until I didn't."

In the distance, a siren sounded. Bertie's eyes roamed, settling on a short, thick fallen branch and then back at Daphne.

A shiver ran through her body. "Um... The arrangement?"

"Nobody else in the world knows. Only Demps and me. And Gina knew bits. So if I tell you, it's our secret." He grimaced and glanced at his left arm. The blood now dripped beneath the sleeve onto his fingers, which were motionless. "That's annoying."

Bertie shuffled to the fallen branch. He leaned down, his fingertips touching the bark.

Daphne edged away from the gum tree. "No point harming me. Your blood is all over the ground and you'll be in jail before you know it."

With a groan, Bertie straightened. His hand was empty.

"Just wanted something to lean on." He managed a short laugh. "I'm the brains, remember. Not the brawn."

"What if we get you some help."

"I'm past help. Might use the tree though to prop me up."

Daphne hobbled further away. She wasn't about to let him near her and if she had to, she would scream the place down. He sighed as he rested against the trunk.

"What arrangement did you have with Dempster?"

"Our secret, right?"

With a nod, Daphne apologised to him in her mind. She'd break his trust the minute she could. The siren had stopped wailing.

"Dempster and I were a lot alike. He grew up hating a family he'd never met. The Tannings. He'd been told the same stories I was. Joseph Tanning stole Mary from our ancestor. And every Tanning since then followed suit. Bunch of liars and thieves." He ground the words out.

"But you said Toby was your friend."

"He was useful. I had it under control and was gradually squirrelling away every dollar he'd invested of. Gina and Bob ruined it but I had enough money hidden in a safe place to partly rebuild the Brooker wealth."

An embezzler. Was it all about money?

Bertie continued, speaking faster as if telling his story for the first time. "Dempster came along when I was unsure of my next move. Money was hidden. Still is. Lisa was spending hers and lots of it was on me and my family. Wasn't about to stop her. But then she married one of them."

"Sam Tanning?"

"Yup. And I knew time was running before they started a

family because the minute they had a kid all the money would flow away from me and mine. Bob was all I had left and then Demps came along. Not my grandson but the nearest thing I'd ever have and he'd been done out of a lifetime of his rightful Brooker name. So we brokered an arrangement to stop anyone who tried to take away my legacy."

There was movement further up the path, behind Bertie and the tree. Police uniforms appearing and disappearing through the bushes.

Bertie stopped talking and his eyes closed. His skin was a sickly shade of grey and the bleeding hadn't slowed.

"Bertie? You told me you love Lisa."

He opened his eyes and his lips turned up. "She's a good girl. A bit emotional and makes bad decisions but yes, I love her."

"Then why would you kill her husbands? And don't remind me it is because of some legacy or for revenge." Daphne lifted her chin. "You and Dempster took away her happiness. What makes you any different from the Tannings?"

His mouth opened and closed. A shaking began in his legs, getting stronger by the second until they started to buckle. Daphne managed to reach him before he collapsed, getting his good arm over her shoulder and using all her strength to keep him upright.

"A little help!" she cried out.

He dropped his head so his mouth was close to her ear. "I was a fool. Tell Lisa I'm sorry." As his body went limp, strong arms caught him. Matty was there.

IN THE REAR VIEW MIRROR

"I promised you we'd leave this town today, and I'm keeping to my promise." John held Daphne's hand so tight it hurt but she wasn't letting go.

The last few hours were dreamlike, which might also be in part due to some painkillers the local doctor gave her after ensuring her ankle wasn't broken. Painkillers and anti-inflammatories plus instructions to rest.

Bluebell was fully operational and ready to leave, but a call from Matty delayed their departure again. John had agreed to wait for half an hour and then he was taking his wife away from Little Bridges once and for all. They sat inside Bluebell to wait, finishing the last of the cookies with some apple cider. Lunch hadn't happened and they'd both decided to give up on finding a meal until on the road.

"I wonder how Bertie is." Daphne hadn't stopped thinking about him since the paramedics strapped him onto a stretcher and took him to hospital with a police escort.

"I'm more concerned about you, my love." John finally

released her hand to refill their glasses and glanced out of the open door. "You should have waited for help."

Daphne smiled. "Do you remember back home when that awful man broke into our house and I ran down the road to see what kind of car he had?"

"How could I forget? But at least then you were on a street where people could see you, not camouflaged by trees and bushes. Thank goodness those women did as you asked and phoned the police."

"Oh. Them."

"Why?"

Would they have stopped a killer?

She shook her head. "Doesn't matter."

"And I heard your message and must have phoned the police a couple of minutes later and thank goodness Matty and Leading Senior Constable Barber knew the general area you were in. Had no idea I could still run so fast!"

The patrol car parked next to the open door.

"Hopefully, he doesn't want another statement." John said.

Apart from the visit to the doctor, Daphne had spent quite a long time making a full statement at the police station. With Bertie's confession the homicide detectives had more to investigate.

"Afternoon. Thanks for hanging around." Matty appeared in the doorway. "May I?"

"Come on in. Iced tea?" Daphne offered, moving over to make room for him to sit. John collected a fresh glass and poured a drink before Matty could reply.

"I have some news. Thanks for this." He sat. "Bertie is undergoing surgery but expected to recover. We were able to retrieve the tub from the river and the phone and yes, it is the one stolen from Gina and used to lure Steve to the pool."

Tears prickled at the back of Daphne's eyes as a sudden wave of relief washed away the tension and stress of the past few days. She didn't speak for fear of crying, but tapped her hands together in a discreet clap. If Matty noticed her emotional response he was too polite to say anything but John caught her eye and smiled.

"We've formerly charged Dempster with two counts of first degree murder pending other charges. He has admitted to stabbing Steve, pushing him into the pool and then using the hose to wash the obvious blood into the water. He hid in the cleaning room until Steve was found. The Brooker and Tanning families have both expressed gratitude to you and asked me to pass that on."

"I would imagine much of this is a shock to the Brookers. Their patriarch behind such heinous crimes for the sake of money and his family name." John said. "Hopefully, they'll move on in time and at least no more murders."

Matty nodded. "There's one more thing. We found the person responsible for slashing your tyres. They've been charged on summons and have already offered to make full restitution for the cost of replacing them. I'd suggest wait until the offer is formerly made and then counter offer to cover your time and any other expenses. Sadly, that's the best way for this person to learn."

"Who did it?" Daphne found her voice. "I thought it was Dempster."

"No. It was Lloyd."

Daphne gasped.

"He was angry at the attention he got from your report

and decided to pay you back. Now, he really has to pay you back."

She'd known Lloyd wasn't a nice person. Not one to be happy at another's misfortune, Daphne nevertheless enjoyed a moment of glee. Nice to see swift justice done.

Matty finished his drink and stood. "Time to let you both get on your way."

"At last." John said, but there was no malice in his tone.

He offered his hand and Matty shook it before turning his gaze onto Daphne.

"We might have got off on the wrong foot, but I've come to respect you, Mrs Jones. You've got good instincts. But no more getting in the way of trouble. Okay?"

"I'll see you out."

The men climbed out and Daphne opened her notebook to a new page to write her final words about Little Bridges.

Family matters but when money and pride become more important, terrible decisions are made. The Brooker and Tanning families may never be friends, but at least they now have one common enemy—the past and its influence. If they can put that behind them then there is a chance for a better future.

"Ready, love?" John was back inside and held out his hand. "Let's get you into the car and we can be off."

"No last minute shopping? No people to say goodbye to?" she teased, letting him help her out of Bluebell.

"I don't think I'll answer that one." John wrapped Daphne in his arms. "There's only one picture I want in my head of this town."

Daphne leaned back and kissed his lips. "Little Bridges in the rear vision mirror?"

He answered with a kiss in return.

THE SHADOW OF DAPH

BOOK TWO

The Shadow of Daph

CHANGE OF PLANS

"Daph, you'll need to check the map again. I'm worried I'll miss the turn off with so little light. We just passed Conways Track." John Jones didn't take his eyes off the narrow road.

Daphne Jones grabbed the map which had fallen into the footwell near her handbag. "Got it. Conways Track? Hm." She traced the route with her finger which John had highlighted in red at their last stop. Then she turned it upside down. "Okie dokie. Another three curves, no, two seeing as you've done one. Another two curves and then there's a bridge. Just after that you need to take a left."

"Is there a street name?"

"Shady Bend Road."

John laughed shortly. "Plenty of shade here." He slowed to navigate another long curve and Daphne glanced in the side mirror at Bluebell. Their beautiful caravan made their travels a little more challenging at times but was a blessing they would never leave behind. Turning the car and caravan around on such a narrow road was not something John would want to try if they missed their turnoff. And not so close to nightfall. Daphne leaned forward to better see the road ahead.

"Kangaroo at two o'clock!"

John touched the brakes as the headlights reflected in the eyes of a grey kangaroo staring at them from the side of the road. "Stay there, Mister Roo." A joey popped its head out of an oversized pouch. "Whoops, sorry. Missus Roo."

When they'd left their last stop a few hours ago, they'd planned on already being settled into a new town, where Daphne would officiate a wonderful wedding on the weekend. But then her phone had rung and within minutes they were on a different road.

"Daph, you said a bridge then a right turn?"

"Left, John. I wish there were some lights along here. One might break down and never be found."

John really needed to put one of those digital location things in the car. A GPS. Maps made little sense to Daphne and she navigated under duress.

"I think that's it!" she pointed ahead. "Over the bridge and almost straight away there's a sign."

A moment later they'd turned onto Shady Bend Road, which curved up a steep hill. Bluebell weighed them down and John changed to a lower gear. According to the car clock it was a little after six, which in late spring was still daylight. It was the heavy canopy of gum, wattle, and blackwood trees towering over the road which made visibility so poor.

"We'll pull in somewhere in the town to find out where we can stop tonight." John said.

"I've got the name of the place but not an address. Shall I check the message?"

"Think we're almost there." Even as he spoke, they

reached the crest of the hill and the trees gave way to houses. Bigger properties at first, then smaller and closer together as they approached a township. The speed limit dropped and houses changed to a row of shops on either side of the road. Unlike the roads they'd left behind, there was hardly a tree in sight. For that matter, hardly a car or a person either.

"Guess it is after closing time for most shops. Is that parking space big enough for us?"

John nosed the car alongside the pavement about halfway through the town. "Good spotting, doll."

"Doesn't look like much is going on here." She checked her phone for the message which had arrived after the phone call. "Shady Bend Camping Ground. Can't be too hard to find?"

"How about we duck into the supermarket over the road? We can get directions and pick up the shopping you wanted." He climbed out and met Daphne on the footpath. After locking the car, he held his arm out. "Be good to get to our camping site before night completely falls."

Daphne tucked her arm through his. "I'll zoom around the supermarket while you get directions. Only need a couple of things for dinner so it won't take long at all."

It was just as well both she and John were flexible with arrangements.

There was no room at the suggested camping ground thanks to a local event which had drawn competitors from around the state. They were directed to an unpowered ground in the next town. At least it was only a few minutes' drive away and the lack of power would be manageable for one or two nights. As John performed his ritual of checking Bluebell was secure and had no ill effects from what had been a relatively short drive, Daphne read the message again.

Dear Daphne, following our phone call I want to thank you profusely for changing your plans to accommodate our late notice request.

The phone call from Fred Yates had surprised Daphne.

The deceased is a local resident of some note and her passing leaves many of our community saddened. On consultation with her daughter, a decision was made to reach out to someone with a proven record of great compassion. Your name was put forward.

Who had recommended her services?

The funeral tomorrow has every arrangement made, but the deceased's daughter asked me to find a suitable person to help say goodbye to our beloved Edwina and celebrate her memory. Attached is information about her life, her place in the community and achievements, along with certain requests.

She'd look at those once they settled in and had the generator going. Easier to view on the laptop.

"Think we're right. Not much point using the awning tonight." John unlocked Bluebell. "Sorry, thought I'd done this."

"Oh, I could have used my key but I was keen to take another look at the message from Mr Yates."

"If I turn on the lamps, are you happy to do a quick check in here while I get the generator going?"

"Can you pass me the shopping first?"

It took little time to unpack the shopping and turn on the lamps which were a clever addition when Bluebell was refurbished. An addition to the usual lighting, these lamps were solar powered from panels on the roof of the caravan. Perfect for using at times like this and meant once the generator was off, they'd still have light.

John kicked the generator into action and then joined her with a smile.

"Not ideal but we're getting better at making do."

She glanced at her watch. "I should get the pasta started."

"What if I do dinner?" John gave her a big hug. "You, my celebrant sleuth, have to prepare for tomorrow."

Daphne grinned. John's funny term always made her smile. "As long as you don't mind. But I'm not here for sleuthing." She squeezed him back and wiggled out of his arms. "I shall find my notebook and get started."

Halfway to the bedroom, she glanced back. "John? Thanks for this. For agreeing without hesitation to come here on a moment's notice."

"Anytime. It is a small detour and will give me an unexpected chance to visit another graveyard. Assuming you don't mind me being there at the same time, albeit in another part?"

John's passion for genealogy fitted well with Daphne's new career. He visited the local graveyards and small churches to work on a project he said little about. But it made him happy and Daphne loved seeing him enjoy doing something for himself.

"You are most welcome. Always."

Notebook and pen in hand, Daphne settled at the table. John set a pot of water on the gas cooktop alongside a deep pan. He chopped lots of tomatoes, onions, mushrooms, and a selection of herbs. As the aromas drifted across, Daphne's tummy rumbled in response. She enjoyed John's cooking and now they were on the road most of the time, he more than shared the load. The only thing he couldn't outdo were her homemade cookies.

She scribbled a shopping list on a spare piece of paper. Flour. Choc chips. Extra butter. Tomorrow would be a busy one but there was always time to do a bit of baking.

After opening the laptop, Daphne located an email from Fred with the extra information and printed the couple of pages out. The little printer was so useful and took up barely any space in one of the cupboards. At the top of the page, she wrote out the timetable for the next day.

10am. Meet with Mr Yates and concerned parties to go over the ceremony. (Allow one hour)

1pm. Quick lunch and get ready.

2pm. Funeral.

In between the meeting and lunch, she'd finalise her words. She had a lot of ideas bubbling in her head based on what she'd read so far and would write them first thing in the morning. Her mind was at its sharpest early in the day. She'd not officiated many funerals but she would make Edwina's send-off special. A memorable day for her family and friends.

Over dinner, Daphne filled John in on more of the details. He wasn't disappointed by the sudden change of destination as this region was on his 'to visit' list anyway. The list he kept on his phone.

"Edwina Drinkwater passed away at her home from natural causes. She's only sixty though, so it seems a bit young for natural causes. Anyway, she has one relative, a daughter. Sonia." Daphne read from the notes she'd hand-written on the printed pages.

"Some more mineral water?" John collected the bottle from the fridge. "Nice with the lime, isn't it?"

"Very. And this pasta is as good as any from a restaurant, love."

Daphne was always the first to compliment a person. Her kind heart and generous soul drew him to her in their last year of high school, and if anything, her love of people was even more obvious with this late life change of career.

"She lived alone, although her daughter has her own cottage on the same property. She had a busy life. Owns a small shop. Oh, this is interesting. She sold the wares of local craftspeople, artists, and amateur cooks. Preserves, jams, cakes...there's a list. And she was president of the Rural Craft, Cooking, and Creation Society. RCCCS. Sounds a bit like the Country Women's Association." Daphne rolled linguine around her fork. "I imagine she'll be missed."

"What else do you know about tomorrow?"

"Mm...this was so nice." Daphne said. "Edwina lived in Shady Bend most of her life. She was divorced but there is no mention about her ex-husband. Sounds like a normal life in a normal town. And she donated to a local wildlife sanctuary."

"I'm sure you will find some beautiful words to comfort her loved ones, Daph. It must make it so much easier when you're officiating for someone who was a nice person."

"Yes. Yes, I think Edwina Drinkwater was a nice woman who will be deeply missed."

NOT MISSED AT ALL

"She was a horrible person and I'm glad she's dead!"

Those were the last words Daphne had expected from the daughter of the deceased, let alone spat with a venom completely at odds with the woman's appearance.

Silence cut through the room like the proverbial knife as all eyes turned in various levels of shock to Sonia Drinkwater. She folded her arms and lifted her chin, defying anyone to disagree. A slender woman with oversized glasses and long straight hair, she gave off a sweet girl-from-the-country vibe. Until she opened her mouth.

Daphne had arrived at the funeral home on time, soft briefcase in hand with her notebook and draft speech ready for approval or adjustments. Shady Bend Funeral Home was set in pretty gardens surrounded by gum trees, with a circular driveway and a central lawn, not far from the middle of the town. Fred Yates was outside the front door with a woman he'd introduced as Tracy Chappell. He was in his early sixties while she was a decade younger, by Daphne's estimation. In a sombre suit, Fred was solemn, balding, and double-chinned. Tracy wore jeans and a T-shirt proclaiming 'Judge and Juror' with a picture on its front of a cake being hit with a gavel.

Fred ushered them inside.

Through double doors was a small entry area with an unattended desk and a bell. Hallways went off in several directions but Fred led them through another set of double doors to a large but quiet reception room with soft lighting and sofas. Sonia, perhaps thirty years old, was already there. She sat cross-legged and didn't get up, but removed her glasses to stare at Daphne.

Ten minutes into the meeting, Daphne asked if there was anything special to highlight about Edwina and the resulting explosion of fury and bitterness ensued. In the sincere hope she wasn't making things worse, Daphne got to her feet and joined Sonia.

"I'm so sorry, dear."

Sonia blinked at Daphne and then a single tear trickled down her cheek. Fred moved fast to provide a box of tissues and Daphne took it with a smile, holding them close to Sonia.

"What would *you* like to happen at the funeral?" Daphne kept her voice soft. "How do you want to say goodbye?"

In the few months of Daphne's new celebrant life, she'd officiated at a handful of funerals, plus a few goodbye ceremonies. Actually, two of the latter and both in a town they'd left only a couple of weeks ago. And that was a whole other story. Although her practical experience might be limited, she had a lifetime of being a people person. Always the shoulder to cry on for friends and acquaintances. The person who would listen and then gently offer kind words. It worked most of the time.

"I'd like...I think that..." Sonia's tone hardened. "I want to see her dropped into that hole and covered up as fast as possible. There's already been far too much money spent on an elaborate casket let alone flowers and all the other costs." She leaned back and crossed her arms as well. "That sounds like the best way to say goodbye. See the back of her."

"Enough, Sonia, give it a rest." This was Tracy. "You'll still get a nice little windfall. Not like anyone will throw you off the property."

The two women glared at each other and Daphne retreated to her previous seat. Whatever history there was should be shelved until after the funeral. She glanced at her notes. There was nothing in them to indicate anything other than a community filled with love and respect for the deceased.

Fred poured water into four glasses from a jug on a stand near the door. "Who would care for some water?"

Daphne nodded and he brought one across.

"Only if there's something...extra in it." Sonia announced.

Tracy rolled her eyes as she got to her feet. "Thanks, Fred." She took a glass from him. "Mrs Jones, I'd like to speak at the funeral. I've known Edwina for decades and we've worked together on committees for longer than I care to admit. So how do we make this happen?"

"Once Sonia approves the ceremony, I'll then add anyone who wishes to speak in order and will introduce them. Do you know of any others?"

Fred sat opposite. "Only two others apart from Tracy. The first is Desmond. Desmond Rogers. He considered Edwina to be a close friend and—"

"Get real." Sonia reached for a handbag and stood. "Nobody liked her so it is all lip service."

"Ilona adored her." Fred said, getting to his own feet. "And Ilona is the other person who wishes to speak. Why not put aside your feelings until after the funeral, Sonia? In a few hours this will all be a memory. Rather than rake up old upsets, shouldn't we all try to get along for this short time and do the right thing?"

Sonia, who had seemed intent on stalking out of the room, came to a halt near Fred. Instead to doing what Daphne had half-expected and continuing with her snipy comments, the younger woman dropped her head and nodded.

"This is a dreadful time, Sonia. Stressful and distressing. But if you can be the bigger person in all of this, you'll respect yourself later on. And if I can do this, so can you."

All of this was quite interesting. It was one thing for a funeral director to offer support and comfort but quite another to counsel a grieving client on how to behave. And what had he meant by if *he* could do this? Sonia returned to her seat. Tracy, meanwhile, was tapping on her phone.

"You mentioned a person called Ilona?" It was time to take control back. "What do I need to know about her so I can ensure she has the appropriate time to speak?"

All three looked at her as if she was supposed to already know.

She didn't.

"Ilona is, was, my mother's closest friend. Probably only real friend." Sonia said. "And she is a wedding celebrant. Like you. Except she is," Sonia gestured quote marks with her fingers, "Too shattered to officiate. So, if she wouldn't pull her head out to look after her best friend's funeral, I had to ask Fred to find someone else."

Do you ever say anything nice about anyone?

"I believe Mrs Drinkwater had a special request." Daphne summoned a smile. "In the notes I received—and I have to thank you, Fred, for such comprehensive information—Mrs Drinkwater wished to bestow gifts on every person who attended the funeral as a reminder of her affection for them."

Something like a choke emanated from Sonia, which Daphne chose to ignore.

"I understand there will be a table set up after the funeral which will include a selection of items from the shop she owned. I think it is a lovely gesture."

It was interesting how each of the other people in the room responded.

Fred nodded the whole time she spoke.

Sonia shook her head.

Tracy put down her phone and ran her tongue over her lips. Her eyes were elsewhere—somewhere faraway. Was she imagining some delicious fare from the shop?

Someone's phone rang and the moment was gone. Fred apologised and hurried from the room, reaching into a pocket. Tracy had a small smile on her face but was back in the present. "I didn't know Edwina had made last wishes. Rather nice of the old girl."

"Old girl. Really? You are almost the same age." Sonia snapped.

Tracy burst out laughing.

Before things got out of hand, Daphne located the draft ceremony. "Sonia, would you mind taking a look? If there are any changes, I can make them now."

"It doesn't matter. Say whatever you wish."

"I'd feel more comfortable knowing you were satisfied with my wording. If you don't mind?"

With a sigh, Sonia took the couple of sheets of paper and read. At least the room was quiet while she did, apart from the low tapping sound as Tracy's focus returned to her phone. Daphne snuck a look at her own but the signal was too low to even send a message. With luck it was better outside, otherwise she had a long wait ahead. John had dropped her there and was going to see if there was a powered camping site anywhere else to move Bluebell. Which led her to a question.

"Excuse me, what is the event on in town? We tried to find a powered site for our caravan last night and had to go to the next town."

"Oh, that's just our local agricultural show." Tracy answered without looking up. "The livestock exhibitors always pile in early to settle their horses and whatnot. Today we begin preliminary judging of the crafts, baking, bottling and so on. Get things ready for the finals."

Was Tracy a judge? Her T-shirt made sense if she was. Daphne hadn't been to a country show in years. Not since... well since her childhood. Animals. Rides with carnival music. Laughter. Sticky sweet treats. People everywhere. Her father yelling. Furious with her.

Daphne's heart thudded.

"So sorry to disappear like that. Had to take the call." Fred returned.

The music subsided. Not that anyone else heard it. She released a breath she'd not meant to hold. Had anyone noticed her hands shake?

"Shall we finalise the details?" Fred asked. "I think your husband is parked outside, Mrs Jones."

Not only was John parked along the grass verge, but a motor scooter was behind him. Daphne was partway along the path to the road when the rider alighted and removed their helmet. A woman.

John stepped out of the car.

"Hello-o. Are you Daphne?" The woman flapped both her arms as though to get Daphne's attention. "I really need to speak with you."

The woman was in her mid-forties, dressed in an ankle length black dress and wearing fresh flowers in bright red hair that flowed to her waist.

"I am Daphne."

"Oh, I thought so! My cousin described you and you are exactly as he said."

Cousin?

"Um...how did he describe me?"

Sure you should ask, Daph?

The other woman smiled, softening her expression. She wasn't pretty as such but had a kindness in her eyes which warmed Daphne to her.

"He said you had cute streaks of colour in your hair, wore fashionable glasses, and know how to carry off a nice suit. He also said you have a beautiful smile." The woman held her hand out. "I'm Ilona."

They shook hands. John rested his arms on the roof of the car.

"I'm so sorry for your loss, Ilona. I understand Mrs Drinkwater was your friend."

"Yes. Edie meant the world to me and I miss her so much." Ilona blinked a few times. Close up, the rims of her eyes were red. "I really can't believe she's gone."

"What can I do to help you? I believe you have asked to speak this afternoon?"

Ilona nodded. "If I don't speak for Edie, nobody will. Oh, I know Sonia and Tracy and perhaps Desmond will stand up but I'm the one who knew her. Do you know what I mean? I was her confidante and understood her."

"Then you must speak. I didn't know her, but with such a close friend I would imagine she'd treasure having your unique words heard. Is there anything in particular you'd like me to know first. Anything I can include in my ceremony to help."

All of a sudden, Ilona threw her arms around Daphne in a hug. "This is why you are here, dear Daphne."

The hug was quick and Ilona stepped back with a hint of embarrassment on her face. "I don't do funerals. Never could. Weddings, naming ceremonies. All the good, happy stuff is fine, but I'm too big a sook to manage to help people say goodbye. But I heard you are wonderful with sad times."

Not sure I'd like that on my website!

"Ilona, who is your cousin?"

"I am so sorry? I thought you knew. Maurice. He met you in Little Bridges."

Her shoulders dropped. As much as she liked Maurice, who owned the local newspaper in Little Bridges, hearing the name of the town was an unwanted reminder of how quickly things can go wrong.

TOO MUCH TO BEAR

"Is that town going to follow us around forever?" Daphne grumbled as she applied makeup in the small bathroom in their caravan. Lunch had been little more than a quick sandwich and there was no time for even one cup of tea. A call from Fred had requested she be at the funeral home earlier than first planned.

"Little Bridges?" John leaned against a cupboard outside the bathroom. "I wouldn't let it upset you. Even though it was stressful, just think of how you helped find a killer. Something to be proud of."

Not long ago, Daphne was the celebrant at a country wedding which went horribly wrong. Against her better judgement she'd become involved in working out who was behind some dreadful crimes. And it was satisfying but hardly the kind of thing she wanted on her calling card!

"I suppose something good came of it. And Maurice was kind to recommend me. We could leave after the funeral if you prefer." Daphne chose a lipstick to match the top she wore. It might seem a bit much for a funeral, but another of

Edwina's requests was that every attendee wore at least one bright colour. Thank goodness Daphne had a lovely hot pink blouse which fit the bill and worked well under the elegant black jacket she'd don at the last minute.

"Wouldn't mind taking some photos this afternoon. There's a gorge not far away with a waterfall. Might get something good enough to print out and frame for the house."

Since retiring as owner and principal realtor of Rivers End Real Estate, John had turned his mind to new activities. Genealogy of course, but also photography plus a renewed interest in river fishing. There were few things which filled her heart more than seeing her husband of forty plus years enjoying their nomadic life.

"If you don't mind, I'll come with you. A waterfall sounds like a perfect place to relax after a sad funeral."

Make up done, Daphne was ready. Jacket, handbag, and briefcase with her embossed ceremony book were all she needed. There were mourners who deserved to help say goodbye and she wasn't about to keep them waiting.

The reception room where Daphne met earlier with Fred, Sonia, and Tracy, was transformed with the comfortable seating pushed back to make space for a long trestle table with smaller tables and plastic chairs dotted around.

On the table was a tower of small plates and plastic glasses, along with napkins and plastic cutlery. Laid out at both ends were plates of scones, slices, cupcakes, and other baked goods, while the middle had been raised with boxes to form a second level. This overflowed with sealed bottles of preserves, jams, fruit, chutneys, sauces, framed artwork, and small gift-wrapped boxes. There was barely room for another plate, yet at the far end a woman managed to wiggle one more in.

"Think we might leave the rest in the kitchen." The woman smiled at Daphne. "Hello, I'm Petra West."

"Nice to meet you, Petra. I'm Daphne, the celebrant."

"Very good of you to come on such short notice. We are all most appreciative." Petra wandered around the table checking everything. "This is for after...well, once poor Edwina is...well, you know."

"It looks delicious. Is all of this locally made?"

"Oh yes. Our little community loves local and Edwina was passionate about us all creating perfect products for the customers. You should try some of the rhubarb and apricot jam on a scone. I had a taste in the kitchen and it is something to behold."

Not a fan of rhubarb, or sampling the wares meant for a wake, Daphne was about to politely refuse when Fred arrived, followed by a younger man dressed in a similar suit.

"Mrs Jones, hello and thank you. I wanted you to meet the pall bearers before we left. The funeral home is providing three of them, including Zeke here. The others are friends of the deceased who volunteered. Zeke, this is Mrs Jones, who will officiate the ceremony."

Daphne and Zeke shook hands but his eyes were on the table.

Fred continued. "I see you've already met Petra. And you spoke with Tracy earlier. Our remaining person is Desmond Rogers who—ah, there you are."

"Apologies. The old car didn't want to start again so it was a case of walk here instead." Desmond Rogers was in his seventies. Not a tall man, his black jacket barely covered a large stomach which wobbled as he shuffled across the floor with a slight limp. Daphne couldn't help comparing his face to that of a bulldog.

"Desmond, this is Mrs Jones, who changed her itinerary to help us out. Desmond is...was, Edwina's neighbour."

Daphne shook Desmond's hand. "My condolences."

"Yes. Sad state of affairs. Heart attack. Expected, but not so soon. Never so soon."

Tracy emerged from another room carrying a tray of filled champagne glasses. "Everyone! Time to make a toast. I have no idea where Sonia is but we haven't got time to wait around for her."

She placed the tray on a table and took a moment to hand out each glass. "Fred. Desmond. Zeke, you're driving so not for you. Ah, Petra, here's yours."

Daphne retreated close to the door, not wanting to intrude on this moment. Once everybody else had a glass, Tracy proposed a toast.

"To living life the way you want. To being the person you enjoy being. To Edwina."

There was a murmur of agreement, some clinks of glasses, and then silence as champagne was sipped.

"Be the person you enjoy being, even when it makes everyone else hate you."

Daphne glanced around. The words were softly spoken by a person in the hallway. A woman about her own age, shorter than Daphne and with short cropped brown hair. Her arms were wrapped around her body and she gazed into the room at the group.

"Hello, dear. Would you care to come in?" Daphne made herself known.

If the other woman was concerned her words had been overheard, she said nothing, but stepped inside and looked at Daphne with interest.

"I like your hair." She announced.

"Well, thank you."

Tracy drifted over with more glasses on the tray. "Mrs Jones, please have some. Hello, Amanda."

"I'm fine, thank you for offering." Daphne said. "Best keep my mind focused on the important time ahead."

"Fair enough." Tracy turned to leave.

"But I'd like one." Amanda reached out for a glass.

Tracy held the tray out of reach and kept walking. Amanda followed, grabbing at the tray. With a crash, it hit the ground, glasses shattering and golden liquid bubbling on the carpet.

"Look what you did!" Tracy hissed at Amanda. "I was trying to avoid disaster but no, you always find a way to mess things up. This special time here is just for the pall bearers of which you are not one."

Petra rushed over with a roll of paper towels and small bin and began carefully collecting pieces of glass. Zeke squatted to help, immediately cutting himself.

"Take more care, Zeke! You'll get blood on the carpet." Tracy scooped up the tray and stalked to the kitchen.

"Don't mind her, hon." Petra wrapped his thumb with a sheet of paper towel and shooed him away with a smile.

Amanda watched on with no outward response. Desmond and Fred kept out of it.

Good thinking. Tensions were running high and in Daphne's experience, stress often showed a side of people they usually hid away. Well, she was learning a lot about the personalities in this room. And the oddest part was how little they actually liked each other, which was not the face they'd all tried to portray. What an interesting funeral this would be.

John wandered into the Shady Bend Cemetery a few minutes before Daphne's start time. His purpose was quite different to hers and he had his phone and a notebook ready to record anything of interest. The cemetery wasn't large and he had no desire to intrude on the funeral so kept his distance up a small hill, but even so, he was unable to avoid seeing the funeral party.

Daphne was graveside, along with a growing group of mourners. All wore black but each had a dash of colour. The woman who rode the motor scooter earlier was still in her long black dress but now had a sash of woven flowers around her waist. Others were less flamboyant. A yellow tie here, a blue set of shoes there. Daphne noticed him and waved discreetly.

After waving back, John turned his attention to the headstones. Here, in this tiny forest town, was there a clue to finding someone from Daphne's life? A father she'd probably never met. It was his secret mission and every little town was an opportunity to search. He took his notebook out and read through some of his scribbles from another graveyard.

There was a noise. A cry followed by a dull thud. And screams. His heart jolted. Something terrible was happening at the funeral.

How comforting John's presence was. Funerals were quite new. She'd attended too many in her lifetime and officiated a few, but it was hard work to separate her emotions from the motions. The sorrow and grief around her were profound and as more people arrived, many openly weeping, her heart cried. Seeing her beloved husband at a distance helped. He always gave her strength.

One of Fred's staff had given her a lift over and they'd arrived before the hearse so she was able to spend a few minutes gathering herself and setting up a little spot for the speakers to stand. The grave was a couple of rows from the carpark, overlooked by beautiful flowering trees. A peaceful place to rest.

Ilona arrived soon after and although she'd offered a sad smile, said nothing as she found a place near the foot of the grave, her eyes glistening.

Within a few minutes there was a crowd. This funeral had no seating, but there was a small table which held a hundred or so yellow roses. Each mourner collected one on their way.

Sonia stalked from the carpark. She wore black with no sign of colour and ignored the roses. She walked right around the grave and chose a spot halfway between Daphne and Ilona.

Fred joined Daphne. "They are on their way. It'll take a little while with Desmond's wonky knee, but he insisted. Better slow than sorry."

Her ceremony book open, Daphne cast an eye over the words. She was here for these sad folk. Here to lay their dear one to rest. It was a time of loss and mourning but also of celebration of a life well lived. A life which had made a difference.

The casket approached. Desmond and Petra at the front. Two of the staff in the middle. Zeke and Tracy at the back with Tracy counting their steps aloud. Left. And right. Left. And right.

Daphne couldn't recall ever seeing someone at the back direct the pallbearers. But Tracy did give the impression of needing to take charge even if she wasn't doing a good job of keeping everyone in step.

The casket wobbled.

Something's wrong.

Petra wasn't in time. Not even close. As they crossed the short grass between graves she faltered, forcing the others to adjust their grips. Tracy didn't look impressed.

"Lift a bit higher, Pet. We're almost there for goodness sake."

They reached the side of grave and a silence fell. There was no birdsong. No breeze in the trees. No whispers from the crowd.

Petra swayed and then leaned against the casket which visibly shook.

"Petra. Stand up." Tracy whispered loudly.

"My stomach. Help...me..."

Petra's skin was red and glistening with sweat. Her eyes rolled into the top of her skull. Releasing the handle, she thudded onto the ground.

Mourners cried out.

The other pallbearers tried to compensate but Desmond overbalanced and let go of his handle, almost falling as well.

The casket dropped with a dull thump onto its side.

There was a collective gasp.

All eyes were on the casket.

On the latch of the lid somehow undone.

On a narrow gap which shouldn't be there.

Everybody stepped back except for Fred, who dropped to his knees beside the lid. From a pocket he drew out car keys, rummaging through them to find a tiny flashlight. He blinked a couple of times as if to gather his courage, and then pointed the light into the gap.

Zeke joined him, squatting to peer into the casket.

"Leave it, Zeke." Fred's elbow shot out as if to force the younger man away. "We'll right it and seal it again."

"But sir..."

"I said leave it alone. Help the others."

"But, how?" Zeke straightened and gazed at Daphne through startled eyes. "It's empty."

A CATASTROPHE

The scene was chaotic.

Petra lay groaning on the grass, clutching her stomach after regaining consciousness.

Desmond was down as well, but sitting upright as Tracy checked his ankle.

Zeke and Fred covered the casket—or at least what they could—with their suit jackets and those from the other funeral home employees.

People were all over the place. Some on their phones, even taking photographs. Others holding on to each other in shock.

"Someone call an ambulance!" Daphne looked for John. He was jogging towards her with his phone out, tapping as he went.

Ilona hadn't moved from the end of the grave. Her face was ashen and her lips mouthed something Daphne couldn't work out. Perhaps it was 'Edie'. Hopefully, she would keep an eye on how close she was to the edge and not take the wrong step.

And Sonia? She was laughing. Tears poured down her face as chortles racked her body.

Amidst the pandemonium, nobody was caring for Petra. Daphne stepped around the casket and lowered herself onto the grass.

"Petra? Can you hear me, dear?"

Petra turned wide, frightened eyes to Daphne, opening and closing her mouth with no words. Her eyelids fluttered and she was unconscious.

Daphne undid the buttons on her jacket and slipped it off to gently cover Petra. The woman was breathing but her skin was hot and clammy. This wasn't fainting. Daphne searched the faces around her, all intent on their own worries. Amanda appeared through the crowd.

"Can you help? Do you know if Petra has any underlying conditions?" Daphne asked.

For a moment Amanda stood there without a word, her eyes darting around, but then she kneeled beside them both. Her hand went to Petra's neck, fingers against her pulse, and she counted against her own watch. John was there, behind her, talking on his phone.

Amanda leaned back. "She needs to get to hospital. And I mean a big hospital with an intensive care unit. We need a rescue helicopter."

John put his phone away and leaned down. "Ambulance is coming."

"Won't be enough." Amanda brushed a strand of hair from Petra's face. "Can you find some blankets. Or a priest."

"A priest?"

"Doubt she'll make it to the hospital. Poor love."

John helped Daphne to her feet. "I have a blanket in the car. Back in a minute."

Amanda began singing to Petra. It was a childhood lullaby Daphne knew but didn't quite remember and a shiver went down her spine. It was bizarre. Amanda rocking in time with the song as she held Petra's hand. Petra lay in a pool of sunlight and Daphne moved to cast a shadow across her. The poor woman didn't need the heat of the day directly on her face.

"Mrs Jones!"

Fred gestured from the other side of the casket.

"Amanda, can you stay with Petra? Please give her some shade." Daphne touched the other woman's shoulder and received a nod in response. "Be right back."

Her handbag and briefcase were still at the head of the grave and she collected them before joining Fred, who had Zeke and his two other staff with him. His tie was crooked and he'd rolled his shirt sleeves up. He glanced at Daphne then turned to Zeke.

"Would you three ensure nobody gets photos or video of this? Just be polite and discreet but we need to protect the deceased's privacy."

The three men fanned out and Fred took a deep breath, closing his eyes for a moment.

"Fred, what a dreadful shock for you all. There's an ambulance on its way."

His eyes opened. "Ambulance? Bit late for that."

"For Petra. She's not in a good way. And I imagine Desmond might need his ankle looked at."

For that matter, Sonia could use someone to check she was alright.

The laughter had subsided to an occasional cackle. Sonia sat cross-legged at the side of the grave, occasionally tossing a blade of grass or piece of dirt in.

"Oh dear. I thought Petra fainted. What is wrong with her? We can't have another scandal here and as for Sonia..." his shoulders slumped. "This will be the final straw for her."

"Another scandal?"

"There's always something. You said an ambulance is coming. What about the police?" He called to Zeke. "Give the police station a ring, mate."

Always some scandal? Daphne had a familiar sensation in her gut. Last time she felt this, she'd soon found herself knee-deep in a murder mystery. Her senses tingled.

"What did you do with her?" An angry, tear-filled voice screamed. Ilona was on the move. Other mourners stepped aside as she powered her way to the casket.

Fred got in between it and Ilona and held his hand up. "Please, please, Ilona, I know you are upset. We are all upset—"

"Upset? Upset?" Ilona stopped short of Fred. The flowers around her waist were gone, leaving her long dress ballooning about her. "Where is she?" She tried to push past Fred to go to the casket and he grabbed onto her arms.

"You can't go there. I promise we'll find out where she is. I promise you."

"This is...this is your fault." With a sob, Ilona wrenched herself away and ran in the opposite direction, long hair whipping behind her.

"Should someone go after her?" Daphne asked. She took a step or two in the same direction but Ilona was a fast runner and was already almost out of sight between trees. "Someone needs to check on her."

Fred's eyes were on Sonia. "She's laughing."

"Shock does odd things to people."

"For goodness sake, Fred, of course she'd find this

funny." Tracy stood on the other side of the casket. "Just ignore her and she'll sort herself out. In the meantime, Desmond needs to see a doctor for his ankle and we really need to get Amanda away from poor Petra." She rolled her eyes. "Why don't you go and find out what you did with Edwina and I'll shoo everyone out of the cemetery."

"I didn't do anything with Edwina." Fred spun around, his face turning even redder. "She was in...well, in there. At least she was last night and everything was done properly. How on earth could this happen to me?" He pulled at the knot of his tie to loosen it and undid the top button. "And no. It isn't up to you to send mourners home. The police will be here and they can decide if the ceremony can continue."

Without the deceased?

Daphne could just see it. The casket would be turned onto its base. The people regathered. And she would resume her place and begin the ceremony. Well, that might work if nobody knew the casket was empty. But they did. And Sonia would laugh hysterically while Ilona cried and Tracy bossed everyone around.

"Daph? I've put the blanket over the lady but she's been left alone. The minute we could hear the siren, the other lady jumped up and dashed away."

"Why would Amanda leave her?" Daphne followed John and so did Tracy and Fred. Petra was barely breathing.

"Amanda knows she shouldn't have even touched her." Tracy kneeled down. "I had no idea she was like this. Sorry, Pet. Help is coming. Where's her handbag? She'll need her phone and stuff in hospital."

"In the hearse. Unless she left them at the funeral home. I'll check." Fred was gone before anyone could reply.

"I don't understand." Daphne said. "Why shouldn't

Amanda have sat with her? She took her pulse so looked as though she has some training."

Tracy laughed shortly. "She does. Used to be the town doctor." She made the motion of someone drinking. "Bit too much of this. Lost her licence. But I reckon our Petra's been poisoned and it wouldn't surprise me one bit if Amanda Sinclair is responsible."

John made two more trips to the car. One to take the blanket back when the paramedics took over, and then to find some water for Daphne. She'd left her bottle in the footwell rather than take it to the ceremony and now, instead of being ready to go home, she had no idea when she could leave.

Once again they were at the scene of a crime...or at the very least, the scene of several awful mishaps.

After putting the water bottle into Daphne's hand and seeing her take a few sips, he excused himself. He'd dropped his notebook up near the trees when the commotion began. It took a few minutes but he spied it on the grass, sprawled open.

He scooped it up. Nearby, a muffled sob alerted him to someone partly hidden behind one of the trees. And she was crying. His heart went out to her. She leaned against the trunk of a tree with her head in her hands and her legs drawn up against her body. It was the woman who'd spoken to Daphne near the car this morning.

John made sure he stepped on a couple of twigs as he approached, so as not to startle her. She glanced up and wiped her eyes.

"I'm John. Daphne's husband. It's Ilona, isn't it? Would you like me to get you some water?"

"Um...no. But you are kind to offer. I'm overwhelmed. I just don't know what to think."

"Understandable. Such a shock."

She nodded. The tears stopped and she took a couple of short, sharp breaths, then stood. Her hand went into a pocket in her dress and she pulled out a tissue. "Nobody else understood Edie like me. People think she was harsh in her judgement of them and perhaps she was, but there was always a reason why. And now they'll all fight it out to get her secret recipe." She blew her nose. "I'm not good with confrontation but if anyone is mean about her, I will say something."

"I would hope nobody would take advantage of the situation to be unkind, but if they do, that is a reflection on them. Not on Edie." John said. "Hopefully, this is all a simple mix up. Possibly the wrong casket was collected. Would you like to go back down there and see if there is any news?"

Her eyes drifted to the grave and John followed her line of sight. People were trailing out of the cemetery. The few who remained were close to the casket. The poor woman the paramedics had just loaded onto their ambulance—handbag tucked under her blanket—had looked gravely ill to John. Not at all responsive to their care and there was talk of meeting a helicopter to transport her to the closest hospital equipped to assist her. Nobody seemed to have an idea what was wrong but he'd overheard the comment from the louder woman. The one about poison.

With every fibre of his being, he wanted it to be untrue.

Daphne gazed up towards them and John raised his hand and waved.

"You should go to her. Your wife has been so lovely and kind and I'm sure this is as much a shock to her as us."

"I can wait a while if you need company." John said.

"No. I think I'll go home and freshen up. They'll have to reschedule because this is highly irregular. Fred has a lot of explaining to do."

On cue, a police car pulled in through the gates.

"I am so sorry Daphne's ceremony was messed with. And thank you."

With that, Ilona sprinted down the hill toward the car park. John headed back to Daphne.

WHERE IS EDWINA?

"Porter and Browne are here." Zeke announced.

Daphne's head shot up. As common as her real maiden name was, it still always made her look. Gave her heart a little lift in case this time... She pushed down the hope. The trouble with pushing away hope was that one day, it might not reappear. But when one discovered their birth certificate had the wrong information on it, and eventually found out what their real surname would have been under different circumstances, well it changed a person.

Two police officers cut through the cemetery, a thirty-something woman, and a fifty-something man. As they neared, Fred rebuttoned his shirt and fixed his tie. His forehead was beaded with perspiration, which Daphne put down to standing in the direct sun for too long. The afternoon was warm enough for a bit of sweat.

Thanks to the efforts of Fred's staff, most mourners had left or were leaving. The ambulance was gone and Daphne's thoughts went out to the woman inside it. One minute Petra

West was chatty and enjoying rhubarb jam and then she was so ill that an ex-doctor recommended a priest.

The revelations from Tracy and Amanda were both odd and concerning. Daphne filed their comments away.

Just in case.

"I'm here, doll. Are you doing alright?" John reached for Daphne's hand.

"Yes, but I don't know what I should be doing." Daphne tugged at his hand. "Let's find some shade."

An expansive flowering tree provided instant relief. And more privacy.

"I spoke to Ilona." John said. "Drink some water, Daph. You look so hot."

Although she knew what he meant, a bubble of mischief —fuelled by a roller coaster of emotions—rose and she couldn't help herself.

"You'd better believe it, young man."

With a wide grin, John put his arms around her and planted a kiss on her lips.

"Ouch! Scorching!"

They both smiled. Forty plus years of marriage created a comfortable and safe place to co-exist, and Daphne loved John as much—if not more—than the day she'd married him not long out of high school.

The moment passed and Daphne sipped on her water, eyes on the events unfolding around the fallen casket. The police officers squatted to take a look as Fred had, while he stood by, running his finger under his collar.

"Do you think Fred had anything to do with the—er—mix up?" John asked.

"I'd like to say no. But he has some serious questions to

answer about this, being the funeral home director. And he is so nervous."

"Losing a client would be nerve-wracking, I imagine."

"How could it happen though? And why. Actually," Daphne glanced at the discussion underway between Fred and an officer, "the why is what interests me. Unless it was a complete error and the wrong casket was collected, then a person, or persons, did this deliberately."

It was a dreadful thought. Best not to dwell on it.

"You said you spoke to Ilona? She was upset with Fred."

"A few tears but she seemed better after we spoke. Not as distraught." John said.

Tracy and Zeke stood a little away from the casket and were deep in conversation, with Zeke's eyes darting back to the casket as he spoke. Fred's other staff were nowhere around.

From the other side of the grave, Sonia stared at the casket, or the people around it. It was too far for Daphne to be certain. The laughter was gone. There were no tears. In fact, nothing but a vacant stare. Edwina was still her mother and instead of the funeral being almost over, she had this new shock to deal with.

Fred nodded in Daphne's direction and the older police officer headed their way. The younger one took photos of the casket.

As he neared, the officer removed his cap and stepped into the shade with a smile.

"Bit warm out there today." He held a hand out to Daphne. "Adam Browne. Leading Senior Constable but Adam works."

"Nice to meet you, although the circumstance could be

better." Daphne shook his hand. "This is John, my husband."

As the men shook hands, Daphne took a closer look at the officer. He had a pleasant face with a ready smile and warm brown eyes. He was completely bald and wore glasses.

"Not what you expected when you agreed to officiate?" he grinned and took out a notepad. "I've no wish to keep you standing around so just wanted to ask a couple of questions, if you don't mind."

"Not at all. I have some myself."

The corners of John's mouth flicked up. Daphne ignored him. He knew her too well and no doubt had already figured out she wasn't about to leave the poor mourners without some form of closure. As long as Edwina could be found, of course.

"Would you run through the events of today? Anything you observed, particularly concerning the casket or the hearse. Or the funeral home. Fred mentioned you were there twice today." Adam said.

"Yes. I met with Fred, Sonia Drinkwater, and Tracy Chappell, to go over the ceremony and discuss the final wishes of the deceased. We spent about an hour in a room in the funeral home. When I was leaving, I met Ilona briefly. But none of the staff at that point."

"Aside from the gravity of the situation, did anything strike you as unusual, or of concern?"

Daphne considered her role as a celebrant to be similar to any professional caregiver. Doctors, counsellors, lawyers, clergy. In some circumstances in a life, a person might say or do something they wanted kept private. Times when emotions ran high. It was a mental balancing act to know when to share what she'd seen and heard. Apart from her chat with Ilona, there'd been others present. Others who would be questioned as well. Nothing to keep a secret.

"Sonia was very upset. Angry. Mostly at her mother which is quite normal under the circumstances."

Adam nodded. "Normal for Sonia. She isn't afraid to speak her mind."

At least her behaviour was unremarkable. No need to get into her comments about being pleased Edwina was dead.

"In that case, then nothing felt out of place. When I returned this afternoon, on Fred's request, I met a number of other people. Apparently, the pallbearers were having a little meet up first."

"Who was present?" Adam wrote in his notepad.

"Fred. Tracy. Desmond Rogers. Zeke. Sorry I don't know his surname. Poor Petra West. And Amanda Sinclair."

Did I just recall all those names? Go me!

Adam glanced up. "Amanda was there?"

"She arrived last."

"But she wasn't a pallbearer." He made a note. "Any observations about that part of the day?"

Let me think.

Petra getting stuck into the food early. Tracy not wanting Amanda to have a glass of champagne. The tray dropping after a minor accident. Cross words spoken. Zeke cutting himself.

But is any of it relevant?

"I got the impression Amanda wasn't welcome there by some people. But I'm a stranger to town and funerals are times of great stress for those involved."

"You are a discreet person, Mrs Jones." Adam said.

"Please call me Daphne. I just had a thought about Petra. She told me—at the funeral home—that I should try the rhubarb and apricot jam on a scone and that she just had. I do hope that isn't why she fell ill. Food poisoning. Or something worse."

"Something worse? Such as?" Adam put away his notepad to give Daphne his full attention.

Back in Little Bridges, after the events at the wedding she'd officiated, Daphne had tried to tell her suspicions to the police officer who'd been first on the scene. It had been less than successful, leaving Daphne feeling she was not being taken seriously, or worse—that her observations were of no value. This was different, because the body in question was deceased before Daphne and John arrived in town. But what if this otherwise pleasant officer also considered she should mind her own business?

Her throat tightened up.

As if he could read her mind, John gently took her water bottle from her hand and undid the lid before giving it back with a soft, "Have a drink."

Grateful for the minute to think and her husband's sensitive response, Daphne sipped.

"It might be a while before we get an update on Petra West, so I'll ask Fred to put aside the—rhubarb jam?" Adam asked.

"Rhubarb and apricot jam." Daphne corrected "I'm sure I'm only speculating but what if something's wrong with it."

"Not much for rhubarb but I imagine other people are." Adam said. "Best to be safe."

His quiet agreement boosted her spirits a little.

"What will happen now, Adam? Who is looking for the deceased?" Daphne asked. "Is there anything we can do to help?"

Adam's phone rang. "Might be able to tell you in a min. Be right back." He wandered off, answering as he walked.

Fred, Zeke, and another of Fred's employees worked in unison to roll the casket onto its base. The other police officer was speaking with Sonia who had her back turned to the scene. There was nobody else around.

"Daphne, John. Thanks for waiting." Adam slid his phone into a pocket as he rejoined them. "That was the funeral home. I've asked them to locate and quarantine the jam in question. There's been a search of the premises and unfortunately, no sign of the deceased. There are no unaccounted for caskets and no other clients." He ran a hand through his non-existent hair. "I'm heading over there now and Fred can come with me. Bodies don't just disappear."

John spoke. "Are we good to go back to our caravan?"

"Yes. I'll grab your contact details in case I need to follow up with any other questions but for now, please try to enjoy our little town. The agricultural show begins this afternoon which is always fun."

After swapping cards, Adam returned to the grave. He spoke to Fred, whose shoulders visibly dropped. The other police officer was finished with Sonia, who'd moved into some shade and sat on the grass. Her eyes had rarely left the casket anytime Daphne looked her way.

"Should I go and see if she needs to talk, John?"

"What if we go home. Give you a chance to freshen up and take a breather. A cup of tea."

Tea did sound nice. Being somewhere away from the shock of the last hour sounded even nicer. This funeral wasn't over. They'd find Edwina. And reschedule. And as long as it didn't interfere with the wedding she was heading to, she'd be ready to help Edwina go to her final resting place.

As long as they can find her.

SIDE TRIP

"Tea is ready." John called as he carried the pot to the table in Bluebell. Two cups and saucers were already in place as well as some lemon tarts he'd found in the fridge. Daphne had barely eaten today and with all the upset at the funeral, a little treat wouldn't go astray.

"Lemon tarts! Good idea." Daphne slid behind the table. She'd changed into what she often called her 'cosy' clothes —three quarter length loose pants and a pretty blouse. She looked much more comfortable like this than her suit on a hot day, as smart and professional as it was.

John joined her at the table and poured the tea. "What an afternoon!"

"Indeed. And I have a feeling this will keep us here longer than expected, so apologies in advance."

"There is nothing to apologise for, Daph. What are the odds of something like this happening?"

"About the same as the events in Little Bridges. We went there for the sole purpose of me officiating a wedding and ended up staying far longer thanks to the treacherous behaviour of people who had murder on their minds." Daphne picked up one of the tarts. "You should see all the food laid out at the funeral home for the wake. No tarts though."

"When you were talking to Leading Senior Constable Browne, I got the feeling you were being careful what you said about the pre-funeral meeting." John poured some tea. "I imagine in a small town where everybody knows everyone, there are old rivalries as well as friendships, and losing a valued member of the community might bring out some ill feelings. And I didn't mean to make that pun."

Daphne nodded. "Well, somebody *did* lose Edwina, quite literally."

For a few minutes they sipped their tea and each enjoyed a lemon tart. Cars filled with families periodically drove past Bluebell along the dirt track. Perhaps to visit the show which was beginning today.

"That hit the spot." Daphne said. "What you said earlier is true. As much as I want to help, I'm rather worried about saying too much. It isn't as though there's been a murder or anything, just a missing body. And an ill woman, of course. But apart from wondering if poor Petra was affected by something in the jam, I really don't know if anything else that happened has anything to do with Edwina's disappearance."

"I'm sure you would say if you had suspicions."

"I would. It was just a bit odd when Amanda Sinclair arrived." Daphne's brow furrowed. "She seemed hesitant about coming into the room but muttered something in response to Tracy's toast. And it wasn't very complimentary to Edwina. Tracy was quite scathing to Amanda when the champagne glasses ended up on the floor."

John opened his mouth to ask what happened just as her phone beeped. He closed it again as she read the message.

"It's from Fred. Says police have a lead on Edwina and can we stay for a possible rescheduling of the funeral for tomorrow, pending the outcome."

"That's positive. Say yes, of course. We were going to be here tonight so if this is resolved then you'll still get to fulfil your appointment." he reached over the table and took one of Daphne's hands. "I know how important it is to you. Finishing your job."

"I hate to think of someone not being properly laid to rest, not to mention what her friends and family are going through with all of this."

And because you are driven to make those around you happy.

"Another cup of tea? Then, how about a visit to this show in Shady Bend?"

When they'd returned to Bluebell earlier, Daphne had glanced at their bed with a small sigh. She was tired. They'd only been travelling for a few weeks and she wasn't quite accustomed to the nomadic life they followed. Although there was much to enjoy about visiting a new place once or twice a week, there were moments she longed for more stability again. A bit less unpredictability.

Be adventurous, Daph!

She managed to sweet-talk herself into a better frame of mind and now, as John found a parking spot among rows of cars in a paddock, she found herself looking forward to the rest of the day. The agricultural show was held on a large sports ground surrounded by bushland. According to the sign as they'd driven in, the show had only opened an hour ago and would end at midnight on Saturday. The air was filled with music and laughter, along with some excited squeals from people on carnival rides, as she and John headed to the main entrance.

"Quite a few people already here." John had changed into shorts and a shirt and wore the floppy white hat he favoured wearing when fishing. "Can't remember the last time we went to a show."

We haven't. Not together anyway.

"I think you took a couple of our foster family over to the one in Green Bay." She said. Her heart was beating a bit too fast and she slid her arm through John's. "What shall we do first?"

"What if we see what's on in the main arena and then plan it all out? Looks like its straight ahead." John paid for their tickets and accepted a small booklet which he slipped into his top pocket.

Arm in arm, they followed the road past old buildings on one side and the entry to the carnival on the other. Country agricultural shows in Australia were an old tradition from the times of farmers and growers competing for more than pride of what they produced, but to find new markets and showcase their animals and goods to buyers. Over time, entertainment in the form of travelling side shows—carnivals—became a common addition which was anticipated by young and old alike in towns often too small to offer much entertainment.

"I do love seeing the horses." Daphne said as the main ground opened up ahead. On perfectly manicured grass, which wouldn't stay that way for long, three rings were marked with temporary roping. In one, judging was underway of a breed of cattle. Led by white coated handlers, the group of red cattle stood calmly as a trio of judges made notes. Another ring was empty, but the third was set up for show jumping and riders without their mounts, walked the course.

They stopped in the shade of a grandstand and John took out the booklet.

"Let's see what's what." He opened it up to a map and then squinted around the ground. "All the buildings around the perimeter are in use. There's a cat show, oh, but that doesn't begin until tomorrow. Livestock apart, there are woodchopping competitions a bit further along from here. They run pretty much every day with the grand final on Saturday. There's an art show."

"Like the sound of that."

"Agree. There's the craft pavilion which has items for sale. And the food hall. Local produce. Baking competitions. Preserves and the like."

What had Tracy said earlier today? Preliminary judging started today.

"I think we should check it all out, love. Not like we have to be anywhere."

They doubled back for a few metres then turned left onto a wide and busy hard dirt path. Families, couples, and groups of teens bustled along in both directions, occasionally stepping aside to allow a horse and rider cross, or make way for an official vehicle to slowly nose through.

The sting was leaving the air as the sun dropped behind the tall trees, making the late afternoon air pleasant. Behind them the music and screams were less intrusive as they put the grandstand between themselves and the carnival. Daphne rotated her shoulders. The carnival wasn't going to hurt her and this was a good opportunity to send whatever old memories had emerged right back where they belonged. Hidden.

"Art show first?"

"Perfect."

After stepping through the open double doors of a stone building, Daphne and John stopped for a moment for their eyes to adjust to the darker interior. There was a hush in here reminiscent of a library. Of the few people wandering, most wore official's vests. The room was split into art in its different mediums, and a section at the far end which immediately took John's attention. Photography.

"Hope you don't mind if we wander down there first?" John was already on his way.

"I'll catch up."

John's interest in photography was a growing passion as he recorded their journey in images. More and more he was experimenting with different techniques using apps on his phone. It all was above her understanding, not because she wasn't smart enough to follow what he did, but because it wasn't fascinating to her as it was to him.

Much as she tried to show her interest, he would enjoy the exhibition more on his own.

She gazed around. Along one side were large easels holding canvases with oil paintings. A table was filled with smaller easels and lots of watercolours. And another table displayed miniatures at one end and an eclectic mix of entries at the other.

The oil paintings ranged from quite stunning to less than ordinary, but Daphne believed art was in the eye of the beholder. It was just that some didn't appeal to her. Perhaps she'd been spoilt over the years, for Rivers End—their home for many years—had two talented artists, Martin Blake and his grandfather, Thomas. Martin specialised in abstracts but was just as capable of producing wonderful portraits. Thomas was known for his emotion-charged seascapes. Haunting work which was sought after even decades after he'd completed it.

Almost at the end of the row was a painting of a woman. It wasn't particularly well executed—in Daphne's opinion—but it was interesting. The woman was staring in a mirror. She was older. Perhaps in her sixties, hair piled on top of her head in a neat bun and her eyes serious. Even angry. Her reflection though smiled back at her, the eyes alive with love and happiness. Quite the contrast.

"As conflicted as the woman herself."

Daphne hadn't noticed anyone close by and turned to the man standing to her right. Desmond, leaning on a cane.

"Hello. How is your ankle?"

He grimaced. "Hurts. But just a bad twist thanks to Miss West."

Rather than point out that Petra was hardly in a condition to have deliberately harmed him when she collapsed, Daphne gestured to the painting.

"Someone you know?"

Desmond snorted. "Yes. My painting, not that it matters or will win anything. Should have entered it into the Archibald instead."

Australia's premier art award might be a bit out of the league of this piece, but there was clearly more to this than Desmond's throwaway comment. Something about the woman was familiar. The expression reminded her of someone she'd met. Someone much younger.

"There's a lot of love in this painting, Mr Rogers. And if

you painted it, then you certainly portray some intense feelings for the subject."

Eyes back on Desmond, Daphne sensed a tension in the man. His mouth was in a straight line, lips hard together. And a muscle in his cheek twitched. As though he was considering her assessment, he stared at the painting.

"You are seeing something that isn't there, Mrs Jones. My neighbour she was, but I had no love for the woman."

"This is Edwina?"

He nodded. "This is Edwina."

ART, OR ARTFUL?

Edwina Drinkwater—or at least, her likeness according to Desmond—was an older version of Sonia, once Daphne took another look with the new information. The same eyes, at least the angry ones.

"Have you been her neighbour for long?" she asked.

"Too long. Decades."

"I am curious." Daphne turned her back on the painting to address Desmond. "I'm being personal, but why paint her if you didn't get on with her?"

Desmond shrugged. "She was two faced and it appealed to the artist in me to capture it in paint. Edwina hated it. Told me I shouldn't have taken her image without permission and she'd sue me if I showed another soul." He suddenly flashed a row of ragged teeth in a rather fearsome smile. "Thought she'd blow a fuse when I said I was entering in this and every art show I could get to."

"What about Sonia? Does she agree with her mother?"

"She doesn't agree with anyone. But I think she quite

likes this painting." Desmond took his phone from a pocket. "Another message. Group chat never ends."

Daphne looked at the painting again as he tapped on his phone. There was a detail she'd not noticed before. The background was faded out a bit but looked like shelves and a counter. A shop? And perhaps those were jars on the shelves. In the reflection was a narrow bottle like one for sauce but it wasn't replicated where it should have been.

"Whoever thought they knew where she'd gone to was wrong." Desmond announced.

"Where Edwina is?"

"Stupid idea to go off looking in the bush. Who'd drag a body out of a casket and leave it lying around under a tree?"

"Is that what they thought?"

"Police got an idea this was some kind of prank. Youngsters having a bit of fun but why would they even bother. Not easy to pick up an embalmed body let alone carry it any distance." He shuddered. "Edwina was probably rejected by the afterlife, rose from the dead, and is on her way home."

Before this conversation became any more macabre, Daphne excused herself and went to find John. As she wound her way past the tables, a familiar sensation raised the hairs on her arms, and she glanced back. Desmond leaned on his cane with both hands, his eyes following her.

Browsing the collection of photographs made John happy. He was surprised by the depth of quality in the entries and returned twice to an image of an old cottage. The house was unloved, in need of paint and repair. But the gardens were spectacular and immaculate. Not a weed in sight and manicured lawns with a sweeping path between long beds filled with flowers and trees. He was taken by a long garden bed of roses alternating red, pink, and yellow varieties. Very striking with the riot of colour against the drab exterior of the house creating an interesting contrast. Something loved. Something neglected.

Judging was complete for the photographs and this one had placed but not won its section. He compared it to the winning entry, a nice enough image of a tree but without the attention to detail of the other one.

I still have much to learn.

Daphne was on her way to meet him but she glanced over her shoulder and he couldn't help but look in the same direction. The older man from the funeral, the one who'd hurt his ankle, stared at Daphne.

His stomach tightened. Something about the man's intensity bothered John. Daphne always knew when someone was watching her and she'd obviously glanced back thanks to her intuition. Something was off about this whole day, between odd behaviour from mourners through to the dropped casket and missing body.

"John? You look worried."

"That man. Did you speak to him?" he asked.

"Desmond. Yes, he was one of the pallbearers and hurt his ankle when the casket fell. And yes, he was watching me walk over here." Daphne took his arm. "Have you seen enough of the photographs?"

"Feeling a bit hungry, actually. Shall we find some food?" John was happy to leave this building and they found a food truck outside and got on the end of the line.

"He painted Edwina." Daphne said.

"Sorry?"

"Oh. Back there I was talking with Desmond. I'd been looking at a painting of a woman and he told me he did it. And that he was no fan of hers but they'd been neighbours for decades."

Maybe he stole her body to get back at her for something.

"So, he didn't like her but did a painting of her." He pushed his unkind thoughts away.

"Said it showed how conflicted a person she was. She was looking in a mirror and the real Edwina was stern and angry but the reflection was happy. But you know what I think?"

They moved forward as people were served and left the line.

"I got the impression that whoever painted it had a strong emotional attachment to the subject, but when I said that Desmond scoffed at the idea. I think he once loved her. Perhaps still does."

They ordered hotdogs and chips and returned to the main field to eat. The show jumping was underway and the grandstand was almost full of spectators but they squeezed into a row near the front. One by one, horses and their riders navigated the arena in a timed competition that left people gasping and clapping. The food wasn't as good as the entertainment and Daphne only finished half of her hotdog.

"Bit on the cold side." She dabbed her lips with a napkin.

"Sorry. We'll make up for it with a nice restaurant meal in the next couple of days."

"I'm not complaining." Daphne took his hand as they headed away from the grandstand. "Besides, we might find some goodies in the produce pavilion."

Evening was closing in and enormous overhead lights powered up with a series of crackles. Further past the art show they located another building, this one up a long ramp and with lots of glass windows. At the entrance, a table was set up with free goodie bags and a smiling woman handed one to each of them.

"Well, this is nice." Daphne said. "Which way should we go?"

"Daphne! Over here."

A female voiced boomed from the far wall.

"Tracy." Daphne didn't sound very enthusiastic but now the woman was bustling towards them it was too late to pretend they hadn't seen her.

Talking to Desmond was one thing, but Tracy was a different matter.

Be nice. Ignore her sharp tongue. Move on quickly.

She was enjoying her visit to the show with John and hadn't considered the woman might be here.

Tracy wore a mid-length brown skirt, long boots, and cream blouse and over that, had a vest with 'Official Judge' on a rosette pinned on the front. She carried a clipboard and was heavily made up. Even at the funeral she'd been less dressed up.

"Daphne, Daphne. I hope you've got some news for me."

"News?"

"Well yes. I'd imagine Fred would let you know first when the rescheduled funeral will be." She frowned. "Guess it means Edwina is still missing in action. Whoops. I mean, inaction. Better not let anyone else hear me joking about it."

That was a joke?

"I saw Desmond a short while ago and he had news that

there was no progress from the police. Something about a group chat?" Daphne said.

"Never understood why someone his age is messing around on social media. I can only imagine what Fred did with her but he'd better find her fast. All of this right in the middle of the biggest event of the year is terribly inconvenient." Tracy grumbled.

Daphne was lost for words. A woman had died and then been removed from her casket by persons unknown. It might have inconvenienced Tracy but it had done a bit more to poor Edwina.

"Anyway, we must do our best to go on. Come and see what I've been doing."

Without waiting for a reply, Tracy strode to a series of long tables. They were set up with multiple levels and on each were individual displays of bottled goods. All had their lids off and a sample of the wares was on a small side plate. Each was numbered and there were handwritten labels on all.

"This competition is always fiercely contested. Until now." Tracy waved an arm dramatically in the direction of the jars. "All of these are from within our own region and use fruit or vegetables from this area, so it is seasonal. There are jams, chutneys, even locally made mustards. And preserved lemons, baby cucumber, cherries...the list goes on. And my job is to select the top three."

"You said 'until now'? Is something different this show?"

Tracy rolled her eyes. "Well, obviously. No entries from Edwina so the competition is fairer. At least as far as the sauces go. And the grand prize."

John wandered along the table, inspecting the display.

"Sauces?" Daphne had no idea what the woman was talking about.

"You must have heard about her secret recipe?"

"Only something Ilona mentioned. But no, I have no idea about a secret recipe."

Tracy laughed. "Edwina would be turning in her grave. Whoops. Too soon? Anyway, she imagined her sauce was world famous and kept the recipe hidden so it wouldn't be stolen. But it doesn't matter, because the absence of her sauce means other people have a go at winning, even if they don't deserve it."

"I see numbers, so each entry is anonymous?" Daphne asked. There was some delicious looking apricot jam which made her mouth water. As long as it didn't include rhubarb.

"Of course. We couldn't have competitors claiming I was prejudiced in my decisions. Mind you," she leaned closer to Daphne to a conspiratorial whisper. "I've judged so many of these competitions that I could probably guess who made what. Good thing I'm not open to bribery."

Good thing nobody overheard you.

"I'm sure everyone would consider you a fair judge. If you've been doing this for so long, they must value your expert opinion." Daphne said, her eyes drifting back to the apricot jam.

Tracy nodded. "Yes. Yes, I'm well respected. At least by most people. Edwina never liked my decisions but she wasn't nearly as good in the kitchen as she believed." She looked over Daphne's shoulder. "Speaking of people whose creations aren't as good as they think...hello there, Sonia. Have to say I'm surprised to see you here."

For the first time, she agreed with Tracy. Sonia was last seen sitting alone under a tree. What a traumatic day she'd had and from Daphne's observation, there was little in the way of comfort offered to her from the other mourners. Not even from Fred, who'd earlier revealed an almost fatherly side when he'd counselled her to calm down. He'd been caught up with his own troubles, of course, but still, was there nobody at the funeral who cared enough to check the daughter of the deceased was coping?

"Haven't you finished judging yet? Or whatever you call judging. People want to know who won."

Sonia was dressed in the same clothes as the funeral—black knee length dress, black tights, and black ankle boots. Her skin was tinged pink, no doubt from sitting in the sun for so long. She didn't bother to look at Daphne or Tracy but gazed up and down the table.

Tracy huffed, clutched the clipboard against her chest, and stalked to the opposite side of the table where she glared at Sonia.

Daphne's heart thumped.

I'd like to tell you both to be nice. It's a difficult time.

Her phone rang and she couldn't grab it out of her handbag fast enough. She stepped away to answer.

"Mrs Jones, this is Leading Senior Constable Browne. Adam."

"Oh yes. How are you? I mean, is there any news?"

"I'm fine thanks. And the answer is yes. And no."

"I see. Well, not really."

John joined her and she mouthed 'Adam' to him.

"We did have a lead earlier which hasn't panned out. It probably was a long shot but we'd had a tip off and it was worth following up." Adam said.

"Do you mean the one about local youngsters playing a rather bizarre prank?"

He chuckled. "Small towns. Can't keep a secret. Although the whereabouts of Edwina Drinkwater is one secret I wish would make it to the Shady Bend grapevine. The main reason for the call is to see if you mind answering a few more questions. In the morning will do, assuming you and your husband aren't planning on leaving before then?"

"The morning is fine. Shall we come to the police station?" Daphne asked.

"If you can. I'll send you a text message with the address. Any time between nine and eleven is great, but if I end up having to attend anything I'll let you know."

They chatted for a minute then Daphne disconnected the call.

"Adam wants to ask a few questions in the morning. I imagine he's trying to fill in the gaps."

"So, no success finding the...er, missing person?"

"Not yet. Do you think we can slip away?"

"Let's try." John took her arm and they zigzagged between displays and people through the pavilion.

Once they were a safe distance away from where they'd been, she risked a look back. Tracy and Sonia were talking. Their body language was no longer angry, in fact, if Daphne hadn't seen so much animosity between the women today, she'd have thought them to be friends. Close friends. Sonia even smiled as she spoke with animation and Tracy patted her arm.

Adam wasn't wrong about small town secrets. From the odd behaviour of several residents today, Shady Bend had its fair share.

A FEAR FROM THE PAST

After another hour of sampling cheese, buying some local wine, and indulging childhood memories with popcorn, they were more than ready to head back to Bluebell.

With the coming of night, visitors spilled through the gates at a rapidly increasing rate until the pathways and road filled with excited faces and laughter. Teenagers grouped together and they might have been the loudest, but they also stepped aside to make room for prams and the occasional wheelchair. Daphne smiled at them. She'd loved being a foster mother to children but really enjoyed having teenagers in the house. There was something special about watching a child grow into young adulthood.

"And then they disappear." She said under her breath.

John turned his head to look at her, a question in his eyes. Hopefully, he hadn't heard. She didn't want to tell him where her thoughts drifted to some days. Her wishful thinking about reuniting with some of their foster children. One in particular.

He squeezed her hand. "We seem to be a long way from the gate. Want to cut through the carnival?"

"Oh. Um, sure." It wouldn't be so bad. There was an almost straight path from where they were now to the road they'd come in on. A Ferris wheel towered over the carnival where ride attendants shouted above music blaring from one ride after another. People lined up at food trucks and rides alike. Lights flashed in time with a procession of recorded silly voices at a shooting range.

"Here, I'll carry your bags." John took the handful of sample and show bags from Daphne and added them to his, then offered her his free hand. "Fancy going on the Ferris wheel?"

"My, oh my. No thank you. Just the idea of being all the way up there is enough to make me dizzy."

"Sorry." John guided them past a fire breather who'd gathered a small crowd around himself. "We've never been to a carnival or anything together and I don't really know why. I always went as a kid. My parents even took us kids to Melbourne Royal Show one year." He grinned. "Never forgot how big it was. Could fit ten of this size shows into it. Twenty. And the showbags were so expensive we were only allowed one each and boy, did we spend our time making those choices."

"Sounds fun."

This was taking a long time, walking through here. Her spare hand moved to her chest, pressing against it. And for some reason she was having trouble swallowing.

"Daph?"

People milled around. The music was loud. Perspiration dripped between her shoulder blades.

"Daphne. Doll, are you alright?"

Why did John sound worried? She smiled at him and nodded.

Get a grip, Daph.

From ahead, a different tune cut through the crowd where painted horses bobbed up and down and around. The music must be the same for every carousel on the planet.

She stopped, her mouth open as she fought for air that just wouldn't reach her lungs.

"Okay. Something isn't right. Are you unwell?" John turned to face her, still holding one of her hands. "Or is it the side show?"

Daphne nodded.

A flicker of a smile crossed his lips. "With the absence of a definitive answer I'm assuming it is the side show."

She nodded again. Her words weren't coming out and if her heart didn't stop thudding so hard, she might fall in a heap right on this spot.

"We can turn back." John scanned the area around them. "Actually, I think we can get behind all of this. Looks as though the fence is just the other side of these tents and at least then we're away from the bulk of the noise. Give it a go?"

He didn't really give her much choice, just gripped her hand more firmly and set off between two food trucks. She held on for dear life. Because, if she lost him...

"Ah. Just as I thought. Step over the cables on the ground. I can see a path through."

True to his word, in a few minutes they were at the boundary fence. It was a relief to stop here, away from the chaos of the carnival. It was still noisy but in the darkness her heart slowed to normal and she swallowed.

John ran his hand over the mesh fence. "This is temporary fencing. Let's see if we can find a gap."

Daphne giggled.

"No giggling, young lady. We are escapees and must find a way out before we're caught." John's voice was stern, which only made Daphne laugh harder. He followed the fence in oversized steps, slightly hunched and darting his head from side to side. All they needed was some comedic spy music. "Aha! We don't even need those giant bolt cutters you keep in your handbag. Or explosives in your pocket. Just let me move this a bit..." he carefully lifted a panel. "And we can slip through before anyone sees."

It didn't take long to step through the space and then John replaced the panel. Without another word, he picked up the bags he'd dropped on the ground and then her hand. The night was lit by an almost full moon which was just as well with the lights of the show behind them. They were on the grassy field not far from the carpark and that is where they headed. Only when they were both in the car and John was pulling out of the carpark did Daphne let out a long sigh.

"I've got you." John reached over and patted her leg. "Never let anything bad happen."

Daphne opened her mouth to say he couldn't be with her every minute but clamped it shut again. Instead, she covered his hand with hers until he needed it for the steering wheel.

Being married to someone for decades teaches you about two important people. The person you married and yourself.

John had no doubt Daphne was the reason he was the man he was proud to be. Her unwavering belief in him had seen him through plenty of tough times and gave him confidence to start their real estate business all those years ago. And he'd become the trusted agent people came back to time and again from watching how she encouraged clients to talk about what they needed, rather than wanted.

Today he'd discovered something new about Daphne. A fear she'd hidden their whole lives, if indeed she even knew it existed before tonight. So, he needed to listen when she was ready to tell him what she needed. And somehow not speculate in the meantime on the reason she'd turned white and looked ready to flee when they were at the carnival.

"I might check my website, love. See if there's anything pending for me." Daphne carried her laptop to the table. "Can't afford to miss a query."

"In that case, I might update our blog. And can I pour you a glass of red wine to finish the evening?" He was already taking wine glasses from the cupboard over the sink and fancied opening one of the bottles they'd picked up at the show.

"Yes please. Have you got some new photos for Bluebell's Blessings?"

Since beginning their travels, John had created a blog for their friends which was getting quite a following. He wrote about each town they visited, highlighting interesting details and adding any funny experiences as well as images he was happy with.

"I have. Was up before dawn this morning and got some interesting shots. I'll show you in a few minutes." He opened the wine and poured the deep red liquid into the glasses. "Anything on your website?"

"There's a query from a couple in Minyip. Why does that sound familiar? Anyway, they have their wedding set for one week before Christmas. What do you think about me accepting?"

John brought the glasses over and sat opposite. "No reason why not. We can leave early the next day and be back in Rivers End that night for our Christmas preparations. And Minyip is familiar because it's been a location for television and movies. In fact, it would be great to visit so can we make sure we're there a couple of days early to do some touristy things?"

Daphne's eyes lit up. "Of course! And now we'll have some time to rewatch some episodes of the Flying Doctors ahead of visiting because I'm sure now that was filmed there. What a treat."

They raised their glasses. "To Minyip!"

For a few minutes they worked on their respective laptops. Daphne was typing rapidly with a smile on her face and she finally had relaxed her shoulders. Talking to her clients always made her happy and he exhaled a breath of relief. She glanced up and tilted her head with an unspoken question.

In response, he lifted his glass. "Are you enjoying the wine?"

"It is yummy. I've told this lovely couple I'd be honoured to officiate their wedding and directed them to the next part of the process, so that's me done for the evening. What about you?"

"There's a comment here from the last blog entry which I thought you'd like to hear. It was the one about you helping solve the crimes in Little Bridges. Shall I read it?"

Daphne closed her laptop, picked up her wine glass, and nodded.

"How thrilling to hear the outcome of what must have been a scary time for the people involved. Be proud of yourself, Daphne, because you made a difference. But, please, dear friend, try to stay away from danger because you are so special to those who know you. All our love, Elizabeth and Angus."

There was a sad smile on Daphne's lips when he looked up again. "Oh, I'm sorry. I thought you'd like to know our friends are keeping an eye on us from afar."

Elizabeth White and Angus McGregor were close friends of theirs who ran Palmerston House, a beautiful old home-turned-bed and breakfast, in Rivers End.

"I'm not sad. At least, I don't want to. Sometimes I realise how far we are from home and I miss it. I miss them." She took a quick sip. "And I'm going to do what they say. Not get into any dangerous situations again."

Something told John she was talking about more than avoiding killers. Her eyes were on her glass, not him. There was a tremor in her tone that only he would ever pick up. What had spooked her at the show?

"I'm pleased to hear you say that. With all the events of today, I'm hoping things are quickly resolved and we can resume our journey to the next wedding."

"We are in complete agreement." She raised her glass. "To resolutions."

Long after John had fallen asleep, Daphne stared at the ceiling, her arms hugging her body and her thoughts racing.

She'd wanted to talk to John about what happened at the show but had nothing to tell him. Some long-forgotten moment from her childhood had been unleashed by sights and sounds she'd hidden away and none of it made sense yet.

But I won't go back to the show. I just can't.

As for getting involved in the fallout from the funeral... no, she wasn't going to do anything except answer the questions the police wanted to ask and hope Edwina's funeral could go ahead very soon. She'd had quite enough of solving crimes and was going to put it all out of her head and get some sleep.

She turned onto her side and closed her eyes. Today had been far too long and too stressful.

You're safe now. John is here. And you can sleep.

She'd make pancakes for breakfast with some maple syrup. She shuffled a bit to get more comfortable and let her mind reach out for slumber. All was quiet.

Tap.

Tap. Tap.

Her eyes opened a little. A tree branch touching the roof?

Knock, knock, knock.

That wasn't any branch. John stirred. Surely nobody was at Bluebell's door at this time of night?

"Daphne? Are you in there?"

Swinging her feet over the side of the bed, Daphne reached for her dressing gown and found slippers for her feet. The voice sounded familiar and before she could call or knock again and wake John, she wanted to see who was there.

She peered through the kitchen window. A shadowy

figure was outside in a long, billowing dress. Daphne hurried to the door and swung it open.

"Ilona? Are you okay?"

Tears streamed down the other woman's face and her long hair was a tangled mess. Daphne climbed down and put her arms around her without even thinking. Poor Ilona. Had something else happened to make her awful day even worse?

"Daph?" John was at the door, rubbing his eyes. "What's going on."

"Ilona is here. Come inside, dear. We'll get you some water."

A couple of minutes later, Ilona was seated at the table with a box of tissues and glass of water, while John and Daph sat opposite. Ilona wiped her eyes with a handful of tissues and then drank the whole glass.

"I'm so...sorry to just turn up. I might be wrong, but I felt a real connection with you, Daphne. I feel we could be friends. And John, you were so kind earlier." She glanced from one to the other and then gulped. "I've had news. Terrible news."

Daphne and John exchanged a glance. Had Edwina been found and something dreadful happened to her remains?

"What is it, Ilona?" Daphne asked.

"It's Petra. She's dead."

A CHANGE OF HEART

Daphne gasped.

Ilona nodded, her eyes brimming with tears again.

"That *is* terrible news." John said. "Do you know...well, what caused it?"

"It had to be a reaction to the new medicine she's been on for her immune disease. There's no actual information yet. But I blame myself. I should have been there at the pre-funeral meeting. If only—"

"Now you listen to me, Ilona," Daphne patted Ilona's arm. "Unless you made Petra ill then you have nothing, not one little thing, to feel bad about."

"But there might be."

"Might be what, dear?" Daphne asked.

"Something to indicate foul play. Isn't that what you sleuths call it?" Ilona pulled a handful of tissues from the box and blew her nose.

John's eyes met hers. Sleuths? Seriously?

"Not sure we're following. Would you like more water?"

John was on his feet and had picked up her glass before she answered.

"Oh, yes. I'm parched. Let me start at the beginning. Well, not that I know if it is the real beginning but as much as I know. Petra is more than she appears. She always has been and I've known her for a good ten years or more since I moved here from Little Bridges. Despite being so sweet and bubbly, there's another side to her and not everyone liked it." She accepted the refilled glass from John with the flicker of a smile.

"What kind of side?" Daphne asked as John sat again.

Ilona glanced around as if checking for eavesdroppers. "She liked to know what everyone was up to. A gossip. And lots of people like to talk about what's going on but she took it to a whole new level by keeping a list of what she called misdeeds. And if that wasn't stupid enough, she told people she was doing this!" She lifted her glass. "At first there were some arguments, particularly at the RCCC, but then most people just ignored her."

"Ilona, do you think Petra was blackmailing anyone with what you called misdeeds? Would someone have meant her harm over their secrets?" In Daphne's experience, people sometimes killed for much less. If Petra's death was suspicious, on the same day Edwina's body disappeared, then something was terribly wrong in this little town. And hadn't Fred mentioned something about a recent scandal?

Despite the hour and the long day she'd had, a small rush of energy perked Daphne up. This might well be a mystery worth exploring.

"Well, if they did, then it will be someone among us. One of those she kept tabs on. Or at least, that's my take on it. Edie always said Petra West was trouble, but that was mainly because she once owed Edie quite a bit of money. For that matter, she was always borrowing ten dollars here or twenty dollars there and somehow all of us indulged her even though she rarely paid us back."

A potential blackmailer who also owed money all over town. Petra West—according to Ilona—was a different person from the one Daphne met. But some people were very good at hiding their true selves.

John, with his cautious nature, wasn't as impressed. "Probably best to wait for the official results before anyone speculates."

He was right. Which sparked a question.

"I know this is a sad subject for you, dear, but with Edwina, Fred mentioned she passed away from natural causes. Would you mind sharing what happened to her?"

After taking another handful of tissues, Ilona nodded. "Nothing so dramatic as with Petra. She was gardening. At home. Apart from her shop, her garden was the big love of her life and she would spend hours out there, even until it was almost dark sometimes. Anyway, Fred went to visit the other night and couldn't raise her at the house. Sonia wasn't home either and for some reason he walked around the garden." A tear dribbled down her cheek. "There she was. Peacefully sitting on the ground against a stone wall. Gardening gloves still on. And deceased. She'd been diagnosed with a serious heart complaint a few months ago which she didn't broadcast and the doctor said it was a heart attack. Never even got to say goodbye."

Silence fell. Ilona dried the tears and stared at the table. Daphne wasn't sure what to say. The other woman's grief was contagious and Daphne's heart hurt for her. How awful for Fred to find Edwina and not even be able to render assistance.

"I really should go and let you both go back to bed. I'm sorry I disturbed you but I just needed..." Ilona stood with a sad sigh. "Although I like living in this area, there's nobody else I could talk to. Not now Edie's gone."

"Are you okay to get home?" John opened the door.

"Thank you, yes. I only live a short walk away and the fresh air will do me good." Ilona stepped onto the ground.

Daphne followed. "We can walk with you."

"Please, no. Besides, you are both in night wear and I don't want to inconvenience you more than I have."

"Then please take care. But can I just ask...was it normal for Fred to visit Edwina at night?" Daphne asked. "They were friends?"

"Friends? Not really. They used to be married."

Married. Which must be why Sonia listened to Fred at the funeral home.

"Sonia is his daughter?" Daphne asked.

"Maybe." Ilona walked away. "Nobody knows for certain. Good night."

Daphne wasn't certain if she'd slept or simply drifted in her thoughts during the hours until dawn. What she did know was there was a mystery tugging at her and depending on the outcome of her visit to the police station, she might have to delve into it.

She got up when John woke and they had a quick coffee together before he wandered off with his phone to take some photos. It was a pity they weren't near a waterway as he loved to fish and it helped him relax.

While John was out, Daphne opened a new notebook she'd recently bought. Her other one was almost filled with a mixture of the notes she always made before a ceremony, and quite a lot of pages dedicated to the events in Little Bridges. It was time to start fresh.

First though, she whipped up pancake batter and put it aside while she sliced a punnet of strawberries. The maple syrup bottle was almost empty so at the last minute she'd toss the berries in some butter and sugar and drizzle what was left over the top. And more coffee. Everything was ready to begin cooking so she took a few minutes to make some notes.

She titled the first page 'Edwina'. Some instinct told her the deceased woman was central to the subsequent disappearance of her body and the passing of Petra. But it was a long stretch of the bow to connect how.

"Start with why, Daph."

Why would someone remove an embalmed body from its casket before burial? She chewed on the end of the pen until she noticed what she was doing and wrote instead.

A prank

To hide something

To cause distress/payback?

For evil purposes

Daphne wasn't about to consider what those evil purposes might be.

"I'm back." John swung the door open and climbed up. "I smell strawberries."

"You do. I've made a pancake batter."

"Perfect." He dropped a kiss on her hair. "I see you are

making a list. Keep going and I'll freshen up and cook while you write."

"I don't expect you to cook!"

He didn't answer until he returned a few minutes later. "I enjoy flipping pancakes. And you can talk to me about your thoughts while I do."

How did I find such a good man?

John heated the crepe pan and tossed some butter in. "Quite a shock about Petra. What do you think?"

"I have the strongest feeling her death is connected to Edwina's disappearance. And I was trying to work out why her body went missing." Daphne read out what she'd written. "Anything I've missed?"

"Ilona said Petra collected information about people. Bad information. What if Petra, or even a third party using Petra's notes, forced someone to do it?"

Daphne wrote down 'blackmail'. "Still doesn't give us an idea of who it might be."

"Not yet." He poured batter and gave her a quick smile. "If there is a crime behind any of this, I imagine you will put some ideas together. What about the other people you've met? How do you view them?"

Good question. "Bit early to rate them as suspects because we don't even know if—or what—crimes have been committed. But I have formed some opinions."

John didn't say a word and Daphne had to smile to herself. He knew her so well.

"I think a few locals have something to hide. Fred. Sonia. Amanda. Tracy. And Desmond. Mostly him so far because he is hiding whatever compelled him to paint Edwina against her wishes. On the other hand, Ilona means well but her grief is clouding her judgement, I feel. She's seeing things that might not be there."

"Quite a few people with something to hide. Should I do something with the strawberries?"

Daphne slid out from behind the table. "Those pancakes look fantastic. Just toss the strawberries in some more butter and a spoon of sugar. I'll get our plates."

When they sat down to eat, their plates were pretty as pictures.

"Thank you, John. I love having breakfast with you in Bluebell."

"Me too. Have to admit I'm enjoying our nomadic life even if it does seem to lead us to some strange events. Events which I thought you said you weren't getting involved in."

True. But Ilona's revelations intrigued her. She picked up her fork. "I'm not."

"So, what about your notes?"

"Them? One never knows when the written word will come in handy. But mark my words, we'll be out of this town before you know it and then those notes will be relegated to a page called 'never happened'."

QUESTION TIME

The police station in Shady Bend was an old stone cottage converted into one large room with two desks. There were a couple of closed doors which might have been a kitchen and bathroom or even an interrogation room, but none had signs. Between the front door and the main room, a wall had been removed and a counter added, along with a locked access door.

At least, it had a lock but when Daphne and John arrived, the door was propped open with an old boot.

"Come in." Adam was finishing a phone call at a desk and gestured to two chairs on the opposite side. "Right. That's very helpful. Yep. Ring me once you know." He hung up and smiled. "Thanks for coming in. That was regarding Petra West and I'm afraid the news isn't good."

"She passed away."

Adam leaned back in his seat. His brows raised.

"We had a visit last night from Ilona with the sad news." Daphne said.

"Ilona told you. Interesting. Did she happen to mention where she got her information?"

John shook his head. "She was pretty upset and didn't mention it. Do you have the cause of death? I mean, only if you are allowed to say."

"No. Yeah. Toxicology isn't back. Thinking it's some kind of reaction or overdose, whether intentional or not and perhaps a prescribed drug. Which is one of the reasons I appreciate you being here early. With this development, I've got some questions about Petra as well as Edwina."

"Most happy to help." Daphne said. "Can I ask a question?"

Adam straightened, pulling his chair closer to the desk. "Go ahead."

"What do you think happened to Edwina?"

He grimaced. "Wish I knew. We have tracker dogs on their way and will do a proper sweep of the bushland around the funeral home. At least it might give us an idea if she was carried on foot for any distance or put into a car."

"Any theories?" Daphne pressed.

"That is two questions. But no, I'm not at the theory phase. Still at the 'what the heck happened' with a dash of 'what possessed someone to do this?' phase." He grinned and put his fingers on the keyboard. "My turn. I've been busy asking a lot of questions, but they've been of people who live in the town and knew Edwina. Most were close to her one way or another and either in a state of shock or hiding something. Too early to tell. So, your take on the day might insert some much-needed clarity."

"Where would you like me to start?" she asked.

"Can you go back over what you've already told me from

when you arrived at the funeral home? From the first meeting."

"I had a mid-morning appointment with Fred, Sonia, and Tracy. The purpose was to go over the ceremony I'd drafted based on information sent through by Fred in a message. Due to the short notice, I had prepared a fairly generic document so was looking forward to having some input from Sonia because of her relationship to the deceased. We were in the funeral home in the reception room. There was some discussion about people who wished to speak at the funeral—Tracy, Desmond, and Ilona. And the last wishes of the deceased." Daphne said.

"Which were?" Adam asked.

"Gifts to the mourners who attended the wake. I believe they were from her shop. A table was prepared filled with bottled goods, small pieces of artwork, framed tapestry and the like."

"Ah. I saw the table at the funeral home." Adam stopped typing to look at Daphne. "Did you see Edwina? Was it an open casket?"

Daphne shook her head. She'd have not wanted to view her if it had been open. "My understanding is there was no viewing."

Was she even in there?

"Adam, Ilona mentioned last night that Edwina was found in her garden. Nothing suspicious as she'd had heart problems for some time. Was there any kind of police involvement?" Daphne asked.

He reached for a file and flicked through. "Fred found her, realised she was deceased, and called her doctor. After examining Edwina, the doctor signed a Cause of Death certificate, which was straightforward and indicated natural causes. No need for us or even an ambulance. And Fred, being our only local funeral director, took care of everything else. Sonia would have been informed and approved Fred being responsible for her mother. Or there may have been a pre-existing arrangement."

The phone on the desk rang. "Sorry. Be right back." Adam answered as he walked to the back of the room.

John touched Daphne's shoulder. "What are you thinking? I can see your brain ticking over."

"Just gathering data."

"As long as you don't find yourself knee-deep in someone else's problems."

She knew what he meant. The last time she'd got involved in helping solve a murder she'd ended up putting herself at risk. Not that the events in Shady Bend were linked to any murder.

Unless Petra's death was intentional by someone else's hand.

Daphne forced her face into what she hoped was a reassuring expression. "Don't own any long boots so best to stay out of knee-deep situations. Do you think there's something familiar about Adam? He reminds me of someone."

"Funny you mention that. I got a sense I'd met him from the beginning. Must have one of those faces."

Adam returned and dropped into his seat with a sigh. "Sorry about that. Trying to get a bit more help up here but we're such a small town we rely on the bigger stations in surrounding towns for numbers and there's a blitz on the highway underway. Might be able to pull a couple of officers off it to assist but in the meantime, it is me and Constable Porter until the dogs and handlers arrive."

"Can we help?" John asked. "Never mind taking a walk in the bushland."

Daphne hid a smile. So much for staying out of things.

"Very kind of you to offer, John. We've already had a civilian sweep of the area but will keep you in mind if we need extra legs and eyes. When do you both intend to leave town?"

After exchanging a glance with John, Daphne spoke. "It depends on when I can perform the ceremony. I would like to speak to Fred about the possibility of holding it regardless of Edwina's whereabouts but I'm not certain on the protocol and have no wish to offend."

With a short laugh, Adam returned to the keyboard. "Guarantee you will offend someone in Shady Bend regardless of your intentions. I've worked in quite a few places in my time and this one takes the cake for being contrary. Nice people but they work against each other a lot of the time."

Daphne filed that away as Adam continued.

"But you have another appointment coming up?"

"I do." Daphne chuckled. "At least, *they* will say 'I do'. I just tell them when to say it. And yes, in four days I have the great honour of marrying a lovely couple in Benalla. We have to leave by Friday morning in order for me to meet with them on Friday afternoon."

Hands off the keyboard, Adam tilted his head as he looked at Daphne. "You have a pretty special job. I know a few celebrants and usually they stay close to home. As Ilona does. Makes sense really as there is always something happening to keep her and those like her busy. But you get to travel as well. And bring—I imagine—your own special brand of love to those who need it."

Oh my.

"She certainly does, Adam. I've known Daphne since high school and there is no other person I know who seems to understand what a person is going through and finds exactly the right way to comfort or support them. And while I would rather she only does happy ceremonies, the care she gives to those grieving is something to behold."

Although the wonderful words warmed her heart, they also made it hard to speak.

With a quick smile, Adam returned to the keyboard. "Back to my questions. You finished at the funeral home. What was next?"

She licked her lips. "Ilona was waiting for me outside the funeral home to have a quick chat about her speaking at the funeral. Then no sooner had we got to Bluebell than I got a call from Fred. He asked if I would go to the pre-funeral get together to meet the pall bearers. So, after a quick lunch and change of clothes, I arrived to find the room transformed for the wake."

"With the table?"

"Yes. All the gifts on a central level and lots of food around the sides."

Adam stopped typing to flick through his notepad.

"You mentioned who else was there. Fred. Zeke. Petra. Tracy. Desmond. Amanda." Adam read his notes from their chat at the cemetery. "Amanda wasn't a pallbearer. Earlier, you suggested a feeling she wasn't welcome. Why is that?"

"She stood outside the door at first, then came in."

Amanda had said something odd when she'd thought nobody was close by. Something in response to Tracy's toast. The words evaded Daphne but they'd been uncomplimentary. With nothing concrete, there was little point mentioning it.

"And there was a small incident between Tracy and Amanda, more of an accident." Daphne said.

"Go on."

"Tracy was carrying a tray with glasses of champagne. I declined to have any, I mean, with such an important ceremony ahead it wasn't appropriate. But Amanda said she'd like one and when Tracy walked away without giving her any, there was a mishap and the tray was dropped."

"Mishap?" Adam stared at her.

"Amanda tried to help herself and the tray overbalanced. Petra cleaned it up. Tracy said something about trying to avoid a disaster and Amanda always finding a way. Oh, and Zeke tried to help but cut himself and Petra sent him off to clean it up. It was an accident but I got the impression Tracy was annoyed Amanda was there."

Yet again, the phone rang. After this call, Adam grabbed his keys from the desk. "Apologies. Dog squad is at the funeral home so can we continue this later?"

A few more minutes and Adam drove off after locking the station. Daphne and John stood on the footpath. Across the road was a café and without so much as a glance at each other they crossed over. If there was one thing they both needed it was a coffee and a chat.

TRUTH IN TALK

"This was a brilliant idea, love." Daphne stirred her coffee and smiled across the table. "Needed to have something to pep me up a bit after the interrupted sleep last night."

The café was almost deserted with only one other customer at a table and one person serving. Looking through the window, John saw the odd car drove by but the street wasn't as busy as he had seen previously.

"I wonder where everyone is."

John grinned. "I was thinking the same thing. Seems a bit on the quiet side. Are you sure you wouldn't like one of these pastries?"

She shook her head. "You go ahead. I'm fine."

"What if we find somewhere nice for dinner tonight? Can't see us leaving today so we might as well enjoy the local fare." John suggested.

"I would love that. Although Shady Bend isn't on the map for its culinary delights, I have a feeling it is under promoted. After what we saw at the show, I'm excited about trying some of the locally made products."

There was movement across the road near the police station as a car pulled up and immediately, a couple climbed out. Both were in jeans, T-shirt, and peaked caps which were pulled down over their eyes and they were too far for John to know if he'd come across them. And it wouldn't matter, except for the way they huddled together part way along the path to the station, looking past each other and back to the road. Not looking. Checking.

"Are you wondering what they're up to?" Daphne asked.

She was also watching the couple, her long fingernails tapping the handle of her coffee cup. Something about the events in this town warned of coming trouble. Not for them, but among the residents. So many at odds with each other and such tension now that one of their own had disappeared and another had died. Daphne wouldn't be able to let go.

"I am. Do you recognise them?" He asked.

"I think the man is Zeke. He works for Fred. The height and build is right but I can't see his face or hair. But the woman is Tracy. I'm certain."

After another check around them, the man scurried to the station, his head down. The woman returned to the footpath and gazed one way, then the other. At the station door, the man rattled the handle then disappeared around a corner.

Daphne had her phone out and was taking photos of them. The peculiar actions of the couple might be innocent, but John had the strongest feeling they were up to no good, and in a minute, he'd need to decide whether to call Adam.

A couple walking a dog headed towards Tracy and she pulled out her phone and spoke on it. She climbed back in the car and once the couple had gone past, the man raced to join her, sliding into the passenger seat.

"Not sure what we just saw. Looking for Adam?" John said. "Why are you screwing up your face like that?"

"That is definitely Zeke and Tracy. They were deep in discussion at the funeral after the casket fell and Petra collapsed. After the police arrived. He was edgy, kept looking at the casket. Yet Tracy was abrupt in how she spoke to Zeke at the pre-funeral meet. Bossy. Bordering on rude. And then there's the apparent dislike between Tracy and Sonia yet we both saw them laughing last night like best friends. Makes one wonder about what Tracy is up to."

It did.

Tracy got out of the driver's side and headed their way. Daphne was suddenly busy stirring her coffee again. If she wanted to avoid being noticed, it didn't work because Tracy saw them both through the window.

She pushed the door open with a bright, "Well, hello you two. Enjoying our little town?"

"Tracy! How nice to see you, dear." Daphne sounded welcoming and John had to admire her ability to make other people feel comfortable.

"Those coffees smell good. Back in a minute."

The minute Tracy stepped to the counter, Daphne leaned towards John and whispered. "Let's find out what she knows."

"Daph."

"It can't hurt."

There was little point objecting. Daphne had a look in her eyes. A glint of curiosity which he knew accompanied her love of puzzles.

"Right. I've ordered mine so might as well catch up

while I wait." Tracy dragged a chair from another table and sat at theirs. "Nobody has found Edwina yet and Petra died. Did you know?"

John nodded, a little shocked by her indifferent tone. "We spoke to Leading Senior Constable Browne this morning."

"You did? Do you know where he is? Even better, where Porter is because I have information for her and the station is shut." She gestured across the road. "Don't want to sit around waiting."

Daphne's lips were pressed together and she gave John the faintest shake of her head. It wasn't their place to say. Not that it was likely to be a secret, but even so.

"No idea? I'll ask someone who does." Tracy tapped at her phone. "Did you have fun at the show? As a judge I'm disappointed so far. The quality of the preserves was particularly ordinary this year which isn't surprising."

"Why is that?" Daphne asked.

"Obviously because Edwina hadn't entered anything. Or she did, but it wasn't displayed posthumously. She generally won most categories and that irked the others." She laughed shortly. "The funny thing though is there has been a rumour lately that she didn't actually make any of them."

John feigned surprise. "Is it just a rumour?"

Tracy raised both eyebrows. "There's *always* truth in talk."

Daph's favourite saying.

"If that is the case, who did make them?" Daphne hadn't blinked an eyelid. In fact, she didn't take her eyes off Tracy. "And what did she usually enter?"

"Second question first. Preserved fruit, from her garden. Jams. With fruit from her garden. Oh, and she and Desmond swapped fruits as he has a decent orchard. Chutney. Her secret sauce. And oil paintings."

"Well, that's a bit different." John said.

"Never saw her paint anything and I always suspected poor Desmond did them for her and then the paintings he signed as his were inevitably beaten for best oil. Perhaps that is why he did that preposterous painting of her this time."

"Anyone else involved, or just Desmond?" Daphne asked.

A puzzled expression crossed Tracy's face. "It is a mystery. Not Desmond when it comes to bottling, but someone close to her. I'd say Sonia if it wasn't so funny. Petra was one of her fiercest competitors. And Ilona is useless. Maybe she got someone in another region to make them and passed them off as her own." She shrugged. Her phone beeped and she checked it. "Adam is at the funeral home with the canine team. Group chat has its upside. But he's not going to find her."

Daphne straightened. "I beg your pardon?"

"If our law-abiding, never-put-a-foot-wrong Adam wanted to find her, he would have already." Tracy pushed her chair back and stood. "I'll find Porter. At least she takes me seriously." She started to leave then turned back. "Oh, I was being sarcastic about Adam. He's crooked and I expect he had something to do with Edwina's disappearance."

With that bombshell dropped, she collected her coffees from the counter and left with a 'Cheerio' as she exited.

As much as Daphne had hoped to avoid Tracy, there was plenty to interest her from their conversation. It irked her that the woman believed Adam was crooked and she'd have liked to ask why.

John paid for their coffees and they set off for a walk around town, arm in arm.

The morning was getting a bit busier with a few more cars passing and it occurred to Daphne that it was still early. Not even ten o'clock. No wonder the place wasn't bustling. If it ever did.

"Shall we see what shops are here?" John asked.

"It won't take long, as the population is only about four hundred. I looked it up."

Beside her, John smiled and she squeezed his arm. "Thanks for your help with Tracy."

"Didn't do much."

"Sure you did, love. Asking her if it was just a rumour about Edwina not making her own goods. Have you considered acting? The surprise on your face was a sight to behold."

His smile turned into a lopsided grin. "You were pretty good yourself."

"Thanks. But she's right. There is always truth in talk. I've always said it. If you cast your mind back to when Christie first walked into our agency, I told her then there was speculation about her great aunt that deserved closer inspection."

"And I suggested it was old gossip to stay away from."

"And *I* was right." She smiled to herself. "Look at all the love and happiness which resulted from following the speculation."

John chuckled. "I give up."

"Besides, the world isn't filled with straight forward answers. The truth about a situation is often clouded by the passage of time or misunderstandings." Daphne stopped smiling. "Even by lies and deception. If everyone was truthful, we wouldn't need to rely on gossip or speculation." Her stomach tensed as sadness crept into her heart. "Why can't people be honest?"

John stopped them both beneath a tree and rested his hands on her shoulders. "This isn't about Shady Bend, or even Rivers End, is it, doll?"

She shook her head. If she answered, she might blurt out the words she'd kept buried for so long. It wasn't John's fault but if she brought up the past—that particular part of the past, he'd blame himself for not trying harder to help her find the truth about her family.

"Daphne Agnes Jones, my sweetheart. I'd give anything to help you find the truth. And I know we lost momentum thanks to building the business up. But the few occasions I've suggested we hire a private detective or the like, you've said no."

This was true. The shock of discovering the man on her birth certificate wasn't her father still resonated after all these years yet she'd come to terms with never finding her real dad. Too many roadblocks had stopped her original search. And the other loss, the foster child she yearned to see again, was another dead end. Privacy laws had to be respected.

"There isn't any point." Daphne whispered. "Sometimes it just hits me again but then I remember I have everything I need." She wrapped her arms around his waist and leaned against him. "I have so much to be thankful for. Our friends. Enough money to live a good life. Bluebell. And you."

John's arms held her tight against his chest and his heart pounded loudly.

"I'm really okay, John. I promise."

If only there was a way.

"And I think we should go and see if Edwina's shop is open." She gently extricated herself from the hug. "Instead of getting all silly, I'd like to gather some more information. Just in case."

There was doubt in John's eyes. She'd worried him.

"I mean it. I'm okay and we're okay. And I would love to track down some of the delicious looking apricot jam from the show last night." She said.

He took her hand. "We'll find that jam. And see what secrets are lurking within this shop of Edwina's."

LITTLE SHOP OF SECRETS

Without a doubt, *Edwina's Secret Sauces & Special Supplies* was one of the quaintest shops Daphne had ever seen. Built from bluestone, it had an iron roof painted dark red to match the timber window frames and door. Two windows were on each side of the door with inviting displays of products.

The door was open and aromas of dried herbs and lavender mingled with spices. It was enough to encourage anyone inside and Daphne and John didn't hesitate.

The interior was every bit as charming as the outside, with wine barrels set up as display tables and a counter made from recycled timber. The floorboards creaked with every step and in the background, a sound system played a track with tranquil raindrops then changed to waves on a beach.

"Oh, this is a darling little shop." Daphne said. "We might be here longer than planned."

"I think we might."

"Are those preserved lemons?" Daphne asked.

"They certainly are! And the best in the country if you ask me."

Daphne and John turned to see who spoke. A young woman, mid-twenties at the most, slipped an old-fashioned shopkeeper's apron over her head and smiled as she tied the strings around her waist. Even her eyes sparkled as she crossed the short distance from a back room to where they stood.

"Welcome to the shop. I'm Constance."

"Nice to meet you, Constance." John said. "This is my wife, Daphne, and I'm John."

"Visiting Shady Bend for the first time?" she asked.

"Do we look like tourists?" Daphne smiled.

"Oh, I grew up here and have worked in the shop for years plus I have a great memory for faces. Don't remember seeing you before, although," she gazed at Daphne. "There's something familiar about you."

And you.

Constance had the warmest brown eyes in a pretty face shaped like a heart. There was a streak of red in her shoulder length dark hair. A bit like Daphne's. Which is probably why she seemed familiar.

"Is there anything in particular you'd like to see, or would you prefer to browse in peace?" Constance asked. "I can discreetly stand behind the counter ready to pounce at your command."

Much to her dismay, Daphne couldn't find any words. Her throat constricted and she nodded. What on earth was going on?

John jumped in. "Daph saw some apricot jam at the show last night. It looked delicious, so do you have any here?"

Constance grinned. "We sure do. In fact, we have over fifty flavours of locally made jam. Almost as many preserves, and yes, those are preserved lemons but they also have a special ingredient which is a touch of ginger. As for relishes and sauces...don't get me started." She hurried to a shelf and reached for a jar. "Apricot jam. One jar? Ten?"

Daphne laughed aloud and her mood shifted. "One will do, thank you. And one of the preserved lemons. What else do you recommend?"

"I recommend experiencing our tasting plate. What if I set one up for you both while you have a look around? Anything either of you are allergic to, or dislike?" With a jar in each hand, Constance headed to the counter.

"No allergies we're aware of, but I'm not keen on rhubarb."

"I'll be honest. Nor am I. Leave it to me and I'll find some goodies." Constance disappeared into a back room.

"You okay, Daph?"

"I am. Had a little moment when I felt a bit emotional but then I realised why. Constance reminds me of Belinda. Same delightful way of speaking."

Belinda was the daughter of one of Daphne's close friends in Rivers End, a bright and bubbly young woman who used to help her mother in the local bakery and now worked for Christie in her beauty salon.

John nodded. "I know what you mean. Both of them have such a friendly approach and don't mind being a little cheeky. Perfect for a shop like this. But I do have a question. Something occurred to me when Constance mentioned she didn't remember seeing us."

"Why wasn't she at the funeral?" Daphne asked. "If

she's worked here for a long time for Edwina, surely she'd attend the funeral?"

"You'd think so."

Daphne and John enjoyed a few minutes browsing laden shelves, selecting a jar of plump cherries and a bottle of locally made olive oil.

"Right-e-o," Constance announced. "These are some of my favourites and are very popular." She placed a wooden board onto the counter. "There are three sweet offerings and three savoury. And a delicious little pickle that goes very well with the cheese I've added."

It was a good thing Daphne hadn't taken up John's earlier offer of a pastry. What a treat this was with tiny dishes with miniature spoons, a few slices of a hard cheese, and some small pieces of crusty white bread.

"Locally made bread. In fact, everything here is made within a thirty-minute drive of Shady Bend, so try a bit of everything." She collected some napkins. "I suggest a piece of cheese on the bread topped with the pickle. And then the same but with the other options. The sweet ones are lovely popped straight into the mouth. Oh, wait a min, I forgot something."

Constance vanished into the back room and in a moment emerged carrying an unlabelled sauce bottle. She poured a small splash of creamy, bright yellow sauce onto the plate and the aroma drifting up was something Daphne had never experienced. Sweet and savoury all at once.

"Dip a piece of bread in the sauce and tell me it isn't the best thing you've ever tasted."

Daphne did. The instant the sauce touched her tongue, layers of flavour played with her tastebuds. She closed her eyes to enjoy it.

"Told you. There's something special about this one. What do you taste?" Constance asked.

Eyes open and mouth sadly empty, Daphne considered the question. "Lemon but not too tangy. Honey but not too sweet. Something earthy. Reminds me of thyme. What is it?"

With a big smile, Constance nodded. "Correct on all three counts. But there are four other ingredients and depending on what the sauce accompanies, you'll enjoy other aspects of it. It goes beautifully with most vegetables but is also special over homemade ice cream."

John dipped a second morsel of bread into the sauce. "Why haven't we seen this on supermarket shelves?"

"Oh. It's a private recipe." Constance said. "Not for mass production. I can sell you one bottle but we have to limit it as there are only a few bottles left."

"Yes, please. Does it have a name?" Daphne already had a sneaking suspicion. There'd been mention of a secret sauce and surely, this had to be the one. "And who is behind the recipe?"

Oddly, Constance blushed and turned her head away. "Um, I should get some water for you both." She collected two bottles of water from a fridge behind the counter. "The recipe belongs...belonged to the owner of this shop." She finally looked at Daphne. "The former owner. Edwina Drinkwater. She recently passed away so I'm not completely sure what will happen to the shop. Or the sauce."

"Dear, I need to come clean." Daphne said. "I was at the funeral. Edwina's. As the celebrant. So John and I visited here because other people said it was such a lovely shop and it is."

"Oh." Constance said. "You probably are wondering why I wasn't at the funeral. I had to be here. Nobody would tell me if I could go to it and Sonia said the shop needed to keep trading. So, I stayed here." There was a glisten in her eyes. "I'd have liked to be there. Edwina was good to me."

Daphne patted her arm. "As it is, you didn't miss the funeral. I expect things will resolve and I'll perform the ceremony and you'll have another chance to go to it."

Constance gazed at Daphne. "I have to do what is right for the shop, though."

"I'm sure if half the town is at the funeral, then you closing the shop for an hour won't be a big ask. Is Sonia taking over from her mother?"

"Probably not. Sonia doesn't like the shop very much but it does pay the bills. Most likely it will be sold. Tracy has always said she'd love to get her hands on it."

Another customer came in.

"Please excuse me, and enjoy the platter."

Daphne's phone beeped as her hand hovered over the plate and she reluctantly reached into her handbag instead of taking another bite. The morsels of flavour were enough to make a person want to stay here all day.

Not to be.

"John? Fred's asking if I can go to the funeral home to discuss Edwina."

He looked as reluctant to leave as Daphne felt. But he nodded. "Let's finish this though and buy what we want. Another few minutes won't hurt, surely?"

"You are a man after my own heart. No point leaving behind what Constance went to such trouble to prepare for us. What are you looking at?"

On the counter behind Daphne was a display of postcards. John's eyes kept going to one on the top row and

Daphne turned to take a better look. It was an old house in a pretty garden.

"I saw this at the show. Much bigger of course, and I was struck by the contrast between house and garden."

"Oh, that's Edwina's place." Constance had finished with her customer. "Sonia takes nice photos and has the best ones made into postcards to sell. Edwina loved her garden a lot and when not here in the shop, was usually pruning, planting, or painting an oil of it." She took one and turned it over. "See, photo by Sonia Drinkwater. Here, have this one. There's a whole box out the back."

"That's very kind of you, but I will pay for it. Also, we have to meet someone so can we gather some goodies?" John asked, accepting the postcard with a smile. "Our visit has been wonderful."

"I'll find a nice big bag to put your many purchases in." Constance grinned. "What would you like?"

While John paid, Daphne took a quick look at a row of paintings near the door. On a higher shelf were oils on canvas without frames, each about the size of a paperback. The theme was flowers of many types from roses to sunflowers.

"Curious." She murmured.

"Ready, love?" John picked up a brightly patterned woven bag, laden with jars and bottles each wrapped in tissue paper.

"Constance, thank you for making our visit special." Overcome with a need to hug the young woman, Daphne managed to lift a hand to wave instead. "I hope we see you again soon, dear."

"Oh, me too! Please come back before you leave town." Constance picked up the board and sauce bottle. "You are most welcome any time."

Back on the street, John and Daphne retracted their steps to the car. The morning was warming up but not unpleasantly and the shops were busier. They made it back to the car before either spoke.

"You're very quiet, Daph. Feeling okay?" John put the bag into the boot.

"Me? Yes, yes fine. Deep in thought." She climbed into the passenger seat and waited until John started the motor. "Did you see the small oil paintings in the shop? A different flower in each one."

"Can't say I did. Why?" He indicated and pulled onto the road.

"Remember I mentioned the painting of Edwina that Desmond entered in the show?"

"The one where she's looking in a mirror and her reflection is different from her face."

"Yes. What struck me at the time was there was a lot of understanding, even love, in that painting but Desmond assured me he felt no such things for Edwina. I wish I'd taken a photo...there was a sauce bottle in it which was like the secret sauce bottle. And the style of the flowers—and I'm no expert—looked a lot like those in Desmond's."

"You think he also painted the ones in the shop? Didn't Tracy say as much earlier?"

"She did. But Constance mentioned painting as one of Edwina's great loves so what if, well, now I am being silly, but do you think Edwina might have painted the one at the art show?" Daphne doubted herself the minute she spoke. There was no reason for Desmond to claim it as his own. Was there?

By now they'd left the main street and were approaching the funeral home. Up ahead, a couple of police vans were parked along the road. Adam's patrol car was in the funeral home driveway. John found a spot under a tree.

"Quite a presence here. Would you like me to come with you?" he asked.

"If you don't mind. I'm not sure how long I'll be though."

"Doesn't matter. And to answer your question about that painting. If you think it is a self-portrait, would it explain why you felt there was some understanding and love woven into the paint? After all, nobody knows a person more than themself, and Edwina might have had a strong sense of self. Just odd if somebody else put their name on it."

There were a lot of odd happenings in Shady Bend apart from a missing body and a sudden death. A secret sauce with no name and apparently nobody to make it anymore. A shop in limbo. Paintings done by one person, if she wasn't mistaken, but accredited to different artists.

"Better go and see what Fred is proposing." Daphne climbed out to a chorus of barking. "Let's hope that means the dog squad have found something."

INTO THIN AIR

The closer they got to the funeral home, the louder the barking. Partway down the driveway, one of the uniformed handlers had a magnificent German Shepherd on a tight hold as the dog strained to get closer to Fred, who was trying to talk over the noise to Adam.

John was a big fan of dogs and he'd thought a few times lately about suggesting to Daphne that they find a travelling companion. Loving them though didn't mean getting in their way when they were working, and the teeth on display from the angry dog reminded him this was a highly trained police officer. Not a civilian canine.

"Let's wait on the grass until we're called over." He and Daphne diverted off the path. "Fred seems to be the focus of our furry friend there."

"And doesn't Fred look upset about the attention!"

She was right. Fred glared at the dog and his hands were clenched. Fear possibly. And why was the dog upset? The handler leaned back on his heels, well in control of his dog and quite happy to let him bark. Something was going on which made no sense. Not yet.

Adam raised a hand to wave and Daphne responded with a big smile. She'd taken to the police officer almost on sight and John had seen how annoyed she'd been when Tracy made the comment about Adam being corrupt. It was a big statement and not a pleasant one. Daphne was an excellent judge of people and John trusted her gut feeling over anyone else's.

"Isn't he the most handsome creature?" Daphne nudged John.

What? Adam?

"Not sure if I feel the same, Daph."

"But look at his muscles."

Hadn't noticed.

"And the way he stands. As if he's ready to spring into action. One would never be afraid with him around."

John patted his stomach. He had to improve his fitness. Obviously.

"I know he's baring his teeth and looking all ferocious, but what a gorgeous doggie he is. Why don't we get another dog? Someone to travel with us?"

Oh. The dog.

With a chuckle at himself, John relaxed. "Happy to have a chat about it once we're back in Bluebell. And yes, he is a magnificent dog and a committed member of the police force."

The conversation between Adam and Fred ended. Adam joined the handler and the dog stopped barking, but watched every move Fred made as he headed up to John and Daphne. He glanced over his shoulder at the dog as he reached them.

"Thanks for coming on short notice. Sorry about that animal. No idea what got into it but it hasn't stopped trying to eat me since I walked outside."

"Have the police located Edwina?" Daphne asked. "There seem to be a few vehicles around."

"Not yet. The dogs can't pick up any scent, apparently. They've been through the funeral home and nothing took their fancy. Not even the food from yesterday which is untouched in the lounge."

Yet the dog was keen on Fred.

"Did they have something of Edwina's to use?"

"No idea, Daphne. All of us, the staff, stayed outside while the police went through with the dogs. Two of them are apparently searching down near the waterfall but Adam said they aren't picking anything up. As for that one." Fred motioned at the dog, who growled, "it must know I can't stand dogs."

John had nothing to say and from the way Daphne straightened her shoulders, neither did she. In his experience dogs were a good judge of character.

"Anyway, Adam says I can plan the wake. We can't do a funeral as such until this dreadful situation is resolved but at least we can fulfil Edwina's wishes and complete the wake. I'm going to speak to Sonia in a few minutes, but if she agrees, would you be willing to adapt your ceremony?"

"Yes, of course I can. I'll remove some of the parts more fitting with a funeral and emphasise the areas that remember Edwina. Is that what you have in mind?" Daphne asked.

He nodded. "Yes. And people can speak and get their gifts, eat, and toast Edwina. And then, even if the worst happens and her body isn't recovered, we'll have had a proper farewell and be able to move on."

Daphne pulled sunglasses from her bag and put them on. "Fred? Why wouldn't her body be found?"

"Just a bit strange that even the dogs aren't picking up a trace. But I'm sure it will be." He checked his watch. "If Sonia agrees and I can round everyone up, can we make a tentative arrangement for this afternoon? Let's say, four?"

"Fred, perhaps give Daph a ring once you confirm the time." John asked. He had no intention of letting Fred expect Daphne to drop everything on short notice again like he had before the funeral. It wasn't fair for Daphne to have a guestimate rather than firm arrangements and a tentative time was just as likely to be moved at the last minute.

"Sure. Sure. I have to go and see Sonia now. Thank you."

Fred took a wide berth around the dog before going inside. Adam patted the handler on the shoulder and made his way to the grassed area. The handler and dog disappeared around the back of the building.

"Sorry about running off on you both earlier." Adam said. "So far we've got exactly nowhere with the dogs, other than the one you just saw taking exception to Fred." He didn't seem at all concerned about the mutual dislike.

"Is there any news at all? Was the funeral home broken into?" Daphne asked, removing the sunglasses she'd only just put on. "Do you think it might have been an inside job?"

Adam's lips flicked up for a second. "Inside job sounds very television cop show. But there was an unlocked exterior door. No idea how long it was unlocked and none of the staff can explain it and sadly, there is no video surveillance on the property. There's no evidence of anyone touching the casket apart from Fred, his staff, and the pallbearers but it had been polished the morning of the funeral so fingerprints might have been unwittingly removed. The dogs aren't interested. Almost as if she never even..." he pressed his lips against each other.

"Never even arrived here?" Daphne suggested. "Do you know for certain she did?"

"Zeke saw her. Paperwork checks out. And Fred is hardly about to pretend Edwina wasn't in the casket. There's no reason for it. No. I'm certain we'll find her in due course."

Daphne opened her mouth as though to say something but closed it and nodded. She glanced at John.

"We might get going, if you don't need us?" John said. "Daphne will be back here in a few hours so needs some time to prepare for the wake. Anyway, if there isn't anything else?"

"Not for now. I have to assist the search for a while, what if I touch base later so we can finish the interview?" Adam said. "Sorry to mess you both around."

He strode away in the direction the police dog and handler went a few minutes ago.

Daphne watched him leave. "Something isn't right, John. Call me suspicious, but I have a feeling there is a whole lot more to this than meets the eye. Too many secrets for such a small town. And so many questions. Shall we go back to Bluebell so I can write them down, love?"

"Now, first off, who else was involved in the funeral home's processes?"

"Processes? Is there time for a pot of tea?" John held the kettle aloft.

"Yes please! So, I'm not an expert and I really don't wish to sound clinical or be offensive, but what else can I say other than body? Deceased might work. Edwina sounds too personal." Daphne tapped the end of her pen against the fingers of her other hand. She had her notebook open at the table.

"Say whatever sounds right to you." John said.

"Okie dokie. I believe that a deceased person is collected by someone from the funeral home and in Edwina's case, probably from her home and by Fred with another staff member or even the doctor to help. The deceased undergoes the embalming procedure and is moved to the casket at the appropriate time. I'm not sure of the time frame for each of these but the funeral was supposed to be yesterday which was what...four days after she passed away. So not long."

"Not sure where this is going. Would you like a biscuit?"

"I think there are a few of my cookies left in the cupboard. Butterscotch if I remember correctly."

John glanced inside. "No. Must have finished them. There's a packet of those chocolate covered ones. What if we open them?" He grabbed the packet. "I know you think they're not healthy but it's only now and then."

"Once this wake is behind us, I'll do some baking. Much nicer to have my homemade cookies on hand. But store bought will be fine. I was sure there were some of mine in there."

John must have eaten them and forgotten to mention it. At least she knew how much he loved her baking and it was no trouble to whip up a batch.

Once John brought the teapot, cups, and a plate of biscuits over, Daphne added a quick note to the paper.

Who saw the deceased?

"I wonder if Adam has asked Fred who else was involved with the deceased?" Daphne helped herself to a biscuit. "That might narrow down the list of suspects and—"

"Whoa. Suspects? Daph, I'm sure the police have things well in hand."

"Going to disagree. Adam has *no* idea. An unlocked door but nobody knows anything about it. Police dogs who cannot pick up the scent of someone who was at the funeral home for several days. A funeral home director who stated he thinks Edwina won't be found. And then there's Tracy calling Adam corrupt. Questions over who is the real artist. And what happened to Petra West?" Daphne realised her voice was spiralling upwards and clamped her lips shut.

John leaned over and kissed her on the cheek. "I pity any criminal who gets on the wrong side of Daphne Jones, celebrant sleuth."

Daphne giggled. She hadn't meant to get worked up but all it took was a couple of words from John and the frustration evaporated.

"Now, eat the biscuit while I pour the tea." John said. "I love how passionate you are about the truth. And I agree with everything you've said. Almost everything. But let the police do their job."

This wasn't anything new John was saying. Daphne had heard it more than once and in more than one situation. But while he was adamant about keeping her distance, more and more often he showed signs of being every bit as fascinated by small town secrets as she was. One of these days he'd have to admit he enjoyed putting puzzles together.

"I'll do my best, John."

His exaggerated sigh almost sent her into a fit of more giggles. She was little more than a kid in a grown woman's body sometimes. No point taking life too seriously. At least, not unless there's a murder involved.

SAYING GOODBYE

A few minutes before the wake began, Daphne put down her ceremony book to go in search of a glass of water. She'd been sitting in the reception room in a quiet corner to get things straight in her mind. Words were one thing, but making sure the emphasis was right was another. She'd spent much of the afternoon rewriting and finessing what she hoped was a memorable farewell for Edwina.

But not too memorable.

There was already plenty of negatives around the passing of Edwina Drinkwater, or at least, the aftermath and no doubt this would be spoken of for years to come.

The room was almost the same as when she'd been here yesterday. Goodness, it felt as though it was days ago, not just over a day. The perishable food for the wake was replaced with plates of fresh offerings but the raised middle remained filled-to-bursting with the now-familiar bottles and jars.

On one side of the room was a service door which she

imagined—and hoped—led to the kitchen. It was where Petra had gone in and out of yesterday, and while Daphne had rehearsed, staff from the funeral home had been a steady procession from there to set up the table.

Daphne went through it into a long, poorly lit hallway with several closed doors on either side. At the very end was another door with a built-in window such as restaurants employ to ensure a safer way of entering and exiting their busy kitchens. Daphne peeked through the window in case someone was coming the other way.

"Oh my!"

There were only two people at the far end of the kitchen and they were in an embrace. Actually, more than an embrace. Full on smooching and hands in places, well, where they shouldn't be in public. Daphne was not a prude but a funeral home kitchen was no place for such antics.

One of them was Zeke and for an instant, Daphne assumed the other person to be Tracy. Despite the big age difference, they'd been seen together a few times and Tracy spoke to the young man with a familiarity a step beyond a working relationship. So, when the kissing stopped and the woman moved away from Zeke, Daphne had to slap a hand across her mouth not to gasp aloud.

Amanda?

Not your business, Daph.

She stepped back and turned away. Being seen watching them would cause embarrassment and might lead to questions about her own motives. No, best to return to the reception room and manage without water for now.

"Daphne?"

Dandelions and ducks! She'd taken too long to make a

decision and been caught only a couple of feet from the door. Smile plastered on, she spun back.

"Hello, dear. I think I'm quite lost. Somebody said the kitchen was around here but I think all of these doors are locked." Not quite a lie. Or the truth. As if to prove her point, she turned the handle on the nearest door which wasn't locked and abruptly closed it. "Wrong room."

"Yes. That's where Fred keeps the embalming chemicals and protective gear. Not really a good place to be poking around."

Was that a touch of suspicion in Amanda's tone?

"The kitchen is behind me. Was there something in particular you wanted?"

"Glass of water. I normally keep a bottle close by but forgot to bring one."

With a sudden smile, Amanda stepped forward and linked her arm through Daphne's. "Why don't we go back to the wake and I'll get you a bottle of icy cold water? There's a stash of them in a fridge near the front desk and nobody will mind me getting one. After all, we can't say goodbye to Edwina without you."

Or without her body, really.

"Everyone is on edge." Amanda chirped away as if doing an update on the weather. "Fred is usually so calm but even he is snapping at people. Even at poor Zeke. I had to intervene."

Is that what they call making out these days?

Amanda continued. "But Fred calmed down when I said if we all stick together, we'll find Edwina. Even made the three of us a plate of scones to say sorry. And how much he appreciates our friendship and support under such awful circumstances."

Fred obviously didn't like upsetting people.

"May I ask you a question, Amanda?"

Amanda tensed, her arm tightening around Daphne's, but her voice remained cheery. "Ask away."

"When poor Petra collapsed, you said she'd need a priest...as if you knew she wouldn't survive. But what made you think that?"

They stopped close to the door back to the wake. Amanda stepped away, a hard expression entering her eyes. "You saw how she was. Short of having a stomach pump graveside, or an emergency response unit, Petra was a goner."

"Stomach pump?"

"Look. I shouldn't say this but the medical examiner will release the details at some point anyway. Petra had a condition and was trying a combination of new drugs. One of them had the side effect of—shall we say—lifting the spirits? My guess is being upset about Edwina, Petra took a couple more than she should to make herself feel better." Amanda said.

"I'm so sorry. You must have been a dear friend to know about her medication." Daphne fished.

Amanda screwed her face up. "Petra was a pest. Nice enough but she liked to be in everyone's business and wasn't above threatening to tell the community about what she'd dug up if you didn't loan her some cash or the like."

"Oh my! She sounds like a criminal. What if someone didn't like her making threats?"

"What. One of us killed her?" Amanda burst out laughing. "I can assure you we all pitied her. She was pathetic."

The door opened and Fred's head appeared. "There you are."

"Sorry, Fred. Just filling Daphne in on how Petra probably died." Amanda scooted past him. "I'll fetch you some water, Daphne."

Fred rolled his eyes. "Amanda has an over active imagination. Now, are you fine to start soon? People are arriving."

Daphne led the way. "Let's go and help everyone say goodbye to Edwina." There'd be time later to jot down these new revelations.

The ceremony went well. There were fewer mourners present than at the funeral, but they solemnly listened to Daphne, nodding in unison or breaking out in murmured agreement. People wore black with the same accent of colour requested for the funeral. Only Ilona looked different, with a shorter and fitted dress and braided flowers through her hair.

"The first person who wishes to speak is Tracy Chappell. Would you like to step up here, Tracy?"

Daphne moved to one side of the podium as Tracy worked her way through the mourners. She put a hand on either side of the podium and leaned forward. Was she about to unleash an impassioned sermon?

"Friends. And others. We are united by Edwina's passing. A few of us were close, dear friends of hers. Most though were only recipients of the wonderful wares from her shop, Edwina's Secret Sauces and Special Supplies. And speaking of her wares, I expect to confirm that I will soon be in possession of the recipe for her signature sauce and continue to make it in her tradition. Although a bit more commercially."

Constance was standing with Ilona and they exchanged a sudden glance. Tracy gazed in their direction and then focused on Desmond. More accurately, she smirked at him and his face reddened as he glowered back.

"But enough of me. Edwina put Shady Bend on the map for preserving. No town does it better and we prove it over and over by taking out so many awards around the state every year. If it can be preserved, bottled, sauced, jammed, or any number of other culinary techniques, then Edwina wanted it in her shop. We all knew Edwina as a tough businesswoman who stood up for what she believed. Even if it offended those around her."

"Tracy!" Fred whispered from the sidelines.

She rolled her eyes. "Righto. Time for me to let someone else speak. I'll miss the old girl. She might never have shared her secret sauce recipe with me until it was too late for her to see how successful it will be in supermarkets, but we had our good times. Hopefully, she'll stop hiding and hop back in her casket where she belongs."

A collective gasp rose from the mourners.

"Don't act all precious. Only saying what you lot would if you weren't so uptight. But while we're on the subject, if any of you have an inkling of what happened to her, tell Porter. And that's a wrap." Tracy stalked away from the podium to the back wall, leaning against it and taking her phone out.

Crossing her fingers that no other speaker would be so... blunt, Daphne nodded to Desmond.

He lumbered across the room, pushing his way through people who muttered and made space. At the podium he tugged on his tie to loosen it and wiped his forehead with a handkerchief. He sweated profusely. The room was uncomfortably warm with so many bodies in it and no air conditioning on but the staff didn't seem to notice.

For that matter, Fred had vanished. The door to the hallway clicked shut. Perhaps he'd had the same thought and gone to turn on the air con.

Desmond cleared his throat. "I am compelled to speak today. Should have been yesterday but some low-life took our Edwina from her rightful place. Here's a first. I agree with Tracy on this point. If you know anything at all, tell the police. Tell our Senior Leading Constable Brown. Or Constable Porter. But be honest." He dabbed his forehead again. "Edwina was my neighbour for decades and we might not always have seen eye to eye, but she was a good neighbour and raised a good kid." He scanned the room, finally resting his eyes on Sonia.

Daphne hadn't noticed her until now. Hair unbrushed, her face was set and her eyes vacant with no repeat of the manic laughter from the previous day. Her clothes looked like she'd slept in them.

"Anyway, one reason I wanted to speak was to make something clear. Some of you believe I've tried to buy Edwina's property and that she refused, straining our relationship. I'm here to say our relationship, in the past year, was close and we made a certain arrangement after her heart condition was diagnosed."

All eyes were on Desmond. Even Sonia blinked and took a deep breath. Tracy lifted her chin.

"People believe Edwina never made a will. Always said she didn't believe in them. But she was clear on what she wanted to happen after her death and in respect to her house and land, it was that I am to have first option to buy it." Desmond nodded as if it was a done deal.

"That's a lie!" Ilona burst out. "Edie wanted Sonia to have a place to live for as long as she wishes."

Desmond shrugged. "Did I say Sonia would have to leave?"

People whispered to each other. Fred appeared through the main door, glancing around and then joining Tracy, who leaned close enough to say something. Probably catching him up on what he'd missed in a way only Tracy could.

This wasn't going to plan at all. Daphne approached Desmond and spoke for his ears only. "If you have any special words about Edwina, please feel free to say them. I'm certain there will be time later to sort out Edwina's wishes."

Daphne hated any kind of confrontation but wasn't going to allow the ceremony to veer any further off track. For a moment Desmond studied her face and Daphne's heart thudded uncomfortably, but then he nodded and addressed the room.

"I apologise if I've upset anyone. It is an emotional time for us all. Just for the record, Sonia will always have security. And I will miss Edwina Drinkwater, even if she did believe she was a better gardener and artist than I."

He stomped away and people complained again as he pressed past.

"Our last speaker is Ilona."

Constance opened her mouth and Ilona touched her arm with a quick shake of her head. If Constance wanted to speak, then Daphne would make sure she had the chance, but it appeared as though Ilona didn't want her to. How strange. What was their relationship?

Ilona hurried to the podium and cast a sad glance at Daphne with a mouthed, *thank you.*

"Edie was my closest friend, but you all know that. For some of you, Edwina Drinkwater was simply the owner of a successful local business, a heavyweight in the culinary arts, and a respected, senior judge at many of this region's competitions. But to me, she was a warm and caring woman who put her heart into the community and would never turn a needy person away. And she did a lot to help the wildlife sanctuary. She leaves behind a beautiful daughter in Sonia, and darling, you made her so proud."

Sonia's eyes were on the floor.

"She also leaves behind the shop which has helped so many of us, either by being able to sell our products through it, or by enjoying its wares. Usually, a bit of both. I believe she had a different vision for her possessions than the ones mentioned earlier, but today is about celebrating Edie and I would like each of you to take a moment this afternoon to remember her in your own way." A tear ran down her face. "Goodbye Edie. I will never forget you."

As she made her way back to Constance, the mourners clapped and some touched tissues to their eyes. Sonia turned and left the room and a moment later, Tracy followed.

"Ah...um, would anyone else care to speak?" Daphne asked.

Ilona whispered something to Constance.

Nobody put their hand up or made moves to approach.

"On behalf of Sonia Drinkwater and the funeral home, thank you for attending today. Edwina requested all attendees have mementos to take home and I believe Fred is able to assist with this. Please spend some time here to celebrate Edwina's life and enjoy the delicious food and drink on the table." Daphne smiled and stepped away from the podium to a brief round of clapping.

She'd collect her bag and slip out and then, it was time to move on to a wedding. To a happier celebration.

PRESERVED

Back in the cemetery in Shady Bend, John stood at the spot where he'd been when he'd seen Ilona by the tree yesterday. Although he had a genuine interest in genealogy, there was more to his regular visits to cemeteries and graveyards than a hobby.

Daphne had another family somewhere. Her mother was no longer alive and her siblings lived on the other side of the country with sporadic communication, usually in the form of a Christmas card. It wasn't that they'd cut Daphne out of their lives, but the revelation that their father was not her father had raised many questions and the fallout of some of the answers changed everything.

Although Daphne rarely mentioned them, or the mystery of her birth certificate, it was a source of deeply kept sadness. Somewhere out there was her biological father, the one left off her birth certificate in favour of the man she'd grown up believing was her real dad.

John sighed. No point pondering the past. His goal was to find her father who somehow was invisible through the regular channels. No mention of him through the genealogy sites, nor even with Births, Deaths, and Marriages. He had some details thanks to Daphne's mother. A name. An occupation. And the frustrating knowledge the man had moved constantly around regional Victoria.

"Thank goodness for your new career, Daph."

While she performed amazing ceremonies, he researched and if she believed it was because he was interested in genealogy, then he let her. It wasn't a lie, but nor was it completely truthful. After all, if he couldn't find out anything to fill in the blanks in her life, then he'd never have got her hopes up.

This town was interesting. Tucked away off a main thoroughfare, it was an important part of a network of communities which shared resources. Apart from the produce, arts, and crafts, Shady Bend was known for its timber. Dense bushland surrounded the region but felling was part of a controversial history. These days, the unique flora and fauna was mostly protected, but fifty or sixty years ago, the timber trade had been considered respectable. And Daphne's father had worked in it, following the work from place to place.

John wandered from headstone to headstone. It was possible Alfred Browne was still alive so it was a sign of other relatives he sought. Alfred's parents or grandparents. So far, he'd found—and discarded—a dozen people called Browne since they'd begun travelling in Bluebell. Tomorrow they would leave Shady Bend and thanks to the bizarre events, he'd not been able to look for a local church where he often found old records.

"But there is Adam Browne."

All John needed was a couple of minutes alone with the police officer to ask a few questions. The man had mentioned he'd worked in other towns so might not even be a local but it was a chance worth taking.

His phone beeped as Daphne sent a message. He had an hour spare.

Going to the far side of the cemetery, John worked his way along rows, checking names on headstones. Many were related, as was so often the case with small towns where founding families expanded over generations.

He'd reached the final row before finding anything interesting. It was a small headstone and he had to bend down to read the engraving.

Moira Browne (nee Peters). Beloved mother of Constance and wife of Adam.

It was dated almost twenty years ago.

John straightened and wrote the information in his notebook. Constance had reminded him and Daphne of someone and now he knew, it was Adam. But Adam also seemed familiar and John couldn't work out why.

He glanced at his watch. Perhaps Adam would be at the police station and wouldn't mind a question or two.

"You're not leaving?" Ilona followed Daphne from the reception room. "I mean, why not stay for a bit?"

"I'd rather not intrude. The wake is for those who knew Edwina, dear."

"You must feel as though you do know her. Even just a little bit. Anyway, Constance has to leave and I'm feeling alone and it would be wonderful to have you around for a few minutes. If you could?" Ilona's eyes were intense. "And you are not intruding."

Daphne checked the time. John had made dinner arrangements in two hours but she wouldn't need long to change. "Let me just send a message to John and I'll be right in."

Ilona threw her arms around Daphne. "I'll make a little plate of goodies for you." She was gone before Daphne could refuse.

"Not sure my jacket will stay done up if I indulge in those goodies." Daphne muttered as she sent a message to let John know she'd be a bit longer.

He replied straight away.

Am gainfully busy. Be there in one hour.

"Gainfully busy? What are you up to, love?"

About to follow Ilona, her attention moved to raised voices from another part of the funeral home. Women's voices in loud, angry whispers.

None of your business, Daph.

Nevertheless, her feet somehow carried her in the direction of the argument rather than back to the wake. A hallway led around a corner where a sign pointed to the restrooms. A bathroom stop was a good excuse if she needed one.

The entire building was made up of hallways, corners, and closed doors. Daphne peeked down a narrow passage where a single light bulb cast eerie shadows as it blinked on and off. An icy shiver ran up her spine and she gripped her briefcase close to her body before stepping into the middle of the hallway. Might as well be bold.

"You shouldn't have said anything. Not about the recipe!"

Sonia's voice stopped Daphne in her tracks.

"Oh for goodness sake." This was Tracy. "The sooner everyone gets used to the idea, the less risk there is."

"Risk? You've put my future at risk by blabbering about it. All I want is to live in my cottage and be left alone but now Desmond and Fred will be breathing down my neck trying to pry the recipe from my hands."

A long silence. Daphne made it almost to the corner.

"So, you do have it?" Tracy said. "All this time, you've led us to believe you don't know where it is—"

"What I know is nobody's business." Sonia's voice faltered. "My mother kept her own secrets and now she's missing. Whoever took her has to be found, Tracy. It isn't right that she's not been buried."

Two sets of footsteps walked away. The women had gone.

"Unless she is."

Daphne spun around in shock. Amanda was behind her with a full-to-the-brim champagne glass in her hand and a peculiar expression on her face. Reminiscent of a child who has discovered where the lollies are hidden.

"Amanda. I didn't hear you."

"No. No, you were too busy eavesdropping." Amanda went past Daphne to look around the corner. "Not very nice of you. I'm beginning to think you were snooping around the kitchen before. Judging me for being involved with such a young man."

Best to ignore that.

"What did you mean? Unless she is?" Daphne asked.

Amanda drank half of the champagne in a couple of mouthfuls then flicked her eyebrows up and down. "Unless she is already buried. Somewhere else. Did anyone think of that?"

No. But now I am.

"Do you know something about it? Is this a rumour around town? In the group chat I keep hearing about?"

Amanda snorted. "Group chat. They kicked me out of it ages ago. Bunch of losers." The rest of the champagne went down her throat. "Do you know I was a respected member of a medical practice? Speaking of rumours, people like Tracy love to start them and keep them going. I've heard through the grapevine I lost my licence."

Daphne had heard it. "Not true?"

"Not true. I just choose not to practice anymore. Tracy loves dropping what she thinks is a bombshell but there is rarely any fact behind them." She touched her forehead with a frown. "Do you think it's hot in here?"

"Not here, but it was in the other room."

A couple of people from the wake went past chatting. Amanda leaned against the wall as if using it to prop her up and held one hand against her stomach.

How much champagne have you had?

"People didn't like Edwina. Only Ilona did, but she likes everyone. Tracy had an odd relationship with Edwina. Not friends but not enemies. Always trying to outdo each other with judging appointments and the like. As for Petra, she made a public accusation that Edwina was not making her own products. Jam in particular."

"What did Edwina say to that?"

"She threatened to sue. Got really nasty for a while with lots of sniping back and forth. Until Fred got in the middle of it."

"Fred? Because he was Edwina's ex?"

"I doubt that mattered. I think he was trying to win points in the hope of getting his hands on the secret recipe for her sauce. He came up with the idea of doing one of those blind tastings. Her jam against Petra's." Amanda rubbed at her stomach. "Scheduled as a fun event at the show, not that it matters now. Did you know Petra kept a little book filled with gossip?" Amanda raised the empty glass. Her hand was shaking. "Think I drank that a bit fast."

"Are you feeling alright, dear? Shall we go and sit somewhere?"

"Stomach hurts. Think I ate something a bit off. But I want to tell you about the book."

"What about it?" Daphne asked.

Amanda's face was turning bright red and sweat beaded on her forehead.

"She gave it to someone for safe keeping a couple of weeks ago. One of the police. But it backfired and someone is using it for their own means."

"Wait, one of the police is using the information in Petra's book?"

"Who else would have poisoned Petra?"

Amanda slid down the wall. "This isn't from a dodgy sandwich."

Daphne dropped to her knees at Amanda's side. "Tell me what's wrong?"

"Me. I did something...wrong." Amanda's eyes fluttered shut and she toppled onto her side.

"Help! Someone, please help!" Daphne screamed.

It was like Petra all over again.

Flushed, clammy skin. Barely breathing. Unconscious.

Daphne draped her jacket over Amanda's torso. She

hunted for her phone to call an ambulance as Fred ran around the corner.

"What the—" He skidded to a stop and grabbed his own phone. "Amanda! I'll ring the ambulance. Can you go and find Zeke? He has medical training."

"I should stay with—"

"No. No, I'll look after her." He reached a hand out to help Daphne up.

Her knees creaked as she stood and she grabbed her bag. "Where is Zeke?"

"Reception room. I think."

Daphne called John as she hurried.

"Ready early?" he answered.

"No. Yes. Its Amanda. She's collapsed. Same as Petra."

"Oh my goodness. Adam, we have to get to the funeral home." John said.

"Adam?"

"Sorry, Daph. I'm with him. Is an ambulance coming?"

"Fred said he'd call one but maybe call as well. In case he forgot." Or in case everyone in this town was out to get someone. "Please hurry."

She hung up as she entered the crowded room. People congregated around the long table and others sat on the stools in groups, some holding plates and others with champagne glasses.

"There you are!" Ilona appeared with two plates piled high with cheese, preserves, and scones. Daphne's stomach rumbled despite everything. "Would you like some champagne? There's plenty of bottles around."

Champagne.

Amanda had drunk a whole glass then collapsed.

Petra also had a glass yesterday and then collapsed an hour later.

"Everyone! Please, please give me your attention!" Daphne clapped her hands together and the conversations stopped as all eyes turned her way. "If you have champagne, I urge you not to drink it. Please put it down and wait until you are told it is safe to drink."

"Daphne? What on earth is going on?" Ilona asked. "I think you're scaring people."

She was. A number of people almost dropped their glasses in their rush to put them down. Others—including Desmond who took a long look at the bubbly liquid—held onto their glass.

"Does anyone know where Zeke is? We need some medical assistance."

"Zeke? Um, I think he's in the kitchen. But, Daphne, I don't under—"

Tracy appeared from nowhere and took Daphne's arm. A little too firmly for comfort. "For goodness sake, what is this nonsense about the champagne? Most of us have had at least a sip and now you're frightening people." She steered Daphne to the door leading to the kitchen. "Let's find Zeke but I want to know what this is about!"

Ilona was right behind and trying to calm everyone. "Just a slight hiccup! Champagne might be old...flat? Anyway, we'll arrange some fresh glasses so keep on enjoying the lovely food."

Unless it was the food!

Daphne tried to turn back but Tracy wasn't letting go and before she knew it, they were in the hallway.

"Right. What is going on?" Tracy released Daphne.

"Amanda has collapsed. Near the restrooms."

"Is that all?" Tracy rolled her eyes. "She's been getting stuck into the drinks since before the ceremony. Told you she likes her alcohol."

"No. No, she is in a bad way. Just like Petra, but Fred asked me to find Zeke as he has medical training."

Ilona hurried past to the kitchen, and returned almost straight away. "He isn't there. Nobody is."

"I'll call him." Tracy dialled.

A phone began to ring. Daphne followed the sound to the door she'd opened earlier. The one to the room with the embalming equipment and chemicals.

"Let me see!" Tracy pushed past Daphne and flung the door open. "Noooo!"

Zeke lay on the floor, phone in his hand and his eyes staring at the ceiling.

A TERRIBLE DAY

Daphne was right behind Tracy. It took a moment to process the scene in front of her. Zeke was lifeless. His skin was red and tiny beads of sweat peppered his forehead. His phone was in his palm. A champagne glass was shattered near the corner and a couple of plastic containers had fallen from the shelf. Had he grabbed at it to stop himself falling?

"Zeke. Zeke. No, no, no, no." Tracy moaned. She sat on the floor at his side and ever so gently closed his eyelids. "Not little Zeke."

"He's her nephew," Ilona whispered. "This can't be happening."

But it was.

Daphne found herself in the hallway, leaning against the wall rapidly blinking her eyes. The thudding of her heart filled her ears and her legs were like pillars of unmoveable concrete.

People ran down the hallway and piled into the room.

Cries.

Movement in and out.

Someone arrived with a first aid kit and Daphne let out a sob at the futility.

Poor Zeke was gone but what about Amanda?

Legs working again, Daphne retraced her steps. The reception room was in chaos. People were forcing their way through a bottleneck at the door. Desmond watched them from near the podium, still holding the glass of champagne.

"Is it true?" he asked.

Daphne had no chance of getting to Amanda until the door was clear. "Why don't you put that down. I am worried there's something wrong with it."

"Do you believe it is poisoned?"

"Um, no. Maybe. I don't know. But surely best to be cautious?"

He held it up again to peer at the contents. "How would one know? It looks like the cheap excuse of sparkling wine it is. Smells it. Almost everybody attending took at least a sip during a speech a few minutes ago."

"Who gave the speech?"

"Sonia."

Well, that was a surprise.

Desmond waddled to a side table and placed his glass on it. "She thanked us all for coming here. Said her mother would have been touched. And encouraged us all to collect our gifts before we left. It always takes her a bit of time to adjust to changes and she's doing better today."

"Do you know where Sonia is?" Daphne asked.

"She left as soon as she stopped talking. It was a bit odd. When she took off earlier, it was through the main door but she came back through the service door."

The opposite way Fred went earlier.

"Was Tracy with her?"

Desmond shook his head and his heavy jowls wobbled. "Tracy has a way of sneaking around so nobody knows where she's come from. She followed Sonia out. Then when you began banging on about the champagne, there she was again. Quite a talent."

Sonia and Tracy had left the area near the restrooms but Daphne had been between them and the main door. If Sonia returned through the service door, then there had to be another way through and she must have passed the room where Zeke was. Had he already been deceased? Or had she heard noises come from behind the closed door and kept going? Or had she killed him?

Get a grip, Daph. That's silly.

"I have to go and check on Amanda." She said.

"What's wrong with Amanda?"

"We were talking and she lost consciousness. Like Petra."

The doorway was clear now. Why had everyone been so quick to leave? Unless they thought it was dangerous here. Perhaps it was. Perhaps the champagne had nothing to do with this and something in the food, or the environment did.

A siren wailed in the distance.

Desmond headed towards the service door and Daphne went in the other direction. A handful of people lingered out here and they stared at her as she rushed past. Along the hallway.

Fred stood with Daphne's jacket looped over his arm and his eyes focused on the floor where Amanda lay.

His own jacket was over her head and shoulders.

Daphne covered her mouth with a hand as the enormity of this struck her.

Murdered.

Three people murdered.

What else could it be?

John parked a bit down the road from the funeral home. There were cars on both sides of the street and people congregated on the grassy area out the front. Adam was already here. The benefits of lights and a siren. He'd driven into the circular driveway and run into the funeral home.

An ambulance turned in and stopped behind the patrol car. Someone was there to meet it. One of the pallbearers from the funeral who worked for Fred. The man waved his arms around as the paramedics unpacked medical bags. He was agitated as he addressed them. "You're too late."

Alarming words. John sprinted.

Inside, the place was almost deserted. No staff to be seen and no Daphne. He was about to phone her when she came around a corner, head down and feet dragging.

"Daphne! You look so upset." He held his arms open and the minute she was close enough, he wrapped her up in them. "Oh, you're shaking. Tell me what happened to Amanda. You said she collapsed like Petra. The paramedics are here."

She mumbled something against his chest.

The paramedics followed the staff member in the direction Daphne had come from.

"See, they're here now."

Daphne pulled back so he was able to see her face. His heart dropped at the sadness in her eyes. "Too late, love. Too late for them both."

"Both?"

"We found Zeke as well. He was already gone."

"Let's go." He took her hand but she didn't move.

"I can't, John. I was with Amanda when she collapsed so there will be questions. And people need comfort."

"Which people?"

"Tracy for one." Now, her eyes glistened and he squeezed her hand. "Zeke was her nephew and she found him."

This was hard to take in. Three people in two days collapsing and dying in one tiny town. All associated with one funeral that went horribly wrong. Was there some illness spreading through the place? Or was it...

"Daphne. I think we should go outside and wait for Adam. This may be a crime scene."

To his relief, she nodded and let him lead her through the front door. Rather than join the other people, he found a bench not far from the entrance under a tree. For a few minutes they sat without speaking, Daphne gripping his hand.

The other police officer—Porter—arrived and instead of going into the funeral home, mingled with the people on the grass. Daphne paid her particular attention.

Why so interested, Daph?

People then began to leave the grounds. When they were all on their way, Porter headed to them and squatted in front of Daphne.

"You've had a bit of a shock, Mrs Jones. I'm Constable Porter. Beth. Everyone calls me Porter though. Adam let me know what happened and said I should ask if you can stay a little while longer. He wouldn't mind a word."

Daphne licked her lips. "We'll sit here."

"Thanks. I'll pop inside and see what's what." Beth straightened. "You should have some water. Try to relax."

Once Beth was out of sight, Daphne reached in her briefcase. "I will have some water. But relaxing is out of the question." She took a long drink then replaced the cap. "We need to be careful."

"Careful?"

She hesitated.

"Daph, I'm worried. I don't even know what happened in there or what you saw, so please, please talk to me." He turned to face her and touched her cheek with his spare hand. "You are my sweetheart and I hurt seeing you upset."

She leaned in to his touch and released a sigh. "I'm reconsidering this new lifestyle of ours. We seem to get ourselves into some dangerous situations."

"I'm listening."

"Certain comments today have been startling. Some about Edwina and her so-called secret sauce. Amanda suggested she is already buried somewhere else. Petra apparently gave her blackmail book to one of the local police and they have been using it for their own means. And I saw Zeke and Amanda kissing before the wake."

Unsure what to comment on first, John chose none of the above. Instead, he shuffled closer to Daphne and put an arm around her shoulders.

"You know what? There's plenty of time to fill me in later. Close your eyes for a few minutes and I'll let you know when Adam arrives."

As Daphne settled against him, John longed to get her back to Bluebell and be on their way. This wasn't the first time they'd come across tragedy and crime, but if he had his way, it would be the last. No more risk for his girl.

A little after seven, John set the table and invited Daphne to join him for a candlelit dinner in Bluebell. Going out tonight was a bit too much. It was great that both John and the restaurant were so flexible about changing to takeaway.

She'd had a shower after they got back half an hour ago while John went into town to collect their meal and she'd let the refreshing water wash away the worst of the feelings. For a few minutes she'd played with a treasured gift they travelled with, a snow globe depicting Rivers End, a reminder of the power of love, family, and home. Now, all she wanted was to sit with her husband and fill him in on what he didn't know.

"Ready?" he called.

"Almost." She gazed in the mirror as she brushed her damp curls. The warm evening air would dry them soon enough and she'd worry about straightening her hair tomorrow. She'd changed into loose pants and top. Perhaps they'd take a walk before dark and all she'd need to add would be some walking shoes.

"Oh, love, this looks just like a restaurant!" She gave John a kiss on his cheek as he opened a bottle of wine. "Tablecloth and nice cutlery and that lovely candle from Christie's beauty salon."

Their friend Christie had a line of scented candles, including the one on the table. 'Jasmine Sea' had special meaning to Christie and her husband, Martin, and brought the heady scent of the sea, mixed with a touch of jasmine, into the caravan.

"Please, take a seat and I'll pour us both a glass. I trust the white is to the lady's taste?" John poured with a flourish and Daphne giggled. He had a way of making everything special and just a little bit humorous and the latter was well and truly welcome. Wine poured, he served entrees kept warm in the little oven and joined her at the table.

"How lovely. I am sorry about not wanting to dine out as planned."

"I would have been more surprised if you had after such an afternoon." John picked up his glass. "To happier days."

"I'll drink to that!"

They ate their entrees and moved onto mains.

"This is delicious." Daphne swallowed her first mouthful. "The combo of goat's cheese and caramelised onion tart is yummy but the little chutney on the side makes it sensational. I wonder who made it."

"The meal?"

"Chutney. Whether it's one sold through Edwina's shop. Or a winner at the agricultural show. I'm beginning to wonder if the murders are connected by the club. The Rural Cooking, Crafting, Creating one."

John was about to take a bite but put it down. "Did you say murders?"

"I did. And I think it high time someone began investigating before anyone else falls victim to the Shady Bend killer."

BUT, WHY?

Daphne enjoyed her meal and waited until John finished his and poured them both a second glass of wine. Giving him indigestion wasn't her intention and she'd needed to think for a while.

"Spill your thoughts, Daph." John leaned back in his seat. "Tell me why you think there's a killer about."

"This town is filled with secrets and not just about the recipe of a sauce which everyone wants to get their hands on. Take Petra for example. She not only was known for keeping track of other people's personal affairs, but she wrote them down in a little book. Amanda was quite cutting about it."

"When did Amanda tell you this?"

"A few minutes before she collapsed. Said Petra gave it to someone a couple of weeks ago."

"Did she say who has it?" John asked.

"That's one of my worries, love. One of the police here have it. Might be Beth Porter or else Adam. But she claims whoever has it is using it for their own means. Blackmail, presumably."

John's mouth dropped open.

"You'll catch flies like that." Daphne observed.

Now you sound like your mother.

"You think one of the police is blackmailing people? That's a big accusation."

"Amanda's accusation, not mine. But it made me think of something Tracy said this morning. About Adam."

John nodded. "I remember. She said he's corrupt, or words to that effect. I don't believe it for a minute."

Which reminded Daphne. "When I phoned from the funeral home, you spoke to Adam. Said you were with him. But why?"

"Let me top that glass up." John opened the bottle. His face had reddened and he was intent on what he was doing. Not on her question.

"John?"

"Hm? Oh. Adam. I went to the cemetery earlier to finish what I was doing the day of the funeral. Ran into him on the way back. And we had a nice chat about Shady Bend. Want a guess at who his daughter is?"

Nice deflection, John Jones.

"His daughter? He must be fifty something at a guess. Could be anyone in their late teens to late twenties, give or take. Can I have another clue?"

"Nope. You're the sleuth." He grinned.

Daughter of Adam. Warm brown eyes.

"Constance?"

John clapped.

"She has his eyes. Interesting. So, she works for Edwina. Worked for Edwina. Now for Sonia, presumably. And Constance has custody of the last bottles of the secret sauce." She tapped the table with her fingernails as she took a sip of wine. More pieces of the puzzle. "There was talk that Edwina didn't make her own goods. And Petra was involved in some kind of competition to see if it was true. Not to mention Petra's way of keeping tabs on people's behaviour."

"Assuming Petra was murdered, you think there's motive because of the book?" John asked.

"Perhaps. But she'd hardly give the book to Adam, whose daughter works for Edwina. I'd love to know where Beth Porter fits in."

Daphne's phone beeped a message. "Sorry. Better check this."

It was from Tracy.

Can you come to the pavilion now? Need to speak with you and I'm busy judging.

"Huh?"

"What is it?" John asked. Daphne showed him the message. "You said she's Zeke's aunt and he just passed away and she's at the show?"

Daphne typed back.

Sorry, unable to come out tonight. Happy to text or speak on the phone.

"I admit I'm a bit curious." John said.

"Me too, but we're not going back to that place."

He hadn't asked her why she'd been so distressed there but she suspected he knew something out of the ordinary had affected her.

Her phone rang.

"Guess she does need to speak to me!" Daphne accepted the call. "Hello, Tracy, I've popped you onto speaker and John is here with me."

There was a lot of background noise. Music. The mutter of a crowd.

"Would have been easier to speak face to face, but this will have to do." Tracy said.

John covered his mouth to hide a smile but the crinkling around his eyes gave it away. Tracy had such a sense of entitlement. Expecting people she'd only met a day ago to change their own plans, drive to another town, pay entry to a show they'd already been to, and find her.

"We've both had some wine, so it wasn't a good idea to drive." Daphne had no idea why she was defending her decision. "We are so sorry about Zeke. Such a dreadful thing to happen."

"It is terribly sad, isn't it? Part of life. Birth, death and so on. Anyway. Sonia got a bit carried away after her impromptu speech earlier and has decided she wants to memorialise Edwina's passing with photos of the people who helped her go to her final resting place." She snorted. "Her mystery resting place."

Daphne had no idea where this was leading and eyed her glass of wine. She had a feeling she'd need it after this.

"Can you be at Edwina's house tomorrow, please? If you can wear what you did at the funeral." Tracy said.

"Oh. Um, I guess I can. Who else will be there?" Daphne asked.

There was a sigh. An exasperated one. "I told you already. The people who helped. Pallbearers, apart from Zeke and Pet. Naturally. Fred. Ilona, I suppose. If you come along, you'll see."

John nodded across the table. He wasn't smiling now, just listening intently.

"What time? And can you send me the address please?"

"I'd say ten. Will text you later with the details. Gotta go because these scones won't judge themselves and I've taken up more time away from judging than I should."

With that, Tracy hung up.

Daphne reached for her glass.

After a special treat of strawberries and cream, Daphne opened her notebook while John logged onto his laptop. He uploaded some photos from his phone.

"I have nothing for your website. I know you prefer to show happy photos on there, but sometimes people need to see some of the more sombre moments. Gives them a sense of confidence in your kindness and care at such a difficult time." John said.

She didn't feel very kind or caring. Just a bit numb.

"I'm not sure about photos of a funeral. Although I do agree potential clients need to see what a funeral might look like with me officiating. This is a part of what I do but after this week..." She bit her lip.

"After this week?"

"I'm giving strong consideration to following Ilona's lead and keeping to happy celebrations. Not at all certain I have what it takes to do more funerals and goodbyes." Daphne wasn't a quitter. If anything, she took setbacks as a challenge. But lately she'd seen the worst of people and it was getting to her.

He patted her hand. "If you decide to restrict your services then I'll support your decision. Nothing matters more than your mental and physical health, so take your time, but know I've got your back."

"I love you, John Jones."

"And I love you. Are you up to going to this photo thing of Sonia's?" John asked as he closed the laptop. "Bit of an odd request."

"Bit of an odd person, is Sonia." Daphne said. "As is Tracy. And Desmond. I wonder what their relationship looks like on a day-to-day basis. Sonia takes photographs and sells them as postcards. And lives in a cottage on her mother's property."

Daphne started a new page in her notebook. "I suppose I'll need to tell Adam, but I'd forgotten about something I heard earlier. Sonia was upset because Tracy made a big deal about the secret sauce when she spoke at the wake. How she expected to be the recipient of the recipe and had big plans for it. Anyway, Sonia called her out claiming Tracy put her at risk because Desmond and Fred would be breathing down her neck trying to get it first."

John frowned and he leaned forward. "At risk? I wonder what kind of risk?"

"No idea."

Daphne wrote some notes based on what she'd just told John. Then added a subheading.

Who wants the sauce and why?

"Well, as interesting as this is, nobody knows if those poor people were murder victims. There may be a logical explanation which has nothing to do with the recipe, or the blackmail book." John said.

"At the funeral home, Adam mentioned there are homicide detectives arriving in the morning. And that the funeral home was off limits to everyone, including Fred, until the detectives made a call on it. The police are treating this like murder."

Under the subheading, Daphne wrote a few lines.

1. *Tracy. Intends to commercialise sauce.*
2. *Desmond. Unknown reason.*
3. *Fred. Possibly thinks he has a right, being Edwina's ex.*
4. *Constance. Because she loves the sauce.*

"You know, Sonia didn't say if she had the recipe or not. Just that it was nobody else's business what she knew. One has to wonder how long this sauce had been the object of so many people's interest." Daphne said.

"Interest or greed? Sounds as if more than one person believed this sauce has the potential to make them money." John glanced through the window. "Still light enough for a walk. Do us good to take a stroll."

Although Daphne preferred to stay right where she was, John was right. Keys and phones collected, they set out in the direction of the back of the camping park.

"I noticed a path through the trees earlier." John pointed. "There's meant to be a stream around here so shall we take a look?"

"I'm sorry you've not got any fishing in, love." Daphne looped her arm through his. "I bet you're looking forward to the conference weekend."

He grinned. "Access to one of the best fishing river's in the state? I am!"

"Still can't believe they invited me." It lifted Daphne's spirits remembering her invitation to the annual Celebrant's Conference next month. It was a weekend at an exclusive resort in the high country with fifty like-minded people and lots of interesting speakers. John was joining a few other spouses for an overnight camping trip fishing. "I might need to walk more and eat less so I can fit into that polka dot dress again."

"Or you could get it adjusted."

Nice thought. Daphne touched her stomach which was too rounded for her liking. No, she'd work on dropping a little weight. Best to care for one's health.

They turned onto the path, which was wide and firm underfoot and wound through pretty bushland. Native flowers abounded and an echidna ambled across without bothering to look at them, John quickly snapped some photos before it vanished again. After a few minutes, bushland gave way to a little village with a handful of houses and one general store.

"Well, I had no idea this was here!" Daphne said. "Such a cute, peaceful spot."

A park was ahead with a pond and gazebo. And in the gazebo, two people were embroiled in a heated argument.

So much for peaceful.

Their voices carried and Daphne gasped. "Ilona and Desmond."

"We should go." John said.

"No. In case it gets out of hand."

"I still cannot believe you think Edie would want you to buy her property!" Ilona sounded furious. "She's always maintained Sonia was to have the two cottages and land. And for the shop to go to—"

"Then she should have made a will." Desmond snarled. He leaned on a walking stick and even from this distance, his face was beet red.

To Daphne's surprise, John led them both closer, keeping to the tree line.

"Well, what if she did? You all assume she didn't. You and Fred and Sonia. Just because there's nothing lodged with a solicitor doesn't mean there's no will. She knew her health was deteriorating and she worried about the future. She also knew you lot would all swoop like vultures so don't be surprised if there is a will." Ilona put her hands on her hips.

"You are bluffing. I have every right to that piece of land and you know it."

"What is he talking about?" John whispered.

"Tell that to Sonia." Ilona said.

"I will. Time she knew the truth. Time everyone knew the truth." Turning his back on Ilona, Desmond stepped down onto the grass.

"Wait!" Ilona flew down to get in front of him. "Sonia won't cope. At least let her get through tomorrow and then we can have a proper meeting. You, Sonia, Fred. Me. Even Tracy if she insists. But we can work through this. Please, Desmond."

"Very well. She can have her photo session and I'll play nice. But sooner or later Edwina's body will turn up and when it does, my bet is it'll prove she didn't have a heart attack. At least, not without some help."

He lumbered away, barely using the walking stick.

Ilona was open mouthed.

Daphne made a move to go to her but John held her arm and nodded in Ilona's direction.

She took out a phone and dialled. "We have a problem. A big, oafish problem."

STAY OR GO?

"The last thing I want to do is worry you. But Desmond is set on telling the world what he believes about Sonia and she'll be the one hurt by it all." Ilona continued.

Daphne and John tip toed their way closer.

"I don't know how to stop him, but he did agree to leave his big announcement until after her session tomorrow. And I want you there. If truth is coming out then you need to be part of it."

Ilona sank onto the bench and listened to the person on the other end of the phone.

Although John had no time for gossip and even less for inflammatory conversation, there was something going on here which he couldn't ignore. People dying. Talk about blackmail and corruption. And secrets everywhere. He had every intention of leaving with Daphne after the photo session tomorrow but until then, wasn't about to turn his back on what might be important information.

Listen to yourself!

He shook his head. Too much time hanging around with Daphne.

"Okay?" Daphne whispered.

Hanging around with Daphne was the best part of his life.

"Shh. Listen."

From their position it was impossible to see Ilona's face, as she was side-on to them and in the shadow of a tree. A shadow being just one of many creeping across the grass as the sun closed in on the horizon. Darkness would fall within minutes.

"What worries me, sweetie, is what will happen if Desmond—or any of the others—puts more pressure on Sonia to hand over the recipe. She's trying hard to be brave but I see her pain and the last thing we want is for her to fall apart because of this. Her state of mind is fragile at the best of times and these are far from the best of times."

Ilona's head bobbed up and down in agreement to whatever was said in return.

"Stay strong. The truth will come out but until Edwina is located, I think we have to protect what is important. Let's talk in the morning."

Ilona hung up the call. She got to her feet and left the park without so much as a glance behind.

"Well, well, well." Daphne said. "What do you make of that?"

"Let's head home as we talk. Didn't think to bring a flashlight."

"I wonder who Ilona was speaking with? She called them 'sweetie', so someone she's close to?" Daphne asked.

"Some people use endearments for everyone but I've not noticed Ilona doing it. We know who it wasn't. Sonia or

Desmond. And who are the 'others' she referred to? Who would pressure Sonia to release her mother's secret recipe, I wonder?"

"All good questions." Daphne took her phone out. "I might turn on the flashlight function because this path is dark." A sudden shaft of light appeared from her phone. "Much better. Where were we? Oh, the others. What we know is that a few people have either expressed an interest in getting it, or a third party has mentioned them."

"Tracy."

"Yes. She jumped straight into my mind. That woman is quite open about wanting to get her hands on it and commercialise the sauce. Why she believes she has any right to it though is a mystery because she comes across as having a real sense of entitlement about it, yet she wasn't close to Edwina." Daphne waved the phone around, and a pair of startled eyes stared back from the undergrowth.

"A wallaby." John observed. "Who else. Fred?"

"Definite maybe. He was married to Edwina although I don't know when. But he may believe he has a right to whatever she created. What doesn't make sense is why he'd try to take it from Sonia. Whether he is her father or not, he was married to her mother. She has priority."

It was a mystery. Not enough facts and far too many snippets of unverified information.

The path curved in the direction of the camping park, the drone of generators filling the air. He would have to pick up some more fuel for theirs tomorrow if they stayed another night. Hopefully, they'd be on their way once Daphne attended the photo session. He'd have suggested giving it a miss but Daphne wasn't one to let people down.

Be honest, John. You're curious about Edwina's property.

To see the place with his own eyes, rather than through a photograph, held a lot of appeal. He might ask Sonia if he might photograph some of the garden.

"Oh. Is that Adam?"

They were in sight of Bluebell. A patrol car was parked behind John and Daphne's car and the interior light was on.

"Looks like it." With a touch of frustration at yet another interruption when Daphne needed a chance to relax, John took her hand. "Let's see why he's here."

"I had no intention of bothering you both tonight." Adam followed Daphne inside Bluebell with John climbing in last and closing the door. "I'll be as quick as I can."

"Sit yourself down and I'll get you a coffee. Or would tea be more to your liking?" Daphne asked, already filling the kettle.

"That's too generous of you."

"You look exhausted. Have you had dinner?" Daphne frowned. She'd not got to making cookies yet. It would have to be store bought.

John motioned for Adam to sit and with a thankful smile, the officer did.

"I just finished a burger while I waited. Coffee sounds wonderful."

Daphne made three coffees while John and Adam chatted about the weather. Warm days were forecast with the possibility of a storm tomorrow night. Best be at the next town by then. She placed the coffees down and a plate of the biscuits, then slid beside John.

"Thank you for this." Adam wrapped his hands around the cup. "Just sitting here for a few minutes is nice." He glanced around. "What a pretty caravan you have."

"We love her. Bluebell." John said with a grin. "Took me a while to get used to towing, but now it feels weird if she's not behind the car."

Daphne blew on her coffee. Why was Adam here? Earlier, when he'd come to talk to her at the bench outside the funeral home, the conversation was brief. He'd asked her a handful of questions about Amanda and Zeke, apologised for keeping her waiting, and left. There'd been no mention of follow up questions or them staying any longer. Of course, he'd had a lot to deal with. A second ambulance arriving. Two bodies removed—from a funeral home of all places. And more patrol cars as out of town police arrived to help set a perimeter around the property.

"This is nice coffee, Daphne." Adam said. "And I do apologise for just dropping in so late."

"How long were you waiting?" John asked.

"Only long enough to eat my burger. I figured you'd gone for a walk seeing as your car was still here. Thought I'd eat and if you hadn't returned, I'd leave a note."

"So, to what do we owe the pleasure of your company?" Daphne offered a small smile but her heart was pitter-pattering too fast. She'd almost reached a sense of acceptance of the events of the afternoon, even with overhearing the odd conversations at the park, but something told her the news ahead wasn't pleasant.

Adam sighed. "I have some news. Preliminary results on Petra West's toxicology screen show levels of a poison. An unusual one related to cyanide."

"Cyanide!" Daphne gasped. "But the symptoms weren't the same. No sudden death after foaming at the mouth...oh, that's more like something from a movie."

Adam grinned. "Very much like a movie. This appears to have a natural source. She ingested something containing enough of the compound to be fatal but there is ongoing testing to identify what that something is."

"Champagne."

"We don't know. And there's not sufficient evidence to point towards this being a deliberate act. Which brings me to Amanda and Zeke." Adam said.

His face was drawn with sadness. He'd known these people and may have been close to some of them, for all Daphne knew. It tugged at her. Even if she hadn't decided yet if he was involved.

"You were with Amanda when she fell ill. I understand this is difficult, but would you mind running through those moments again. Earlier, I had a million things going on and want to be certain of your observations. I might write this down." He took out his notepad.

Daphne did her best to remember every detail as she recounted the awful minutes around Amanda's collapse. How she said her stomach hurt. And appeared lightheaded. Her flushed skin. Her final words to Daphne.

"She did something wrong?" Adam repeated. "Nothing else?"

"Nothing else. And then Fred arrived and told me to find Zeke. That he had medical training."

"You mentioned Amanda suggesting Edwina is already buried. There's just no evidence, not from our preliminary investigation, supporting her being removed from the funeral home."

"When the casket fell, Zeke had a quick look through the crack where the lid opened. He was dumbfounded. And I do mean that. He looked straight at me with a look of confusion and said the casket was empty." Daphne said.

"Yes, I spoke to him at length and he was shocked about it. I have no doubt he knew nothing about Edwina's disappearance."

She pushed her cup away, undrunk. "What about Fred? Did he suspect Zeke of having anything to do with moving the body?"

"Doubt Zeke, or any of the other staff for that matter, had the chance to move it. Fred insisted on managing every aspect of Edwina's time at the funeral home. They were married for a long time and he felt it was the one thing he could do for her to maintain her dignity and pay his own respects. Zeke is actually the only one who saw Edwina there."

"But Zeke did confirm he saw her?"

"Yes. And he helped collect her that nigh." Adam flashed a sudden smile. "No need to imagine Fred with a shovel in her garden. And you must remember there was a doctor's certificate signed so her remains definitely went to the funeral home."

Fragments of conversations played on Daphne's mind. Now wasn't the time to consider them. She needed a quiet caravan and her notebook.

"Adam, what is being done to ensure nobody else gets ill?" John asked. "I ask because a lot of people were at the wake."

"Nobody else has reported any signs of illness, thank goodness. If, and it is a big if, it was the champagne, then it might have been restricted to one bottle. The contaminant appears to only have been ingested by Amanda and Zeke which suggests they unfortunately drank from the same bottle."

"But...Petra." Daphne said.

Adam's shoulders slumped. "I know. And this is the problem. We don't have a conclusive answer to what we're looking for. A forensics unit will arrive first thing tomorrow and that will help. I have officers watching the funeral home tonight to make sure nobody goes in. All the champagne bottles were moved to a storeroom and are locked inside, along with glasses and anything else the team thought needed attention."

"You did remove the jam?" Daphne asked as a thought struck her.

"Jam?"

"The rhubarb and apricot jam from the other day." She reminded Adam.

"You know, we couldn't find any at all in the funeral home and Fred had no idea about it. None of the staff did. I wonder if Petra was confused with another variety?"

How would someone who makes jam ever confuse the flavours? Something wasn't right here. Did Petra take the jar home, perhaps? Perhaps someone should check her house.

"Do you think it was intentional? I mean, is there a reason anyone would target those three people in particular?" Daphne might not see the connection but Adam, with his knowledge of the town, would have to have an opinion on it.

He shook his head. "Been trying to work it out for hours. Petra had some character traits which made her unpopular at times, but I can't see anyone killing her over them.

Amanda hadn't been part of the 'in' group in ages. How Zeke fits in I have no idea."

But I do.

"Er...did you know they had something, um, going on?"

"Going on?"

Daphne filled him in on how she'd accidentally come across Amanda and Zeke in the kitchen.

"Now I've heard everything." Adam said. "Why anything surprises me in this town—anyway, I've taken up enough of your time." He stood. "You've been very helpful. Again."

"We met your beautiful daughter today." Daphne said.

The lines of tiredness on Adam's face disappeared as his eyes lit up.

"Did you go to the shop?"

"We did." John opened the door. "Came home with a bag of delightful wares and the taste of many samples on our lips."

"Connie likes looking after her customers. And she loves that shop. Glad you met her." He stepped down and Daphne and John joined him. "Be a pity if Sonia sells. For both of them, really."

A moment later he was driving away, waving through the window as the patrol car nosed along the dirt road. Daphne stared after him.

"Coming in, doll?"

"I wonder what he meant."

"Meant about what?" John held the door for Daphne.

"About it being a pity for both Constance and for Sonia if the shop is sold. Do you think he just meant it would be sad to see Edwina's shop go?" Daphne made it inside and collected the coffee cups as John locked the door.

"Well, what else would he mean?"

That there might be a fourth death in town if his daughter risked losing her beloved job? That with Sonia out of the way, Constance might have a shot at keeping it?

"Nothing, dear. Nothing at all."

CLUES AND SECRETS

John was up early and snuck out of Bluebell. He waited near the door for a minute, listening. Hoping he'd not disturbed Daph.

The air was warm. Humid. No wonder there was a forecast of a storm later. With a bit of luck, they'd be in Benalla and the storm wouldn't follow. He knew Daphne tried to be brave but had never overcome her fear of thunder. There'd been one time she'd pushed all those feelings aside. A stormy night in Rivers End. Christie was lost at sea and a rescue was underway on the beach. Along with many of the townsfolk, Daphne had braved the terrible conditions to set up a station complete with medical supplies, food, water, and lots of blankets. He'd rarely been prouder of her than on that night.

With a shake of his head to dispel the rather gloomy thoughts, John followed the path they'd taken last night. It was light enough to walk without a flashlight and John took his time, hoping to come across more of the wildlife. But he made it all the way to the park before he saw anything worth photographing.

A fine mist rose from the pond. Through the trees, the first rays of light transformed the mist into hovering gold droplets and John hurried to capture the gorgeous image before it disappeared. All too quickly the mist evaporated, leaving a family of ducks in charge of the water.

He wandered to the gazebo and perched on a seat to see what he'd got, smiling at the crystal-clear photographs. These were as good as he'd ever shot.

The gazebo was large enough for a dozen or so people to sit or mingle, with a high, curved roof and open sides, two steps up from the ground. At the side of the steps was a board with information about the region and John stopped to read.

In the middle was an illustrated map covering Shady Bend, this town, and two others in close proximity. Walking paths were highlighted and interesting spots indicated.

"Shady Gorge. Windy Orchard Peak...sounds unsuitable for growing fruit." He traced a path to another town which had different shops highlighted. "Fresh produce. Herbs and flowers. Timber furniture...wait on." John peered closer. "Alfie's Timber Creations. Alfie."

He stepped back and took a photo of the board. Then scratched his head. Thanks to the panicked phone call from Daphne yesterday, he'd had no chance to ask Adam about anything other than his finding in the cemetery.

"I noticed a headstone for Moira Browne." He'd said when he caught up with Adam at the police station.

The other man's smile had dropped. "We lost her when Connie was a young child. Still miss her every day."

And then the phone rang and he'd not had the opportunity to ask if Adam was related to an Alfred Browne. He needed to ask someone or for that matter, visit the shop himself. Just not with Daphne.

John glanced at the lightening sky and left the gazebo. There had to be a way to see for himself. If he left Daphne at Edwina's then he'd have time.

Had he found her father? His step was lighter than usual. If locating Alfred Browne came from their detour to Shady Bend, then some of the distress of the past few days was worth it. As long as Alfred wanted to see Daphne, of course.

One problem at a time.

A few minutes before ten, John parked outside the address Tracy had messaged to Daphne. There were no other cars in sight. And no people.

"We're a bit early, John. I'm happy to wait for one of the others to arrive if you want to go exploring."

"Are you sure? I don't mind waiting with you."

Ever since John had arrived back at Bluebell this morning, he'd been distracted. He'd mentioned some peak or orchard or something and said how much he'd enjoy taking some photos. Which struck Daphne as odd after he'd been so keen to visit Edwina's place.

"No, you go take photos and there might still be time for you to take some here." She climbed out and leaned back in to give him a kiss. "Have fun."

She watched him drive away until the street was quiet. In fact, there was no sign of any movement anywhere along here. Admittedly it was more of a country lane than a street, with wide, overgrown grass verges in place of footpaths and only a handful of cottages set back from their gates. Very pretty in its own way. There was no shelter out here though and the temperature was climbing. If she went up the driveway, she could stand beneath a rather imposing oak tree and wait.

A glance at her watch told she had a few minutes before the starting time so she picked up her soft briefcase and stepped through the open gate. Made of timber, the gate was old and in need of repairs, with some boards barely hanging on. It had been pushed into its open position long enough that grass had grown up through the panels.

The driveway was steep.

One step at a time, Daph.

Pity she'd not worn more sensible shoes but who'd have known there'd be a hill to climb?

She sucked in air. "Almost...there."

And then she was at the tree and took a minute to catch her breath leaning against its wide trunk.

From here the house—or cottage, rather—from the postcard, was a short distance away. Between Daphne and the cottage was one of the most beautiful gardens she'd seen. The postcard didn't do it justice.

For a moment, Daphne breathed deeply of the fresh air and allowed the country atmosphere to soak in. Grass tickled her ankles. The slightest of breezes rustled the branches above her. Far away, a cow lowed. So serene.

If John wasn't here to take photos, then she'd take some for him. Her phone camera wasn't as snazzy as his, but it wasn't a slouch either. She pointed, focused, and snapped away for a few minutes, zooming in on different garden beds, trees, or little touches. There were plenty of the latter, from stone benches with a backdrop of a weeping silver birch to tasteful ornaments peeking through colourful groundcovers.

A movement near the cottage caught her eye through the lens and after taking another shot, she lowered the phone. The front door was ajar.

Tracy had said the cottage was empty as Edwina had lived alone. Sonia's home was on the far side of the land but it might be her inside, getting things ready for the photo shoot. Which really should be starting any minute.

"Might ask Sonia if I'm too early." What if Tracy had given her the wrong time?

Daphne left the shade.

The driveway was topped with large loose pebbles making it difficult to walk in small heels, so Daphne cut across the lawn. Compared to the lower part of the property, the lawn was lush and short. How tempting to kick off her shoes and sink her toes into the soft grass.

But she ignored the temptation and made her way past a ceramic bird bath, disturbing a couple of rosellas in the midst of cleaning themselves.

The outside of the cottage was in need of some love. The metal roof was rusted on the ends overhanging a small verandah. Weatherboards—like the gate—needed new paint at the very least, with some rotted through where water stains ended. Window frames had seen better days and the windows themselves were grimy. The comparison to the immaculate and obviously loved gardens was stark. And strange.

There was no screen door, just a plain wooden door which was open about halfway. Daphne raised her hand to knock.

"Why are you here?" The words were screamed from inside. Sonia.

"Oh, I'm sorry—" Daphne took a step back.

"Are you trying to steal the recipe?" Sonia sounded furious.

"No, dear, I just—" Daphne started.

"You have no right to be in my mother's home."

But how can she see me?

"Leave now. Before I...I, phone for help." There was less conviction in Sonia's tone.

A muffled voice, a different voice, spoke. Too softly to hear the words but it was a male voice. Daphne was sure.

"Oh my very goodness, she wasn't yelling at me." Daphne whispered.

Somewhere, a door slammed. Daphne retreated, retracting her steps across the grass. No further sounds came from the cottage and by the time Daphne reached the tree, a car was pulling into the driveway. Tracy was at the wheel with passengers in the front and back.

Play it cool.

She plastered on a bright smile and followed the car to where Tracy was climbing out. "Beat us here, Daphne! Good show." She opened the back door. "Out you get, you lot."

'You lot' was Fred, and the two pallbearers who worked for Fred. And from the front seat, a woman with a camera climbed out. She barely nodded at Daphne before heading onto the lawn.

A motor scooter chugged up the incline carrying Ilona, her long black dress hitched up exposing her legs and horse-riding boots. She wore a backpack.

"Right. Now we need Desmond and Sonia." Tracy said.

"Sonia's in the cottage."

"She is?" Tracy glanced at the open front door. "You've been inside?"

Daphne shook her head. "No. I was going to knock but..." Perhaps she should be careful with her words. "Um, I heard her in there and decided not to intrude."

Tracy raised her eyebrows.

Ilona opened her backpack and swapped the boots for slip on shoes. "Can't ride with these on."

"Nobody cares about your footwear." Tracy said. "I'll round the others up."

Off she strode, up the driveway with no trouble on the pebbles.

"Despite how she talks, she's not all bad." Ilona said. She'd pulled a long sash decorated with real flowers from the backpack and was winding it around her waist. "I officiated at her wedding a few years ago and she was a different woman. Pleasant. Thoughtful. Sonia was her bridesmaid, believe it or not."

Not the Tracy of today then.

Ilona continued as she dug around for a hairbrush. "Lost her husband only a year later. Car accident—hit by a truck which then kept going. Don't think she ever forgave poor Adam for not finding the other driver. Wasn't his fault."

Daphne added this to her mental file. If Tracy felt that way about Adam it might account for her belief he was corrupt. Might be nothing to do with recent events.

"How awful for her."

"Yes. And she was in the car. So were Edie and Sonia, all on their way back from judging a show in another town." Ilona hung her head and her shoulders slumped. "Sonia had a head injury and has never really recovered. Tracy swings between silly guilt about Sonia being hurt in their car, and impatience that she hasn't got better. That night changed everybody."

Such a tragedy would be hard to move on from, injuries or not.

"I'm sure it means a lot to Tracy that you are always so kind to her."

"Oh. You are so sweet." Ilona hugged Daphne, then returned to dragging the hairbrush through her long hair, frowning as it snagged. "When are you and John leaving town?"

"We hope this afternoon, depending on whether the police want any further interviews. I have a wedding in Benalla this weekend and would love the chance to visit a hairdresser and for John to get some fishing in."

"Such a pity all of this has happened. Edie disappearing and poor Pet, and Amanda and Zeke." Ilona gave up trying to tame her hair and tossed the hairbrush away. "Any other time you'd love being in Shady Bend. Lovely food. You've been to the shop?"

Daphne couldn't help smiling. "If you mean Edwina's then yes. And we had the most wonderful tasting plate and bought a lot more than intended. Constance is so nice."

Tracy was waving at them.

"Let's hope this isn't too stressful." Ilona left her backpack under a tree beside her scooter as she and Daphne walked over to the lawn. "Constance is a darling. Sounds silly but she's a bit like a daughter to me. I'd hoped she would be here but she feels she can't close the shop again after being at the wake."

So, you were speaking with Constance last night. How interesting.

Why had Ilona wanted Constance to attend the photo

session? She'd not been at the funeral. Was this concerning the shop and who would end up with ownership?

The woman with the camera was taking test shots in a couple of places. Fred's staff stood around. Fred was nowhere to be seen.

"We're missing Desmond so I've given him the hurry up on the group chat. Fred's in the cottage getting Sonia sorted." Tracy said with a glance at her watch. "Need to get a move on because I'm judging this afternoon and can't stand around here all day."

It was beside the point that she'd arrived after the arranged time but Daphne wasn't about to mention anything so provocative. Best to play nice. And hope it wouldn't be too long as the sun was beating down quite hard now. A trickle of perspiration ran down Daphne's spine. Great.

PHOTOGRAPHIC EVIDENCE

Almost ten minutes later, the front door flung all the way open and Sonia stalked out, head high. Fred followed, pulling the door closed as he left the cottage.

"Well, thank goodness. Now we just need Desmond." Tracy said as she checked her phone. "Odd. He usually replies straight away."

"Then let's begin without him." Sonia went past the small group to a lovely display of roses. "Here. This was Mum's favourite part of the garden so we'll take the photos here."

Each rose was about five feet tall, a bed of red, pink, and yellow plants. In a semi-circle around perfect lawn, they were charming. Something about them wasn't quite right though. As healthy as the ones on either end were, a couple towards the middle had drooping leaves.

"Not here, Sonia." This was Fred. He stood apart from everyone and pointed to the stone bench. "How nice to have some people sitting and others standing."

Sonia rolled her eyes, crossed her arms, and planted her feet.

The photographer returned. “This is the best spot.”

Fred frowned but didn’t reply. He wandered over to Daphne. “You must wish you’d never taken my original phone call.”

And miss all of this?

“Goodness. It is hardly your fault this turned into such a...” Daphne clamped her lips shut to avoid saying ‘mess’.

“Disaster. Tragedy upon tragedy in our small town.” Fred nodded. “There’s nothing more keeping you here. At least, once this final obligation is done and I want you to know I appreciate your understanding. There’s some extra funds transferred to your account to compensate for all the extra time.”

“Oh. Oh, well, I didn’t expect that. But thank you.”

An old car, spluttering as it struggled up the incline, stopped as close to the cottage as it could. The motor sounded dreadful and its exhaust dragged. The door creaked as it opened and Desmond pulled himself out using the door to support his weight. All eyes turned his way but Daphne was interested in Sonia’s reaction and it was worth waiting for. The younger woman stiffened and her chin lifted.

“Sorry everyone. Took forever to get the car started. Thought I’d need to walk across.”

Something about Sonia’s expression told Daphne what she’d suspected. It was Desmond who’d been in the cottage before. The person who’d upset Sonia to the point of her screaming at him. Words about him not supposed to be in the cottage. And was he trying to find the recipe. The secret sauce recipe? What was it about the ingredients of a sauce which made half the people in Shady Bend act so oddly?

"If you'd have told me, I would have driven around and collected you, Desmond. Rather than hold proceedings up." Tracy moved to the middle of the rose area. "Right. Everyone, get into places. Tallest in the middle."

Daphne quickly sent John a message. "About to start. Usual shenanigans but getting some very interesting intel. Will reveal all later!"

She muted the phone and put it away as Tracy gestured for her to stand between Ilona at the end and Desmond. Then came one of the pallbearers, Fred, Tracy, the other pallbearer, and Sonia.

"This isn't what I want!" Sonia announced.

"Just for once stop being so dramatic. We'll swap everyone around in a minute." Tracy glared at Sonia.

So did Desmond.

Talk about needing a knife to cut the tension! Ah, this reminded her. She needed to make cookies today. Why that particular thought appeared she had no idea but she knew it was long overdue to refill the cookie jar with her yummy treats. She might make two flavours.

"Daphne? You need to smile." The photographer said.

It was to commemorate someone's passing. Why smile? But Daphne did as she was asked. They all did, apart from Sonia, who looked disinterested.

"We might get individual photos now." The photographer said. "Who is first?"

Nobody moved.

"For goodness sake. Everybody exit the area. Sonia. You go first. Stand or sit or leap about but get your photo taken." Tracy was back to being bossy boots.

One by one, everyone took a turn. Ilona was last and just

as she smiled at the camera, her sash fell off. Flower blossoms went everywhere and she kneeled to gather them. Several rolled onto the garden bed beneath the roses and she leaned in to collect them.

"Leave them!"

Fred was at her side in an instant.

"I'll do it. You sort out your dress."

Ilona moved to one side, fiddling with the sash. The pallbearers, photographer, and Sonia congregated near the front of the cottage. But Desmond and Tracy remained with Daphne. The other two gazed at Fred as he reached under the plants, snatching them back and avoiding touching the dirt with his hands.

"Quite right there, Fred?" Tracy asked.

"Can't have someone else's flowers contaminating these roses. Edwina would be mortified if they pick up some disease or other."

"My blossoms aren't diseased, Fred. You know I take great care of my plants." Ilona said. She tied the sash again and although there were a few empty spots, at least the bright colours stood out against her black dress. "The petals will decompose if you leave them there. Probably help them, seeing how sad those leaves are. Is nobody watering them now?"

Fred straightened with his hands full of flower heads. "I'll put these in the compost. Don't wait for me."

Before anyone had a chance to respond he disappeared between this garden bed and the next, dropping some blossoms as he went. Daphne scooped them up and followed. His behaviour interested her. The garden did as well.

She found Fred around the side of the cottage near an

ornamental stone wall. He'd stopped and was gazing at it, his hands against his chest, clenching the blossoms. The wall was about three feet high, built of some light-coloured blocks of stone, and made a barrier between this part of the garden and an orchard of fruit trees.

Was this where Edwina died?

Daphne slipped behind a bush, watching through the branches so as not to disturb Fred. He'd found Edwina against a stone wall, already deceased. By his body language, this spot meant something. How awful to find her there. Even divorced, they'd apparently remained friends.

Suddenly he leaned closer to the top of the wall, peering at it. He dropped the blossoms and took a handkerchief from a pocket, wetting the corner with his tongue. Fred applied the wet patch with vigour to a small area of the stone wall, scrubbing and then muttered a curse word. He shoved the handkerchief away and grabbed the fallen flowers before stomping off and disappearing through a gate.

Grabbing her phone and somehow managing with one spare hand, Daphne zoomed in as far as she could on the spot but all she got was a blur.

She closed in on the wall, snapping photos without focusing because her hand was shaking and she struggled to walk making a call let alone get the most from a camera.

Please don't come back yet. Please don't.

Almost there. Almost.

From behind the gate, another curse.

She stopped abruptly and zoomed in to take one photo before shoving the phone away.

"What are you doing here?" Fred opened the gate.

"Ah. Wondered where you are. You dropped these back in the rose garden and I thought I should save you another trip to the compost." She held out the blossoms, which were rather worse for wear thanks to squashing them into one hand.

He gaze her a curious look. Did he believe her?

"Thanks. Here, I'll take them. You go back."

"I don't mind coming with you. Or waiting here."

"No! I mean, Sonia wanted some photos of you and her together." He took the blossoms. "Getting so hot now it can't be pleasant in your jacket. I know I'd like to take mine off. I'll catch up."

He really didn't want her here.

"Yes, it certainly is warm. And humid."

Fred went to the gate but instead of going through, stood.

With a smile, Daphne retraced her steps, glancing over her shoulder when she was on the other side of the bush. He'd gone. It wasn't worth risking being caught again. Hopefully she had one good image of whatever he'd been so interested in.

Alfie's Timber Creations was frustratingly hard to locate.

John had driven past the caravan park where they were staying, beyond the tiny town with the pond and gazebo, and followed a winding road into a valley. There was only a petrol station, the smallest supermarket he'd ever seen, and a pub along the main street. John parked and checked the photograph he'd taken of the map. It was far from exact so he did an internet search. This gave him an address and after more than a couple of wrong turns, he stopped near a yard with a shed along a narrow dirt road.

Surrounded by high chain fencing, there was a faded sign on a locked gate.

Alfie's Timber Creations.

The shed was fairly large with double doors that were locked with a heavy padlock. Only the sight of a couple of hanging pots with healthy flowers restored the hope this wasn't an abandoned property.

Still, it didn't help him find answers.

He wandered the length of the fence. There were no other signs. No opening hours or contact details.

A couple of boys riding pushbikes went past then circled back.

"Not open today, mister." One of the boys pulled up, cleverly keeping balance by adjusting his weight and moving the pedals back and forth. "Tomorrow. Maybe."

"Thank you. Do you know who works there?"

"Old dude. Cranky as."

The other boy rode off.

"What's his name?" They wouldn't be here tomorrow. "Do you know where he lives."

"Somewhere up the hill. But you don't want to visit. Told you he's cranky." The boy followed his friend.

"Thanks." John did want to visit. Cranky or not, John needed to know the man's identity. But if he was Daphne's father, arriving unannounced on his doorstep was not the right way to make first contact. Talking to Adam might be the best solution.

Back at the gate, he took a couple of photographs. Perhaps he could ask Ilona. Out of all the people he'd met, only she and Adam and Constance seemed trustworthy. As long as she didn't tell Daphne until he'd had a chance to follow things up because if her hopes were raised and nothing came of it... He couldn't bear to break her heart.

"You've been through enough already."

He'd think it through. But have to think fast because Daphne was ready to leave Shady Bend and he wasn't inclined to encourage her to stay a minute longer than they needed to.

BEST LAID PLANS

"We can't leave yet." Daphne had almost thrown herself into the car when John pulled up where he'd dropped her earlier. "Let's get back to Bluebell."

He glanced up the incline. "No chance of me getting some photos, I guess?"

"Negatory. Not this time. But I took a few."

An old car rattled down the driveway and John waited until it turned onto the road before he pulled out. It went the opposite direction with Desmond behind the wheel.

"How did it go?"

Daphne kind of snorted. "Care to take any guesses?"

He smiled and accelerated. "Let me see. Tracy bossed everyone around. Sonia pouted a lot. Ilona was sweet and probably cried. Fred kept everybody on track."

"Not bad. You got the first two right. Ilona is sweet, of course, but no tears. She had some wardrobe malfunctions which kept her occupied. And Fred? He was weird." Daphne undid her jacket. "I should have taken this off."

"I can pull over."

"I'll be fine. Not far to go and then I'm changing and having a tall glass of iced tea."

The remainder of the short trip was in silence as Daphne tapped at her phone. John parked next to Bluebell and they climbed out. If anything, the temperature had risen since he'd left Alfie's and the air was dripping with humidity.

Daphne dropped her briefcase onto the seat at the table. "Be right back."

John poured glasses of iced tea and sat at the table, doing another search on his phone. This one was on the name 'Alfie Browne'. He began scrolling the list.

"Feel better already." Daphne was in looser clothes and had bare feet. She picked up her glass and sipped. "Thanks, love. Needed this. Did you get some nice photographs?"

"Photos? Oh. Not as many as I hoped for." He closed the search and put the phone on the table.

"Pity. I got a few. Some of the gardens because everyone was late and I walked up to the cottage. And overheard Sonia terribly upset with someone. Desmond. At least, I'm pretty sure."

"Pretty sure?"

"The front door was partly open and I heard Sonia yelling at someone. And the muffled voice, a man, who then left through a back door. But when Desmond arrived in his car, quite late, she wasn't happy to see him. Whoever was in the cottage, they weren't invited. She accused them of trying to steal the recipe."

"The secret sauce recipe? What is so special about it?"

"My question exactly. I have the strangest feeling this sauce of Edwina's has something to do with the unfortunate deaths." Daphne said.

"You think the sauce killed them?"

She shook her head. "Goodness me, no. But maybe their greed did. And there's more."

Daphne told John about Fred's peculiar behaviour around the rose garden and then at the stone wall.

"Did you get close enough to see what he was trying to clean?" This was a turn of events. Fred came across as a man in control of his environment. Even the disappearance of Edwina's body did little more than put him on edge.

"I tried to get photos." She opened the gallery on her phone. "I was behind a bush at first."

John chuckled.

"Well, I couldn't very well make an appearance if he was doing something suspicious. Ah, here we go." She handed the phone over.

There were lots of photos of the garden, which was even more beautiful than John imagined. He wanted to stop at each one but kept flicking through until there was one of a branch. Close up. The next few were out of focus but there was a figure in the background.

"This is good." He turned the phone to show Daphne a clear image. Fred rubbed at something on the wall with his handkerchief. Zooming in didn't reveal what though.

Another dozen images later—all random shots of grass, sky, and Daphne's feet—there was one of the wall. He pinched the screen and zoomed until it was too fuzzy, then backed out.

"Anything?"

John stood. "I'll get my laptop. Might be clearer."

"Because I have a theory."

"Keep talking." John collected the laptop from the cupboard.

"Adam said Fred found Edwina slumped against the wall. She'd had a fatal heart attack."

John connected Daphne's phone to the laptop and downloaded the images she'd taken today.

"What if it wasn't a heart attack?" she asked.

"What else would it be?"

"Maybe she fell and hit her head. And for some reason when Fred found her, he didn't notice and assumed it was her heart."

"But the doctor would have noticed. Bit hard to overlook a head injury."

Daphne tapped at the table top with her nails and her eyes had the familiar faraway look signalling she was puzzling something out.

The photos began to populate the screen and John enlarged the one he was interested in. Viewing it on the larger screen helped to a degree but it wasn't sharp enough to be certain. He'd like to go there himself and take a look. And take photos with his phone, which he'd bought mainly for the outstanding camera quality.

"John, I don't know. The way Fred was today...and Edwina's missing body. What if her death was not from natural causes, and the doctor was in on it? What if Fred killed Edwina and then he covered it up?"

He rotated the screen so she could see. "I'm beginning to think you might be onto something."

"We have to show this to the police." Daphne checked the screen for the third time. Still the same close up of the stone wall. And still the same reddish-brown splashes dried into it. "It may not be blood, but they need to make that determination."

"Would you like to go to the station?"

"I think so. Can we take the laptop?"

John nodded.

"What a dreadful turn of events if it is blood. If someone had a hand in poor Edwina's passing."

Daphne went in search of sandals. She was slipping as a sleuth. Fred was never once in her sights as a potential killer and this was all something of a shock. If her theory was right, had he been responsible for hiding Edwina's body? But why? Surely a proper burial following all the rules was the least suspicious course of action.

What is he hiding?

She pushed the thoughts aside as they drove to the police station.

Several cars, patrol and otherwise, took most of the parking in front of the station so John pulled into a spot further up the road and they walked back.

Inside, a meeting was underway. Adam, Porter, and half a dozen uniformed police stood around a whiteboard. A plain clothes officer was speaking and she stopped mid-speech when she noticed Daphne and John waiting at the counter. Adam followed her gaze and excused himself. The other officer resumed what she was saying.

"Sorry. Just in the middle of a briefing. How can I help?" Adam spoke quietly.

"Actually, we hope we can help." Daphne said. "I don't know where you are with investigating Edwina's disappearance, and this may or may not assist, but it should raise more questions. Which hopefully lead to answers."

Oh dear. That sounded complicated.

"Not sure I follow."

John set his laptop on the counter and opened it.

"I was at Edwina's cottage earlier. For a photo session with Sonia and some other people. Long story short, I followed Fred at one point and found him doing rather an odd—"

"Wait. Go back a bit. You followed Fred?" Adam's pained expression made Daphne pause and take a breath.

I've done it again.

"Well, he dropped some flowers and I tried to catch up as he had them and then I saw what he was doing and hid behind a bush and...anyway. He took out a handkerchief and tried to clean part of the stone wall."

"None of that made sense, but go ahead. What am I looking at?" he stared at the laptop screen as John showed him the original photograph of the wall. John zoomed in and suddenly, Adam was on alert. He leaned in to look better. "Can you zoom more?"

"Not without losing focus."

Adam turned. "Detective. Porter. May I borrow you both?"

The women approached and the rest of the group followed at a distance, interested, no doubt, in why there was an interruption.

"Detective Malone, this is Daphne and John Jones."

"The celebrant. You've been very helpful." Detective Malone nodded. "I understood you were leaving town today."

"Yes. Well, we still plan on that. But Daphne took a photograph this morning and we thought it best to show it to Adam." John said.

Adam repeated, more or less, what Daphne had told him

apart from the muddled bits and then he, Detective Malone, and Porter huddled around the laptop. The others tried to peer over their shoulders. After a few words which Daphne couldn't make out, Adam straightened. "May we have a copy of this?"

"I'll send it to your email. Do you want all the ones Daph took today?"

"Anything you think might be of interest."

The other police returned to the whiteboard.

"We're not any further along finding Edwina. What we are working on is locating the source of the poison ingested by Petra, Zeke, and Amanda. There's no further illness, thank goodness." Adam glanced at the whiteboard. "What we know is all three consumed similar foods and drinks a short time before succumbing to the poison."

"Champagne? Jam?" Daphne asked.

Adam rolled his eyes. "Mrs Jones."

"I thought you normally call me Daphne. I just keep my eyes and ears open."

"I've emailed all of those across to you." John closed the laptop. "We shouldn't take up any more of your time."

"You've done the right thing." Adam ran a hand over his head. "Please stop hiding behind bushes though."

"I tell her the same thing." John said. "Mind you, if Daphne has a hunch, it's usually right."

I'd like to kiss you right now.

She didn't. "Adam, I think you should look at Fred more closely. I feel there's more to him than meets the eye."

"I'll visit the cottage shortly. Take one of the forensic officers up."

"Thank you." Daphne smiled at Adam. "We'll let you get back to work."

Halfway to the car, John stopped. “I left my phone on the counter. Jump in the car and I’ll be right behind you.” Before she could say a word, he’d gone. Wasn’t like him to forget anything but it had been quite an exciting morning.

Rather than get into the heat of the car, she waited in the shade of a tree and glanced at the sky. Clear. Not a cloud. With a bit of luck, the forecast storm would fizzle out. There was enough going on in Shady Bend without adding thunder and lightning.

John was taking a while. Odd if he’d just gone to get his phone. She was about to find him when he, and Adam, emerged from the station. They stopped just outside the door and shook hands and Adam gazed at Daphne. He lifted a hand and she waved back. Such a nice man. He couldn’t possibly be corrupt but then again, sometimes the person you least suspect turns out to be the bad guy.

COOKIES AND CARDBOARD

"I'm thinking one batch of vanilla and sultanas, and one of chocolate with added choc chips." Daphne pulled two baking trays from the bottom cupboard. She had the ingredients lined up on the counter and the oven was heating, thanks to the generator going outside.

John had his head in his laptop. In fact, he'd hardly moved or said a word in the last half hour.

"And one batch with river pebbles and another with cut up pieces of paper."

Nothing.

"Tracy is going to judge them. She'll decide which one is the most delicious and then she'll want to steal my secret recipe."

"Sound delicious, doll."

It was all Daphne could do not to burst out laughing. John was so distracted she could have said almost anything. He must have realised she was looking at him for he lifted his head.

"Sorry, what did you say?"

"Would you like a pot of tea while I bake?"

He smiled. "Are you sure that's what you said? And yes, I would love that."

She filled the kettle. "What are you up to?"

"Genealogy research. That little cemetery piqued my interest about a name I saw and now I'm following a family tree." He closed the laptop. "Would you like a hand?"

"I've got everything under control. Seeing as we're staying one more night, I might as well put my time to good use. But you never really said, John. Why are we staying another night?"

After they arrived back at Bluebell, Daphne had begun packing Bluebell's interior ready for travel. Instead of going outside to do the same, as was his routine, John took Daphne's hands. "Leave it until morning, Daph. I have a feeling if we leave, we're going to have to turn around and come back."

His words weren't a complete surprise. Not when there was an unsolved case here. Several unsolved cases. Deep in her bones was the answer. Well, perhaps not in her bones, but that was how strong her commitment to finding the answers was.

John reopened the laptop. "Couple of things made me reconsider leaving today. I've had a look at the weather forecast and it seems as if the storm will miss Shady Bend but give poor Benalla a hammering. Not a fan of getting Bluebell settled at a new ground in those conditions."

"That is reason enough on its own." Daphne shook flour from the packet into a large bowl. "What else?"

"Er. Remember I ducked back to the station for my phone?"

"Yes. I waved to Adam when you both came outside again."

"Oh. Yes. Well. Anyway, he was about to go to Edwina's cottage."

"I know that, dear. Remember I was there when he said so?"

What is going on, John Jones?

"So you were. Did you say you needed a hand?"

Daphne turned around, flour on her hands and a grin on her face. "Would you mind making the tea? I seem to have messy fingers."

"Cookies?"

"Unless you'd rather wait for tea until they're cooked? Won't be too long." She could have sworn he was frowning. This was becoming a bit of a regular occurrence. Either some odd grimace or cookies disappearing when she'd known there was some left. Must be her imagination because John loved her cookies. Everyone did.

"I should enter them into the show."

John got up and reached for the teapot. "Don't do that!"

"Don't enter my cookies in the show?"

Daphne lifted her hands from the board, her heart skipping a beat. Were they really so bad?

He kissed her cheek. "Less for me if you do."

Her heart sighed. He did love them. Perhaps there was enough here to make three varieties.

Despite John's earlier enthusiasm, Daphne snuck a glance his way when he bit into the first warm cookie. He caught her looking and turned up the sides of his lips, which couldn't be easy with his mouth full. Her phone rang and she put down her own cookie before even getting a taste.

"Daphne Jones speaking."

"Daphne, it's Ilona." Her voice was both loud and stressed and Daphne held the phone away from her ear. "I'm at Petra's house and I think something is wrong here."

"Slow down a bit. Why are you at Petra's?"

"Oh. I've been tending her garden and feeding her sheep until arrangements are made. She has three sheep. One just climbed through the fence. But I think someone's been in her house and hoped you might come."

John leaned forward and Daphne put the phone onto speaker.

"Ilona, this is John. Are you in danger?"

"No. No, I don't think so. And before you ask, I have spoken to Adam and he'll be along in a bit but has his hands full. But something odd is going on. There's a parcel outside the door."

"Like a delivery?"

"Yes. It is broken. Open in one corner. And there are...jars inside."

This wasn't getting any clearer to understand.

"I know I'm not making any sense but I can show you. I mean if you would come around, I would be very grateful for your opinion." Ilona said.

"Our opinion?"

There was a long pause with only the baaing of sheep through the phone.

"Ilona?"

"I'm not sure who to trust anymore, Daphne. But I know

I can trust you and John. You don't have any stakes here. Would you come and see, and tell me if I'm overreacting?"

John was nodding.

"Yes, dear. Send the address and we'll come right away."

Almost the instant she hung up, the phone dinged a message.

John was already on his feet, leaving behind the cookie with just one bite missing.

Petra West's house was the last home down a winding laneway not far from the ground where the country show was being held. From here, music and excited screams of those brave enough to try the scary rides was at odds with the occasional baaing of sheep somewhere behind the house. The garden was pretty with daisies growing through long fine grass and a collection of fruit trees scattered around.

"I'm surprised fruit does so well here." Daphne waited as John locked the car. "For some reason, Shady Bend sounds too...dark. How silly of me. It's like Edwina's property having an orchard. They are in a sheltered but sunny area and with the cold winters up here are probably in an ideal situation to thrive."

Ilona's motor scooter was parked in front of a single garage but there was no sign of her, so Daphne led the way to the front door. The parcel which concerned Ilona so much was larger than Daphne expected and looked heavy. Someone had dropped it and the cardboard corner had come apart leaving a wide gap.

"Should we look?" Daphne asked.

John didn't get a chance to answer as Ilona hurried towards them from around the corner of the house. She was in overalls and muddy boots and her hair was escaping from a ponytail.

"Sorry. I had to round her up, the sheep that is, the one who escaped and then I found I'd left the hose on and so much mud." She glanced at her boots. "But at least she's back in her paddock. I see you found the box."

A shriek of terror from some poor soul probably upside down on a ride at the show made all three of them jump.

"Have to go there this afternoon and I'm already over the noise!" Ilona said. "Anyway, this is the quandary. A box addressed to Petra which raises a whole lot of questions. Did you see inside?"

John shook his head. "If it's addressed to Petra..."

"She's not going to care at this point." Ilona pointed out. "You can see without touching. They are jars."

"Like bottling jars?" Daphne asked.

"Yes. So, what is strange about it? Petra used to be one of the most competitive makers of jams and bottled fruit in the region. For years she won just about everything and then everything changed. She still entered every so often but rarely won. As if she just didn't care anymore." Ilona nudged the box with her toe, leaving a muddy mark.

"So, you think it odd she'd have a delivery of jars?" John asked.

"A bit. But it isn't the bottles as such. Can you see the bundle on top? Here, if you slightly widen the gap," Ilona used both hands to do so, "there. Those are labels, already printed and ready to attach once the bottles are filled."

Daphne peered in but her eyesight wasn't good enough

to read the label. She got her phone out and turned on the flashlight. Much better.

She gasped and stepped back.

"Daph?" John looked inside. "Does that say...no."

"Yes." Ilona put her hands on her hips. "Yes, it says *Edwina's Secret Sauces & Special Supplies*. Why. That is my question. Why would Petra be receiving jars meant for Edwina?"

There'd been speculation, accusations, about Edwina. Did she paint her own paintings? Or was it Desmond? And the jams and preserved fruit and chutneys and sauces...were the rumours true?

"Ilona, you were close to Edwina. Does this resonate with you? I've heard stories."

"About Edie not making what she put her name to?" Ilona stared off towards the show as more screams cut through the air. "Of course it resonates. I asked Edie about it one time and she said not to believe everything I hear. It wasn't a denial. Nor admission. But she'd have told me if she wanted me to know."

"You never saw any signs? Like these jars?" John asked.

Ilona turned to them. "I seek to see the best in people. Perhaps that is naïve. It may be the rumours were true but even so, it doesn't change how much I loved Edie. She was my friend, flaws and all. If Petra was working for her, then there was a good reason and with her heart condition she'd felt a sense of doom. This might all have been a contingency plan to keep income coming in for Sonia."

A patrol car pulled up outside.

"Good. I didn't want to go inside alone."

Constable Porter joined them. She glanced at the box

and raised a questioning eyebrow. "Ilona, you mentioned a break in."

"I think so." Ilona pulled a key from a pocket. "Petra gave me a key when she went away so I could feed the sheep and water her indoor plants. Told me to hang on to it for future jobs." She looked at Daphne. "I do house sitting and pet walking on the side."

"And..." Porter checked her watch.

"And I can see through the window here," Ilona pointed at a vertical glass panel beside the front door, "there's a mess inside. Petra kept her place immaculate."

Everyone tried to peer through the glass at the same time, over the top of the box.

"Shall I open the door?" Ilona inserted her key. "Oh. It isn't locked."

Porter stepped up. "Let me." She turned the door handle and it opened. "You all stay here please." She unclipped her holster and stepped inside. "Police. Constable Beth Porter entering the house."

She disappeared into the house. With the door open, the mess was apparent. A potted plant knocked over with dirt scattered across carpet. Drawers in a hallway table were open, their contents hanging out. Someone was looking for something and didn't care if they made it obvious.

Ilona looked as if she was going to follow and Daphne put a hand on her arm. "Best let the police do their job. Make sure nobody is still inside."

"I'm sure they aren't. We've been talking out here for a while so anyone in their right mind would have left through the back door. But you're right. They'll need to fingerprint the place but I just hate seeing the plant like that."

"Can we step under a tree? Bit hot out here." Daphne

didn't wait for an answer. If it got any stickier, she'd melt. The other two followed, John taking out his phone. They stopped beneath a golden ash in view of the front door and John took some photos. He was getting as bad as she was. Record everything. Miss nothing.

Suspect everyone.

WHAT FRED DID

John wasn't taking random photographs. A glint in the grass caught his eye as he'd left the doorway, somewhere beyond the tree. Even zoomed in it was unclear what caused the reflection which for all he knew might be nothing more than a piece of rubbish flown over from the show. Life with Daphne taught him to record anything suspicious. Better to delete unwanted images than wish you'd taken them.

Porter was still inside the house so he wandered in the direction of the object. The grass was even longer in this part of the garden and if the sun hadn't caught it at the exact moment he'd looked the right way, he'd never have seen it.

A key.

He squatted to better see.

It was a house key on its own. Not even a loop to attach it to a keyring.

"John? Is everything alright?" Daphne was heading his way.

He straightened. "There's a house key here. I might stay

with it if you don't mind letting Constable Porter know once she's out of the house."

Daphne peered into the grass. "Oh my. You are so clever finding it. Do you think whoever let themselves into the house then threw the key away? Or maybe it dropped out of their pocket or something."

"There's Porter. She's coming over."

So was Ilona. Porter was on the phone and came to a halt a few feet away as she continued a conversation. "No sign of break in. Yeah. Unlocked. Oh really? Huh, well there you go. Righto." She hung up. "What's everyone looking at?"

"Key." Daphne pointed.

Ilona moved closer. "Oh. That is one of Petra's. I'm certain."

"Interesting." Porter took some photos of her own, then slipped the key into an evidence bag. "Why does it have 'one' written on it? Any idea, Ilona?"

"Yes. She had three keys. One was hers. Two was mine. Three was hidden for emergencies. How did anyone get hold of her own house key?" Ilona teared up. "And why would someone go into her house and trash it?"

Daphne put an arm around Ilona's shoulders. "We'll get to the bottom of it, dear."

"No." Porter started back to the house. "The police will get to the bottom of it."

"And we will help them." Daphne whispered.

"I heard that." Porter called over her shoulder. "If you want to know what happened at Edwina's, you'd better catch up."

"First of all, let's set some ground rules. No repeating what I tell you. And no going into the house. Okay?"

Everyone nodded at Porter. They were all beneath another tree closer to the house and she stood facing them, hands on her hips.

"There's a unit heading up here, including some of the forensic team who are in Shady Bend investigating other matters. Adam is busy at the station but because Desmond arrived right in the middle of it and has overheard certain information which he's already said he has no intention of keeping to himself, he says I can share what happened up at her cottage. Edwina's."

"What? What happened?" Ilona was still fragile, Daphne sensed it. Being here was clearly playing on her emotions and whatever barrier she'd erected to get her through this time was crumbling.

"Do you remember this morning, at the photo shoot, that I followed Fred with some of the flowers you lost?" Daphne asked.

"Not really. I was trying to fix the sash and then I noticed you appear from around the side of the cottage."

"Daphne noticed there was an odd mark on the stone wall." Porter said. "She took a photo and Adam and one of the forensic team were up there a bit earlier to take a better look."

"What kind of odd mark? Was it where Fred found Edwina?" Ilona's voice squeaked and Daphne grabbed her hand. "Is this about her body?"

"Not precisely. Look, at this point, Fred is at the station chatting to Adam and Detective Malone. All I can pass on is that there was some blood found on the wall. We don't know if it belongs to Edwina, but Fred has come forward and said he wasn't entirely honest about how he found her. That she had a cut on her head and he thought she'd had a heart attack and fallen against the wall. Whether she died from the heart condition or the fall we will only know if her body is recovered."

Tears dripped down Ilona's cheeks.

"How about you sit here in the shade." John suggested. "Do you have some water somewhere?"

Ilona sank onto the grass with a shake of her head. "I don't need water. I need Edie back and for all of this to go away." She pulled a tissue from a pocket. "I don't understand why Fred didn't say what really happened at the beginning. Why would he lie?"

Why indeed?

Rather than allow Ilona's grief to worm its way into her heart, Daphne put her mind to work. Fred had acted suspiciously at the stone wall. Now he revealed he had lied about how he found Edwina. But what would prompt such a lie? Was he afraid people might believe he'd been responsible? Or was there a reason he didn't want her cause of death investigated?

Daphne's fingers itched to get a pen and her notebook.

"No need to hang around here." Porter said. "We'll call if we have any questions."

Ilona gazed up. "I want to stay. I need to check the sheep and make sure the fence is holding where I repaired it. And what about the box?"

"The delivery? One of us can put it inside once crime scene does their thing."

"Neither Petra nor Edwina are going to use the contents." Ilona looked down at the grass and played with a blade. "Jars might as well go to Sonia."

This surprised Porter. "Sonia?"

Daphne explained about the labels.

"You think Petra was making the jams and stuff? And then putting a shop label on, which implied they were made by Edwina? Well, I never." Porter's phone beeped and she walked away.

So did Ilona's but she ignored it.

And again.

"Message, dear?"

"Just the group chat, Daphne."

All three of them looked at each other and Ilona tapped at her phone. If group chat was going, was it about Fred?

"Oh. Oh, dear, here Daphne, would you read it. I'm a bit afraid of what I might see."

Daphne took the phone. "I just scroll down?"

"Uh huh. Bit like a text message but more people involved."

There were more dings.

Daphne read aloud.

"Desmond is the author. Sender. He says you lot are in for a shock."

"That's what he said?" John asked.

"There's already replies so I'll read them in order." Daphne sat on the grass beside Ilona. The messages were going back and forth at speed.

Tracy: Feeling bored, Des? Read a book.

Desmond: Nobody asked you.

Tracy: You did. You said, 'you lot' and I am part of this chat.

Sonia: Is there any point to this?

Tracy: Nope.

Desmond: Fine. But I know what just happened at Edwina's.

Daphne glanced up. "There's some angry faces from both Tracy and Sonia. Who else is part of the chat, Ilona?"

"Fred. He won't be thrilled if Desmond is about to spill the beans. Me, of course. Constance. But she'll be working and won't touch her phone in the shop, good girl she is."

"There's more."

Desmond: Freddie's been a bad boy.

Tracy: Get to the facts.

Sonia: Is this about Mum?

Desmond: We should get together. Tell you in person.

Tracy: Hang on. If that's the case, come to the show. I can't leave.

Sonia: Is it about Mum?

Desmond: Let's meet at the show. Six?

Tracy: Five. Got the jam-off event at six. Better be worth it. I'm busy you know. Not like you two.

"Oh my. There's a poked tongue face thingy from Desmond. I thought these people were adults." Daphne raised both eyebrows. Ding. Ding. Ding.

Desmond: Be near the front gate at five. I'll bring the news.

Sonia: I'd rather watch grass grow.

Desmond: Then you also miss out on the truth about your father.

Ilona gasped and scrambled to her feet. "He can't tell her! Not there. And not without me as a support."

The group chat was off. "Tell her what?" Daphne asked. Was this the secret Desmond and Ilona had touched on at the park the other evening? She handed the phone back and caught Ilona's eye. "What is the truth about Sonia's father?"

But Ilona looked away. "Not for me to tell. Sorry."

"Does Sonia want to know?"

"She won't say. Edwina let her believe it was Fred but

Desmond thinks he knows who it really is. Guess being neighbours for decades one might see things. But rather than dredging up the past, I believe these things are best left alone." Ilona walked towards the house, calling over her shoulder. "Need to check the sheep."

John held out his hands for Daphne. "What do you think."

She took them and climbed to her feet with only a couple of groans.

"About Desmond telling Sonia whatever this secret is? She deserves the truth. I know what it feels like to believe one thing and then discover it was all a lie. Not pleasant. But even if she wants to know, what if the real father doesn't want her to know? Or doesn't know himself? Now that could throw the cat among the pigeons."

Arm in arm, Daphne and John made their way back to their car. Ilona was nowhere to be seen. Porter was at the front door and nodded goodbye. John was quiet.

As they nosed down the road, Adam's patrol car went the other way and he waved.

John raised his hand in return. "Daph. Do you think it possible a man wouldn't want to know he had a daughter?"

Was he worrying so much about Sonia? How sweet of him.

"I have to wonder about a man who was involved with a woman and didn't stay around long enough to know he was a father. He might not be the kind of father a girl would want."

There was no answer from John. The wrinkling of his forehead was a giveaway that something was playing on his mind. Daphne patted his leg and he smiled. For a minute.

FRED'S EXPLANATION

As they waited to turn onto the main road to go back to Bluebell, a car rounded a curve on the wrong side of the road.

"Did you see that?" John shouted.

The car moved back into its lane and sped past.

Daphne had and she peered at the driver. "Is that Fred?"

"Think it is. Sorry I yelled. Shocked me."

"Follow him." Daphne said. "I think we should."

John glanced at her. He'd say no. He'd say they needed to mind their own business and not get any more involved in the goings on in Shady Bend than necessary. And he'd be right, of course.

But he grinned.

"You, my sweetheart, are a bad influence." He pulled onto the road and followed at a distance.

Well. Wonders do happen.

"He wasn't being very careful," she said. "Thank goodness nobody was coming the other way.

"Downright dangerous. Wonder if he's upset at having to come clean about Edwina."

With no indicator on, the car ahead turned into a side street.

"That's the way to the cottage." Daphne leaned forward. "Surely he wouldn't go back there?"

But he did. His car was halfway up the driveway when they drove past. John went a bit further along to where the road inclined and he did a U-turn.

"I can see the front of Edwina's cottage from here, love." Daphne pointed.

"Let's pull over. Might get my phone out."

John Jones you are becoming an excellent sleuth.

Car parked, they both got out and slipped beneath the cover of a tree. From this elevated spot, there was a view back to Shady Bend over trees and houses. It was interesting how the landscape varied between bushland and orchards.

"Wonder if he's visiting Sonia. Perhaps to tell her the truth." John trained his phone camera on Fred, who was out of his car but motionless at the bonnet. "He's staring at something."

"Any idea what?" Daphne couldn't tell from this distance but it was in the general direction of the garden. There was no other movement. Not even a rustle of branches because the air was still. She glanced up through the canopy. Although the sky was blue, she shivered. There might not be a storm coming but something else in this community was terribly wrong.

Fred moved towards the cottage then stopped again. He pulled something from a pocket.

"He's checking a message. I think." John relayed what he saw through the advantage of his zoomed in camera.

"Hopefully not checking the group chat!"

If Fred read what Desmond had said about him, who knew how he'd react. For that matter, what else was Fred hiding? In Daphne's experience, people rarely kept one secret. If they had something to hide it was likely to creep into many areas of their life and affect more than the main problem. And if he hid *how* Edwina died, was it possible he hid where she was now?

"John?"

"Can't see if he's on group chat. But he is scrolling so my guess is he is." John said.

"No. I mean, that's no good. But do you think we need to let Adam know that Fred is here? What if he tampers with anything?"

John lowered the phone to look at Daphne. "What's worrying you?"

"A feeling."

"About?"

"Fred is dishonest. He lied about something as important as a woman's death."

"And you are thinking about what else he's lied about?"

You know me so well.

She nodded.

"Why don't you send Adam a text message while I keep an eye on Fred?" John suggested.

"I will."

Daphne searched for Adam's number.

"Um...we might need to get back in the car." John pointed. "Sonia is heading his way and she's not looking happy to see him."

From around the corner of the cottage, Sonia stormed across the grass.

"Oh dear. Let's go."

By the time John parked beside Fred's car, the other two had vanished. But once they climbed out, it was easy to find them. Sonia was yelling at Fred.

"We should wait for Adam." John looked worried.

Daphne had finished her text message on the short car ride but not heard anything back. Poor Adam must be tired of running from one place to the other thanks to this whole mess with Edwina.

"Don't you dare touch me!" Sonia screeched.

John was already running before Daphne took a step. So much for waiting. She puffed her way across the grass, skirting around the edge of garden beds and the bird bath.

Sonia and Fred were near the wall. Fred held his hands up near his shoulders, palms facing Sonia as if to prove he wasn't going to touch her. Sonia's face was distraught and tears poured down her face as she stepped side to side in agitation, arms wrapped around her body. She glanced at John and Daphne as they halted nearby then back to Fred.

"You killed my mother."

"Of course not! What a ridiculous thing to say, Sonia. You know I considered Edwina a dear friend after the divorce. But I did make a mistake, a big error of judgement, and for that I am so sorry."

Daphne put a hand on John's arm and they exchanged a quick look. Hopefully he understood she wanted to listen and only intervene if absolutely necessary.

"Mistake? Mum didn't have a heart attack and now we might never know what really happened. Why would you lie about something so important? You were married to her. And I always thought you cared about her."

"It's because I cared about her that I covered up what happened. Sonia, I wanted to protect her reputation."

Sonia stopped stepping side to side and dropped her arms. She waited for Fred to continue but he didn't, instead, he turned his attention to Daphne.

"Why are you both here?"

"We—"

"You meddled in my business. Followed me and hid in the bushes, no less, taking photographs of a private moment. And now everything has to come out about Edwina."

John took a step in front of Daphne. "Let's all stay calm."

Calm? Daphne's heart raced too fast to be calm. Being confronted was uncomfortable and upsetting but she'd done nothing wrong and if anyone should be hanging their head it was Fred.

An uneasy silence fell. Fred glared at John.

"Fred, tell me what really happened to Mum. Tell me now." Sonia's tears had stopped and she blew her nose. "What about her reputation?"

From his defensive stance and angry expression, it was unlikely he was going to say anything.

Then Sonia reached out and took Fred's hand. "Please. For my sake, please tell me what really happened."

Yes, Fred. Tell us all.

As quickly as he'd angered, Fred returned to his normal demeanour. Quiet. Respectful in his manner. The corners of his mouth curled up as he shot an apologetic look at Daphne. Whatever his faults, he cared for Sonia.

"I should have told you from the start."

"Told me what? You make it sound as though Mum was doing something illegal."

"No. Nothing like that." Fred sighed and took a few steps away from the wall. "I did find her there." He gestured. "But she'd fallen. Hit her head. There was quite a cut and I reckon she felt nothing. It was quick."

Sonia's forehead was deeply creased. "I don't understand. Why not just say so?"

"Because she'd been drinking. A lot by the look of the empty bottle where I found her."

"Mum didn't drink. You know she always said the driver who caused the accident had to be drunk to hit the car we were in and keep going. She swore off alcohol."

"Well, she was drinking. Between that and her heart meds it must have messed with her balance because she'd hit the wall and passed away within minutes. At least, that's what the doctor said. I didn't want people thinking badly of her. I didn't want you thinking badly of her, Sonia. Not as the last memory of your mum."

A doctor went along with this?

Not the time to ask. Sonia was weeping again and Fred put his arms around her. It was a touching moment but Daphne had a whole notebook of new questions to attend to. She leaned near John and whispered, "Shall we go?"

"Can you understand why I lied, Sonia? Please say yes." Fred's voice was gentle.

"Kinda. But it hurts you didn't tell the truth."

"No more lies, Sonia. I promise."

"We missed lunch, doll. Let me make us something now." It would keep him busy for a few minutes. Give Daph a chance to pull her thoughts together and write down some thoughts.

She was at the table, notebook open and pen turning in her fingers. "Just some tea would be lovely. But you have something."

He wasn't hungry.

Too much was playing on his mind. Not to mention his churning stomach. After filling the kettle and leaving it to boil, he went through the motions of adding tea leaves to the teapot and getting out the cups and saucers. In case Daphne was hungrier than she realised, he opened the container she kept her cookies in and placed it in the middle of the table. It didn't matter that they weren't the best cookies in the world. She made them with love and to him, that alone outweighed any shortcomings they had.

"What are your thoughts, love?" Daphne helped herself to a cookie. "What a strange series of events."

"Strange indeed. And I think it raises more questions."

"Agree. Do you think Fred will be in trouble with the police for lying? Would it be considered obstruction of an investigation?"

"Better answered by someone with legal training but I can't imagine he wouldn't be censured on one level or another. And think of the damage to his own reputation let alone if he finds himself in breach of professional codes of conduct."

Once the tea was ready, John joined Daphne at the table. She'd filled a page.

"Care to share?" he asked.

"There are so many moving parts, John. People withholding the truth. Others stirring things up to amuse themselves. And good people like Ilona seemingly caught in the middle. I'm trying to work out if Edwina's disappearance has anything in common with the three unfortunate deaths."

Daphne used the end of the pen to point at the top line. "Fred is connected to each person who has died in Shady Bend in the last few days. Putting aside the fact of him living in a very small town and knowing everyone, I feel this deserves a closer look. He found Edwina. Petra was a pall-bearer and helped set things up for the wake. Zeke worked for Fred. And Amanda..." she trailed off with a thoughtful expression. "What does she have in common with all of this?"

"You told me when she arrived at the pre-funeral gathering that she was not expected and some people were surprised at her appearing." John said. "But at the actual wake, she was helping with the food. Didn't you mention Fred made some odd comment about her?"

Daphne flicked back through several pages of notes. "Yes. He said Amanda has an over-active imagination. Yet he made scones for her and Zeke after he'd had words with the latter. Oh." Her mouth dropped open and her eyes met John's. "What if he poisoned them?"

"Poisoned Amanda and Zeke? Why would he do such a thing?"

"And Petra." Daphne added.

"Wait on. You're suggesting Fred not only made a false report about Edwina's death, and somehow lost her body, but he killed off three members of the community. Fred? The mild-mannered funeral director?"

"Hm." After putting down her pen, Daphne reached for her tea. "It is far-fetched. And really, there's no reason to believe those three died from anything other than a terrible accident. I wonder if Adam has any news about how they ingested the poison."

"No doubt he'd say if he did. Well, when he could because he's had a busy day."

"Yes. I might give him an hour or so and then call."

Call Adam? Not a good idea.

Best to distract Daphne. "Tell me what else you've been writing down. Here, have another cookie."

CHASING THE TRUTH

The second cookie wasn't nearly as tasty as Daphne expected and she left most of it on the plate. Recently she'd begun to critically observe the flavours she came up with and this one just didn't seem to work. John, on the other hand, was munching his as if it were the most delicious thing he'd ever tasted.

"I may have gone overboard with the vanilla."

John shook his head and did a thumbs up.

Whatever is going on, John?

If it was the mystery then she'd back off. Upsetting her husband was at the bottom of the list of things she didn't like to do. Not just at the bottom, but buried far beneath layers of concrete. Concrete reinforced with titanium or whatever the strongest steel might be. With a deep and murky swamp on top for good measure. With crocodiles.

She giggled and John looked at her over the top of his glasses.

"What is the strongest steel?" she asked.

He blinked. "Titanium? I can find out."

"I'm being silly. My mind is at the point of going around in circles which occasionally leads to strange places. Going back to this," she tapped the notebook. "What interests me is why a doctor signed a certificate supporting Fred's original claim about Edwina. Surely, they'd be required to do a proper examination and something such as a head wound must raise questions. Well, I think it would."

"Unless there was no doctor."

John had one of those expressions on his face. The lines on his forehead creased more than usual as he contemplated the problem. Daphne could guarantee his own mind was working overtime. He poured them both more tea and continued.

"Hear me out. Fred arrives at Edwina's after dark, which is quite late at this time of year. She's sadly passed away. At first, he thinks she's succumbed to a known heart condition but perhaps he touches her—they'd been married and he might have reacted without thinking. At this point he notices the head injury or possibly smells alcohol. Instead of actually calling for a doctor, he takes her to the funeral home and tidies her up."

"Then calls a doctor?"

"Yes. Someone he trusts."

She had another thought. "Or he called this trusted doctor, told them he'd found Edwina, possibly even sent a photo of her, and they signed the certificate without even coming to her place."

Who would do such a thing?

"We should ask Adam who the doctor was."

John took her hand. "No. No, he has enough to contend

with. Between missing bodies, mystery deaths, and dishonest funeral home directors, he doesn't need us adding to his burden."

The phone rang.

"Speaking of Adam..." Daphne answered. "Just the man I want to speak with. I'm popping you onto speaker if you don't mind. John's here." She placed the phone between them.

"Daphne. Hello, John. Why do you need to speak to me?"

John leaned forward. "Nothing urgent. What can we do to help?"

Nothing urgent? What is more urgent than solving this case?

Adam's voice sounded tired, even through the phone. "Sorry to bother you both."

"Never a bother." Daphne said. "Was everything alright when you arrived? We thought it best to let you know what was going on."

"You did the right thing. I had clearly told Fred to stay away from the property and make himself available for another interview once Detective Malone arrives back from another enquiry. He was waiting in his car when I got here and is upset he lost his temper with you."

"Will he be in trouble over this?" Daphne asked.

"Can't say. I thought you'd like to know we received a report about the source of the poison."

Both of them leaned forward to better listen.

"Seems to be from jam."

Daphne gasped.

"I know. You thought that from the beginning." Adam said. "Looks as though somebody added apricot kernels to their batch. Not a good idea at the best of times. There is a poison called...um, amygdalin inside the kernel. Nasty stuff."

"Adam, do you know where it came from? And if there's any still around?"

He sighed heavily. "Sad to say we located several suspicious jars in Petra's kitchen."

Or somebody might have planted them there.

"Ilona recognised the house key John found." Daphne said. "Someone had been in her house so what if that someone was leaving something behind instead of stealing anything? And the same someone trashed the place to make it look like a robbery."

Adam chuckled.

Daphne frowned.

"You've missed your calling, Daphne. I'm considering all possibilities. Petra's not here to defend herself so we have to take great care to look at things from all sides."

"I don't mean to step on your toes." She hadn't intended to take offence but was sure Adam and John both heard it in her voice. "You are a wonderful police officer and very good at your job."

"You're not stepping on anything. And you are too kind. There are some who think the opposite of me so I'll happily take the compliment."

Did he mean Tracy? Daphne knew in her bones there was nothing corrupt about Adam Browne.

John cleared his throat. "Quick question, Adam. Any chance this was all a terrible accident? Petra might have miscalculated the ingredients and then brought a jar along to the wake with no clue she was about to poison herself?"

"Not just herself." Daphne added. "When Amanda and

Zeke had scones in the kitchen with Fred, they must have used the same jar. Fred was lucky."

There were voices in the background from Adam's end of the call. "I'm going to have to go. Detective Malone is here and Fred just arrived. But yes, it is possible it wasn't deliberate. I'll be in touch." He hung up.

As Daphne retrieved her phone, John stood. "Might make us another pot. Got a feeling we're going to need it."

"There's a fair bit of info about apricot kernels online, Daph." John's laptop was open and he scrolled with one hand while holding an almost empty teacup with the other. "Some people believe they can assist with cancer treatments."

"Even though they're toxic?"

"All about the dosage. And there are techniques for making jam which include the use of them. Not recommended but I wonder if that's what happened and too much was used?"

There were so many 'what ifs' right now. Enough to have covered a whole page of her notebook.

"Something is missing, John. There must be a connection between all of these seemingly separate issues. For example, we have a tussle over the secret recipe for a sauce with nobody admitting to having it."

"Although Sonia implied she does."

"Correct. Then there are two people who are allegedly at odds over their jam making skills to the point of a competition being organised to decide the victor but it must have been a front. A cover for the fact Petra made Edwina's products. I do wonder why not make them under her own label if they were so good?"

John swilled around the last of his tea. "Edwina had the name. The reputation. And the shop. Petra, on the other hand, owed people money and kept her little blackmail book. Maybe Edwina made Petra pay her debt off by working for her."

"So where is the book?" Daphne felt her mouth drop open. Was it really with the police or was that a lie? Who had told her...Tracy?

"Hellooo...anyone home?" Ilona called from outside.

"Come in, dear."

Ilona closed the door after herself. "Think we'll get a storm? So humid."

"Take a seat." John closed his laptop and stood. "Would you like some tea? Or we have some nice apple cider."

"Ooh, apple cider sounds good, thank you." Ilona slid opposite Daphne and glanced at the notebook. "Preparing for the next ceremony?"

"This is my list of questions about what's going on in this little town." Daphne closed the book. "Speculation. Did you sort out the fence at Petra's?"

"Yes, with a hand from one of the police. Both of us ended up covered in mud but the sheep are safe again. Can't go into Petra's until the forensic people finish and I'll be glad to tidy up for her. Well, not for her. But you know what I mean."

John placed a glass on the table then joined Daphne on her side.

"Thanks. I need to apologise for running off earlier. At Petra's. Sometimes my feelings get too much and I'm better off being alone for a bit. Like after the casket dropped at the funeral and they realised Edie wasn't inside. Anyway, I can't tell you who Sonia's father is because I don't know. Edwina never said it and I never asked."

Daphne nodded. "I can understand you being protective of Sonia. Does everyone think she has custody of Edwina's secret recipe?"

Ilona erupted into peals of laughter.

Had this all been a bit too much for her?

Picking up her glass, Ilona got the giggles under control and took a sip. "Sonia has nothing to do with the recipe. She doesn't even like the taste of it but what she does like is stirring up Tracy and some of the others. Even Fred believes Sonia has it. But can you imagine anyone keeping something so important on a handwritten note and only having one copy?"

"Do you know who has it?" Daphne asked. It was worth the question. Ilona was close to the recipe's creator and had good local knowledge. "Did Petra make the sauce as well?"

"Petra was talented but I doubt she had the finesse for it. Can't really say." She looked at her drink.

"So you know, but prefer to keep the information private?"

Looking up again, Ilona frowned. "It isn't my secret to reveal. And until we find where Edie is, it seems wrong to bring it out in the open. I imagine she covers the recipe in her will. Same as the property and the shop."

"I keep hearing there is no will." John said.

"Oh, there is. But I genuinely have no idea who has a copy. If her solicitor doesn't, and Sonia doesn't, then who would?" Ilona finished her drink.

"Fred?" Daphne suggested.

"No. They might have given the appearance of remaining friends but I can assure you it was for Sonia's benefit. She might have known Fred wasn't her biological dad, but he did okay as a stepfather and after the car accident, stability was paramount to keeping Sonia from going off the deep end. Edie used to say to me it was his best feature, the way he treated Sonia." She smiled. "Fred and Sonia were closer than Edie and Sonia. Edie kept everyone at a distance and she wasn't perfect, but I loved her."

A buzzing sound took Ilona's attention and she pulled a phone from her pocket. "My reminder. Have another house to visit to put some chickens away in case we do get a storm later." She got to her feet. "Thanks for the drink, and the chat. Will I see you before you leave?"

Daphne and John got up as well, and John opened the door and climbed down. The women followed.

"We're heading out early, aren't we, John?" Daphne asked.

"Mid-morning. At the latest."

That late?

"Well, it's probably too much to hope for, but I'd like to think Edwina will be found before you go. And whoever broke into Petra's house."

John shaded his eyes from the sun. "Did you work out how the house key got into the wrong hands? You were quite adamant it was her own copy."

Ilona shook her head. "Oddest thing. All I can think is it fell from her handbag at or after the funeral and someone took advantage of it. Bit strange there was only that key found. Got to run. I'll send you a message later, if you like, once this little meeting at the show happens? Update you."

"Yes, please. Is it at five?"

"I think." Her phone buzzed again. "See you later!"

She sprinted away.

"Does she have to run everywhere? She's making me tired watching her!" Daphne said. John didn't answer. He was gazing into the distance, arms crossed. Thinking.

A GRAVE AFFAIR

"Wonder if we should have brought flowers. Not that she's there yet, but with the grave filled in and the headstone already installed..."

Daphne and John were in Shady Bend Cemetery and had stopped near Edwina's designated resting place. There was a temporary fence around it and a sign to keep off. Not that anyone would want to step all over an unfinished plot. Surely.

"I'm sure there will be plenty of floral tributes once she's found." John said.

"You know, I have the strangest sensation about this. As if I know where she is but can't quite put the thought together enough to make sense."

John took Daphne's hand and they headed away from the plot. "I understand what you mean. Which is why we're here."

About time he explained. After Ilona left, he'd barely said a word, just gone back into Bluebell and washed up the teacups and glass. Daphne left him to work through whatever was troubling him and drew a picture in her notebook. It was a very rough map of from where the police station stood at one end of the town to where they'd seen Ilona and Desmond in the park the other night. Halfway through adding comments, John picked up the car keys.

And now, with no explanation other than he needed to visit the cemetery, here they were. They went up to the trees at the top of the low hill.

"Care to fill me in?" she asked, a little out of breath. Low hill it might be but John had gone at a cracking pace.

"Something happened after the casket was dropped. Something I saw from up here, where I was doing my research." He gazed around. "Over here a bit."

There was a clear view of the area further down. Edwina's grave. The carpark.

"So, what did you see, love? I remember you running down the hill when everyone was screaming and carrying on. Was it then?"

With a shake of his head, John wandered to a tree. He stood there, staring at the base of the trunk.

"I was talking to Ilona. Remember how she ran up here, all distressed? I found her when I came to retrieve my notebook which I'd dropped in the earlier panic." Once again, John gazed in the distance. Towards the carpark.

He'd come up here when Petra was being loaded onto the stretcher. Everyone was fussing around her. Tracy was looking for something.

"Where is her handbag." Daphne said.

"What did you say?" John's full attention was on Daphne and she searched her memories.

"Tracy said Petra would need her phone and wallet and

stuff at the hospital. As a pallbearer she'd left everything in the hearse."

"In her handbag?"

"Yes. Fred went to get it...oh, John!"

Their eyes locked together.

"Daph, I remember. Petra's handbag was on the stretcher with her."

"After Fred went to get it from the hearse. And he took a while."

"Long enough to get a key off a keyring?"

There was no need to respond. They both knew the answer.

They'd sat in the car for a few minutes, each deep in their own thoughts. Daphne suspected who'd broken into Petra's house. But why? Why would Fred do such a thing? Taking a key from an ill woman's handbag implied he already had a plan in mind.

"John? Assuming Fred took her house key just after Petra collapsed, one has to ask whether he was responsible for her death."

"Maybe. But how could he be certain she'd pass away? Even if he'd poisoned her, she was alive when the paramedics were leaving so why would getting her house key matter so much?"

"We need to ask Adam if all of Petra's keys are missing." Daphne reached for her phone.

"I think we should work this out before talking to the police. Last thing we want is to offer a half-baked idea."

John didn't look at Daphne and again, she sensed something wasn't right.

Casting her mind back, she recalled this part-distracted, part-withdrawal of John's began when he'd returned to the police station to collect his phone. He'd stood outside with Adam for a moment in discussion. Had something been said which he didn't want to discuss with her? Something about the case.

"Love?" Daphne took one of his hands. "Please tell me what's troubling you. I wouldn't press, but lately you've been quiet and even worried. Is it because I'm getting involved where I shouldn't? Because I'll stop and we can leave right now, and—"

"I'm okay." John smiled and squeezed her hand. "I am thinking something through but it isn't about the case and I think we need to stay tonight."

"But you're not going to share what the problem is."

"I promise I will. Very soon." He leaned over and kissed her lips. "Trust me."

"I do trust you."

But I want to know!

"Going back to the problem at hand, we both agree we saw Fred with Petra's handbag on the day of the funeral. The day Petra collapsed."

Daphne wound down her window. If they were going to sit in the car, she needed some fresh air.

"If the police find he did remove her house key and use it, what was the purpose?"

"Plant the jars of poisonous jam. Look for the blackmail book." Daphne said. "Petra might have kept notes about Fred. Maybe suspected he was up to no good. I really feel we need to bring this to Adam's attention. Didn't he say they were interviewing Fred at the moment?"

Sonia walked past, not seeing them as she carried a huge bouquet of yellow roses towards Edwina's grave. She climbed through the temporary fencing and stood for a moment or two, eyes on the headstone. Then, she placed the flowers on the ground and climbed back out without a backward glance. Halfway back to the carpark, she answered a phone call and walked as she talked.

"Left Mum some flowers...is there still no news?"

"We shouldn't listen." John whispered.

Daphne pretended she hadn't heard.

"I never said you were responsible for her going missing, Fred. Never." Sonia stopped and turned to face the cemetery.

Very thoughtful of you to stand within earshot.

"You told them what?"

Daphne would have given anything to hear the other end of the conversation.

"But why would Zeke and Amanda steal Mum? You can't really believe that! And then what? They simultaneously took poison out of remorse...yes, I am being sarcastic."

She listened for a while and her shoulders slumped. Her head nodded a couple of times. "Okay, okay. Whatever, Fred. I'm not up for this." She hung up and then squatted, dropping her head into her hands.

Before she could stop herself, or John could, Daphne was out of the car. Poor Sonia. So much to deal with and now the one person she trusted was proving less than honest.

"Sonia? It's just Daphne."

Sonia glanced over her shoulder.

"John and I were in our car. Just over there. We didn't mean to overhear but you seem sad." Daphne reached Sonia and went in front of her. She knew better than to attempt to squat. There'd be no coming back from such a risky manoeuvre.

"I bet you got a kick out of eavesdropping."

"It wasn't intentional, dear. You walked right past us with those lovely roses earlier."

With an exaggerated sigh, Sonia straightened and glanced at the car. John was near the bonnet, tapping on his phone.

"Fine. You didn't mean to listen in on my private conversation. I suppose you have questions. I mean, aren't you some kind of super sleuth or something? That's what Ilona's cousin said to her."

"Hardly. Just a keen observer of humans. All I came over for was to ask if you are doing okay. There's been such a lot for you to deal with between losing your mother—"

"Literally. Go on."

"Yes, well. And the three friends in quick succession. And Fred's revelation about how he really found your mother."

"I wish somebody would find Mum now. Let her rest properly. But the others weren't my friends. Petra did stuff for Mum. Same as Desmond. And others. But Petra was sneaky and not very nice. Zeke was okay but he'd do whatever Amanda told him to and as for her..." Sonia's eyes hardened. "Good riddance."

Oh my!

Daphne stepped back at the venom in the other woman's tone.

"She was useless helping Mum with her heart condition. Signed prescriptions for her without even checking her pulse or running any tests. I wish she had lost her licence instead of just leaving the practice."

As quickly as she'd angered, her mood shifted and again, her shoulders slumped. After a look back at the grave, Sonia walked past Daphne who was trying to process what she'd just heard.

"Sonia, wait a minute." Daphne followed. "One question and I won't trouble you any further." She caught up with Sonia at an old mini. "Do you know who signed your mother's Cause of Death certificate?"

Driver's door open, Sonia stopped long enough to roll her eyes. "Not very smart for a sleuth, are you? Who else but her own doctor. Amanda signed it of course."

As Sonia drove out of the car park, Daphne's mind was in overdrive. And the direction it was taking was disturbing. Very disturbing indeed.

HANDBAGS AND ROSES

"Adam's flat out, Mrs Jones." Porter attended the counter at the police station. She was alone from the look of things. "He's with the forensic investigators and could be hours yet, so unless it is urgent?"

"John and I recalled something from the funeral and thought it might be useful information." Was this a mistake? She and John might put two and two together and come up with four, but since when did the police—trained investigators doing their job—need the advice of a retired couple with too much time on their hands? "I'm sorry. I don't mean to waste your time and should let you get back to work."

Daphne forced a smile and made for the front door. This was twice today she'd doubted her reasoning. Seen herself from another perspective. A meddler. A nuisance who was tolerated because she'd been unwittingly put in the middle of events.

"Mrs Jones? Daphne, I'm happy to leave a note for Adam. We can use all the help we can get."

"You're sure? I don't wish to be a pest."

Porter laughed. "That is the last thing you are. You've helped a lot so come and tell me what's on your mind."

John was outside. He'd mentioned needing to make a phone call and after all the texting at the cemetery, Daphne had the feeling it might be to do with their real estate agency back in Rivers End. Although the young man running things was capable, on occasion he and John conferred about properties or clients.

"Very well." Daphne placed her handbag on the counter. "I'm not expecting you to tell me any details, but if you haven't already uncovered how Petra's house key got into the hands of the person who entered and trashed her house, then we may have the answer."

Porter raised her eyebrows. "Let me grab a notepad." She went to her desk. "On my own at the moment. Too much going on in our little town and we've had to split the resources."

"Between Petra's house and Edwina's house?"

"Oh, not Edwina's. They're finished up there. But yes, Petra's house as well as back at the funeral home." She returned, opened the notepad and pulled a pen out of a plastic cup on the counter. "Right. Go ahead."

"On the day of the funeral, I was officiating, as you know. John—my husband—was in the cemetery as well. Genealogy is his hobby and he was up the little hill. If we fast forward to after the casket was dropped and after Petra collapsed, both of us observed the same person with her handbag. We just hadn't compared notes and in fact, John hadn't given it any thought until we were back up there today and it jogged his memory."

"I'm all ears."

"The paramedics were putting Petra onto the stretcher and Tracy was looking for her belongings. Said she'd need her phone and purse at the hospital."

"So, it was Tracy with the handbag?"

"Negatory. It was Fred."

Pen poised to write, Porter's eyes shot back to Daphne's.

"Say again."

"I heard Fred say he'd collect Petra's handbag from the hearse. And John saw him give it to the paramedics who placed it beside her. Now we certainly don't know that he removed the key but he did take a few minutes to retrieve the handbag."

After jotting down a few lines, Porter pulled out her phone. "Just a minute, please." She wrote and sent a message. "I've let Adam know. He's at the funeral home with the dogs again. Well, one dog."

"Oh, let me guess. The one who took such a dislike to Fred the other day."

"Got it in one."

"Fred told us he didn't like dogs and the police dog must have sensed it. But it struck me as odd that the dog couldn't pick up the trail of someone who'd been at the funeral home for several days—Edwina—yet was so intent on Fred. Did you ever find the rhubarb and apricot jam Petra ate the day of the funeral?"

"No. We did look even though the staff did a search as soon as Adam alerted them to the possibility the jar was contaminated. Fred was adamant there was none of that flavour on the premises."

"Fred?"

Was that why the police dog was so upset? What if Fred

had handled the jar to dispose of it and the dog could sense the poison?

"Mrs Jones. Daphne. I'm going to have to make some phone calls if you could excuse me. Unless you have more information?"

Porter's expression begged Daphne to leave. She fiddled with the pen and glanced at her phone. She might be thinking the same thoughts and not give anything away to a civilian.

"No, dear. Well, apart from Sonia telling me that Amanda signed Edwina's Cause of Death certificate. Which seems a bit convenient."

"Sorry. How?"

"Did Amanda even attend the cottage that night? She signed something to say Edwina died from a heart condition. But Fred admitted Edwina had a head injury which wasn't included on the certificate. Do we even know for certain Amanda saw the body?"

Porter's phone beeped but she ignored it. "Are you thinking Fred had something to do with Edwina's death?"

"Surely it is possible. And if Amanda lied, then Fred might have needed to make sure the truth never came out."

"You think he poisoned Amanda. What about Petra and Zeke?" Beth's phone rang.

"I'll leave you with that thought."

No point keeping Constable Porter from answering her call. Daphne had said her piece. If there was anything useful in it, then she had to trust the police would add it to their information base. It was out of her hands. She'd done enough and it was time to head back to Bluebell for their last night here.

When Daphne emerged from the police station, she wore a look of satisfaction which brought John a moment of relief. He'd wanted to be in there with her for support and to back up her statement. But there was someone he needed to speak with and the timing clashed. Whether he'd made the right decision remained to be seen.

"Finished with your call?" Daphne joined him beneath a tree near the car. "Everything alright?"

"Yes, and yes. Would you care for a cold drink at the café?"

"Yes please!"

Leaving the car where it was, they crossed the road but the café was closed and John checked his watch. "Goodness me. Hadn't noticed how late it is. They closed an hour ago so what about some bottled water from the supermarket?"

They decided to walk the block or so as the weather was finally cooling down and as they did, Daphne repeated the conversation with Porter.

"She seemed shocked about Fred handling Petra's handbag. Oh, and the police dog, the one which disliked Fred, is back at the funeral home for some reason. Wouldn't be surprised if there's an arrest in the cards."

Once they had their water, they sat on a bench beneath the awning of another shop. The street was quiet as the day wound down. Shady Bend was a nice place to visit. To sit for a while. Or would be if there wasn't at least one criminal on the loose.

"It was different in Little Bridges," Daphne said. "There was a family feud and it made it so much easier to pinpoint who had real motive to kill, even though it was a surprise once we found out. But here, well there isn't a clear picture of why this happened."

"Edwina? Or the others?"

"Still feel it is all connected. When I was at the cottage for Sonia's photo shoot, I wondered how someone who cared so much for their garden would let other aspects of their life fall apart. I think that garden is at risk of falling apart." Daphne sighed and opened her water bottle.

"I don't understand? Do you think it won't be cared for?"

"Not going by the poor roses." Daphne said.

"Which roses?"

"Oh, the ones from the postcard. Remember I said Sonia insisted we have our photo taken in front of them and I noticed the middle three or four plants were on the droopy side. I took a photo."

She took her phone out and scrolled through her gallery. "Here we go. See how the leaves look so sad. And it was only these four in the middle. Not so obvious from a distance." Daphne found an image of the whole rose bed.

"That's not right."

"I know. Almost as if someone watered the ones on each end and not the middle."

John shook his head. "I mean the colours. I'm sure in the large photograph at the show that the roses were alternating. Pink, yellow, red. See how each one on the end is red, then the next is yellow, then pink and so on until we get to these four."

Red, yellow, pink, red became red, red, pink, yellow.

He used his fingers to pinch the screen and zoom in, this time to the ground beneath the roses.

"New mulch on those roses. Look, the mulch under the others is faded but under those central four or five there's a fresh covering. Could be they're not getting enough water beneath it. But the colours..."

He was certain he was right. He'd loved the photo at the show and paid it quite a lot of attention, enjoying the little touches in it, such as the patterns of colours.

"I know how we can check." Daphne said as she stood.

"Not sure we should be going to the cottage."

"Didn't you buy a postcard of the same photograph?"

"Clever cookie. Yes, I did." John got to his feet. "We can drive home and take a look."

"Or, seeing how close we are to Edwina's shop, we could drop in and take a look at the postcard stand."

John put an arm around Daphne's shoulders and kissed her cheek. "Even better."

He was probably wrong. There was no reason to believe there was anything out of place in the rose garden. Apart from droopy leaves, new mulch, and the possibility of roses dug up and replanted. Nothing out of place at all.

IN HER GARDEN

"I wonder why the canine unit is back at the funeral home. Do you think they're searching for Edwina again, or trying to find if there is any more poisonous jam hidden away?" Daphne asked as they crossed the last street before Edwina's shop.

"Good question. Guess it depends on what came of the interview with Fred as well as any forensic results the police have had in."

A car slowed as it passed them. Fred glared through the window at Daphne and a shiver shot up her spine. He'd probably had quite enough of seeing her wherever he went. Well, they'd be gone soon and she, for one, wasn't going to miss the funeral home director. As nice as he'd been to her in the beginning, it was becoming clear there was more to the man than met the eye. For all she knew, he might have murdered Edwina and the other three.

"Okay?" John opened the door to the shop. "You look a bit troubled."

No point worrying you with my silly thoughts.

"I really like some of the people here. And the area. I'd like to come back one day but only as a tourist."

"Did you say tourist?" Constance welcomed them with a huge smile. "I love tourists. I love every customer actually and am so happy you've both returned for more of our delectable goodies."

It was like seeing a dear friend again, stepping in here. The same sense of familiarity from the other day returned and Daphne's heart filled up at the genuine friendliness of the young woman.

"We'd love to see what else you have, not that we've had a chance yet to open even one of the products from the last visit."

"Not even the special sauce?" Constance asked in surprise.

"Special occasion. You did mention it was in short supply." John wandered over to the postcards. "Do you happen to know when the photo was taken from this one?" He picked up the postcard of Edwina's garden and cottage. "How long ago?"

"About a month ago. Sonia showed it to Edwina on her phone the day she took it, here in the shop. She was so happy but Edwina told her she should have waited until the cottage was repainted. They had a bit of a spat about it because every year Edwina says she'll have it painted in summer and then it never happens. Sonia said she was entering it in the show and Edwina told her not to expect to win."

"It didn't." John said. He showed Daphne. "See the roses."

He had an excellent memory. The roses alternated between pink, yellow, and red. No two plants of the same colours were beside each other and the plants appeared strong and healthy.

Constance joined them, her eyes darting to the postcard. "Is something wrong?"

"Dear, are you aware of anyone moving these roses around? Perhaps some of them were diseased or something and needed replacing?" Daphne asked.

"Haven't heard anything like that and I'm sure Edwina would have told me. She talked about her garden more than anything else and there is no way her plants would be diseased or the like. If she wasn't in the garden, she was talking about it which is why some of us..." Constance bit her lip.

"Daph, I might just make a quick call about that thing we discussed on the way here."

John went outside and as he dialled, he wandered out of sight.

"Which is why some of you do what?" Was Constance in on the arrangement of making products under Edwina's name? "John and I were at Petra's house earlier. Ilona asked us to go there while she waited for the police to arrive. Outside the front door was a box, a bit battered from being dropped by the delivery driver by the looks of things. But we could easily see the contents."

Constance abruptly turned and walked to the other side of the counter. Her lips were pressed against each other and her face had paled. She fussed with her apron for a while and Daphne gave her time to think.

"It's not what you think." Constance blurted. "Edwina was very talented but when she was diagnosed with her heart condition it was if everything changed for her. She lost interest in making her jams and preserves and even in painting. Some of us helped out. You need to understand Edwina made this town a destination and she was so afraid of letting it down. Of this shop failing because of her illness." Tears brightened her eyes.

"I didn't mean to upset you. How kind of you and the—others—to help keep things going. But now she's gone, people won't expect her name on products."

"There's so much to sort out. People are saying the shop won't continue to trade."

"It won't."

Both women swung around. Fred stood inside the door.

"What makes you think that?" Daphne asked.

Her heart pounded but she wasn't about to allow this man to stop her finding the truth despite his somewhat belligerent stance with his legs apart and arms crossed.

Trust yourself, Daph. Be brave.

"Fred, why wouldn't the shop keep running?"

"The real question is why *would* it. Edwina is dead. Sonia doesn't want to run it. That leaves nobody. It'll be sold off to repay debt."

"What kind of debt?" Daph asked. John came into view outside, still on the phone. He glanced in and stopped when he saw Fred, who at that moment took a couple of steps forward. John said something and hung up the call.

"Me. She owed me money from our divorce and we had an arrangement that I'd be paid back out of the sale of this and that the property will come to me."

Constance laughed. This took Fred's attention away from Daphne and she quickly caught John's eye and did a tiny shake of her head. Fred might let something slip if he thought he had a limited audience.

"Nothing funny about this, Constance. You're about to

lose your job and not even your bully of a father can stop that."

"Dad isn't a bully, Fred. And this shop isn't going anywhere."

"Is that right?" Fred sneered at Constance and Daphne stepped around the counter to stand beside her. "Look at the two of you. Think you're both so smart but I have letters signed by Edwina and without a will—"

"There is a will!"

"She never made one, Constance."

"It might be missing at the moment but I've seen it which is why I know this shop is safe and so is Sonia's home."

Fred's arms dropped to his sides and a strangely comical expression of confusion replaced his smugness. He shook his head. Muttered something. And then took another step.

John walked in. "I'm back, Daph. Have you got some more of the special sauce?"

Silence fell. John stayed near the door. Daphne grabbed Constance's hand behind the counter and squeezed it. Fred put both his hands on the counter, his eyes going from John to Constance.

In the distance, a siren wailed.

"This will. What does it say about the recipe?" Fred asked. "She owes it to me. I'm the one who supported her getting this place off the ground. I paid for everything when all she had was kitchen skills and a vision. Do you know I even poured money into her precious garden? And I raised someone else's child as my own."

Daphne released Constance's hand and forced herself to go around the end of the counter. John looked alarmed but she had questions to ask. Best done without a barrier.

"Sonia seems to care a great deal about you, Fred. Wouldn't you want her to keep the property she's always lived on?"

"The thing none of you understand is Desmond wants to buy the place to extend his orchard. He'll leave Sonia's cottage alone but bulldoze Edwina's and dig up her garden. But she told me I could have it if I keep her garden. Of course, I'll keep her garden." With something like a sob, Fred covered his face with his hands.

The siren was closer and John glanced through the window.

"Fred? When did Edwina say you could have the property?"

He dropped his hands and straightened. "Right before I pushed her. I didn't mean to. We were arguing about Desmond. Again. And she yelled at me I could have the blasted property but it would never change the fact he was Sonia's father."

Constance gasped and her hand flew to her mouth.

Not common knowledge then?

"I didn't mean to hurt her." Fred shook his head. "Never meant it."

The siren stopped.

"And you buried her in the rose garden." Daphne said with a calmness she certainly didn't feel. To the contrary, her legs shook and her stomach did somersaults. She'd need a lie down after this. "And Amanda signed a certificate without seeing her body."

He nodded. All the fight was gone. "Amanda was drunk and didn't even remember. At least not until Zeke mentioned not having to replace any embalming products like he normally would. He began to question whether

Edwina was ever there so I paid him a bundle of cash to say he'd helped collect her and had seen her at the funeral home. But then he wanted more. Things went downhill fast."

Adam let himself in. His eyes shot to Constance who gave him a tiny smile. A little of the tension on his face drained away. Daphne wasn't finished but at least Adam was here to listen.

"So, Zeke wanted more hush money and he was involved with Amanda. You made them scones with jam and cream. Where was the jam from, Fred?" Daphne crossed her fingers behind her back. Would he keep talking now Adam was here?

As if he'd held onto secrets for too long, Fred poured it all out. "Petra did something with the apricot and rhubarb jam. She told me she found an old recipe using a small amount of ground apricot kernels and thought she'd add a few extra for good measure. Added it when the jam was almost cool. Silly woman didn't bother to check about the danger and by the time she told me, she'd already eaten some. I put the jar in my pocket intending to dispose of it but then she died."

"Were you afraid you'd be blamed?"

"I've said enough."

Adam stepped forward. "Fred, I need you to accompany me to the police station."

As if seeing Adam for the first time, Fred gazed up at him. "Three times in one day."

"You might have told me this earlier, mate." Adam took handcuffs out. "Do I need these?"

"Rather you didn't if you don't mind. Have a reputation to uphold."

Porter burst through the door, followed by another uniformed police officer. She stopped, looking from one to the other.

“Mind taking Fred in? Put him in the interrogation room and stand guard. I’ll be along soon.”

Fred stumbled out with the other two officers holding his arms.

Adam hurried around the counter to wrap Constance in a hug. Over her shoulder, he nodded to Daphne and mouthed ‘thank you’.

Those shaky legs weren’t getting any better and Daphne grabbed at the counter top as they threatened to give away. John was there in an instant and slid his hands under her arms and Adam dragged a stool around from the back.

And then Daphne burst into tears.

NOT FAIR

After a glass of water and a small piece of fudge which Constance insisted she eat, Daphne was steady as a rock again. Or close enough.

"I'm going to go to the station and charge Fred." There was worry in Adam's eyes when he looked at Daphne. "Are you going straight home?"

John took Daphne's hand. "Just stopping long enough to get something easy for dinner and we'll head back. You don't need us for anything tonight? I'd like to get Daph home and fed."

Daphne laughed and the other three looked at her. "You make it sound like I'm an over-tired toddler. I'm fine, all of you stop worrying."

Constance gave her a quick hug. "You are amazing. The way you persuaded Fred to tell you all of his secrets was like watching a movie. A really good detective movie. Dad, what if I join the police force?"

"No."

Everyone laughed.

"Connie, isn't it closing time? Do you want me to stay?" Adam glanced at his watch.

"Go arrest Fred. I'll close up and then I'm going to the show."

After Adam left, John grabbed the shop sign from outside for Constance.

"Are you sure you are doing alright, dear? That was quite a shock." Daphne asked.

"Oh, I'm fine. But I'd never have guessed Fred was a killer and had no idea about Desmond. Does Sonia even know?"

"I think so. Well, he was going to tell her at five, wasn't he? At the gates to the show. Actually, do you need a lift there, Constance? We're going right past." John offered. "I can pop into the supermarket now and be back in five. If you're okay waiting, Daph?"

"Actually, a lift would be good. Meeting a friend so getting home is fine." Constance followed John to the front door. "I'll lock us in."

As Constance counted the takings, Daphne found herself drawn to the small oil paintings on the shelf. Was there anything left which Edwina really created? Any paintings, or produce? How sad to lose interest in a lifelong passion thanks to health concerns. And how kind of others to try and keep her wishes alive.

"May I ask something? And don't feel obliged to answer because I've already heard you refuse to tell Fred, but..."

Constance grinned as she folded a money bag. "The recipe for the secret sauce?"

"Am I that obvious?"

"It's what everyone wants to know." Constance leaned on the counter. "Tracy and Fred and Desmond and Petra.

And others. Always asking Edwina to sell it to them. To let them commercialise it. And she would have except it was never hers to sell."

The smile on the younger woman's face said it all. There was a quiet pride in her expression and Daphne clapped her hands in delight.

"You created the recipe!"

"I did. And I was all of sixteen at the time so Dad and Edwina came to a legal arrangement about her selling it under the shop brand. I make it and take a sizeable share of the proceeds and now Edwina is gone, I'll receive documentation to prove my ownership. Once the current batch is sold, I will begin selling under my own label."

"You are clever as well as kind and friendly and brave and beautiful."

Constance blushed and picked up the money bag. "Must run in the family. I'll be right back." She disappeared into the back room.

Run in the family? Adam might be most of those things but Daphne wouldn't describe him as beautiful. Or did she mean her mother? Either way, Constance was a wonderful young woman and she was very pleased to know her. It made the whole time in Shady Bend worthwhile.

John was able to park not far from the front gate of the showgrounds to let Constance out.

"I'll see you tomorrow?" Constance climbed out. "Can't wait to go and see who the winners are."

"Have fun, and yes, we'll pop in before we leave." Daphne said.

Constance waved and walked away, then stopped to look at her phone. “Hey! I just got asked to be a surprise judge!”

“That’s exciting! What for?”

“The jam-off event. Me, Ilona, and Tracy. See you!”

With that she was sprinting off.

John started the motor and Daphne’s hand flung out to grip his knee.

“No. We have to stop her.”

“Why would we do that?”

Daphne undid her seatbelt. “This jam-off is the event Fred designed to judge whether Edwina or Petra’s jam was the best. But there’s no competition because—”

“Petra made them both!” John turned off the motor and was out of the car in an instant. “It is almost six.”

Daphne got out in a bit of a panic, spilling the contents of her handbag all over the ground. “Oh dear. John, you run after her. I don’t have Connie’s number so I’ll phone Adam and Ilona and be right behind you.”

By the time she’d thrown everything back in her bag, John was out of sight. Daphne paid for a ticket and tried to dial as she walked. Never a good idea and after almost colliding with a post, she stopped to one side of the path. Her hands were shaking so much she had to put her password back in twice and then rang Ilona. The call rang out. No message bank. She tried Tracy and this time it was picked up. Thank goodness.

“Tracy is busy. If you must bother her, leave a message but make it snappy.”

“Oh no. Um, This is Daphne. Do not let anyone taste the jam! This is an emergency.” She hung up. Tracy would likely ignore her anyway.

Adam didn't answer but Porter did, and promised to call Constance and send a patrol car. Now she could follow John. He'd likely have taken the quickest route which was straight through the side show. Daphne turned the other way. If she hurried, she'd get there in time. Her phone rang.

Heavy breathing. "Daph..."

"John! What's wrong!"

He sounded awful.

"I'm okay. Turned my ankle in a pothole. Can only hobble. You need to get there."

"But...yes. Okay. Going."

Chin up, Daphne shoved the phone in her handbag as she turned back. There was no chance of reaching that pavilion by six o'clock if she took the long way.

The side show loomed. First were fairy floss sellers and popcorn machines. Not a problem at all. Then some rides. Bumper cars. Giant teacups.

I could use a cup of tea. With a good splash of sherry in it!

Along here it was busy. Kids and adults and lots of teens all out for fun. Some lined up for rides and others for a chance to win something. Clown head turned side to side, mouths open to catch a ball. Disappointed faces mingled with excited ones.

She gulped, pushing down a giant lump of ice in her chest.

The music. The same music from the merry-go-round from the other day. And from her distant memories.

You have to save Constance!

One step. Two. Another.

Shouting. An angry man yelling.

"Daphne! Daphne, you show yourself!"

Heart in her mouth, Daphne spun around.

Nobody was calling her.

But now she was frozen in place, her feet stuck to the ground and her throat tight. Horses went up and down. Lights and music. Chaos.

"Can you help me find my daddy?" A small hand held Daphne's. She looked down in shock. It was a little boy, maybe five or six years old, with big, scared eyes.

People brushed past.

"What's your name?" she croaked.

"John."

"Well, that is a fine name, John. Let's find your dad."

Up past the merry-go-round was a show official, sauntering in the other direction.

"We'll ask the man with the orange vest. Okay?"

The little boy nodded and they started off.

Past the merry-go-round.

John gripped her hand. Poor little mite.

Past the Ferris wheel.

Almost out of the side show. The official was just ahead.

"Excuse me, there's a little boy—"

"John! John, I'm here, son."

From behind came the call. The little boy released her hand and was running. She couldn't look. But she had to.

A young man opened his arms as John ran towards him, little legs pumping to get there.

"Don't...hurt...him." She whispered, her arms drawing up around herself. "Don't hurt..."

John's father lifted him and spun him around with a broad smile. "Gotcha! Stay closer, dude. Thanks, lady!" He joined the crowd and John waved at her as they disappeared.

She touched her face. It was wet with tears. But deep

inside something had changed. The lump of ice had melted. Whatever happened back then, all those years ago, didn't matter anymore. The man she'd known as her father wasn't like the dad of the little boy. But he'd still been the man she called Dad.

And the pavilion was only twenty metres away.

John's ankle shot pain up his leg every time he put weight on it but he couldn't stop. Daphne hadn't gone past him so she must have been too far behind to make it in time. He was sure six o'clock had come and gone and if they were too late to stop the jam-off, what would happen? Would there be time to get anyone to hospital? To counteract the poison?

He shuffled up the ramp holding the railing and finally made it through the doors, blinking as his eyes adjusted.

At the far end of the building was a table with people seated and a selection of jams in front of them. Constance scooped up a spoonful.

"Staaap!"

The entire pavilion hushed. People turned. And most importantly, Constance dropped the spoon with a clang.

A breath whooshed out of him as Daphne wound her way through onlookers until she reached the table. She picked up the lids and one by one, twisted them back on the jars. "There'll be no jam tasting today!"

FAMILIES AND FRIENDS

Even though John was awake early, he didn't go far from Bluebell. Instead, he opened a camp chair and sat outside the door. Before long he'd wake Daphne, but for now, he had some thinking to do.

In a couple of hours, there was a small chance Daphne might finally meet her biological father. She didn't know about it. And she didn't because there was no guarantee Alfie would be there at the arranged meeting place. His one phone call with the man was awkward and left John with more questions than ever. There'd not been animosity, but nor was there surprise or excitement.

Had he done the wrong thing by contacting Alfie without telling his wife? Recently, she'd made comments about not wanting to know a man who didn't care if he had a child. And John had a strong feeling Alfie knew about Daphne.

There was no going back, but the next question was whether to explain his actions before he took Daphne to the gazebo in the park, a place all parties agreed on. All parties being him and Alfie, and Adam and Constance. Or did he take her there and try to explain at the time? It seemed unfair on Daphne.

"Why are you so sad?" Daphne climbed down the steps, wrapped in her dressing gown with her hair all curly after a shower last night.

John stood, taking care with his sore ankle, and gave her a kiss. "Not sad. Thinking."

"About yesterday?"

"No."

She tilted her head with a question and the love in her eyes gave him the answers he sought.

"What if I make you some coffee and we sit and talk for a while. There's something you need to know."

To call the past few days eventful was an understatement, but John's news shadowed it all. Daphne sipped her coffee as he spoke, using the action to keep her from jumping in and asking questions. There'd be time for that.

"I managed to get his phone number but it took a few tries to reach him. And I really don't want to get your hopes up about him actually coming to meet with us. He has a reputation as a cranky old man, not my words, and apart from his woodworking shop is a reclusive type."

John was nervous about this. He should have told her he was following leads after her father and now she understood why he'd been so distracted.

"Daph? I hope I've done the right thing."

She put down her cup and took his hand. "You've done the right thing. I always wondered if part of your interest in genealogy was looking for him but I never expected him to be alive, let alone found. You're a fine detective, John Jones."

He didn't seem quite convinced.

"Nobody else would have done this. My mother refused to help me look. And my siblings...well, they thought I was disrespecting my stepfather by wanting to know more." She leaned towards him and squeezed his hand. "I now know he is alive. And if I get to meet him, that is icing on the cake."

At last, a smile broke though and John lifted her hand and kissed her fingers.

"In that case, are you up for a bit of a walk in an hour?"

As it was, Daphne drove them both. John had insisted he would still drive towing Bluebell later which would become a problem if he made his ankle worse by lots of walking. The drive only took a couple of minutes and they wandered to the gazebo, which was empty.

"Bit early, Daph. Let's sit."

"Will we get a chance to say goodbye to Constance on the way out?" Daphne perched on the edge of a seat as nerves suddenly flooded her. "Thank goodness we got to her in time."

"You got to her. Daph, I've rarely been as proud of you as yesterday when you not only faced your fears but smashed them. When I heard you tell everyone to stop what they were doing I was so relieved."

"I think it was 'staaap'. But it worked, even if Tracy kept saying I should leave and stop drinking."

"But to her credit, once she knew there was a real threat with the jam she was like a drill sergeant. Find a box.

Tighten the lids. Secure the jars in the box. And she did apologise. Sort of."

Tracy's grunted, "Cheers. You did okay," was about as good as Daphne would get.

Ilona had been the opposite, thanking Daphne and John over and over. And then weeping when Adam arrived and gave the news that they knew where Edwina was buried. Sonia was absent as was Desmond.

"She kind of knew, in her heart, that he was her father." Ilona had said. "Sonia wasn't upset and he stopped all the bluff and bravado and they went to get a coffee. I think they'll be fine."

Now, as a car nosed into the carpark, Daphne put the memories aside. Was this Alfie Browne? What would she say? Or do? Which question first? Her head was a riot of thoughts clashing against each other.

But it was only Adam in his patrol car. He climbed out and waved. Was it some development in the case? Did he need to arrange an interview?

"How does Adam know we're here?"

"Not just Adam, Daph."

She stood and stared.

Constance got out of the back seat and opened the passenger door. She also waved with a huge grin and the truth hit Daphne.

"They are my relatives?"

"Adam is your cousin, doll."

Her throat constricted and she stopped breathing. Her heart was beating but so fast it hurt.

A frail man with lots of white hair and a limp held onto Constance's arm as they crossed the grass beside Adam. Daphne couldn't stay still and ran towards them but she could barely see where she was going and took off her glasses to wipe away the offending tears.

"Hiya, cousin." Adam joked and gave her a hug. "Best surprise I've ever had."

Constance reached for Daphne's hand and placed it on her arm, where Alfie's hand rested. "Daphne Jones, let me introduce my great uncle, and your father, Mister Alfred Browne."

Steady brown eyes gazed back at her in a face worn by time. The smallest flicker at the edge of his lips told her everything she'd needed to know. She didn't need questions. And she didn't need answers just now. She had her dad.

"Adam tells me you helped bring Fred Yates to justice. Never liked him." Alfie held Daphne's hand as they sat alone on a bench. The others were over at the pond talking.

"I just observed some things."

"Not going to lie to you, Daphne. I knew about you. Always did. But I wasn't welcome and never was good with staying in one place. Not until I settled here."

"Where you grew up. And you had siblings here."

"Adam was a kid without a dad, due to my brother passing away. He made up a little for my mistake."

Every ounce of joy seeped out of Daphne. This was worse than never meeting him. She couldn't unhear his admission.

"What's wrong, lass. Look like someone stole your dreams."

"I was a...a mistake?"

Alfie frowned. And then he put his hands on her shoulders. "You are no mistake. Me leaving you? That was the biggest mistake of my life."

"When will you and John come back to visit? Or move here? That would be good! Ilona doesn't want to be a celebrant anymore so you can take over." Constance had her arm through Daphne's as they all walked to the cars.

"I have quite a few bookings for a while, but John and I will look at the schedule tonight and see where we can make visits."

"Well, there have to be a lot. Something happened yesterday."

"Oh?"

"Petra's book? The one everybody was so afraid of? Well, she gave it to Dad a few weeks ago because she was trying to work on herself. Stop being a pain. He promised to lock it up until she wanted it back and so he did. And he remembered about it last night and guess what was inside?"

I am scared to ask.

"Edwina's will. I'd say Edwina figured it was safe with Petra because few people liked her and they had their arrangement with the products. Anyway, she left me the shop so I'm going to be very busy taking it to the next level."

"Starting with Connie's Special Sauce."

Neither of them spoke until Daphne parked beside Bluebell. There'd been more tears with goodbyes and some for happiness and now there was a whole lot of planning ahead.

"Thank you, love." Daphne turned the engine off. "You've given me a family."

"Couldn't be happier. I'm just sorry we can't stay longer."

"Can't let my bride and groom down."

They climbed out.

"I'll prepare Bluebell for travel. Should be ready in half an hour or so."

Daphne stood in the sunshine watching him as he began the tasks he'd turned into a fine art over the past few months. How she loved this man. He'd been her rock for all their marriage and she knew him as well as any person could know another person.

And I can never repay you for doing what nobody else would. You found my father.

He'd helped make her whole. But she'd helped herself as well. Carnivals might not be her go-to but she'd never fear them again.

"Everything okay? Maybe you should get out of the sun."

"Negatory. I think it is high time I stepped out of the shade.

TALES OF LIFE AND DAPH

BOOK THREE

Tales of Life and Daph

WHAT HAPPENS IN THE GARDEN, STAYS IN THE GARDEN

If it wasn't for the mysterious note, Daphne would be asleep by now, enjoying the rare luxury of silk sheets and a whole king-size four poster bed to herself. She might have left the French doors open to the balcony to let the warm night air in. Or she might have closed the doors and slept with only a sheet covering her night wear. The choice was hers.

If it wasn't for the mysterious note, she'd have read more of the paperback she'd begun as she enjoyed a late evening cup of tea. Or she might have indulged in a spa bath before donning the hotel dressing gown and writing notes about the people she'd met today to share with John tomorrow. More choices she'd have enjoyed making.

But there *was* a note which left *choice* out of the equation!

Daphne stopped near the dark, deserted tennis courts and checked the note in question using the flashlight on her phone.

There was a map—hand drawn squiggles which represented the hotel and its outer buildings, along with a couple of paths. If she was reading this right, she needed to head to the English garden behind the high hedges.

A shiver ran up her spine to her neck and the tiny hairs stood up. Turning off the flashlight, she gazed around. Was there someone in the shadows, watching her? More likely the tingle of fear was a response to her solitary venture.

Alone in the dark in a strange place. Good one, Daph.

But by the time she'd seen the envelope on the floor slipped beneath the door to her suite, the hotel was quiet. It was past midnight and her gentle tap on the door of the next suite got no response. She didn't know which rooms belonged to anyone else she'd met during the evening and the reception desk had a 'back at six a.m.' sign on it.

Had her neighbour been awake, she would have had someone to show the note to. Get another opinion. And possibly some company on this trek through the grounds of a secluded hotel. But he wasn't.

When nothing moved around her, she turned the flashlight back on and drew a deep breath. Above the map were handwritten instructions and it was those which had compelled her to put on sensible shoes and let herself out of the hotel at this hour.

Come to the fountain at the top of the mountain.

It was the first line in a poem of sorts.

The rest of it was about singing and dancing in the dark and more invitation to meet. And seeing who had left the hotel a few minutes ago left her no option but to follow.

"Next time don't look out of the window." She muttered, raised the flashlight to light her way, and got going again.

Between the high, perfectly manicured hedges was an archway of climbing roses leading into the English garden. Daphne hesitated, peering into the gloom. Above her, heavy clouds scuttled along, threatening rain. She flashed the light around and squealed as a figure loomed close by.

Get a grip, Daph. It's a statue!

Now her heart was thudding. This was a terrible idea. Out here so far from the hotel in the dead of night. It was time to go back before she scared herself again.

But she couldn't. Not until she located the note writer.

She forced her feet to cross the grass to the five-tiered fountain.

All was quiet.

"Well, that is odd."

The fountain wasn't splashing. No water flowed. Did the staff turn it off at night?

As she reached the fountain the clouds parted and moonlight streamed onto the garden highlighting the statues and benches. The garden beds.

And the body face down in the water.

A body wearing a red velvet jacket.

A LITTLE BIT PERFECT

EARLIER THAT DAY...

"Two nights in a luxury queen suite with valley views. All meals including sumptuous breakfasts and the gala dinner. Champagne on arrival. Heated pool. Spa treatments by appointment. Oh my, John, pinch me!"

Daphne Jones didn't mean the last bit but she couldn't stop smiling. She and John had rarely stayed in a hotel let alone a five-star exclusive retreat in the mountains but this is exactly where they were heading. This very minute. Or they would be once John was finished settling Bluebell and the car in at the secure carpark partway up the mountain. A dozen or more vehicles were already here but not another soul in sight, except for the driver of the 4WD who waited near his vehicle.

"Have you got everything, Daph? Nothing left inside you'll need because once we're up there, we can't duck back down at will."

"I'll check again. Just in case."

She climbed into their caravan and headed first to the bedroom. The bed was neatly made, ready for their return. The narrow side tables on either side were clear of everything other than the paperback she'd read for a few minutes earlier and she reached for it before pulling back her hand.

"Silly idea. No time for reading!"

Nothing of importance remained in the bathroom. Her makeup bag was already in her suitcase in the 4WD. So was John's shaver and her hair dryer. Probably a five-star hotel would have hair dryers but better to be safe than sorry.

She checked the rest of Bluebell and ended up in the kitchen, frowning at one of those annoying nagging feelings she'd forgotten something.

"Ready, doll?" John called.

"Be right there."

When I remember.

It was something important. Something to share...

"Dandelions and ducks!" She opened the small pantry and pulled out two containers. "Fancy leaving you behind."

John stuck his head in with a smile. Then he saw what Daphne carried and it disappeared.

"Are you sure you want to take them? There'll be plenty to eat there."

She passed him the containers. "They're not just food. They are for making friends with. Everyone loves cookies."

"You might offend the chef bringing your own supplies."

"I'll make sure the chef gets first bite then. One can make friends with more than the other guests."

John sighed. She was sure it was a sigh. But he nodded and carried the containers to the 4WD and found space in his duffel bag for them. She closed Bluebell's door and locked it, then ran a hand over the bright blue and white exterior. "We won't be long. You have a nice rest."

The driver glanced at his watch and she got the message. The poor man had been there for an hour and probably wanted a cup of tea. Perhaps a cookie might help? But John opened the door for her.

It took her a minute to work out the best way to get in. Her right foot on the running plate didn't let her get traction so she switched legs, reached up for the handle on the inside, and pulled. John gave her a little push and she was in. Much higher than their car. John got in from the other side and they put on their seatbelts as the driver hoisted himself up with more style than they'd shown.

"I'm Colin. Col. The road up the mountain is narrow and a bit winding in spots but it'll give you some decent views. If either of you feel car sick give me plenty of notice. Can't always stop and I'd rather not have to clean up after you. Apart from that, sit back and enjoy the trip. Be there in about twenty minutes."

Colin was a solid man in his forties. He wore tan shorts and shirt with the hotel logo on a pocket and had dark sunglasses on a broad, stubbled face.

As they pulled out of the fenced carpark, a similar 4WD approached and Colin raised his hand as they passed.

"That's my wife. Cherry. She'll bring the next couple up."

Daphne glanced behind as the 4WD nosed onto a dirt road. Bluebell and their car, along with the vehicles of the other guests, would be locked in at night time. Not that it was likely any car thieves would venture to this remote spot but one never knew. Another car drove in. It must be a procession of 4WD's up and down to the hotel because nobody was permitted to use the road other than the staff of the resort and every guest was ferried there by one of these vehicles.

"Don't remember seeing you folk before. First visit?" Col had to raise his voice over the motor as he navigated onto another road, this one even narrower than the last.

"Yes! I'm here for the Celebrating Celebrants conference."

The invitation to attend had surprised Daphne. And baffled her. She'd been a registered celebrant for more than a year but only recently retired from the real estate agency she and John owned and had operated for decades in their home town of Rivers End. Being on the road with Bluebell gave her the freedom to accept more appointments and she was almost booked out for several months ahead.

"I wonder why they've invited me?" She'd asked John at the time. "It says there are only fifty invites and I'd have thought I'd be a long way down the list."

Well, I'm here now and cannot wait to get started!

The invitation included free access to every aspect of the conference including the gala dinner and a discounted accommodation and meals package. The latter was to be paid for on arrival and Daphne had dug into her savings for this lovely little holiday.

Col glanced into his rear vision mirror at John.

"You going out to the river? Saw you have some decent fishing rods back there."

John leaned forward. "I've signed up for a fishing trip. Staying out overnight."

"You'll love it. Best fishing in the state if you ask me."

As the men continued their discussion about fishing and rivers, Daphne peered through the window. They were climbing up a steep part of the road and every so often a break in the trees to her left offered an enticing flash of the landscape below.

This morning they'd departed from a town more than four hour's drive away after dawn and it was now early afternoon. Along the way they'd stopped for an early lunch and bit of a wander around an old gold mining town. It was one of the best parts of her new career as an officiant, seeing firsthand the beautiful countryside and quaint towns in her home state of Victoria. The terrain changed constantly and she never tired of the variety.

The past two hours of the trip was across flat land with little to see but endless paddocks and distant hills. As they got closer, those hills became a mountain range which rose high above the plains. And now, here they were following a winding and steep road surrounded by native trees and bushland.

She took her phone out to take some photos.

"Reception is hit and miss up here." Col said. "There's a couple of spots that work most of the time, but don't expect too much."

Sounds perfect.

No phone. No emails. No cooking. No cleaning.

And no murders!

The 4WD bounced around too much to get a clear photo so she put the phone away and drew out the invitation to read again. She still wasn't certain why she'd been invited. According to the information on the association's website, the annual event was open to celebrants in Victoria who'd been full members for five years or more, which Daphne hadn't been. In addition, a handful of new celebrants were invited who'd been recommended by one of their clients.

I wonder who?

There was nothing on the invitation to indicate this. Her first clients were Christie and Martin in Rivers End close to a year ago and then she and John were busy with the real estate agency for some months, so she'd only officiated at a couple of weddings until they hit the road with Bluebell. Nobody stood out.

Of course, some of the ceremonies stood out, but for all the wrong reasons.

Family feuds. Rivalries. Murders.

Surely nobody involved in those events would recommend Daphne, who'd been at the centre of them and unintentionally ruffled feathers with her own brand of sleuthing.

There was a jolt and the 4WD swayed as its wheels on her side sprayed a cloud of dust.

"Sorry. Keep asking for that bit of road to get some attention. The minute there's rain it deteriorates and the sides are getting soft. But we're almost there." Col had both hands tightly on the steering wheel.

They slowed down to take a hairpin bend and the vista below opened up through a gap in the trees. With a small gasp, she grabbed the handle in the door. This was so high up! With the twists and turns, it hadn't been obvious how much they were climbing but beneath them the plains reached to the horizon, where a heat haze blurred the meeting of land and sky. A small town below was like a toy village. No wonder they'd had to leave Bluebell and their car behind.

A moment later, the road flattened out and widened and Col nosed through a narrower entrance with heavy metal gates on either side and what appeared to be some kind of security system. On one side a discreet sign read 'Hearthstone High Country Retreat'.

Bushland and dust gave way to an open lawn dotted with shaped bushes. They followed a long, paved driveway with graceful weeping birches on either side which led to a building. A two-storey reddish brown brick building.

I'm transported to Bridgerton!

"Welcome to Hearthstone." Col pulled up outside the double doors. "Hope you like things a bit fancy. This was built to include the best of several styles with optimum comfort."

A woman wearing a formal black suit and bowtie opened the door on Daphne's side. "Mrs Jones? We're so happy to see you." She offered a hand and Daphne took it to help herself climb down. "Your luggage will be taken to your suite, so please follow me to reception."

John appeared from the back of the vehicle.

"Mr Jones. Please. This way."

The woman headed for the double doors.

Col opened the back of the 4WD as a young man, also in black, pushed a trolley over. "We'll get this up to you."

"Thank you for the lift, Col." John said.

"Pleasure. Enjoy the stay."

John looped Daphne's arm through his. "Ready, doll?"

She gazed up at the building. Close up the hotel was less like the house in Bridgerton than her first impression. There were large windows and balconies on the upper floor.

"I hope so! This is very fancy."

Even a bit intimidating in its formality.

The woman who'd greeted them held the door open with a smile.

Daphne didn't need a second invitation.

The foyer of the hotel was a throwback to a distant era—and one from another part of the world. A patterned, highly polished timber floor. Enormous, sparkling chandeliers. A sweeping staircase to a mezzanine level. Scattered armchairs. And a marble reception counter where the concierge left them.

No other patrons were in the foyer.

Maybe we stepped back in time!

"Mr and Mrs Jones? I'm Mandy and am so happy to welcome you both." A young woman with flawless makeup and brown hair slicked into a tight bun smiled from across the counter. She also wore a black suit with the logo on a pocket. "Was the ride up the hill comfortable?"

Hill was an understatement.

John nodded. "Col was an excellent driver, thank you."

"What an impressive building!" Daphne gazed around, noticing huge oil paintings on the walls.

"We like it. The current owners are a husband and wife who both love different eras and when they couldn't agree on which one to build, came up with a rather fun combination which is full of luxury."

"Not at all what you expect hidden away up here." Daphne said.

"Your suite has a welcome pack inside which includes information about the grounds, different activities, room service menu should you decide to order in, and complimentary vouchers for the day spa and the fishing trip."

"Complimentary?" This didn't make sense. "I understood those were extras to pay for on arrival, along with the accommodation." She opened her handbag. "I have my credit card—"

Mandy smiled. "No need. They've been taken care of. There are no hidden charges and nothing to do now other than enjoy your time with us."

"But...who?"

"I'm afraid I can't help with that information." Mandy handed over two keys. "Your suite is on the upper floor, number seventy-six. Behind the staircase you'll find the elevator and when you alight, turn right, and follow the signs. If there is anything at all I can help with, dial seven on the phone in the suite."

Free?

John accepted the keys. "Thank you, Mandy. Do you happen to know when Daphne is expected for the conference? We didn't get much information."

"There is an itinerary in the suite. Officially the conference begins in the morning but a number of patrons are already here and out enjoying the grounds or a spa treatment. I believe there is a meet and greet in the bar later."

The phone rang and Mandy excused herself.

As they waited for the elevator, John kissed her cheek. "Someone is very generous."

"Oh my, they certainly are. And I shall make sure I pay it forward."

"Always kind hearted. Well, here's the lift. Shall we go and see what's in store for us?" John asked as the doors opened.

She nodded but her mind was racing. What had she possibly done to deserve this?

A ROOM WITH MANY VIEWS

John used his key to open door seventy-six and pushed it wide to let Daphne go in first. She'd been quiet on the short ride in the elevator and not commented when the doors opened to a spacious lounge area with another chandelier and its own balcony.

Are you worrying about who paid for this?

It was a surprise. When the invitation arrived some weeks ago, there was accompanying information about the cost and it wasn't an inexpensive weekend. Daphne though was determined to pay for it from the money she'd saved over the past few months. In the past he'd always paid for everything. They were an old-fashioned couple that way and it came from John's desire to never put Daphne in a position of feeling money was an issue, like she had growing up. Goodness knows she'd contributed equally over their marriage and although he was better with money, she was better with people and making their clients return time and again.

He closed the door in his wake and followed her down a

short hall. As the space opened up, he found himself smiling.

"Would you look at this?"

They'd rarely gone far from home in the past. The occasional visit to the city was about as far as they'd travelled until Bluebell came along. But this room...this suite, was amazing.

It was situated on a corner of the building and the main living area was as big as Bluebell's total size. A small dining table was near a discreet counter with a fridge, kettle, and coffee machine. Then a sofa and two armchairs with coffee tables nestled close to a well-stocked bookcase. Finally, a couple of tub style chairs faced an expansive window looking over the trees back to where they'd driven from today. A spectacular view.

"Love, come in here!" Daphne called from another room.

This was the bedroom and it wasn't the four-poster bed that had Daphne excited, nor the day sofa, and not even what looked like a decadent bathroom, but the balcony.

John stepped through French doors onto decorative tiles. The outlook was to the front of the hotel, over the gardens of the estate from the driveway across to tennis courts, a croquet lawn, and a swimming pool. Beyond those, the bushland returned and the peak of the mountain towered above them.

"Imagine this in winter!"

"You are so excited, Daph. And it would be incredible to see this all with a blanket of snow but I'm pleased it is summer."

Daphne leaned against him. "Bet you can't wait to get going."

"For once I'd like to be in two places at one time." He

chuckled and put an arm around Daphne. "I can hear the river calling but would just be as happy to wander around here and have dinner with you."

She went quiet again. They were rarely apart and he couldn't remember the last time they'd not slept in the same bed.

"If you'd rather I stay—"

"Don't be silly!" Daphne dug him in the ribs with her elbow. Lightly. "I'm perfectly alright here for one night and will be busy. And I want you to have the best fishing trip ever, love. I mean it."

Another 4WD rattled along the driveway, stopping much where Col had a little earlier. Three people climbed out as well as the driver. Three women and when the concierge walked across, they all greeted her as if old friends.

"Not first timers, I'd say." Daphne commented. "I'm getting nervous about meeting all these established officiants."

He took her hand and they wandered inside, back to the living room. "You will charm them all by being yourself. When would you like to go back downstairs? I see all our luggage is already here. Except my rods."

"Perhaps if we take a look at the itinerary...oh, I didn't see that!" Daphne dashed across to the dining table where a bottle of champagne was in an ice bucket. There were two glasses and a basket with chocolates and fruit. "I have an idea. Rather than open it today when you are going to be hiking soon, what if it goes into the fridge and we'll have a glass when you get back?"

"Good thinking. And speaking of me heading off, I might change into my hiking clothes if you don't mind."

Daphne was busy putting the bottle into the fridge. "Don't mind one bit. I'm going to take a look at the information pack here."

At least she was back to her normal self. He'd been serious about staying with her if she was uncomfortable being on her own for a night. But Daph was treating this like an adventure. And she'd have a wonderful time.

Once John returned to the bedroom, Daphne rested her hands on the back of a dining chair and released a long breath in a whoosh. Everything here was perfect and she couldn't wait to explore outside and meet the other attendees. But still...

If only I knew why this is free.

She pulled the chair out and sat, opening a folder titled 'Hearthstone High Country Retreat Welcome Packet.'

There was a map of the hotel. One elevator. Two floors plus an entertainment area on the roof beside the restaurant. Most of the accommodation was on their level with the exception of the manager's quarters on the lower floor. Also on the bottom floor was the conference room, a bar, and café.

A second map covered the expansive grounds. Backing onto the bushland behind the hotel was the general staff quarters and garages for the vehicles. As they'd seen from the balcony there were several areas for recreation. Close to the main building was the standalone day spa and what a lovely selection of treatments were on offer. Massages, hairdressing, makeup, and more...personal treatments. There was a recommendation to book as soon as possible to ensure an appointment but she would wait until John headed off.

Next was the itinerary of the conference. The first session began at ten in the morning. There was an invitation to attend a 'meet and greet' at the bar at six today which seemed a good idea. At this point, she knew nobody except by names she'd seen thanks to the association's website. Afterwards, she had options of a table in the restaurant or ordering room service. Something to decide later.

"I'm ready, Daph. And had a text message from reception to say we leave in half an hour." John joined her at the table. "Looks like a lot of reading there."

She smiled. "Do you have any idea of how busy I'm going to be? Once you leave, I'll book something nice at the day spa. I want to go for a walk around the grounds and then be back here to change for the meet up at the bar downstairs at six. I hope they like me."

John covered her hand with his. "No self-doubt. Okay? Meeting new people is your thing. Think of them as potential clients and you'll be in your element."

He was right. People were her passion and it wasn't as if she had to deal with feuding families or missing bodies. This was a fun event and she would enjoy every second. A little bubble of excitement had her tapping her toes beneath the table.

"And what about tomorrow?" he asked.

"I might have breakfast on the balcony. And then there is a full day of sessions. You'll be back late afternoon?"

He nodded. "Far as I know we have an hour of hiking each way and the camping area is already set up, so straight into fishing. We cook what we catch and any excess goes into a portable fridge to bring back. Once I'm back I'll be diving straight into the shower to offload all the fishy and river smell and into my suit and then we, my sweetheart, will have a ball at the gala dinner."

"Which reminds me I need to get my clothes hung up in case any need pressing. Can't get all dressed up for a ball and have creases in my skirt." She stood. "Do you know what your accommodation is like?"

"Only that it is a tent. But no idea how big or small so might be a nostalgic trip to those occasional weekends when I headed into the Otway Ranges to fish." John laughed as he got to his feet. "I might return tomorrow with bags under my eyes from no sleep from laying on the ground after forgetting how to make a camp bed."

"I have faith in you, love. You are good with your hands."

Those hands were suddenly on either side of her face, gently lifting her chin so he could kiss her lips. Her heart pitter-pattered and she closed her eyes. If he kept this up, he'd be late for his departure. But then he released her and when she flickered her lids open, he was smiling.

"I'd better get going. Need to check my fishing gear is down there seeing as it isn't here."

"Want me to walk you down?"

"You go and unpack. That way, you can start your adventure as well." John kissed her nose. "Have fun. And no sleuthing."

"No sleuthing at all. As long as there are no murders."

He gave her one of those 'don't even go there' looks.

"The only investigating I intend on is checking the menu and finding out what the gossip is." She said.

John groaned and she burst into peals of laughter.

Daphne waved to John from the balcony. He waved back after putting a handful of fishing gear down. A small group was gathered. All were men and most looked to be around John's age. Each carried their own fishing equipment and backpacks. This was a meeting of sorts, perhaps a pre-hike chat about processes and one man held court. He was thirty or so with shoulder length hair and a muscular build. Beside him, another man ticked items off a clipboard. Both of these men wore the same style of tan shorts and shirt Col had.

John pulled his floppy white hat from a pocket and after winking at Daphne, put it on his head. A moment later the group was walking away, off in the direction of the tennis courts. John glanced back and she blew him a kiss.

How strange to watch him leave, knowing she'd be on her own until this time tomorrow.

Not alone, Daph. There are forty-nine other celebrants to meet.

He was out of sight.

A little piece of her went with him.

"Have fun, love." She whispered. "Stay safe."

A breeze ruffled her hair and she wrinkled her nose as smoke wafted from somewhere. Almost like cigarette smoke.

"Do you expect him to fall into the river?"

Daphne spun around. Was someone in the suite?

A PECULIAR THING

"Over here, buttercup." The voice continued with a deep chuckle. "I'm beside you, not behind you."

What on earth?

A trail of wispy smoke bridged the gap to the next balcony where a man leaned against the railing, smoking. He was at least seventy, white hair pulled back in a short ponytail and wearing a long white dressing gown with the hotel logo blazoned on the left. He grinned as she looked him up and down.

"Isn't the hotel a smoke free zone?" she spoke before she had a chance to filter the words. Confronting anyone wasn't her thing but he'd given her a small scare and her heart was only just settling down to a normal beat.

"Probably."

She didn't have a response. Not one he'd appreciate. And what had he meant about her expecting John to fall in the river?

"Anyway. It is just a cigar. A rather expensive one and I *am* outside."

A cigar. Her father—her stepfather—used to smoke them on occasion, when he had a raise at work or his football team won something. Not her biological father, who'd she'd only recently met for the first time, but the man who'd raised her. A man long gone.

"I doubt John will fall in the river. He is a careful man. To answer your question."

The man sucked on the cigar and blew smoke in the opposite direction. There wasn't much left of it and he stubbed it in a small personal ashtray, dropped the remains in, and closed it. "Then why worry about him?"

It was none of his business.

"We are rarely apart."

Good work, Daph. None of his business!

"You are so sweet. No wonder your clients adore you enough to have written the winning nomination."

"The winning...I'm sorry. Who are you?"

The man bowed. "Rupert Witherspoon."

"Oh. But you're the..."

He smiled. "President? I am indeed. And you are Daphne Jones. Known for beautiful weddings, heartfelt funerals, and a spot of sleuthing."

How to respond was taken out of her hands as a beeping sound emanated from his dressing gown pocket. He pulled out a phone. "Time for my medication. Shall I keep a seat for you at the bar?"

"I, er..."

Rupert winked and disappeared into his suite, leaving nothing but the faint remains of his cigar smoke.

Rather than inhale any more of the toxic air, she stepped inside and closed the French door behind herself, perhaps with a little more force than intended. What a peculiar man

Rupert was. She'd seen his name on the association newsletters and the like but never a photo.

"Eccentric or just strange?" she muttered. "Buttercup! I'm no buttercup."

Rupert had been reminded to take his medication. Might be to improve his manners?

A smile came to her face and she chuckled as she collected her handbag. Time she had a look around.

There were more people checking in as Daphne made her way through the foyer and a couple of the seats were occupied with chatting visitors. Outside, another 4WD with guests pulled up. It wouldn't be long and she'd get to meet some of the other celebrants. But for now, she had plans to wander around the grounds.

The driveway was circular and a path forked away with a small sign to the day spa. Until last year, Daphne had rarely bothered with facials and the like. She had her own regime and looked after herself, or so she'd thought. But then her friend Christie opened a beauty salon in Rivers End and insisted Daphne enjoy some free treatments. After one, she was hooked. Who knew how relaxing a facial was? Or a full body massage.

Being on the road gave less opportunities although visiting a hairdresser was one indulgence she did keep. She was fine doing her own skin care and makeup but not keeping the greys away and managing the flash of colour she liked in her brown curls. Her hand went to her head. Not curls so much these days. Christie had shown her how to straighten her hair a certain way which made it shine and feel soft and that was now her preferred style.

The building housing the day spa was like a mini version of the hotel, with the same brick work and a blackboard near the door with specials. In Daphne's handbag were three vouchers for free services. Any services.

As she stood reading, a door opened and woman with a cheery face emerged. She wore a white uniform and had lots of black hair escaping from a bun on top of her head.

"Hello there! Would you care to make an appointment? I'm Maisie and I run the spa."

"Oh, yes please. I'm Daphne."

Stepping out to hold the door open, Maisie gestured. "Please, come in and we can find the perfect treatment for you."

Inside was a complete surprise. Modern, muted pastel colours. A thick, soft carpet in cream. And beautiful photographs of wildlife adorning the walls. There was a small reception desk, three or four comfy chairs with a coffee table filled with magazines, a coffee machine, and a couple of closed doors. Maisie went behind the counter.

"What takes your fancy, Daphne? A full body massage? Hot stone treatment? There are a dozen or so options."

"Actually, I did have something in mind for Sunday morning, if you are open?"

"Always open. I live up here and don't mind working odd hours." Maisie was in her forties and had such a nice smile. It was impossible not to warm to her. "What were you thinking?"

"My husband is on the fishing trip until tomorrow afternoon and then we have the gala dinner to attend. But I wondered if I could book us both in for a massage before we leave on Sunday? If that isn't inconvenient?"

Maisie opened a book and ran her finger down a page. "Is nine too early? My assistant is here a bit before then so we can look after you both at the same time. We'll need forty-five minutes and you will both feel so relaxed you'll want a nap."

"Sounds perfect. Although we'll need to head off soon after so don't relax John too much as he drives when we're towing Bluebell."

"Bluebell is a caravan?" Maisie hunted around the counter for something.

"She is. Our blue and white home away from home. Do you need a pen?"

"Pencil. Ah, there you are." Maisie reached down to the carpet. "What is your room number, Daphne?"

"Seventy-six."

"Such a nice suite! I love the views from it. And do you have any vouchers?"

Daphne had them in her hand. "There's one for each of us."

"You're here for the conference. And there's one spare. What about something for you?" her finger returned to the page. "Not much today I'm afraid, everyone wants a treatment it seems. But there's a break in the conference timetable between twelve and two tomorrow. I could do a neck massage. Or a nice hand massage. Or refresh your make up?"

Now that she thought about it, her neck was a little stiff.

Maisie continued. "Tell me when you arrive. They all take the same length of time. So, what about one fifteen?

Give you time to have lunch and I'll have you out of here half an hour later."

It was all so easy to do, this new, if temporary, life of being indulged. Treated like royalty. Between the beautiful suite, the welcome package, and not one but two-day spa appointments, Daphne wanted to do a little dance. She left Maisie with a wave and continued her exploration.

The tennis courts were full, with people waiting nearby in small groups. Several teams played croquet. A lovely, natural looking swimming pool had a dozen or so guests floating on blow up shapes or else lounging on sun beds. Past all of this was a secluded garden in the style of those she'd seen on television in English shows about grand homes or else footage of the royal family. Manicured, green, and very formal.

Nobody else was around and Daphne settled on a stone bench beneath an expansive tree. High, perfectly trimmed hedges kept the sounds of the tennis court and pool at bay. A large, five-tiered fountain cascaded into a shallow pool surrounded by more red bricks. At its top was a peculiar looking statue of a man. He stood straight-backed, wearing a bowler hat and suit, with a briefcase in one hand and he pointed, with the other, back toward the main building. From here it was impossible to see over the hedges to the exact place he indicated.

The strange contrasts added to the charm of the property.

Daphne's phone beeped and she unlocked it.

We are at the river. They call the tents glamming tents. Very swish, will send a pic soon.

She messaged John.

Sounds fancy! I'm sitting in a very English garden.

After taking a couple of photos she tapped send. There was only a couple of bars on her phone and the message didn't go. They'd been warned mobile coverage was sketchy. At least she knew John was safe and ready for his long-awaited fishing time.

She wandered back to the hotel, cutting across lawns broken up with flower beds. At the edge of the driveway, she stopped as an emptiness filled her stomach. Not hunger. It was a sense of being alone. Daphne didn't mind being on her own, but this was different.

You're too used to John being with you all the time.

This was true. Not only had they spent many years working in close proximity, but in recent months they'd spent no more than a couple of hours apart.

He'll be back tomorrow.

So why did that empty feeling sink lower? She glanced around, expecting to find someone watching her but everyone was going about their business. There was no reason for dread. Nothing was going to happen to John unless he fell into the river like Rupert Witherspoon had suggested. And John was too careful for that.

What she needed was a refreshing shower, a change of clothes, and a trip to the bar to meet up with the other attendees. No moping around or imagining the worst. This was her time and nothing was going to stop her enjoying every minute.

DINNER WITH A DIFFERENCE

"There she is!" Rupert's voice boomed across a room filled with people, laughter, and chatting. He rose from a barstool and waved at Daphne, who had paused in the doorway at the sight of so many strangers.

There was no going back now and she planted a smile on her face and weaved past other tables and seats in his direction.

He stepped forward and kissed her cheek as if they were long lost friends. "Don't you look lovely? Fresh as a daisy."

"Oh? Well, thank you." She'd taken twenty minutes to decide on her favourite wide legged black pants with a white blouse patterned with pretty butterflies. And for once she'd chosen a higher heeled shoe. Confidence. All about confidence.

Rupert wore a red velvet jacket over a silk shirt with its top two buttons undone which exposed a few white chest hairs and a gold chain, and his hair was loose from its pony-tail. Somehow, the look suited him.

"Daphne Jones, let me introduce you to some of the

wonderful people behind the association. This is Audrey Sutton, Gloria Long, and Stacy Chester. What would you care to drink, Daphne? A glass of champagne?"

"Just some sweet white wine, thank you."

He pulled over a barstool from an empty table. "Sit, and get to know each other."

Rupert disappeared toward the bar and Daphne perched on the edge of the rather high barstool, gripping her handbag.

Three sets of eyes scrutinised her. Three mouths pursed up. And then glances were exchanged. This was disconcerting. Nobody spoke. Well, somebody had to.

"I'm so excited to be here. And I think I've heard all of your names before." She settled a bit more comfortably on the stool. "Audrey, am I right that you are the vice president?"

The woman she addressed nodded. Silver hair in a sleek chignon, she couldn't have been more than forty. Elegant drop earrings with multiple diamonds complemented a pendant. Daphne knew her gemstones and her estimation of the value of the set would have deterred her from ever wearing them without a bodyguard.

"And Gloria, you are the treasurer?"

"Yes, honey. I manage the funds." Gloria was around her own age. With rich brown hair in a classic bob, she had long fingers covered in rings and a thickset waist.

The third woman reached her hand over the table to shake. "I'm Stacy. I look after the members and was the person who had the privilege of seeing the glowing recommendation about you which resulted in the complimentary tickets and free accommodation. So nice to meet you!" Younger than any of them, Stacy spoke fast and was thin with shoulder length, straight brown hair, and small round glasses. In a bright yellow blouse and blue skirt, she didn't wear makeup and barely made eye contact with Daphne, grabbing a glass and sipping as soon as the handshake finished.

"It is lovely to meet you. Are you all celebrants?"

"Only Gloria, and of course, Rupert." Audrey said. She played with the stem of a martini. "My husband is a celebrant and I enjoy being able to serve the association but my thing is wedding gowns, which does fit well with all of this."

Rupert returned with a glass of wine which he set before Daphne, and some red concoction with an umbrella for himself. "When Audrey says wedding gowns, she means Sutton Brides."

She recognised the name as being a chain of top end bridal shops. Suddenly, the diamonds made sense. Daphne had heard more than one bride wish they could afford a Sutton gown.

"Why don't you tell us about yourself?" Rupert settled on his barstool and curled both hands around his drink. "We know little about you prior to joining the association and since you did, you've made quite a splash."

Not sure if I want this on my bio.

"Um, well, I married my high school sweetheart and we ran a business together for a long time. Rivers End Real Estate. John is well thought of in real estate circles. We retired and refurbished a caravan and now we travel so I can officiate. He fishes, and takes photographs, and loves genealogy."

"And do you have a family back in Rivers End?" Stacy asked, eyes still on her drink.

"Sadly, no children. We fostered for many years."

"Can't imagine putting up with someone else's kid." Audrey said. "Bad enough having one's own."

What a sad way to feel.

"How many children do you have, Audrey?" Daphne asked sweetly.

"Me? None, thank goodness. Happy to be an aunt but happier to keep it that way."

"You are missing out on so much, honey." Gloria said. "My five kids are the reason I get up every day."

"To make them breakfast and pack their lunches." Audrey countered.

"Well, they all have their own families now so no more packing lunches but I do miss it. Daphne, you mentioned you fostered? I imagine that was rewarding?"

It was the best time in Daphne's life, apart from the recent move to the nomadic life. Bringing stability and gentle boundaries to the lives of displaced youngsters, seeing their confidence and self-respect grow...rewarding didn't begin to express it. Even when they moved on, it was almost always with a happiness for their new start. Almost always.

"Daphne?"

Gloria spoke again.

"Oh, sorry! Yes. Rewarding on many levels."

Even when one of them leaves a hole in your heart.

She drank some wine. "Thank you, Rupert."

"Let's have a toast." Rupert raised his glass. "To new friends and delightful company!"

An hour later, all five were seated around a different table in the restaurant.

Rupert invited the women to join him for dinner and Daphne had to admit she had warmed up to him. And liked the women. Although Audrey was harder to get to know, as she was tapping away on her phone for most of the time. The reception was better in the bar and when Daphne visited the ladies, she sent a quick message to John to wish him a nice evening.

The restaurant was on the roof of the hotel, with plenty of floor to ceiling windows to capture the wonderful views in what was left of the long evening light. Most tables were full and there was much waving and called greetings between people who clearly knew each other. With an annual conference it made sense celebrants would become friends when attending. Though she was being quiet. It was somewhat overwhelming.

Talk turned to the conference itself and immediately, Audrey excused herself. "Time to circulate."

Once she'd moved to another table, Stacy finally looked up with a small smile. "Much better."

"Aw, you mustn't let her bother you, Stace." Gloria patted Stacy's shoulder. "Everyone knows what she's like."

I don't. But I can guess.

Rupert said nothing. His eyes drifted to Audrey then to Daphne, smiling when she tilted her head in question. He filled a glass with wine for himself and topped up Daphne's without asking.

"Anyway, I'm looking forward to the first session," Stacy said. "Managing a wedding day crisis."

Gloria laughed. "Would have been handy when I did my very first wedding. Bride didn't even show up, leaving a confused groom and a garden filled with arguing relatives. Ah, the good old days."

"Daphne should have been the presenter." Stacy was a different person without Audrey around. Her eyes sparkled and she smiled. "You had a murder!"

"True. But I'd rather it had been a straight forward ceremony. I muddled through rather than anything else and am keen to take notes."

"You are too humble. I happen to know you have helped solve murders in two towns and put yourself in the path of danger both time. Which you shouldn't do, not really, but I do admire you!" Stacy said. "I wish I was nearly as brave."

Dinner arrived. Plates piled high with battered or grilled fish, depending on preference, hand cut potato wedges, and aioli for dipping.

"Freshly caught from the river." Rupert noted. "Which hopefully nobody has fallen into." He grinned at Daphne and she smiled back at the small joke.

Audrey returned when she noticed her plate had arrived. Stacy dropped her eyes again and concentrated on her plate. What on earth was going on between the two women? Stacy was either afraid of Audrey, or there'd been bad feelings between them. Not that Audrey gave any indicator she cared. If anything, there was the hint of a smile on her lips. Or was it a sneer?

Stop seeing things that aren't there.

"When does Darren arrive, Audrey?" Gloria asked.

Audrey glanced at her diamond encrusted watch. "Who knows. He had a wedding today which is a four-hour drive away. I might go and make sure one of the staff is waiting down at the carpark."

"I heard you arrange it earlier, Auds." Rupert said. "No point hassling them."

"Reminding. *Rupes*. Reminding. There's a distinct lack of respect toward me from certain members of the front desk staff and I won't have my husband left standing about in the dark on his own." She stood, picking up her glass of wine. "The food is ordinary. For now." With that she stalked away in stilettos which wobbled as she weaved around tables.

"Apologies, Daphne." Rupert sighed. "Audrey will be much happier once her husband arrives. She worries about him—"

"You mean she imagines he's off with someone else." Stacy spoke to her plate.

Rupert waved that away. "Regardless. We are all one big celebrant and partners family. Now, people. Dinner won't eat itself."

Well, well, well. There were cracks in the veneer of the executive. Rupert calling them all family rang alarm bells. In Daphne's experience, families were the worst when it came to secrets, grudges, and deception. Not that anything would or could go wrong here in this beautiful hotel.

Never.

MIDNIGHT MOVES

Dessert was so delicious Daphne wished she could send a plate of it to John. Three tiny offerings. A chocolate mousse. A crème Brule. And the creamiest vanilla ice cream ever.

"All made in-house." Gloria mentioned as she scooped up some of her mousse. "It surely is one of the reasons we book here year after year."

"This and the view." Rupert added.

He had removed his jacket and rolled up his sleeves before dessert arrived. The restaurant was warm with so many guests and plenty of waiting staff hurrying to and from the kitchen. Daphne appreciated her choice of clothing and stayed hydrated with water in between glasses of wine. Of which she'd had three. Any more and she knew she'd get the giggles.

Audrey had returned from her trip downstairs to reception but joined another group and was laughing a lot. There were ongoing calls for toasts and clinking of glasses coming from that direction. Stacy had glanced over when Audrey first came back to the roof, but then she relaxed. Or it might be the five or six glasses of wine she'd consumed. Not one to judge, Daphne let the others talk, nodding if they looked her way. It was pleasant and friendly and she was happy she'd come out to dinner tonight.

Guests began to leave and wait staff cleared the tables.

"Let's sit out on the roof." Rupert was already on his feet, jacket in one hand and glass in the other. "Pleasant weather tonight."

"I might say goodnight." This was Gloria. "Like Daphne, my husband is off fishing and I have a paperback I'm keen to finish seeing as I have the room to myself."

Spending time with a book was tempting and there was a nice selection in the suite. But she was relaxed and comfortable with the little group and not ready to head back yet. Daphne stood.

"I've enjoyed your company, Gloria. I imagine our husbands are swapping fishing stories around a campfire."

"Ted loves a good yarn so I think you are right."

With Stacy and Rupert, Daphne wandered from the restaurant. A handful of other guests were seated out here so they found a table and chairs at the furthest end and settled down. The air was still warm and the sky cloudy. It didn't feel like rain was coming but it was a pity not to stargaze from this elevated position.

"This is almost the best part of being a member." Stacy stretched her arms wide and high. "Good company. Mostly. And this place."

"How often have you been here?"

"This is the fifth conference here and I've attended each one."

"Did you say earlier you aren't a celebrant?"

"Not the best job for me. I'm too shy sometimes and don't have the way with words people like you and Rupert do."

Rupert patted Stacy's arm. "Sweet of you to say." He turned to Daphne. "Stacy is the only paid member of the association. Although all the executives have a small expense account, we are all volunteers. But Stacy is employed to manage the legal aspects of the association and anything which falls outside the scope of the volunteers. Most of us are busy and Stacy makes our lives easier."

"Which means I get to see the good, bad, and the ugly! I deal with compliments and complaints. I'm the person who members go to if they are having any issues either with their work or with another member...which rarely happens, thank goodness. And I get to read all the glowing testimonials from clients." Stacy picked up her empty wine glass and frowned at it. "And this year, many have come from your own. I might get another. Anyone else?"

"Um, no. I'm fine thanks." Daphne said.

Stacy disappeared into the restaurant.

"Are you less worried about John?" Rupert asked.

"John is a capable man."

"And you have a big heart."

This was true. Daphne loved people and loved giving and making others happy. She wasn't a proud woman but she was realistic and knew herself pretty well at her age.

A burst of loud laughter had both of them turning to look at a table closer to the restaurant. Audrey was on her feet, somewhat unsteady, glass raised. "To people who can't find their way up a mountain. To Darren!"

"Oh dear. So, he hasn't arrived." Rupert said. "She might laugh about it but Audrey will be fuming. I should consider having a cigar on my balcony to make myself scarce before she asks me to gather a search party."

Rupert was an interesting man. His voice was cultured—for want of a better term. Private education. Old money. Over dinner he'd mentioned a career in law and his early retirement to pursue his passion for art and officiating. There was no Mrs Witherspoon, and no children. He had three cats and lived on a houseboat. He also cared about those in the association he presided over.

"Stacy is nice." Daphne said.

"She is. But she sometimes allows other people's opinions to weigh on her."

About to ask if he meant Audrey's opinions, the reappearance of Stacy reminded Daphne she wasn't here to snoop into other people's lives. It wasn't as though there was a crime to solve.

"Well, that was a waste of the walk because the bar is closed, so I'm going to my room. You are both welcome to join me to raid the mini bar." Stacy reached for her handbag.

"Thank you for the offer, but I hear my bed calling, dear." Daphne pushed herself to her feet. "Never slept in a four-poster bed so I want to make the most of it."

Rupert stood. "Goodnight then. I shall finish my drink. Watch out for the moon for a while in case it makes an appearance. I shall see you ladies tomorrow."

When Stacy and Daphne reached the elevator, she turned. Rupert leaned against the brickwork surrounding the seated area, staring off into the night.

They stepped out of the elevator on the accommodation floor and Stacy went straight to the window overlooking the front of the hotel. It was a pleasant spot here with armchairs and coffee tables.

"Such a nice evening, even with the clouds. We should get a bottle of wine and find somewhere to drink it under a tree."

"Outside?"

"Like a night time picnic. But with wine. Or champagne. Except I drank mine yesterday." She turned with a wide smile. "Did you get a bottle as part of your welcome package?"

Yes. And it is staying in the fridge to share with John.

"Which is your room, Stacy? Would you like me to walk there with you?"

"Oh, you don't need to mother me. I'm just happy. I guess I'll see you in the morning."

"If you're sure."

"I am. Goodnight, Daphne. It's been a lot of fun."

Not entirely convinced, Daphne nevertheless needed to use her bathroom and figured Stacy was safe enough to find her way to her room. At the far corner she glanced back and Stacy waved.

Her suite was a welcome sight and she kicked off her shoes with a sigh.

She popped on the kettle then hurried to the bathroom. A few minutes later she returned, makeup off and ready for a cuppa. A quick check of her phone was a little disappointing. Nothing from John. And only one bar of reception.

"Sleep tight, love." She blew a kiss into the air.

She opened the French doors and took a look out at the night but the sound of a door closing nearby reminded her that Rupert intended to have a cigar and she wasn't inclined to let the smoke drift into the suite. She closed the doors again.

While the tea brewed, she ran a finger over the selection of books, pulling out a few to read their back cover.

"A missing man. No body. No clues. And a daughter determined to find the truth. *Last Known Contact.* Oh, you sound promising." She tucked the book under her arm and carried her cup to one of the seats near the window. "Nothing like a mystery to solve while I drink my tea."

How pleasant this was. A beautiful suite with soft, thick carpet to curl her toes into. A nice cup of tea. And a new book.

Deeply engrossed in the fifth chapter, she jumped at a sound from the hallway. Reading a suspense late at night was enough to make anyone a little jumpy. But it was as though someone had stopped outside her door. Leaned on it, or turned the handle.

"John?"

Daphne scrambled to her feet. Had something happened and he was back? He hadn't taken the extra key.

"Is that you, John?"

No answer. And all was quiet. She opened the door and peered down the hallway. Nobody and nothing. Just her imagination.

After closing the door, she stepped on something flat and pliable.

"Oh, my. Where did you come from?"

She scooped up an envelope and carried it back to her chair, where the light was better. It hadn't been there when she came in. Well, she was pretty sure it wasn't. A note from reception? Or someone from the conference?

The envelope was plain and sealed so she opened it and drew out a folded piece of paper. There was writing on one side. Actually, there was a map on half of the paper and writing above it.

"Grab your shoes and find me. S.C.." She read aloud. "Stacy?"

There was a poem.

Come to the fountain
at the top of the mountain
We will dance and sing
Until morning we bring
Meet me now if you dare
For sweet moments to share

"What on earth?" Little made sense. "Until morning we bring? Not very good poetry. Or the ramblings of someone who drank too much!"

If it was Stacy, then she'd better go and check the woman was all right because she'd had a fair bit to drink and might fall into the fountain if she was galivanting around it inebriated.

The map was a rough overlay of the grounds of the hotel. The tennis court and day spa were marked with an X. As was the English garden where she'd sat this afternoon to enjoy the quiet. Yesterday afternoon. It was after midnight.

She peered through the window and sure enough, there was Stacy heading into the darkness toward the tennis court.

Daphne went in search of sensible shoes.

THE FOUNTAIN ATOP A MOUNTAIN

Daphne collected her phone, the note, and the key for the door. Nothing worse than finding herself locked out on her return. She went out onto the balcony in the hope of seeing Rupert but his French doors were closed and no lights shone through.

Despite this, she tapped on his suite door a moment later. Perhaps he'd help her find Stacy but all was silent and even when she leaned her ear against the door, there was not even the sound of snoring. Assuming he snored, of course.

She walked down the stairs rather than wait for what she'd discovered was a slow elevator. The office behind the reception desk was closed and although the sign she'd seen earlier about opening again at six had an emergency phone number, she was hardly going to wake someone over this.

Outside, she followed the driveway until the path to the garden veered off. She crunched her way over the small pebbles, passing the day spa and then stopping near the dark, deserted tennis courts.

This was one of the spots marked on the map with an X.

She opened the flashlight app on her phone and flicked the light around. No movement or sign of anything out of the ordinary.

Whatever that might be.

The poem said nothing about tennis courts though.

A shiver ran up her spine and she turned off the flashlight and gazed around. Surely nobody was watching her?

"Stacy?"

Silence. What if there was someone else out here? Out here in the dark in the middle of the night.

Alone in the dark in a strange place. Good one, Daph.

She was here now. Daphne turned the flashlight back on.

"Find Stacy and go to bed." She muttered and started walking again, before she could change her mind.

Ahead, the high, perfectly manicured hedges were like a wall. There was an archway leading in and beneath it, Daphne hesitated, peering into the gloom.

"Stacy? It's Daphne Jones."

Her flashlight moved around her in a semi-circle as she looked to signs of Stacy. As she turned, her peripheral vision picked up the shape of a person looming in the dark and she squealed and almost dropped her phone.

Get a grip, Daph. It's a statue!

Statue or not, between that and the low, scuttling clouds, this garden was getting creepier by the minute. Putting a hand over her heart which thudded painfully, she took a couple of long breaths through her nose. Her friend Charlotte was a psychiatrist and once told her gulping air through her mouth after a scare might make her feel worse as it sparks off a person's fight or flight instinct. Good advice.

As her fright subsided, she considered her options. The most appealing one was to retrace her steps and hightail it back to the comfort and safety of her suite. But what if Stacy was no longer in a condition to get back on her own?

Best to check the fountain. It would only take a minute.

All was quiet.

"Well, that is odd."

The fountain wasn't splashing. No water flowed.

Moonlight suddenly streamed through a break in the clouds.

A person sat on the bricks surrounding the base of the fountain. A woman, staring into the water.

"Stacy? What's wrong, dear?"

Stacy raised an arm and pointed into the fountain without looking at Daphne, who hurried to join her. She peered into the water and her heart stopped.

Oh no. Oh no!

There was a red jacket floating on the surface.

Was it covering a body?

A body in the water?

"Rupert!"

The clouds closed up again, plunging the garden back into murky darkness.

"Stacy! Stacy, look at me!"

Stacy did more than that. She jumped to her feet and grabbed Daphne's hands with wet, icy cold fingers. Her glasses were missing and her eyes, as she leaned close, were wide and alarmed.

"Need...need, help. Please. Get help."

"Are you alright, Stacy? Are you hurt?"

"I'm okay. But its too late for..." she gulped. "Please get someone."

Releasing Daphne's hands, Stacy turned back to the fountain.

There were no bars on Daphne's phone.

"I'll be right back."

She turned and ran back through the archway.

Someone called her name and she glanced back. Nobody. Just an over-active imagination.

Her feet flew along the pebbled path.

Past the tennis courts.

In sight of the hotel, she had to slow down as a stitch clutched at her side.

Keep going.

The sweet yet irritating smell of cigar smoke reached her nostrils and her eyes shot up to Rupert's balcony.

It was in darkness, as was the suite. But smoke drifted away from the building and there was the slightest movement as a chair scraped on tiles.

"Daphne? Is that you down there?"

Mouth open, she stopped dead, sucking in air.

"Whatever are you doing out there so late?" he asked.

Rupert leaned over the balcony.

Relief poured into her. "You're not dead!"

A pause and then a chuckle. "I sincerely hope not, buttercup. Did you join Stacy at her mini bar?"

Everything began to spin and she had to brace her legs

as the world tilted. What was going on? If it wasn't Rupert in the fountain, then who?

"I'm coming down, Daphne. Find a spot to sit and I'll be there in a minute."

Sit? There wasn't time to sit. Some poor soul had died and she had to get help.

She focused on her breathing. Long, slow, deep breaths. She took her glasses off and blinked a few times, then slid them on again. The ground was steady. She wasn't going to fall. This was all a terrible shock but she had to pull herself together and find a way to make sense of this.

Except...who was in the fountain?

If only John was here.

"Daphne? Tell me what's wrong." Rupert—wrapped up in the same dressing gown as earlier in the day—hurried from the hotel.

"I...there is so much to tell you. But I'm not drunk. The fountain. I was in my suite. And the note. And I found her there. And the body."

Rupert put his hands on her shoulders and leaned down to make her look at his eyes. "What body?"

Her mouth opened and shut again and she grabbed one of his hands from her shoulder. "Come and see." She tugged at him when he hesitated. "Stacy."

"Stacy? Oh my—"

"Not her. I don't know who. But she's there. In shock."

Despite his attire, and a pair of slippers on his feet, Rupert wasted no more time and Daphne had to jog to keep up with him. They made it back to the English garden and to the fountain even faster than she'd managed in reverse moments ago.

"Where's Stacy?" Rupert removed his slippers. "Do you have any light?"

Between gasps for oxygen—this running back and forth was exhausting—Daphne turned her phone's flashlight on and waved it around. No sign of anyone.

"Can you shine it in here, please?" Rupert stepped into the fountain.

"Should you do that? This might be a crime scene."

Daphne turned the light onto the red velvet coat as Rupert leaned down. Water lapped up his calves, the dressing gown just out of danger of dipping in. It was the strangest thing. The coat had floated further around the fountain but where was the body?

Rupert grunted as he dragged the jacket out. "Ruined." Water poured from it as he stepped out and laid it on the grass.

"I don't understand." She walked right around the fountain, flashlight on the water. "Where is the body?

"Which body, Daphne? And where is Stacy?"

An excellent question.

"The top of the bricks are wet here." She was on the opposite side to Rupert and he joined her, slippers in one hand as he tried to dry his other hand on the dressing gown. "All along this side."

Rupert put his slippers on, grimacing as they stuck to his damp feet. "I would appreciate an explanation for all of this. My jacket in the fountain. You running around like you've seen a ghost. And what does Stacy have to do with this?"

Her mind raced. Stacy was here earlier. They'd spoken. Had physical contact. And there'd been a body...or had there? The jacket. Yes. But had she actually seen a person under the surface?

"Daphne! Oh, Rupert. Rupert, you're alive!"

Stacy sort-of sprinted from the opposite direction. She was unsteady on her feet and her arms waved around.

"Of course, I'm alive." Rupert muttered then he grabbed Stacy as she threw herself at him. Well, fell in his direction. He helped her stand upright. "Why do both of you believe I am deceased? Come on, ladies, it's enough to make a man feel he's more than just slightly over the hill!"

"It was your jacket in the fountain. I saw it and thought it was you in there." Daphne said. "But Stacy, where is the body? Was there really a body in there?"

"Didn't you hear me calling? I hadn't wanted to leave." Stacy pointed in the direction she'd run from. "They must have carried him through there. I came after you to ask you to look out for my glasses. I lost them somewhere. But I got as far as the tennis courts and couldn't see you and came back to find...to find, nothing."

Rupert glanced at Daphne with a frown. Worry, perhaps. "How about we go back to the hotel and get you warmed up, Stace? Your hands are freezing."

"Yes and I can make you some tea." Daphne said.

"But we need to find whoever was in the fountain. Can we call the police?"

"Not from here, dear. No signal."

"Then you both need to come with me and help look. I'm sure whoever took the body went through the gap in the corner."

"Who is dead and why would anyone take their body?" Rupert asked.

Oh no, not this again! Not after last time.

Only recently, Daphne had attended a funeral where the deceased failed to arrive for their own burial. This wasn't the same though. There had been someone in the water. Hadn't there? With each passing moment she second guessed herself a bit more. She'd seen the jacket with both arms moving in the water. Stacy had said there was a body. But had she seen one? A foot, or hand? Hair?

"Stacy. Did you slide a note under my door earlier?" she asked, reaching into her pocket where she'd shoved it earlier.

"Of course not. I don't even know which room you have."

"It's just that someone left a map pointing here with a poem and signed S.C. I thought you were out here all alone and after you'd had so much to..." she bit her lip.

"You think I am drunk?" Stacy threw her arms in the air. "What? That I imagined all of this? Well, fine then." She stormed off—not very convincingly—into the darkness in the wrong direction before doing a U-turn and stalking past Daphne and Rupert, again apparently lost. "We won't bother looking for murderers and body thieves."

"Shall we help her find the way back?" Rupert asked. "Won't be the first time she's had adventures after a few wines."

Much as she wanted more information about that, Daphne nodded and they set out after Stacy.

NOBODY. NO BODY

With all her heart, Daphne wished John were here with her. She'd checked her phone for coverage several times but there wasn't enough to make a call, although she did try to send a message. It failed to go but probably would eventually.

She sat in the lobby of the hotel with Stacy and Rupert. All had cups of tea thanks to Maisie, who'd been the staff member rostered on for emergencies. Rupert hadn't hesitated to step behind the reception desk and use the landline to call for help. Maisie had told them to stay put and then she'd woken other staff.

By now it was after one in the morning and exhaustion had chased off any remaining adrenaline. Stacy nodded off in an armchair, covered by a blanket Maisie had found, and Mandy appeared, followed by Col.

After going over the events of the past hour or so with them, Daphne still had no idea what she'd seen earlier. Col went to wake another of the staff to go on a search around the fountain. Mandy was quiet until after he'd left and

Maisie had gone to get more tea. Then, she moved to a seat closer to Daphne and Rupert.

"We need to get Stacy back to her room. No point upsetting her if anyone else comes down and starts asking questions." Mandy glanced at Rupert. "I doubt Col will find anything. This is just like last year. Do you remember?"

He nodded. "She was convinced somebody had stolen the association's laptop she had left in the conference room. Got it in her head it was somewhere outside at night and eventually we found her wandering along a bush track."

Mandy got to her feet. "I'll get a key to her room and be back, if you don't mind helping me wake her."

Once she was gone, Rupert leaned toward Daphne. "How did you know where she was?"

"I saw her leave the hotel. But before then, I heard someone at my door and found the note slid under it. When I saw the initials, I thought it must be her. She'd suggested when we left the roof that we take a bottle of champagne out and have a picnic."

He rolled his eyes. "I think our Stacy has had too much to drink tonight. You didn't actually see a body?"

Had she?

"I saw your jacket. The arms were floating as if your... I mean, a body, was in them. How did it get into the fountain, I wonder?"

"I left it on the roof. Didn't even remember until I dragged it out of the water. Ah, here's Col." Rupert stood and offered his hand to Daphne and she took it gratefully to let him help her up. All that running left both her knees aching and there was a definite crunch from one of them.

Col and another man came through the hotel door, locking it behind themselves. Col gave his flashlight to his co-worker, who walked past everyone with a shake of his head as though expressing he was unimpressed to be dragged from his bed.

"Nothing. Went up through the corner of the garden but there's no sign anyone was around. Found this." Col raised a hand holding an unopened champagne bottle. "Think our friend there forgot it." He put the bottle on a side table. "Want a hand getting her back to her room. Again?"

"Is that you, Col Colly Colin?" Stacy raised her head. "And Rupie. Are we going to open the bottle?"

"Not tonight. How about Col and I get you back to the comfort of your room? You can settle down for a proper sleep."

"Sure. I am tired." She pushed aside the blanket and yawned. "My glasses are missing. I might go for a quick walk and find them."

Mandy was back. "We'll track them down in daylight. Come on, then. Time for bed. I'll help Rupert."

"I have my keys." Col rattled a large metal ring of keys clipped to his belt but when Mandy didn't answer he shrugged and headed in the direction the other man had gone.

Stacy sang to herself as Mandy helped her to her feet and Rupert took her arm. He gave Daphne a half-smile as they slowly made their way to the elevator and mouthed, 'breakfast?' She nodded back even though at this point she had no idea what would happen in the morning.

Maisie appeared with tea and looked around. "Oh. Well, would you like some more?"

Daphne blinked a few times. What she wanted was to have a cry. Not from emotion but tiredness. But she didn't want to offend the other woman, who'd been so helpful and acted as though looking after errant guests in the small hours was normal.

"You know, I think you might enjoy a sleep more than more caffeine. Would you like me to walk up with you?" Maisie put the tray down with a smile. "What a difficult evening you've had. I can assure you it isn't normally like this here. And I'm quite sure there is no mysterious body to be found. Poor Stacy just had a bit of a shock."

Haven't we all?

"May I have a raincheck on the tea? I really would like to climb into bed."

"Well, seeing as we have a beauty appointment tomorrow, I shall make sure to arrange the nicest tea leaves, and a few little treats to enjoy when you arrive." Maisie led the way to the elevator and pressed the up button. "You try and get a few hours' sleep before the conference begins."

The conference was last on her list of things to worry about. Daphne forced a smile. "Thank you for being so helpful. I'll see you tomorrow. Today. Later." The doors opened and she stepped inside.

An annoying, incessant tapping noise woke Daphne. She pulled the sheet over her head. How soft were these sheets? Eyes tightly shut, sleep called again. Just another few minutes and then she'd get up.

"Daphne...wake up call."

Pushing the sheet aside, Daphne sat up and opened her eyes, squinting at the light.

"I'll leave my door open." It was Rupert, outside her

front door. "Come and join Gloria and me for breakfast in twenty minutes. We all need to talk."

"Okie dokie. Be there in twenty." She managed to call out although her throat was dry. Twenty minutes to shower, dry her hair, do make up and throw on clothes? No time for her morning coffee. A glass of water would have to do.

Out of bed, she stretched and winced as the creaky knee complained. Her ankles ached and her neck was sore. Thank goodness for the appointment later with Maisie. Definitely a neck massage. She couldn't resist a quick look from the balcony. A couple of people were out running and one of the hotel's 4WD's nosed past them in the direction of the gate. Cherry was driving. More guests must be on their way. It was a nice morning with blue skies.

It was more than twenty minutes later when she tapped on Rupert's open door, running her other hand through curls which refused to sit right. She'd foregone the makeup and straightening and was thankful it was only a bit after seven so she still had time to finish getting ready.

"There you are, Daphne. Go through to the living room." Rupert didn't look as though he'd had only a few hours' sleep. He wore a linen shirt and pants and his hair was in a small bun at his nape.

Gloria was seated at a small dining table and she waved as Daphne approached. "Morning, honey. Come and sit down and Rupert can make you a coffee."

"What would you like?" Rupert had closed the front door and was now at a coffee machine. He had a proper—if tiny—kitchen. "Black. Cappuccino. Latte?"

"Oh, a latte would be wonderful, thank you." Daphne joined Gloria at the table which was filled with enticing bowls of sliced fruit, yoghurt, and a plate of pastries.

Gloria reached for the fruit and began spooning some into a smaller bowl. "There's eggs, bacon, toast and the like under the cloches on the trolley, so help yourself to whatever you fancy." She nodded at a waiter's trolley to one side. "I keep saying the food here is one of the best reasons to visit."

"As well as the suite. The bed was rather nice."

"I imagine after such an adventure last night that any bed would have felt good."

Adventure was one word for it. Once Daphne had reached her suite, she'd virtually fallen into bed. Even her clothes ended up on the floor, something she would never normally do.

"One latte." Rupert placed a glass mug near Daphne. "Please eat. I ordered some of everything so there is plenty of food. I guessed you might have an appetite after all that running around during the night."

"Thank you. And yes. I am starving."

All of them attended to filling plates or bowls and ate for a few minutes in silence. Gloria was right about the food being delicious. Perfectly scrambled eggs, golden toast, and yummy fried tomatoes. And a pancake. Daphne had to stop herself after one in case she didn't fit into the dress she'd chosen for today.

Rupert dabbed his lips with a napkin then folded it and put it on his empty plate. "Nice way to start our busy day. This is a bit of a tradition, having breakfast in one of our suites—by that I mean mine, Gloria's, Audrey's, or Stacy's. With the situation overnight, I need to talk about Stacy without her here."

"And Audrey would enjoy this more than she should." Gloria added.

"I've updated Gloria on my recollection of events. Would you fill us both in on what happened from your perspective? I'll make us all another coffee first. Shall we sit on the balcony?"

A few minutes later, each with a coffee, they settled on Rupert's balcony which was twice the size of Daphne's and had access from the living area and the bedroom. A small group of hotel staff, including Col, were walking in the direction of the English garden.

"What if there was a body?" Daphne said, before she could filter the question.

"Did you see one?"

"I saw your jacket. That is crystal clear. The way it was in the water...it appeared to be covering something and Stacy was adamant it was a body. But it was dark and when I went to take a closer look she jumped up and was agitated. Wanted me to get help." Try as she might, Daphne couldn't visualise a body in the water. Just the jacket. "So, I came back here with the intention of knocking on doors for someone to help me if I couldn't raise anyone by phone."

"Except you saw me."

"I could smell you."

Daphne bit her lip. How rude she was.

But Rupert threw back his head and laughed.

"Cigars again?" Gloria shook her head. "Just as well the hotel staff like you so much, breaking the rules at whim and bringing people here who have created havoc more than once."

He stopped laughing. "We aren't responsible for the actions of other adults."

Gloria raised one eyebrow and sipped her coffee.

"You don't just mean Stacy, do you?" he asked. Without

waiting for an answer, he turned to Daphne. "We only met yesterday but it is clear how intuitive you are. I imagine you won't be surprised to hear Audrey has made life uncomfortable for Stacy in her role with the association."

"I gathered there is some ill feeling between them."

Tread lightly, Daph.

Gloria and Rupert exchanged a glance and he nodded. "Last year, the night of the gala dinner—but after it officially ended—Audrey got worked up when Darren disappeared without a word. He was helping Stacy look for the laptop she'd thought was missing from the conference room. Turned out Audrey had picked it up for safe keeping but nobody knew that."

"Why would she be upset about her husband helping look for association property?"

"She didn't care about the laptop. Audrey is rather possessive of Darren. He's considerably her senior and has been married several times. She tends to imagine the worst." Gloria said. "Anyway, she had words with both Darren and Stacy, rather publicly, and since then Stacy goes quiet when Audrey is around."

"I imagine they come into contact though. With both having roles in the association?" Daphne asked.

"We only meet once a month—so not often. The role of the vice president is hardly onerous and she's not always present. I've yet to miss a meeting and am hands on, so Audrey doesn't have a lot to do with the day-to-day management of the association."

A position of power without much power. Daphne had come across people who took on a role on a committee or in a group more for the prestige of the title.

"That gives you insight into the awkwardness last night.

When the two women are together, they are civil and represent the association appropriately." Gloria said. "Until Stacy decides she needs to wander around in the dead of night."

"Dead being the question." Rupert pointed in the direction Col and the others had taken.

"Has the hotel contacted the police?" Just in case.

Rupert nodded. "Yes. The closest station is about twenty kilometres away. Two towns from here."

"They might want to take their own look around and speak with Stacy and me. Not that I have much to offer."

"If there's nothing out of the ordinary uncovered in daylight and you can't confirm sighting a corpse in the fountain, then we have to put it down to Stacy having too much to drink. But we'll need to address this with her."

There was an ominous tone in Rupert's words. He glanced at his watch.

"I'm going to head down and do some last-minute preparations so will see you for the first session, Daphne."

Gloria held up her half full cup. "I shall sit here and finish this. I'll lock the door."

Daphne stood. "And I must make myself presentable. Thank you for a lovely breakfast and company."

And a mystery. Maybe more than one.

AN ANGRY WOMAN

In the slow elevator on the way downstairs, a flutter of nerves surprised Daphne.

But I look nice. Hair and makeup done. And doesn't my dress fit well?

The latter was thanks to a few weeks of watching her food choices and walking a bit faster and further every day and it was worth it all to slip into her red polka dot dress and zip it up without too much holding her breath.

Although she'd been made to feel welcome by those she'd so far met, this was all new. Fifty or so people she hadn't met, most of them celebrants and no doubt far more experienced than she was. What if the speakers asked the audience questions and chose her?

Smile and nod a lot.

John always said she was a natural people person.

"Time to prove him right, Daphne Jones." She whispered as the doors opened in the foyer.

The first thing she saw was a large sign with an arrow pointing further into the hotel than she'd been. "Welcome to Celebrating Celebrants." There was a cute picture of a bride and groom on the sign.

She followed the arrow down a wide hallway to where a table was set up with a woman sitting behind it, beside open double doors. The woman smiled as Daphne approached.

"Good morning and welcome! I'm Nancy. Now, I'm afraid I'm not very good at this but let's find you on the list and get you a lanyard." Nancy pushed a box filled with named lanyards closer. "Stacy normally handles the check-ins but hasn't appeared, so can you have a look for yours and I'll tick you off? What was your name?"

"Daphne Jones." She found her lanyard and put it over her head.

"Oh. You're her." Nancy stared.

Not certain she liked the sound of this, Daphne plastered on a wide smile. "I'm who?"

"You know." Nancy looked both ways, leaned forward, and whispered. "The sleuth."

Oh dear.

"Not really. I'm a celebrant. Retired from a real estate business. Past foster mother. Proud wife of a wonderful man. But hardly a sleuth."

"Not what I hear. No, I hear you solve crimes and help the police." Nancy returned to finding Daphne's name. "Ah, there you are." She put a tick against it. "Are you going to find any criminals here?"

The image of Rupert's jacket floating in the fountain flashed through her mind.

"I am quite certain this beautiful hotel has no criminals at all. In fact, I can't wait to listen to all the speakers and learn more about being a celebrant. So nice to meet you, Nancy."

"You too. But I think there is something going on. After all, there were cars driving about and people wandering around right up until the wee hours of this morning. That isn't how innocent people act."

A small group approached along the hallway and Daphne smiled and stepped through the doorway, relieved for the excuse to leave Nancy to her musings. Hopefully, nobody else knew anything about her. What she'd said was true. She was here to learn.

"Ah, there's my buttercup."

I'm really not your buttercup.

Rupert waved from the front of the room, which was large with chandeliers and windows covered with heavy curtains. He was adjusting a microphone at a podium on a low stage. There were rows of seats separated by an aisle leading to him and Daphne followed it. Only a couple of other people were in the room and they sat in the back row, talking.

"Hello again. Nancy said she hasn't seen Stacy yet. Is she alright?"

"Had a quick chat with her after our breakfast. There. Think that will stay still." He finished with the microphone. "She is adamant there is a body. Upset even that there isn't a police presence here. I told her someone has told the police and suggested she get a bit more sleep and come down during the morning tea break."

"And there isn't? Signs of...you know."

He shook his head. "Col and his team did a thorough search in and around the garden and nothing. Thank goodness."

"Yes."

Rupert folded his arms and smiled. "You look nice. Polka dots are in. Are you looking forward to the conference?"

"I am. But I'm also a bit...well, I feel I'm such a newbie."

He laughed. "Not one thing to worry about, Mrs Jones. Between you and me, most of the attendees are here for the food and the conversation. A lot only see each other at the conferences so there is catching up to be done and gossip to share. Most of them are friendly but don't be concerned if they are too busy with each other to get to know you."

"I have cookies."

Rupert's eyes lit up. "Where are you hiding them?"

"Upstairs. I made a couple of batches to bring as an ice breaker. Unless you think it is silly."

"Nothing silly about cookies. We have a break between both morning sessions and there is a table being set up in the foyer with some nibblies, so why not add them to the offerings."

There was nothing she wanted more. Well, apart from seeing John and working out exactly what happened last night. But cookies to share was a good start.

Daphne found a seat on the outside end of a middle row as the room filled. It wasn't long before Rupert made a short welcome speech and introduced the first speaker. She took out her notebook and pen. This was what she'd looked forward to and she wasn't going to miss a word.

The minute the clapping stopped, Daphne slipped out of the room and hurried to her suite. She collected the top container of cookies and was about to leave with them when her phone beeped. A message from John. She wanted to read it then and there but if she didn't get these onto the table it would be too late.

Back downstairs she found a spot on the table between scones and muffins and opened the lid. People were milling about in the hallway, getting coffee or tea, so she moved further along where it was quieter and checked the message.

Only just got this, doll. Are you okay or would you like me to come back?

"Goodness, no."

She tapped out a reply.

It was all a false alarm and everything is going well here. Just attended the first session. How is the fishing?

The response was quick. At least the reception was improved from last night.

Pleased to hear all is well. Fishing is brilliant. Good company and food. Have you made some new friends?

Not certain she could yet classify anyone as a friend, she glanced at the table as she considered her response. People were helping themselves to the cookies. That was nice.

Had a lovely breakfast with the president and the treasurer. Neck massage at lunch time. People are helping themselves to my cookies as we speak!

She fancied one herself with a cup of coffee. Although she'd had two lattes at breakfast, she was still tired and needed a caffeine kick. John sent back a love heart emoji and she replied with one of her own.

There was just time to pour a coffee before Rupert called everyone back in. Others were carrying their cups and nibblies and there were no cookies left. Not sure whether to be disappointed or elated, she chose the latter. If people loved her cookies, then she'd done a good job.

Partway through this session, she saw Stacy snuck in. She stood at the back of the room looking around as if searching for someone. Heads turned and she quickly found a seat. It was good she was up and about and hopefully less upset than when Daphne last saw her.

The speaker was entertaining as she showed slides of some of the more elaborate weddings she'd officiated, including a cliff top affair as a thunderstorm rolled in. The photographs were stunning but Daphne would have struggled to stay out in the open if there was lightning. Not a fan of storms when she was safely inside, let alone out at the mercy of the elements.

All too soon, Rupert was asking for a round of applause and announcing the lunch break. The room cleared faster than it had for morning tea and when Daphne followed, she understood why. Where morning tea had been served, a larger table was now in place with a buffet lunch and there was already a long line which she joined. She checked the time. Her appointment with Maisie was for one fifteen which was just under forty-five minutes away.

"Daphne. Daphne, I'm so glad you are still here."

Stacy was right behind her, her voice low and anxious, and Daphne turned to look at her. Up close, the other woman's eyes were red-rimmed behind her glasses and she wore no makeup.

"You found your glasses, dear."

"Oh. Oh, yes, they were in my room. But I don't remember leaving them there."

Her face was so worried that Daphne wanted to hug her, but perhaps here wasn't the place.

"Everyone is telling me I am mistaken about last night but you were there. You saw."

A jacket in the water.

"Let's get some lunch and we can chat away from everyone."

"You don't want to be seen here with me? With the mad woman?" Stacy's voice rose and people turned around. A couple of them whispered to each other which agitated Stacy further. "Yes, a mad woman who imagines dead bodies that mysteriously disappear."

More whispers.

Daphne took Stacy's arm. "Why don't we go for a walk. Let's check the fountain ourselves."

"What's the point when nobody believes me." Stacy stiffened. "Great. Just what I need."

Audrey headed their way, her eyes on Stacy and the glimmer of a smile on her lips. A rather unkind smile, in Daphne's opinion. This wasn't going to be pleasant.

"Then let's go for that walk." Daphne lowered her voice. "Don't allow her to distress you because I am not going to stand for any nonsense. You've done nothing wrong, so lift your chin and come with me. Please."

Gratitude brightened Stacy's face and she did just that, raising her head and smiling at Daphne as though they were having a lovely—and normal—conversation.

"Well, well. If it isn't our little panic merchant."

Audrey planted herself between them and freedom. Short of pushing through the line, there was little to do but wait for the vice president to move.

"Good morning. Did your husband arrive safely?"

Audrey's face hardened. "I was going to ask Stacy if she'd seen him."

"Huh? Why would I?"

"Oh, I don't know. Middle of the night. Sneaking around outside. Claiming some crime has been committed. My husband nowhere to be seen. Ring any bells, Stacy?"

Stacy's head dropped, her eyes on the ground.

All around them, other guests were watching. Nobody was at the buffet as people inched close to listen in.

"Audrey, I'm not sure here is the place to—" Daphne began.

"Excuse me? You've been a celebrant for two minutes and know nothing about the historical, and hysterical, behaviour of this woman! A woman we pay to manage our membership."

Audrey was wearing the same earrings as last night and the angrier she got, the more they swung from side to side. There was a stone missing from one. Surely it was there during dinner? Yes, the more Daphne looked at it, the more she was convinced the diamond had disappeared overnight. Like the body.

She forced down the urge to giggle. Angry people did that to her.

"Are you even listening to me, Daphne?" Audrey demanded, folding her arms.

Everyone is listening to you.

The earring stopped jingling about. Daphne straightened her back. "Stacy and I are going for a walk outside. Would you let us pass, please?" Keeping one's tone calm and rational usually took the wind from the sails of an unreasonable person. At least, that was her experience with the occasional difficult customer they'd had at work. Her aim was always to defuse rather than defend.

"Listen. I came over here to speak with Stacy so you go

and toddle off and eat one of your awful cookies on your walk. But Stacy stays."

Awful cookies? A chill settled in Daphne's stomach.

Stacy reached for her arm. Her head was still down and her anxiety showed in the tight grip she had on Daphne. Time for this silliness to stop. She smiled at the people closest to her in the line.

"May we squeeze past?"

There was an immediate gap made.

"Thank you so much. I do hope you enjoy the lunch. It looks delicious."

Expecting the vice president to object or follow, Daphne, with Stacy still attached, hurried past the table and into the foyer. She glanced behind where Audrey still stood, arms crossed, glaring in their direction.

WHEN COOKIES AREN'T ENOUGH

"I can't do this anymore."

They were almost across the foyer when Stacy released Daphne's arm and stopped, raising her head to gaze around as though surprised at where they were.

Back in the hallway, Audrey was in conversation with Rupert, waving her arms around and sending death glares at Daphne and Stacy.

"I need to go back to my room. I need to pack."

They headed for the stairs and reached the accommodation floor without speaking. Audrey's behaviour was both strange and appalling. Leaving Stacy on her own didn't feel right.

"Let's go to my suite, Stacy. I'll make us some tea and I have some cookies to share. Or you can simply sit on the balcony alone if you don't want me fussing over you. Give you a chance to work out if you really wish to go."

Stacy followed without a word and when they reached her suite, she saw there were tears streaking her face.

"Oh, you poor dear, let's get you inside."

That accomplished, Stacy asked to use the bathroom. By the time she emerged, face washed but her eyes still bright, Daphne had put cookies onto a plate from the little cupboard beneath the counter and was pouring tea.

"I hope tea is fine. I can make coffee. Or water?"

"Tea is good."

Stacy carried the cups to the table near the window. "I'd rather sit here, if you don't mind."

"Not at all." Daphne put the cookies down and sat. "There's sugar and milk if you want. And please have a cookie. Did you have breakfast?"

"No. I had an orange juice when I spoke to Rupe but when he didn't believe me either...I crawled back into bed and had a cry. Of all people, he should believe me."

Of all people? Interesting.

"Is it possible he seemed to not believe you because so far there's no evidence to support you?"

Stacy looked straight at Daphne, cup halfway to her lips. "You don't support me. You were there but somehow have forgotten what you saw." It sounded a lot like an accusation. "If I hadn't just heard you take Audrey to task, I would have thought she'd got to you. Made you change your story."

"Nobody has that kind of power over me, Stacy. If I had seen a body, I would say so but all I remember is Rupert's jacket floating in the fountain. Can you tell me exactly what happened? Why were you even out there?"

After taking a sip of tea, Stacy put down the cup. "I'd better not say. It was a silly idea, stupid really. I just always hoped, and I thought the time was right...but anyway, I was out there. Around the time I reached the tennis courts I realised I wasn't wearing my glasses and they weren't in my pocket. I mean, I often take them off when I'm just walking or not having to read anything, but I do need them. So, I started back to the hotel but heard something."

"What kind of something?"

"Like a cry. Not someone crying. But like someone had a dreadful shock and cried out. It was a man. I'm pretty sure, anyway."

"Did you go to see?"

Stacy nodded. "I called out that I was coming and ran toward the sound and didn't even consider it might not be a good idea. But when I got to where the sound was, up in the English garden, it was quiet. No people or noises. And I noticed the fountain wasn't bubbling or anything which I thought was weird. Anyway, I still hoped...well, I can't say why but I had a reason to wait at the fountain so I did."

Meet me now if you dare.

Had she been waiting for someone for a secret rendezvous? Was Stacy hoping to meet up with another guest but accidentally slipped her note under the wrong door?

"What did you find at the fountain?" she asked.

Tears welled up in Stacy's eyes and Daphne got up to collect a box of tissues.

"Here you are, dear. Take your time."

Speaking of time, she had to either cancel the day spa appointment or leave soon.

Stacy blew her nose with a muffled 'thanks'.

"I was looking at the sky hoping the clouds would go away so I could see the stars. But from the corner of my eye, I noticed something in the water and had the most dreadful shock to see Rupe's jacket. The one he'd worn at dinner. I thought someone had thrown it in there as prank but when

I reached for it, I felt something under it. Something firm. And then there was a hand beneath the surface."

"You saw a hand?"

Well, this changed things.

"Yes. For an instant before the jacket moved with the water and covered it. I was so shocked I sat down and then you found me." Stacy raised her hands to look at her outstretched fingers. They were shaking. "It was a male hand. Thicker fingers. I guess if I only saw it for a second then you wouldn't have. I'm sorry."

"Would you like a cookie?" Not sure what to say, food seemed the best idea. Her own stomach was churning but not from hunger. There was more to this mystery than met the eye.

Stacy shook her head then stood. "I'm going to my room to think. Audrey has wanted me gone from the association for years and this time I think she'll find a way. I got the feeling Rupert was cross with me and that is unbearable."

"Here's my phone number." Daphne found one of her business cards and handed it to Stacy. "Anytime, dear, just call me. I am about to have a neck massage but if you need me and I don't answer, leave me a message."

After opening the door, Daphne checked the hall in case Audrey was waiting but there was nobody in sight. Stacy stepped out and her mouth dropped open.

"What's wrong?"

"Um. Er. Nothing." Her eyes went from Daphne to Rupert's door. "Thank you for being so kind to me."

She turned and hurried away.

An odd response. Had Stacy just put two and two together? If she'd meant for Rupert to get the note and mistaken the suite numbers...well, well, well.

Although she was worried about being late for her appointment, the chance to speak with Col arose as Daphne exited the hotel. He'd just finished a conversation with one of the guests and smiled as she approached.

"Mrs Jones. Feeling okay after the late night?"

"I am, thank you. And you can't have had a lot of sleep, between being woken to search the grounds and then up early for a second sweep."

He nodded. "Feeling tired but it's just part of the job."

"I wondered if you know when the police are coming."

"Police?" He scratched the top of his head. It was impossible to see his eyes behind black sunglasses but he finally nodded again. "They remember the last false alarm with Stacy Chester and asked if we believed her. I don't. And my men and I have spent a couple of hours out in the bush as well and there's nothing but her drunken ramblings. And the bottle of champagne she took with her."

"So, nobody is coming to speak with her. Or me?" This didn't sound right at all.

"I expect someone will be along at some point but it isn't a priority."

"Well, perhaps it needs to be. Stacy saw a hand in the water."

With a heavy sigh, Col removed his sunglasses and rolled his eyes. "She never said that to me. I'll call the police station myself but I think she needs her eyes checked."

"She wasn't wearing her glasses at the time, but even so, a hand is quite a shocking thing to see in a fountain." At least he was going to follow it up. These things were best left to the police. No need for her to poke around.

"Hello and welcome again, Daphne."

Maisie looked fresher than Daphne felt, considering the night they'd had. Tiredness was beginning to slow her down but she'd managed to get to the day spa with a couple of minutes to spare. It was terribly humid now and dark clouds were looming in the distance.

"Did you decide between hand and neck massage?"

"Neck please. It is feeling tight."

"Well, follow me and I'll take care of that. Not surprising after all the goings on during the night!"

In no time, Daphne was face down on a massage table after changing from her dress into a towel to give Maisie access to her neck and shoulders. The room was softly lit with the same pastel colours as the reception area. Scented candles added to the sense of peace and relaxation. If only she had an hour. Or two.

And no worries.

"Comfortable, Daphne?" Maisie asked as she warmed some oil between her hands. "I'll have you out of here all calm and happy and in time for the next session."

As Maisie began to work on her neck, Daphne closed her eyes. The next session was a panel discussion about best practices and ethics. Surely ethics included how one presents themselves in public, particularly their dealings with other people. Even though Audrey was not a celebrant, she was married to one, was vice president, and through her bridal business was an important part of the wedding industry. Deliberately seeking out Stacy to revile her in front of her peers was far removed from ethical behaviour. At least to Daphne.

The half hour flew as Maisie's fingers worked their magic.

"I'll head back out now so you can dress but come and collect my little care package before you leave."

Almost back in her dress, voices from the next room drifted through the wall. Two women were discussing the scene Audrey made.

"Was embarrassing to watch. Stacy won't stand up for herself and we all know Audrey can be a right so and so when it suits her. At least she had someone looking out for her."

Another woman tutted. "What a mess, Joan."

"Exactly. But this Daphne Jones woman didn't take any nonsense from Audrey. Quite impressive."

A little surge of pride brought a smile to her face and she zipped up her dress as the same voice continued.

"Pity about her baking skills, though." Joan continued.

"What do you mean?"

"She took it upon herself to bring homemade cookies to morning tea."

"Well, that is sweet of her." Joan said.

"You have no idea. They were awful."

Awful?

Tears prickled at the back of her eyes as the other women burst into laughter. She shoved her feet into her shoes, put her glasses on, and grabbed her handbag, smoothing her hair in the mirror. Her face was red and she noticed she was holding her breath.

Awful. First Audrey and now this woman said so. Her cookies were awful.

She somehow managed to smile and say thank you to

Maisie, who gave her a paper carry bag to take back to her room.

And once she was in her suite, she stood there, in the middle of the living area.

What to do?

If two people hated her cookies so much, then perhaps everybody else did. They might have spent the lunch break comparing notes about how bad they were. About her baking skills or apparent lack thereof.

"How can I do this? How can I go back?"

Even as the tide of despair washed over her, she hurried into the bathroom and took off her glasses. She wasn't going to cry. And she wasn't going to take this to heart. Not without further investigation.

"You are strong, Daphne Jones." She told her reflection. "You have a good heart and a clever mind. You care about others. And you deserve to treat yourself with respect."

All true.

"And Stacy has it much harder right now so instead of being afraid of what other people think, go and show her how to hold her head up."

All good and well to give herself a pep talk but this was upsetting. She'd made cookies for years. Decades. All based on her own mother's recipe. Those cookies would appear anytime something was wrong, such as the arguments between her parents. A plate would suddenly be on the kitchen table and the children would help themselves and find a quiet spot to hide until the adults calmed down.

The palms of her hands hurt. Her hands were so tightly curled that her nails dug into her skin. Drawing in a long breath, she straightened her fingers. Funny how an old memory can still affect you after all this time. She breathed out, repeated, and then found her glasses.

"John loves you. And he loves your cookies."

She smiled at herself until the sadness lifted. She splashed her face with some cold water. Glasses back on, she poured some water and drank it before reapplying her lipstick. It was time for the next session.

STORMY WEATHER

Overhead, the sky had darkened as storm clouds rolled in. John hurried up packing to leave. Nobody wanted to be out here when the weather changed even if the tents were secure. More than secure, they were downright comfortable. He'd never slept in a proper bed inside a tent but these were large, permanent structures and had all the bells and whistles.

His backpack done, he checked he'd left nothing behind and made his bed. He knew someone would come along and change the bedding before the next intake of guests but he couldn't walk away and leave a mess.

At the entrance he turned back for a final look. Much as he'd missed Daph, he wasn't going to lie about how much he'd enjoyed the past twenty-four hours. Fishing in a fantastic river at his own pace. Taking photos of the river as well as a beautiful, secluded clearing he'd found, filled with native flowers. And the meals. Relaxed around a campfire eating what they'd caught, perfectly cooked by one of the guides, who happened to be a chef.

"Hope you had as good a time, doll."

Outside, the other men had gathered as they waited for the all-clear to leave. He joined Ted, who'd become a friend on the trek up here. They'd fished within sight of each other and then swapped stories over dinner. John had no doubt they'd keep in touch between their camaraderie and their wives being celebrants.

"This is my fifth trip here and I reckon this was the best." Ted said. He was married to the club's treasurer, Gloria, and talked about her all the time. "Now all we need is for those girls of ours to decide to come back again and we can begin a new tradition."

"I reckon next time I'd want a few days up here. Would love to show Daphne the clearing I found and go for some bushwalks. She'd get a kick out of the tent."

Ted grinned. "You really do everything together? And how long have you been married?"

"Forty something years. Daphne is a person who is easy to be around." John meant it. He'd met her at the end of high school and they'd rarely been apart since. They never argued and always had each other's back and he was grateful, every day, to have her in his life.

They set off a few minutes later in a line of sorts, between one guide at the front and one at the back. Did they occasionally misplace a guest? John almost chuckled aloud at the thought of how they'd explain losing someone out here. As middle aged to senior men they were unlikely to take risks. Or wander far away enough to miss a meal.

Speaking of meals...already on its way to the hotel was a portable fridge filled with this morning's catches. These would be served as part of the gala dinner.

"Think we'll be lucky to get back before the rain." Ted caught up with John. "At least the conference is all indoors."

John glanced up. He wasn't worried about being out in it. But Daphne had a fear of storms. With luck, it would pass by without her noticing.

Going past the lunch table reminded Daphne she'd not eaten but there was no time now with Rupert holding the door open for her.

"Sorry. Am I late?"

"On time."

He closed the door and leaned down to speak quietly. Not that anyone would hear because attendees were still milling around and the chatter was quite loud.

"Stacy still wants to leave. She told me you were kind to her and I thank you for helping her when Audrey was going off. I just couldn't get there in time to intervene." Rupert's forehead was drawn. He must feel he was right in the middle of this.

"Should she leave before the police speak to her?"

"I imagine they have better things to do than come all the way up here based on the drunken imaginings of someone who has done similar in the past."

Did he know about the hand?

"When is she leaving?" she asked.

"Unsure. She said she wanted to sleep for a while before the long drive back, so I've asked Mandy to put one of the drivers on call for later this afternoon."

"Is there anything I can do to help?"

Rupert's face creased into a smile. "My dear lady, you've

done more than most of the association and yet you are our newest member. I would like to think you can now enjoy the remainder of the sessions and then the dinner without another thought about the unpleasantness of the past few hours."

Unverified bodies. Angry vice presidents. Cookie haters.

"I am looking forward to this evening, and to introducing you to John."

"You will both be at my table. Ah, looks like I'm required." With that, Rupert made his way toward the small stage, clapping his hands. "Find your seats. Starting in two minutes."

Daphne returned to her earlier seat, aware of a few glances in her direction. Whether it was about cookies or Stacy she didn't know. What other people thought was not her business so she made herself comfortable and got her notebook out. This was a brand new one she'd purchased just for the conference. She did love a nice notebook.

The panel discussion turned out to be serious and even a bit on the boring side. Rupert and Gloria were joined by Nancy, who was a retired business lawyer and turned out to be a bit hard of hearing, so there was much repeating of questions. The only time ethics was mentioned was regarding overbooking of clients.

Fortunately, this was a short session and the next one began as soon as the stage was cleared. Much more interesting was this masterclass on writing beautiful ceremonies no matter the occasion. There were step by step formulas, ways to use emotive words, how to involve one's clients in writing the ceremony, and several examples of unique ones. Daphne scribbled in her notebook as fast as she could, not wanting to miss a word.

The speaker finished to loud applause and Rupert joined them on stage. But he didn't get as far as saying anything as a long, deep rumble of thunder rattled the windows.

A few people squealed and then laughed.

Rupert spread his arms out. "What a grand entrance I make."

More laughter.

But Daphne wasn't laughing and gripped her notebook against her chest. John was out in this. His tent would be no protection. Or what if he was on the way back? The terrain was rough and a tree might get hit by lightning.

The lights dimmed then came back. Then went again.

A flash of lightning was followed by the patter of raindrops.

"We might take a short break. Let's meet back here in fifteen minutes and hope our power is restored."

That suited Daphne and she was on her feet and first out of the double doors. Not waiting for the elevator, she scurried up the steps, dragging on the railing, as more thunder rumbled. The rain was heavier with every minute and as she let herself into the suite, a huge flash of lightning hit something close by and she screamed.

From the living room window the scene was wild as trees bent against a tirade of wind. In the distance, the storm forked lightning into the flat ground below.

She rushed to the bedroom and peered through the French doors. The rain was like a sheet but through it a line of people emerged from near the tennis courts, hurrying toward the hotel.

"John!"

From the bathroom she grabbed some towels and remembered to pick up her key as she left the suite. What dreadful weather to be out in. But he was almost here and that made her feet fly down the stairs.

Front doors held open by staff, the returning men burst into the foyer. All were soaked to the skin but they laughed and began to clap each other on the back.

You're safe.

John grinned at her as he shrugged off his backpack. Hotel staff were fussing around with towels and she carried hers across to him.

"Hello, love. You look like you fell in the river. Rupert warned me you might."

"Rupert did? Not very encouraging."

"I told him you wouldn't."

"Knew you'd have my back."

Water dripped down his face and his clothes stuck to his body but nothing was going to stop Daphne landing a kiss on his lips.

And then she handed him the towels.

The lights came back on.

"Looks like I have to go, John. You said you'd want a shower but I thought you meant in the suite, not outdoors."

"Taking care of the environment."

"Here's my key. Yours is in the suite." She couldn't resist another quick kiss. "I'll see you in under an hour."

"And I promise to be dry by then."

People were returning to the conference room. The storm was easing. And John was back. Everything in Daphne's world was better again.

AFTERMATH OF THE STORM

"One of the vehicles is missing."

Daphne's ears pricked up at a conversation between staff at the reception counter. She slowed down. The conference could wait a minute.

"What exactly do you mean by missing?" It was Mandy speaking, her back to the foyer and her hands on her hips as she faced another uniformed woman. "And whose vehicle?"

"Cherry's. She went down to the carpark and hasn't returned."

"Why did she go there? We have no guests coming in today."

The other woman shrugged.

"Can't we raise her?"

"Not so far."

Daphne stopped, pretending to check her phone for something.

Mandy sounded worried. "When did she leave? I hope she didn't drive down during the storm?"

"Col said it was around lunchtime. He wants to go to look for her."

"Not until the storm has cleared. Can you please find him for me?" Mandy turned and picked up the landline phone. "I'll see if any of our contacts in town can check the carpark for us."

Not wanting to be caught eavesdropping, Daphne headed for the conference room.

Almost at the doors—which were closed—she remembered something and doubled back. Mandy was on the phone and made eye contact with a brief smile.

"I'm sure that's the explanation. And if you see her, would you give me a call?"

After replacing the receiver, Mandy smiled again, but she looked worried. "How can I help?"

"I couldn't help overhearing about the missing 4WD and I remembered seeing one of the cars leaving earlier."

"Oh, you did? Around lunchtime?"

"No. I was about to meet Rupert and Gloria for breakfast so it was before eight. Closer to seven."

Mandy's brow furrowed and she reached for a book with 'Staff Communication' written on the front.

"Well, that is odd." She flicked through the pages then ran her finger down to an entry. "This was last night and is written by Col when he returned from the carpark for the final time. Our staff write down where, when, and why they use a vehicle and he's said...returned to garage at eleven in the evening after the guest failed to show. Note with contact details left on carpark gate should guest arrive later. Gate locked and security activated."

"Isn't that late for a guest?"

With a nod, Mandy closed the book. "And unusual."

A missing guest. Who became a body, perhaps?

There was that little tingle of anticipation in her stomach. Could this be part of the mystery?

"I imagine a guest not arriving is a bit of a worry. The roads aren't the best and driving late at night..." Daphne left the rest to Mandy's imagination in the hope of more information. She crossed the fingers of one hand between her body and the counter.

"His wife mentioned this morning he'd had to cancel joining her at the last minute. Anyway, thanks for letting me know about the time you saw the shuttle. There'll be an explanation."

"I'd better get back to the conference."

Daphne knew she'd missed the beginning of the final session but this information might matter. One never knew when a snippet of something would be a clue to solving a case.

No case. No clues. Stop sleuthing!

She managed to get to her seat without disrupting the session. Audrey was at the podium and for a moment, Daphne wished she'd skipped this one. After the earlier nastiness, she'd lost all respect for the vice president. But leaving would draw attention and she wasn't about to give Audrey the satisfaction.

"Our wonderful association has been a support system for celebrants for over a decade. As one of several organisations of likeminded people in a rapidly changing world, we understand the importance of providing more to our clients. Ceremonies which are a cut above. Memorable events which everyone around those involved will talk about for months. Offering more."

Audrey paused and gazed around. Her eyes met

Daphne's and her lips puckered for a minute before she continued.

"And by more, I refer to holding ourselves to a higher standard. Our reputation as an association and as individual celebrants reflects on us all. If we step outside the boundaries of our profession then we let everyone down."

She turned a page on the podium.

"An example would be a celebrant who fails to arrive at their appointed ceremony in a timely manner. Or one who overrides the wishes of the client in favour of their own beliefs."

She directed an unpleasant smile at Daphne.

"And most of us would never involve ourselves in matters that were not our business, or attract the attention of the media from our actions. Would we?"

The long pause stirred the audience and some turned to see who Audrey stared at.

Heat rose from her neck to her forehead. Everyone was looking at her.

"Audrey?" Gloria spoke from one of the front seats and Audrey shuffled whatever papers she had in front of her.

"We are fortunate to have the services of a capable treasurer in Gloria Long, who has held the position for a...*long* time." Audrey giggled at her own poor attempt of a joke. "The association's finances are in good health so the committee has supported an idea of mine which will help us all."

You could resign.

She forced her shoulders to relax. Her fingers to unclench. Her breathing to deepen. There was something seriously not right about the vice president and Daphne had an idea of what might be prompting the scathing comments.

Was it Darren who didn't arrive late last night and you don't know where he is?

"Imagine if we could offer our clients a broader range of services than just a ceremony. If they can go to your website and see floral displays and honeymoon destinations and hire cars and wedding venues then you become far more to them than someone officiating on their special day."

"Some of us already recommend local supplementary businesses, Audrey. So, what's different about this?" A person called out the question.

"I'm pleased you asked. Let me ask you all a question first. What do you get from putting somebody else's business on your website or passing their details on to a client?"

A few people murmured to each other and another spoke. "They send clients to me so it's a reciprocal arrangement."

"So, you send business to them and they refer business to you?" Audrey had both hands on the podium.

She was an impressive woman when she wasn't being mean. Apart from her immaculate presentation she had a confidence about her which gave weight to her words. She'd changed her attire since this morning and wore white pants and a matching jacket over a lilac blouse. Her earrings were now gold hoops.

"Then I am so sorry I didn't put this idea forward earlier because you have all been missing out. Imagine how much money a florist makes from a wedding or a funeral? Or a function centre? And you?" she laughed shortly. "Celebrants are underpaid as it is but you are throwing money to these peripheral businesses for a pittance in return."

More chatter, louder, which seemed to be what Audrey wanted for she waited with a slight smile. After a minute, she held a hand up, palm forward and the room quietened.

"There is a better way. Imagine getting a small percentage of every successful referral. Possibly a set amount. All for doing what you already are when you refer clients to another business. And not just wedding related. What about limousines or accommodation for bachelor parties and hen's nights?"

The original speaker stood up. It was a young woman with bright red hair. "Audrey, I'm sorry to interrupt, but this feels a bit...I don't know...distasteful. And too commercial. Speaking for myself, I refer to businesses who I personally know and can whole-heartedly recommend and I'm not going to go to them demanding a fee for doing so!"

"Perfectly fine for you, or anyone here, to continue as is. But as you rightly stated, you are speaking for yourself while I am speaking for the association you belong to."

Gloria coughed. Twice.

"Is this some money grab from the association? Because I won't remain a member if so." The younger woman's tone was sharp.

Rupert, who'd sat quietly off to one side of the stage climbed to his feet. "Jessica, I can assure you this is not a money grab. And although Audrey has the committee's support to discuss this concept today, it isn't approved as yet. The last thing I'd want to see is you, or any of our members, leave, so please hear Audrey out. All members will be contacted in a week or two with further details and a survey and I promise our involvement will only go forward if the majority want it."

Jessica sat. Rupert stayed on his feet, moving to lean against a wall.

Audrey glanced at him and raised her eyebrows before taking a sip of water.

"Apologies for any misunderstanding. I'll give you an outline of what I envision. I think it is fair to say I am well known and regarded in the wedding industry and I have many, many contacts across the different business which come together to create someone's dream wedding. My intention is to create a hub, if you like, filled with photographers and travel agents and function centres...you get the drift. They'll be broken down by region and that is where you all come in." She held her arms wide open. "You will have your own page on a central website, all beautifully set out, with complementary businesses local to you having something like a calling card on your page. Oh, I really wish I had a mocked-up page to show you but my laptop didn't arrive last night."

Does Darren have it? If so, no wonder Audrey was so agitated. It might have nothing to do with her thinking the worst about him and Stacy and everything to do with not having the full presentation materials for the session.

"Nevertheless, this hub is on its way to reality and I am offering all of you the opportunity to get in at the very beginning. The association, assuming this is approved, will pay a one-off fee which will allow members to have their individual pages on it for an initial free year, followed by a heavily discounted rate to continue."

Jessica stood again and there was a flutter of giggles and a couple of groans. The young woman cast a glare at those laughing. "This hub of yours. It is going ahead with or without us?"

"Yes. The website is under construction and there is a lot of money about to be invested into making this a nationally recognised resource." Audrey spread her arms apart. "It will be a virtual wedding expo and *the* place to be."

"You've not explained why we should have a page there. And why should we have these businesses on our page who we may not have any knowledge of, or affiliation with."

"Every time your page results in a successful connection you'll receive a finder's fee. You'll make a passive income to use however you wish."

"For a few dollars it isn't worth risking your reputation referring to somebody who might have poor business practices." Jessica noted.

Audrey laughed. "Few dollars? No, precious. You'll start at low three figures per referral and the sky is the limit considering how many moving parts there are for each ceremony. The wedding industry is far more lucrative than you know and it is about time you started exploiting it."

Daphne reached the top of the stairs but before getting to the corner to the lounge area, she stopped and flattened herself against the wall out of sight.

Gloria and Rupert were talking and it was about Audrey.

They'd left the conference room the second the session ended. People were crowding around Audrey asking question and she was smiling and nodding. Jessica had also rushed out. Poor Jessica. They'd never spoken but it was clear she had strong feelings about how she ran her business and wasn't a fan of Audrey's approach.

"Well, I wish he'd arrived. If nothing else you and I could

have looked at this model of Audrey's before the session and got her to approach how she shared the information differently." Gloria said.

"I phoned him yesterday when I got here to wish him luck with the wedding he had on. He was sweating on her laptop finishing some massive update so he could pack it and seeing as he disagrees with most of Audrey's plan I imagine him being here would have created more friction." He made a scoffing sound. "As if we need more friction. Audrey is on thin ice in my books."

Thank goodness they are paying attention. Poor Stacy needs all the support she can get.

"She's taken such an odd dislike to Daphne and I'm not at all sure why. Daphne is so nice." Gloria's words were a surprise.

"Yes. She's a sweetheart and I won't have any further digs at her by Audrey. I think it is time—"

Footsteps stomping up the stairs interrupted whatever Rupert was going to say. Daphne coughed and emerged, digging around in her handbag.

"Oh. Hello. Just looking for that key and then I remembered I gave it to John when he arrived back from the fishing trip. Soaking wet! Did you see your Ted?" she asked Gloria, aware she was babbling.

"I didn't know they were back. Excuse me." Gloria smiled and went in the opposite direction to Daphne's suite.

Other people wandered past from downstairs and Daphne waved to Rupert. "Better go check on John."

"See you both at six."

Yes. Yes, they would. At least being in the same room as Audrey wouldn't be so bad now John was here.

BEFORE THE DINNER

"Champagne ready to open. Glasses chilled. Fruit sliced. Chocolates being chocolates." John checked off his list. "My clothes are ready. Ah, need to get my shoes out."

On his way to the bedroom there was a tap on the door.

"It's only me."

John opened the door. "There is no 'only' about you."

Daphne grinned and headed for the living room while he closed the door. "Oh my! What is all this, love?"

"I hoped you might join me in a pre-dinner drink?"

She dropped her handbag onto a chair and reached her arms out for a hug. "Sounds wonderful. And much needed."

"Missed you." He had. And he'd missed cuddling her. He squeezed her until she giggled and then he kissed the tip of her nose.

"We have a lot to catch up on but if you can give me five minutes, I have something to do." She said.

"Take as long as you like getting ready. We have just over an hour."

After wiggling out of the hug, Daphne went to her

handbag and pulled out one of her notebooks. “Getting ready will need to wait. I have a few notes to record before I forget.”

“In that case, shall I pour us a glass of champagne?” John asked.

“Indeedy.” She sat at the table and rummaged in her bag for a pen. “There you are.”

While he opened and poured the bubbly, she had her head down writing. He carried the glasses over and handed her one with a ‘cheers’.

“Cheers. Mmm...nice.”

She put down the glass and gave him a funny look. One he recognised. Something had happened during the night, this much he knew. A false alarm about a body in a fountain from a person who’d had a bit too much to drink. Surely in the short time he’d been away she hadn’t found herself a mystery.

He sat opposite. “You’re not making notes about the conference.”

“You know me too well.”

There were worry lines around her eyes he’d not noticed when she came in. She caught at her bottom lip with her teeth and he reached his hand across the table to take one of hers. “Tell me everything.”

This made her laugh at least and she closed the notebook.

“I can offer an abridged version given the short time window we have.” She glanced outside. “At least the weather has cleared.”

The storm had passed as quickly as it began and only the glistening trees gave away the recent downpour.

“You sent me a text message about a missing body.

Somebody in a fountain. Don't tell me you've found the body?" he asked.

He loved Daphne with all his heart and would do anything to help her, but lately they'd been involved with several mysteries around weddings and funerals. The last twenty-four hours was a delight without anything to worry about except which spot to stand in to fish, or whether to have dessert.

She shook her head. "No. We found Rupert's jacket in the fountain. It is red and made of velvet so easy to identify. And by we, I mean Stacy Chester found it—she works for the association, managing the membership and most of the administration side. But she'd left me a note under the door and I saw her leave the hotel in the dead of night so I followed and—"

"Whoa. Hang on a sec. You followed someone in the middle of the night? What note?"

"Here." Daphne slid it out of an envelope on the table. "I'm pretty sure Stacy wrote this but she denies it."

The poem didn't make much sense apart from being an invitation of sorts.

"This was under your door but she says it isn't hers?"

"Well, she's not seen it. But she told me she didn't know which room is mine and then earlier today, after Audrey upset her, Stacy was here and had a moment when she noticed Rupert is in the next suite. I have a theory."

"And my head is spinning, doll. Can you go back to the fountain?"

Daphne outlined what she thought she saw and then what Stacy claimed to see. How she wasn't certain there was more than the jacket in the water and Stacy's claim someone moved the body. No wonder Daphne was keeping notes. This was right up her alley.

"And now I am concerned about the wellbeing of Darren Sutton. Audrey's husband. He should have arrived last night but didn't. So, what if it was him in the fountain? What if he did arrive but somebody killed him and then moved the body?"

"Didn't you say the hotel staff went out to search?"

"They did. Unless one of them is in on it. One of the hotel's 4WD left this morning and hasn't returned." Daphne took another sip.

"Okay. We have no body but a guest who was a no-show. One alleged sighting of this body by someone who'd had a lot to drink. A search party finding nothing to back her story *and* a history of her acting a little oddly up here."

"I wish I'd thought to take photos last night. And I didn't wake up until Rupert knocked to invite me to breakfast with him and Gloria so I haven't been back up there." She sighed and tapped her fingers on the glass.

John checked the time. "Feel like a quick walk? Rain's gone."

Daphne's smile made the offer worthwhile. Now to dispel her concerns and put the mystery aside.

She'd changed into sensible walking shoes, which looked a little odd with her polka dot dress but that was too bad. Most of the guests were probably preparing for the gala dinner and the hotel staff would have seen stranger attire than hers. They'd need to be back in about twenty minutes to allow changing and freshening up time. It was humid out here and steam rose from the path as the sun heated it.

"I'd already been to the English garden. After you left yesterday, I went for a lovely walk around the grounds and sat there for a while enjoying the peacefulness."

"The whole property is an interesting mix of natural growth, like all the gum trees and native flowers, and the manicured gardens." John said. "Even the hotel is a combination of styles which somehow works."

The archway came into view and Daphne slowed. What if there had been some poor soul in the water and she'd not taken the time to discover who it was?

"I came in this way through the hedges. And it was so dark because there was a heavy cloud cover and the moon only appeared every so often. I stopped here, near this statue, which gave me quite the fright!" She laughed. "Thought it was somebody standing there."

John said nothing. His lips were pressed together.

"In hindsight I shouldn't have come out here alone, love."

He glanced at her with a half-smile.

"And I wouldn't have, not just from the note. But seeing Stacy disappear into the dark and knowing she'd had a lot to drink...I couldn't have left her out here alone."

"Except you think the note was meant for someone else. For Rupert?"

"I'm drawing a long bow."

In the late afternoon sun, the water in the fountain sparkled.

"Still not working."

"Have you seen it in action?" John strolled around the base.

"Yes. It cascaded nicely during my afternoon visit. But last night I noticed how quiet it was and wondered if the staff turn it off at night."

"No need. See this?" he pointed at the top of the fountain. "On the bowler hat."

Daphne had to step back to see high enough. There were a couple of small, flat boxes facing up. "Solar panels. Like on top of Bluebell."

"Something may have come undone inside. You said there was a jacket in the bottom so there might be a blockage from it." John took his phone out and began taking photos. The fountain, including the water from different sides and angles. The statue. And around them both. Hedges. Statues. Benches.

"And Stacy came from which corner when you arrived with Rupert?" he asked.

"There." She pointed. "Col and another staff member said they had a good look but there was no sign of anyone, or anything to indicate recent movement. It all seems unreal now."

Phone away, John put an arm around her shoulder. "Must have given you quite a scare. Not sure I'd have kept my head."

"If you'd seen me running back to the hotel you might not be so kind. I was sure Rupert was dead in the fountain but it was only his jacket."

"Which got there...how?"

An excellent question.

"Well, he wore it to dinner but we were all sitting outside on the roof and it was warm so he took it off. He told me he must have left it there by accident so presumably, a person unknown picked it up."

"Why? Was it some prank?"

I am so glad you are back.

"He seems well liked. But this association has a lot going on under the surface," she glanced at the water. "So to speak. I overheard him say to Gloria that Audrey was on thin ice with him."

What was going on among the committee? Daphne had served on a few in her time and managed to stay clear of petty politics and power plays. But other people took themselves more seriously and in-fighting wasn't uncommon.

"We need to head back, Daph. I'll need some time to make myself beautiful."

"You are already beautiful, Mr Jones."

"Not nearly as lovely as Mrs Jones, though."

Hand in hand, laughing, they walked away from the fountain. A sudden chill shot up Daphne's spine and she glanced back. Nothing and nobody in the garden area.

Except she knew.

Someone was watching again.

DESSERT SURPRISE

On the way to dinner from their suite, Daphne gave John the lowdown on who was who. "Rupert is loud and kind and a bit eccentric. I really like Gloria. She's Ted's wife and the treasurer. Down to earth and nice. We're sitting with them, so Rupert told me. And hopefully Audrey will sit elsewhere."

"I take it she isn't the friendliest of people?"

"Unfortunately, she's taken a dislike to me."

John stopped them both. They were almost at the upstairs lounge area. "Care to elaborate?"

Daphne preferred people to make their own judgements rather than sway them with her point of view. She lived her life, giving others the benefit of the doubt. But this was different.

"Remember, I said earlier Audrey was upset with Stacy? Well, I was there and Stacy was afraid of her so I acted as a bit of a buffer between them. I suggested it wasn't the place to have a go at Stacy, not with most of the other celebrants watching on and she got a bit...snippy."

Thinking about it made her blood pressure rise.

With a smile, John kissed her lips. “Always looking out for someone else.”

They continued down the stairs.

“And what about Stacy. Is she alright now?”

“Not really. Last I heard she was going home before the dinner.”

“Daphne! Daphne, wait up!”

Stacy ran to meet them.

“Scratch my last comment.” Daphne whispered. “Hello. I thought you were leaving, dear.”

“I would but there’s storm damage on the road with a giant tree down and no access. Not even for the police coming up here. So, I’ve pulled myself together, dressed myself up, and intend to enjoy the evening.”

Dressed up was an understatement with a fully sequined pantsuit and matching shoes.

She put her hand out to John. “I’m Stacy Chester. You must be John.”

They shook hands.

“Are you going to sit with us?” Daphne asked.

“No, I’m not feeling welcome at the executive table. Might join Jessica and some of the others who aren’t Audrey fans. Could use a bit of solidarity. It’s been nice to meet you, John. And you look gorgeous, Daphne.”

With that, she tore down the steps as though on a mission. Hopefully, it wasn’t to find more alcohol.

“She’s right.” John took Daphne’s hand as they reached the bottom steps. “You do look gorgeous and I’m so proud to be your date tonight.”

“Aw, love. You’ll make me blush.” Her heart overflowed with love for this man. “And you are so handsome in your suit. I admit I’ve missed seeing you in it since we retired.”

He leaned in. "Maybe I need to wear it more often?"

She giggled and squeezed his hand. John made everything good in her life. But she was quietly proud of how the dress she'd recently bought made her look and feel. Not quite floor length, it had soft, flowing lines and was blue—the same blue as the highlights in her hair—with a lacy bodice. A pair of heels and she was ready to dance.

The gala dinner was in the conference room and as they entered, she almost gasped at the difference a couple of hours had made. Set around a dance floor, tables of eight were decorated with candles and flowers. The stage was softly lit with a large screen rotating beautiful scenes of nature in time to low music. White aproned staff carried bottles of wine to the tables and the mood was festive.

A tingle of excitement pushed away all the other feelings and worries of the past day.

But a little thought niggled in her mind. Stacy had implied there was no way up or down the mountain. Exactly how long had that been the case?

As principal of Rivers End Real Estate, John had attended his share of conferences over the years. When he'd gone without Daphne, particularly when they'd been fostering children and she refused to leave them with anyone else, he'd learned what he could, networked, and been happy to go home without staying a minute more than required.

Tonight was different. This was her new world and she was shining. In the past few weeks, she'd been firm about walking more and eating less and although he loved her regardless of a few extra kilos here and there, she was keen to be healthier. And that was something he wholeheartedly embraced. He patted his own stomach which had flattened thanks to keeping pace with his wife.

A tall man with white hair on his shoulders stood and waved and Daphne led the way to his table. He wore a forest green velvet jacket and bowtie to match and wasted no time kissing Daphne's cheek.

"Don't you look divine, Mrs Jones." He held a hand out to John. "I'm Rupert Witherspoon and your lovely wife never believed for a minute you would fall in the river."

"Nice to meet you. And thankful I managed to avoid such a catastrophe."

Ted and Gloria arrived and introductions followed. Ted and John elected to sit next to each other to continue a discussion about fishing, and Gloria settled on the other side of Daphne, with Rupert next. There were three empty seats at the table.

"Hope you won't find this too boring, John." Ted said. "Lots of speeches between courses and then there's the awards."

"Awards?"

Ted gave him a look of disbelief. "Does nobody tell the newbies anything these days? There'll be awards for different categories. Best ceremony with heart. Or humour. You get the drift. All based on comments from clients who elect to fill in a short feedback form. Daphne will have left them with her clients."

He didn't recall her doing so. She was unlikely to do anything if she felt it might put someone out.

"We used to do similar with our real estate clients, not that Daphne ever called them a feedback form. I think it was a 'how did we do' thing. And these are then voted on? Or how does it work?"

"Stacy manages them. She reads everything that comes into the association whether a feedback form or a legal letter. First point of call really and nothing gets past her. Be a pity if this little incident sees her out of a job."

John had no intention of sharing his thoughts on the matter. Not when he had so little information to go on. But he wasn't against listening.

Ted continued. "With the awards, Stacy makes a short list for each category and then the committee votes. She's the only one who knows the winner until each envelope is opened. Not even executive know who they've voted on."

"Makes for a fair result."

"It does." Ted glanced around as though to check nobody was close enough to hear. "But it also gives one person an awful lot of power."

"Looks like we're missing two people." Gloria looked around their table.

"Stacy is over with Jessica. I don't think she's comfortable being here if Audrey is."

Gloria leaned closer. "Honey, if Audrey gives you a hard time, you let me know and I'll have a quiet word. She's upset about her husband not attending but that is no reason to act mean."

Audrey chose that moment to arrive, throwing herself onto the seat beside Rupert and launching into a whispered conversation with him. She'd changed again. Her hair was in soft waves around her face and her dress was black and floor length and tight in all the right places. Why she'd ever believe her husband would stray made no sense to Daphne. Audrey was a smart and beautiful woman. But she had shown an unkind side so who knew what their relationship was like. Living with somebody who wasn't your friend was unthinkable.

I'm so lucky.

She glanced at John. He listened intently as Ted regaled him with a story about a fishing trip in Tasmania and she had to smile. If nothing else, coming here had been good for him. He was supportive of her new career and never complained about longer than expected stays or sudden changes of plan.

"I should have just brought the thing with me, Rupert." Audrey no longer seemed concerned with being overheard. "Darren insisted he'd bring the laptop once it completed an update but I think he had no intention of coming here."

"Last time I spoke with him he did. We planned a game of tennis tomorrow. And a swim."

"Yes. You two old fogeys enjoy wasting your time." Her words might have been on the rude side but she smiled at Rupert and he grinned in return. "I'll remind him he missed out on beating you with his backhand and that there are less opportunities with every passing year."

Rupert threw his head back and laughed.

By now, Daphne was getting used to his easy-going nature and ability to laugh at himself. But Audrey confused her, as did her relationship with Rupert. They clearly had known each other for a long time and it seemed as though her husband and Rupert were good friends. Was the woman so stressed about her husband—or the laptop—that she was behaving out of character toward others?

Rupert, quickly followed by John, reached for bottles of wine from ice buckets scattered around the table, and began filling glasses. Audrey checked her phone and put it face down on the table before picking up her glass and sipping. Her eyes roamed the room, resting on Stacy who was drinking and laughing.

"Why didn't Darren join us, honey?" Gloria asked.

Audrey sighed dramatically and looked at her. "He said he was too tired to drive up. That was last night. Not even late. I suggested he reconsider because he would be missed and got the impression he'd changed his mind. But alas, he didn't."

"And you've spoken today? You must have wanted your laptop."

"I would love to have had the laptop, Gloria, but it doesn't seem to have made a negative impact. After my session I've been inundated with people falling over themselves to get in on the ground floor of my new venture."

Money talks.

"And what about you, Daphne? Are you going to join the fun?" Audrey said.

John jumped up and reached his hand across the table. "I'm John Jones. You must be Audrey Sutton? A friend of ours has one of your beautiful wedding gowns."

Audrey's mouth fell open and then she shook John's hand.

He sat back down and Daphne put a hand on his leg and squeezed. How had he remembered Elizabeth White, their friend in Rivers End, had bought a Sutton gown for her upcoming wedding? Even she'd forgotten.

"Well, I'm most happy to hear that, John. Daphne, you should have told me."

I've been too busy protecting Stacy from you.

"I'm sure I would have got around to it." she turned to Rupert. "I heard a tree fell across the road down the mountain."

"Several, actually. And some of the road gave way. One of the hotel staff is stranded on the other side. I imagine there are plenty of people working on clearing and fixing the road for those leaving tomorrow."

"But we're every bit as stranded." Audrey contorted her face into mock fear. "Let's hope there isn't a real murderer on the loose up here." Her phone buzzed and she picked it up. As she read her message, her face didn't change, but when she put the phone down again, she shot a look of pure venom at Daphne. "Who told the police they saw a hand in the fountain?"

All talk at the table stopped and all eyes turned onto Audrey. She appeared happy to have the attention—again. John put a hand over Daphne's and she held back whatever she was going to say.

"Was this hand disembodied?" Rupert sounded amused but those worry lines were back around his eyes. "And is it the hand responsible for tossing my expensive, and much loved, jacket into the water?"

"I'm not joking and as president you should take this more seriously." Audrey snapped. "The police are apparently attempting to get up here sometime tonight."

Gloria seemed unimpressed by the other woman's mood. "Why is this a problem? If the police are here then they can investigate the strange events of early this morning. *They* are then able to remove any thoughts of foul play."

"Foul play? Are you some deluded fan of Agatha Christie? The only foul play was somebody thinking it funny to put Rupert's jacket into the fountain. Clearly it was all a joke and I know exactly who did it." Audrey finished her drink and held the glass out for someone—anyone—to refill. "Little Miss Panic-Pants will do anything to get your attention back, Rupert. But she might have gone too far this time."

THE WALLS CLOSE IN

Rupert excused himself without responding to Audrey, or refilling her glass. John did the latter, which kept her attention on him rather than Rupert, who had caught Stacy's eye and gestured, with a nod of his head, in the direction of the hallway.

Without a beat, she followed and the door closed behind them.

What I would give to listen in...

"Daphne, would you care to visit the ladies room?"

Gloria was already halfway to her feet and Daphne wasn't about to be left behind. If Gloria wanted what she did then who was she to interfere?

"Be right back, love." She said to John.

It was obvious he'd seen what she had because there was a slightly pained expression on his face. But the corners of his lips turned up.

"Oh, maybe I should join you." Audrey reached for her phone.

"I was hoping you might tell me more about this new

venture of yours." John began. "I'm a small business owner and love hearing about enterprising initiatives."

Last seen, Audrey had moved to Daphne's seat and was chatting to John. That should keep her occupied for a while. She went through the doors and Gloria grabbed her arm, making her jump.

"Shh." Gloria whispered. "I *have* to know."

Before Daphne could respond, Gloria had set off in the other direction. The hallways were long, with a few corners and 'Hotel Staff Only' signs on several doors. They reached an open door to the outside and the familiar smell of cigar smoke signalled Rupert's presence close by.

"There's a smoking area out here behind the screen."

Then Gloria was on the move again and Daphne had little choice but to follow. No point one of them being there alone.

"You do realise I'm more than forty years your senior, darling?"

Rupert's voice carried as they found a spot behind a tall bush. They couldn't see him or Stacy which hopefully meant they wouldn't be caught listening.

"Age doesn't matter. Only the heart." Stacy replied. "Anyway, I don't get your point. Audrey is out to get me so stop going on about a note."

"Might need to ask Daphne if we can see it again. It was dark last time I glanced at it. Because if it isn't your handwriting then of course we'll need to dig around and see who is behind this."

"I vote for Audrey."

Rupert chuckled.

"Is my job at stake, Rupe?" There was a wobble in Stacy's voice. "I really did see a hand in the fountain."

"I don't know. Once the police get here, we might get some answers but so far Col and his crew have searched high and low and there isn't a trace of a body. Now before you get upset with me, look at it from my perspective. You were in the English garden at the fountain where you believe you saw a dead body. You say you didn't write the note so why exactly were you out there?"

A long silence followed.

Was Stacy working out how to dig herself out of a hole after denying her involvement?

"Look, I'm not comfortable discussing this, Rupert, but I promise you I did not put your jacket in the fountain. I'd never damage anyone's property, least of all yours. May I go back inside now?"

"I'll finish the cigar and be along in time to make the opening announcements. But, Stacy?"

"What."

"Honesty is best. I know it is hard if feelings are involved but don't let that stop you standing up for the truth."

"It hurts me you think I'm not. Really hurts. Even last year nobody believed me about the missing laptop except for Darren." She ended the sentence with a sob and a second later her footsteps hurried inside.

"Oh, Stace..." Rupert murmured.

Gloria and Daphne exchanged a glance but before they could go, heavier footsteps went past in Rupert's direction.

"Ah, Colin. Any news?"

"Nah. Road is too blocked to clear in the dark. Can't even get around it with a motorcycle thanks to where the trees fell. Straight rock up one side and straight down on the other with a chunk out of the surface." Col laughed.

"Couldn't pick a better spot to fall if someone wanted to keep everyone out. Or in."

"I see. Must make it difficult to remove the body before the police arrive."

Gloria and Daphne clamped their hands over their mouths at the same time.

Col stopped laughing. "Not funny, mate."

"Is it Darren?"

"Is what Darren? Do you mean Darren Sutton? Mate, he never arrived. Remember it was me waiting for hours in the bottom carpark."

"I'm just stirring you up. Must have been a pain sitting down there until eleven at night and all for nothing."

"His no-show bothered others more than me. Housekeeping had his suite ready and one of the chefs was still up to finish the meal Mr Sutton requested. You want to stir someone up, find the chef. But it's just part of the job. And also, part of the job is locking the garage which is where I was going. Good night." Col sounded a little less annoyed than earlier.

There were no more sounds, just the occasional whiff of smoke. A tickle began at the back of Daphne's nose and she put her fingers on its end and squeezed. How would they explain their eavesdropping if she sneezed?

At last Rupert headed indoors and Daphne held her nose until she was sure he was gone.

"We'll give it a min and go back. Are you quite alright, honey?"

Daphne tested a sniff and all was good again. "Had the worst tickle thanks to his smoke."

"I tell him off about that habit every chance I get. He doesn't listen."

"Gloria, why would Darren Sutton have a separate suite to Audrey?"

"He's an insomniac. And like Stacy, is a bit of a wanderer at night so might go for a walk at odd hours. He once told me when he got his pacemaker it messed with his body clock."

What if he was up at the fountain and something awful happened...but how did he arrive at the hotel if Col didn't bring him? And why would anyone hide his body?

"Let's get back before they send a search party. Rupert will wait for us because I have to announce one of the awards."

Awards?

But Gloria was already off at a faster pace than looked possible with her high heels.

There was a lot to consider. Pity she couldn't run upstairs and get a notebook.

Audrey was back in her own seat and Rupert was at the podium reading notes. John and Ted were again chatting and nobody seemed to notice when Daphne sat and reached for her wine glass. On the other side of the room, waiters served entrees table by table.

Daphne rubbed her stomach when it growled. She'd had a piece of fruit and one chocolate in their suite but nothing else for hours.

"Good evening to you all. Celebrants and partners. Welcome to the gala dinner and awards night from your committee and executive. I'm Rupert Witherspoon."

There was a ripple of laughter. As if anyone didn't know the president.

"I see our entrees are being served so will make this quick. We'd like to extend our thanks to the hotel staff and management for once again creating a warm and comfortable environment for our conference. And to the committee, I wish to make my own special thanks for the hard work undertaken over the past year."

There was clapping until Rupert raised a sealed envelope.

"This is first award of the evening. I'd like to ask our treasurer up to present it. Gloria, will you join me?"

More clapping as Gloria pushed her chair back and made her way to the podium with a wide smile. She accepted the envelope from Rupert, who took a few steps to one side.

"Look at you all! Isn't this a lovely evening in this lovely hotel? Well, because I can see entrees heading to my table, I'm going to hurry along and announce the winner of our fundraising category. As you know, each year we run a different effort and our most recent one was dear to my heart, being a wonderful raffle for prizes from Victorian chocolate makers. Yum. One person sold such a lot of tickets and I'm pleased to celebrate their contribution."

She opened the envelope and slid a folded sheet of paper out.

"I love this bit because I have no idea who the winner is. Oh, and there is a lovely glass trophy on offer."

Gloria unfolded the paper.

"How cute. It appears to be written in a poem."

Even as Gloria drew a breath to speak, a premonition of doom clutched Daphne's stomach.

"There's no way in and no way out
No matter how you try
Before midnight there is no doubt
That one of you will...die."

The entire room gasped.

"No, but...what is this? Rupert?" Gloria handed the sheet of paper to him as he reached her. She fanned herself with the envelope.

Reaching for John's hand, Daphne knew this was from the original poet, if one wanted to be so generous. Or else someone able to copy a style. She glanced over at Stacy. She wasn't in her seat.

"Guests, please calm down." Rupert spoke over the rising talk. "This is clearly a joke. A very poor taste in joke. Nobody is dying unless the author meant dying of laughter at such a lame poem."

"But what if there's a serial killer loose?" Somebody called from a back table and a few people murmured in agreement.

"As nobody has died, how can there be a serial killer?"

Jessica stood. "Stacy saw a body in the fountain. That sounds like a murder victim to me!"

"Sit down, Jessica. Nobody wants to hear your theories." Audrey also stood. "What a ridiculous situation. Who gave you the envelope, Rupert?"

Jessica sat with a thump.

"All the envelopes are together in the box." He gestured to a shoebox sized metal box with a lock. The lid was open. "I was here when Stacy unlocked it."

"Well, what do you have to say, Stacy?" Audrey demanded, turning to look at the table where the other woman had been seated. "Where is she?"

People looked around.

"Jessica, when did you last see her?" Rupert asked.

"She followed you out."

"But after that."

"You came back but she didn't." Jessica leaped to her feet and pointed at Rupert. "What have you done to her?"

FINGERS POINTING EVERYWHERE

The next few minutes were chaotic.

People yelling at each other from one side of the room to the other.

Other people crying.

And some running out of the room.

"Daph? When you said we'd have a relaxing weekend in the mountains, is this what you expected?"

They hadn't moved from their chairs but Ted had gone to the podium to escort an upset Gloria back to the table, settling her beside him and getting her a glass of water while she continued to fan her face with the envelope.

"Gloria, dear? Perhaps we should pop that envelope into a plastic bag. In case the police need it." Daphne said in a calm voice.

As if it burned her fingers, Gloria dropped the envelope, which fortunately landed on the table. "Oh no, what if I contaminated evidence?"

"I'm sure you haven't. But you have had a bit of a shock."

"Stop mothering everyone, Daphne!" Audrey was still on

her feet. "Gloria, what on earth possessed you to read that out aloud? Look at what you've done."

Ted glared at Audrey. "I'll stop you right there, Mrs Sutton. Keep your nasty words to yourself."

Gloria kissed Ted's cheek and he reddened.

"He's like you, John. Always the first to defend the woman he loves." Daphne whispered. "And this is not what I expected at all!"

The waiters, who had been about to serve their table, stood in confusion with their plates aloft. As bizarre as this situation was, there was no point in good food going to waste and John got up and had a word to one of the staff. In a minute, the entrees were in place.

"Excuse me. Is there any chance you'd have a zip lock-able bag or similar? Big enough to put this envelope in?" Daphne pointed to the offending item. The waiter she'd addressed nodded and hurried away. "Do you think it is wrong that I'd like to eat?"

"Not at all. I'm starving."

The room gradually quietened. Rupert was off the podium talking to Mandy who had hurried in at all the commotion. She shook her head and nodded and tapped on her phone.

The entrée—a mini tart filled with locally made goat's cheese and caramelised onion with a relish on the side—was delicious, all things considered. And the food was welcome, even if a few people gave them odd looks for eating. Gloria hadn't touched hers but Ted's was long gone.

"How can you people eat at a time like this?" Audrey finally sat. "All this noise and anger."

"And nothing we can do until Rupert works out what is going on." Daphne pushed her plate aside. "I missed lunch,

Audrey. And that was because I was on the receiving end of someone else's anger."

Well. Wasn't Daph doing well standing up for herself?

"Okay. I get the hint and apologise for being unpleasant to you. Stacy and I have a long history and I've been dreadfully worried about Darren, but you just happened to bear the brunt of it all."

"I accept your apology." Daphne smiled. "Have you had an update on Darren?"

"What? Oh, where he is? Well, I assume he went home but we've not spoken since early yesterday evening. The reception is bad up here which is one of the first things I'll fix when I..." she clamped her lips shut.

John would have loved to ask, 'when she did *what*'.

Daphne wasn't as hesitant.

"Oh, are you moving here? If you buy the hotel, it would make the most wonderful place to run your new wedding hub from. Once you fixed the phone coverage up." She spoke with total innocence and a particular sweetness. Sleuth questioning mode activated.

Audrey had just taken a mouthful of wine and almost spat it out. After wiping her lips, she stood and picked up her phone.

"Who told you such a thing? Oh, never mind. Believe what you want. You and Stacy and Rupert. I'm about done with this silly little association."

With that she stormed out of the room, even trying to slam one of the doors in her wake. She was not given that satisfaction as the doors closed at their own pace.

Rupert climbed back on the stage. For a moment he gazed around the room, his face pained by whatever was going through his mind. John barely knew him but had the feeling this was a man who was genuine and cared about people. What a dreadful situation to be put in.

"Ladies and gentlemen, can I have your attention please. Thank you." Rupert waited as a few people returned to their seats. "Thank you for staying. I understand a few of our guests tonight have chosen to remove themselves from the room and I will be going to find them and make sure they are doing alright. But I want to say how sorry I am, how sorry your committee is, that some unknown person has interrupted our special evening. Rest assured, I will get to the bottom of this. Now, I've spoken with Mandy, who you all know. Neither of us believe there is any risk to any of you but she is contacting the police as well as getting all her staff involved."

His calm manner was working magic on many of the guests. They visibly relaxed. Only a handful, Jessica for one, held themselves tightly and glared in his direction.

"As hard as it might seem, I would count it as a personal favour if each and every one of you remained here for our gala dinner. We have beautiful courses to come and much to celebrate. I promise you will be safe."

There was one comment of 'how can you promise that' which was shushed by other guests. He'd won them over. That and the need people have for normalcy. Much easier to believe someone was playing a twisted joke than there was a killer on the prowl.

Waiters began clearing the entrée plates, which on some tables, guests frantically began to eat from. Normal talk continued. The music came back on. And Rupert returned to the table.

The first thing he did was push away his wine glass and swallow some water. Then put his fork on his uneaten plate.

He glanced around the table, his eyes resting on Gloria, his mouth in a straight line.

"I'm fine, honey. Just gave me a shock." She said.

"I am so sorry."

"How is this your fault?" Daphne asked.

"You've seen firsthand how dysfunctional we are. I should have taken this more seriously. Where's Audrey?"

"Off in a huff," Gloria said. "I'm more concerned where Stacy is."

He nodded. "Agree. Are you up to keeping things going here while I look for them both? And see how the others are?"

Gloria looked down and Ted put a hand over hers. "Happy to take over until you return, Rupert. Pretty sure I remember how to keep people in a room."

Rupert and Gloria laughed. It made no sense to John and from Daphne's face, nor to her, but the mood lightened and Rupert stood. "Thank you."

"We'll help." Daphne was up in an instant. "More chance of finding them all if we split up. Coming, love?"

If it would speed up the process of settling the guests down and bringing on the main dishes...of course he was.

No. She was not to blame for Audrey's outburst and subsequent departure. But still, she could have worded things better. There was a lot going on in the background and somehow the so-called body in the fountain was connected to this scare.

In the hallway, doors closed behind them, Rupert

suddenly stopped and leaned against one of the walls, his shoulders slumped.

"Are you unwell?"

"Like Darren, I have a pacemaker. That's how we met. In a hospital twenty years ago. Unlike Darren, who is back to an almost normal life, I still need some medications to help things remain stable."

"Do you need something now?" John asked, putting a hand on Rupert's shoulder. "Happy to get what you need if you don't mind me going into your room."

"Thank you, but I have them on me. A glass of water though?"

John went back into the room.

"I'll be alright in a few minutes. This stress isn't helping." Rupert said.

"At the risk of increasing your stress levels..."

Rupert managed a small smile. "You want my risk assessment?"

"I do."

"Someone is stirring up trouble. What better way than to create havoc at our premier event where we have most of our members present."

"Any theories why? Or who?"

"None."

She didn't believe him for a minute. He knew these people better than anyone and must have some insight into whether the brewing storm between Stacy and Audrey was at tipping point.

Mixing your metaphors, Daph.

"What about Darren?"

"What about him."

How to word this? "Audrey said she last spoke to him early last night. And thought he might have decided to join her after all. But then no contact. Is it worth checking in with him?"

Rupert took his phone from a pant pocket. He held it at arm's length and dialled. "Let's ask him where he is." The phone was on speaker and the number rang a few times before going to voicemail.

"I'm Darren Sutton and I love that you called. Leave your words behind and I'll listen to them all."

Rupert rolled his eyes. "Daz, it's Rupe. People need to hear from you. Call me."

"Leave your words behind?"

"I know. Terrible attempt at poetry."

They looked at each other. Then Rupert shook his head.

"Everyone who knows Darren teases him for his dreadful rhymes. But he didn't just threaten to kill someone and nor did he leave you a note to meet him at the fountain. He's never met you so even—*even*—if he had arrived here and somehow not been seen by his wife or all the other people who know him, why would he ask you to meet him at the fountain?"

"What if it was a mistake? My door? The note was meant for someone else and the person got the room numbers wrong."

John returned with a full glass of water. "Sorry it took so long."

Rupert returned his phone to one pocket and pulled a small pill container from another. After swallowing a pill, he straightened. "Thank you. These won't take too long to work so I'll push on." He left the glass on the table outside the doors. "I want to see if Mandy has news from the police."

Reception was almost as chaotic as the conference room had been. Several guests were lined up and luggage was scattered around the foyer. There were staff behind and around the counter, some on phones and others trying to reason with the guests. Bits and pieces of conversations highlighted just how seriously some had taken the poem.

"We are so sorry but there literally is no way down the mountain until the road is cleared."

"I understand you are upset but we don't have access to a helicopter..."

"You have to call the army! Call the Premier! Anyone who can save us."

"How will you protect us? We need to lock the doors!"

Mandy hurried to them, stray hairs escaping from her normally perfect bun. "I don't know what to tell people. But I can't have them yelling at my staff so if there is anything you can do?"

"I'll speak in a minute. Anything from the police?"

"There are two officers who are going to walk up. They are waiting for a lift as far as the blockage from one of the emergency service workers but it will take them a couple of hours to hike up here. We can't even pick them up partway as the road is too dangerous. They know we've had a written threat."

"Did they suggest any action to take?"

"To keep people calm. Continue as usual. Not let anyone wander around outside alone." She glanced over her shoulder to where one of the guests was banging on the counter with their hands. "But how do I keep them calm?"

Rupert clapped his hands until everyone was looking at him.

"I understand you're scared but I'm asking as your president, and as your friend, to take a breath. The staff are doing their best so treat them with respect. Please."

"But there's a killer loose!" a woman cried out.

"No. There's a note. A stupid joke designed to upset everyone. I'd very much appreciate you all standing up against whoever wrote that note by coming back to the dinner. Mandy needs a chance to speak to all of her staff to put a safety plan in place and this..." he waved his arms around, "is simply slowing the process."

Another woman pointed at Daphne. "This is your fault."

"Sorry?" Daphne managed.

"Audrey was right about us celebrants needing to stay out of other people's business but you don't! You get involved and bring the police into it so of course you've got a target on your back and I just hope the person finds you and not an innocent bystander! If anyone deserves to die, it is you."

There was a shocked silence from everyone, guests, staff, and Daphne. John put his arm around her shoulders.

"Oh, what a load of rubbish!" Rupert almost bellowed. "Daphne has done nothing wrong so keep your nasty opinions to yourself, Joan."

So, this was Joan. Who hated her cookies.

"For that matter, we have a code of conduct which you've overstepped so I'll be wanting a word later on. This is quite enough."

One by one, the guests moved away from reception to congregate in the seated area. Although several cast looks of fury at Rupert, nobody challenged him. He winked at Daphne and she took a few deep breaths.

"Thanks, Rupert." Mandy said. "I've asked Col to keep

the team he's put together outside the hotel to make sure nobody goes in or out who doesn't belong here."

"Have you seen Audrey or Stacy?" Daphne asked. It was all very well calming the upset patrons but those two women, in her opinion, held the key to the strange goings on. "I'm happy to knock on their doors if you let me know their room numbers."

Mandy frowned. "Neither of them. Why?"

"Stacy hasn't been seen since before the er, poem, was read out. Audrey left soon after. We want to be sure they are both safe and sound." Rupert said. "Let's go and look upstairs. Mandy, can you let Col know to keep a look out for them?"

A moment later they were on the accommodation floor. Rupert went to the seats and dropped into one. "Bit of a racing heart. I'll be okay in a couple of minutes."

"Do you need medical attention?" John asked.

"Not at all. This happens now and then. Bad timing though. Stacy is in room twenty-three. Audrey is in room sixty-six. It might be quicker if you split up."

"Not a chance." John said. "We shouldn't even be leaving you alone."

Now was not the time for being overly cautious. "I think Rupert is right. We're quite safe here, love. Within calling distance really. What if we take a room each and meet back here? And if we find the ladies, they can come with us."

Before John had a chance to argue, she was on the move. "Whose room is this way, Rupert?"

"Audrey. Sixty-six."

BEHIND CLOSED DOORS

Daphne followed the hallway which headed to the back of the building. Then a left. This was a dead end with four suites. The one at the end was sixty-six and there was no response to her knock.

"Audrey? Are you in there?"

Silence.

She tried the door.

Locked.

After checking nobody was coming, she leaned her ear against the door and although she counted to twenty, there wasn't a sound.

Next door was suite sixty-seven. This was the one prepared for Darren.

She tapped even though it was silly to do so, because he wasn't here in the hotel.

Of course, there was no response. She had better catch up with John. See if he'd had better luck. But first...she tried the handle.

The door opened.

Don't do it, Daph.

She pushed it wider. "Hello there. Anyone in?"

Silence.

It wouldn't hurt to look around. She closed the door behind herself, deciding against turning on any lights. Nobody was here.

So why was there a laptop bag on a chair?

Her bravery didn't extend to looking inside. And being in an unoccupied room was one thing but snooping around in someone's belongings quite another.

Her phone beeped and her heart jumped into her mouth. Or so it felt. But it was John.

Any luck? No sign of Stacy so heading back to Rupert.

She quickly typed back.

None. On my way.

There must be a simple explanation for the laptop bag. It might belong to Audrey and she'd left it in here for some reason. But she'd said Darren had the laptop. Unless this was a different one. Yes. That would explain it. Time to leave.

Under the door she could see the light from the outside hallway. And it was enough light to see an envelope pushed against the wall. Almost as if it had been dropped. Or pushed aside by a foot as someone came in and closed the door. It looked like the envelope from last night. The one slipped beneath her own door. Unable to stop herself, she picked it up. It was impossible to see if there was writing on it so what to do?

"I cannot believe this is happening!"

Daphne shrank against the wall, even though the door to the hallway was closed.

Audrey was close by.

"Well, it means the police are totally involved now. Before it was all about Miss Husband Chaser stirring things up. Nobody believed her, not even that interfering wannabe sleuth."

Moi?

This had to be a phone call.

"Hang on, I'm looking for my key."

A couple of curse words were uttered.

"Once Stacy blabbed about the so-called hand in the fountain it became a problem we need to solve. You need to solve. Yes, that *is* what I mean."

The next sound was of a door closing.

Daphne waited. Listening and counting. When she reached one hundred, she let herself out after making sure the hallway was clear. She closed the door to Darren's suite with great care not to make a sound.

She straightened and released a breath she'd not realised she was holding.

The door to suite sixty-six flung open and Audrey stared at her.

"And just what do you think you are doing?"

"I might go find Daphne. As long as you are okay here?" John's worry level was rising after returning to the lounge area and finding only Rupert.

"Go right ahead. I'm feeling much better and will try calling Stacy again."

The elevator doors opened and one of the housekeeping staff stepped out. She carried Rupert's red velvet jacket which was in perfect condition. "Mr Witherspoon. I was going to hang this in your room."

"Would you mind? Looks as though you've given it new life."

"No more soaking it in the fountain. Fabric is dry clean only. And I kept the circle from the pocket." She took a plastic bag from the inside chest pocket and offered it to Rupert. "Thought it was a big coin but not."

He frowned, turning the bag to see both sides of a flat disc a few centimetres across. "Not mine."

"It was in the pocket. I'll put this away for you." The woman left them.

"May I?" John took the bag. "I've seen these. Had a foster son who was obsessed with magnets." He held it near his watch which had a metal band and it latched on. It took him more effort than expected to separate the items. "Strong as well."

"Would you hold onto it please? Magnets are not friends of pacemakers."

"Of course. I'll be back shortly."

As John left, he slipped the magnet into his pants pocket. What an odd thing to find but if Rupert didn't own it, then there must have been a mix up in the laundry.

He followed the direction Daphne took, checking his messages again. The bars were down again so she might have had no reception. He should never have let her go off without him. Not that he believed there was a killer on the loose. Although that woman, Joan, wishing Daphne to be the target cut deeply.

Turning a corner, he found her. She was standing at the end of the short hallway sliding something into her handbag. Before he could call out, the door at the end opened with some force and Audrey emerged. Daphne visibly started.

"And just what do you think you are doing?" Audrey demanded.

"Hello, dear. I knocked and called but you didn't respond."

"But what are you doing at the door to my husband's suite?"

Daphne glanced at a door to one side. "That belongs to Darren? I was about to knock on the doors on either side."

What are you up to, Daph?

"What on earth for. Are you selling cookies?" The smirk on Audrey's face made John walk faster. "I'd suggest stick to being a retiree."

"Ladies." John slid an arm around Daphne's waist just as she stepped forward. "It is obvious you are safe, Audrey, so we will go."

"Since when is it the job of amateurs to look for criminals?"

Daphne wasn't budging but her whole body tensed. In a sweeter-than-sweet tone she smiled at Audrey as she spoke. "Since the criminals began to show themselves. Such an interesting way to describe yourself. Don't forget to lock the door." She glanced at John. "Shall we?"

The door slammed behind them as they left the hallway and once around the corner, Daphne stopped dead. "Oh my. That was too close."

"What was."

She opened her handbag and showed him. There was an unopened envelope, somewhat crumbled and with part of a footprint on it.

"Daph..."

"I know. But I had to."

"But where? And how. I'm not sure I even want to know."

"Sorry. The opportunity presented itself. And thanks for rescuing me from Audrey. Did you hear her? She referred to herself as a criminal."

"Don't think she'd intended it to sound that way."

"Did you locate Stacy?"

"Not yet. Shall we go back to Rupert?"

But Rupert wasn't there. John rang his number and he answered.

"Back downstairs, John. There's been a...development if you and Daphne would care to join me at reception." His voice wavered.

"I heard what he said, love. But can we quickly open this? I know it's important. Very important."

Daphne plonked herself on one of the seats and gazed at him with a pleading expression. How could he possibly stop her? Besides, he was interested in the contents of this envelope.

Since the moment Audrey caught her in the hallway—or possibly from the moment she'd overheard the strange telephone conversation—Daphne's heartbeat was heavy and fast. Better not be the next one to need a pacemaker but at this rate, anything was possible.

She carefully opened the envelope and slid out a single sheet of paper, folded the same way as the one from Stacy. Or whoever was pretending to be Stacy.

"My theory is that whoever wrote the first note didn't

mean it to be seen by me. I figured it was meant for Rupert. The way Stacy reacted when she noticed our suite is next to his made me wonder if she was the author, despite her denials. Now, I'm not so sure."

This note was simple. No map. No poem.

My secret love,

I made a terrible error by mistaking which room you were in.

We should be together. You'll be happier without her.

Will you forgive me and let us find our future?

S.C.

"Well."

They stared at each other.

"Indeed." John said.

"I thought Stacy was keen on Rupert. I even heard him remind her he is forty years older than she is, so possibly he is under the same impression."

"There seems a lot of catching up to do, Daph. Starting with where you found this envelope."

"In Darren's room. The one next to Audrey's, and don't look at me like that. It was unlocked and I was just checking Audrey wasn't in there upset or murdered or something. It was on the floor against the wall so who knows how long it was there."

Or who put it there.

"And there's more."

He sighed.

"Sorry, love. Audrey spoke to someone on the phone and she told them to solve the problem. That was after mentioning—"

The beeping of her phone interrupted.

"Rupert again."

John stood. "Let's see what this new development is. Hopefully, something to do with dinner."

Oh, love. You haven't eaten in hours thanks to my wild goose chases.

"You must be starved. And isn't it the fish from your trip being served tonight?"

"Yes and yes, but none of this is your doing. Well, apart from removing what may be evidence from someone else's room. And apparently getting intel about Rupert and Stacy... how exactly did you hear that conversation?"

A little less guilt-ridden, she took the arm he offered. "Gloria and I overheard them talking."

"Weren't you both going to the ladies?"

"Well. No. Gloria was deliberately going to listen in and I had to make sure she didn't get caught. It was an odd conversation with Stacy denying she wrote the note and blaming Audrey. Says she's out to get her. And after she left, Col came along and he and Rupert talked about how bad the road was." What was it Rupert had said? Oh yes. "Rupert said something about how that must make it difficult to get Darren's body off the mountain."

"Huh? And you didn't think that is suspicious?"

"Rupert was trying to get a rise out of Col and managed it quite well. But there is a discrepancy about Darren. Col mentioned the chef was waiting on his arrival to make a meal for him, and Col had sat at the bottom carpark for a couple of hours. So, he was expected. Yet Audrey said she last spoke to him early in the evening and tried to talk him into changing his mind about coming."

There was something else. They reached the top of the stairs and started down.

"The first night here, I was sitting out on the rooftop

with some of the others and Audrey made a toast to people who couldn't find their way up a mountain. She mentioned Darren and burst into laughter. That was after ten."

"Perhaps he called the hotel directly rather than Audrey? But it is strange."

Strange wasn't the word for it. Somebody or several somebodies was up to no good.

GRIM NEWS

Rupert was at the foot of the stairs with Col and Mandy. His colour was better than earlier but deep lines etched his forehead. "We've had some news. A bit disturbing, actually."

"Not about Stacy?"

"No. Although she seems to have vanished."

There was nobody else in the foyer now apart from staff. The guests had either retreated to their rooms or returned to the dinner and there was faint music drifting from the conference room.

Rupert continued. "One of the staff took a call from a resident of the local town. They've found a car which sounds like Darren's."

"His car?" Daphne said. Her stomach tensed.

"Looks as if it veered off the road and ended up in the river. They can't reach it to see if he's in..." Rupert dropped his head.

Daphne put her hand on his arm. Darren was his friend.

"There are emergency services heading there. Nothing indicates he's in the car. But the front of it is partly submerged. We all hope it isn't Mr Sutton." Mandy's eyes glistened. "He's such a gentleman."

Col tapped on his phone the whole time.

"Did Cherry make it back safely?" Daphne asked.

Everyone, including Col, looked at her.

"She left early this morning but I never heard if she returned before the road closed."

Col returned to his phone. "No need to worry about my wife. She's ex-army and tough as nails. Probably could move those trees with her bare hands."

Mandy managed a short laugh and nodded. "He isn't far off the mark. While we're on the subject of Cherry, I'd like to know why she left so early."

"Was close to lunchtime, boss."

"I saw her drive out before breakfast." Daphne said.

"You're mistaken." Col hadn't looked up from the screen.

"Col?" Mandy asked. "What was the purpose of Cherry's trip?"

He slid the phone into a pocket and gave Mandy his attention. "One of the guests she transported on Friday was carsick and she wanted to get to the carwash and do a proper clean before letting anyone in it again. Must have got the time wrong." His phone beeped. "We're checking the grounds for Stacy and I'm needed."

"Keep in touch please." Mandy said.

Col grabbed a backpack Daphne hadn't noticed and dragged it over his shoulder, back on his phone as he strode away.

I'd love to take a quick look at his call history.

John touched her arm and when she glanced at him, he had a question in his eyes. Probably along the lines of 'what conclusions are you drawing from nothing', or 'why don't you stop solving everyone else's problems'.

"Solving!"

"Solving what, buttercup?"

Much as she needed to put a stop to Rupert's casual endearment, now was not the time. Not when he might be about to find out his friend was dead.

"Um...solving the mystery of baking better cookies."

That's what you come up with?

"Your cookies are fine, doll." John said with a frown. The frown might have been directed more at Rupert than her.

"Not according to Joan or Audrey. Both proclaimed them to be...quote, awful. I would love to speak to your chef, Mandy. When he or she is not in the middle of a banquet, of course."

"Um. Sure. I might check the gala dinner now everyone is back in there. Excuse me." Mandy hurried up the hallway.

Rupert took out his phone. "I'm going to try Stacy again. She needs to know about...Darren." With a small shake of his head, he dialled. It went to her voicemail which was merely a beep. "Stace, something's happened. It's about Darren and I'd rather tell you face to face. No more hiding. We need to talk."

Phone back in his pants pocket he looked from John to Daphne.

"What is your take on all of this?"

"Mine?"

She'd not sorted a lot in her mind yet, nor gone through notes with John. And there was a lot to take in.

"At some point you need to go back to the dinner and receive an award, Daphne. I saw the different comments from your clients, including one lady who said you'd put yourself at risk to bring her husband's killer to justice. And another whose friend had been buried in the wrong place and you helped work out where. People love you. Heart and mind."

Tears sprung into her eyes and she blinked fast. Had she really made such a difference? She knew who would have written those things but was stunned, particularly as one of them had been a main suspect of the police and had not made Daphne's time easy.

"I don't know what to say." She managed.

"Only what's in that sleuthing mind of yours."

Mandy approached, carrying a tray laden with plates and glasses. "Mains for you three. And sparkling water. Come on, I'll put this down for you."

They followed to where she set everything on a coffee table in a quiet spot and they quickly pulled chairs around it. The meal smelled so good that it took no time for them to each take a few bites of delicate fish in a creamy sauce and perfect morsels of vegetables. Simple but delicious. John finished his in no time but Daphne, although hungry, wanted to continue what Rupert had started, so she offered John the rest of hers.

She took a sip of water and dabbed her lips with a napkin, then settled back in the chair. "Not certain that my mind has a lot to do with this but my gut leads me to make certain conclusions."

"I'm listening." Rupert pushed his own plate aside. "Please. Share your theories."

Stomach feeling much happier, John drank his glass of water, thankful for Mandy's thoughtfulness. The staff here were so lovely.

"Normally, I talk things through with John. It helps me sort out what is pure speculation and what might be based in truth. But everything is happening so quickly that I feel as if there are a hundred observations all vying for attention. So please, forgive me if I ramble."

Daphne clearly had lots going on in her head and was working on her unique type of magic; making connections which passed by other people. Certainly, by himself too often.

"I'll try not to bore you with what you already know so stop me if I do. In the space of thirty-six hours, actually, less than that, the following have happened." She held up one hand and counted her fingers. "Stacy says she saw a body in the fountain. One which subsequently vanished. Your own jacket was taken by persons unknown and dropped into the water. Audrey's husband was coming here, then not coming here, then coming here again. Except he didn't and now, I'm so sorry Rupert, he may have been in a car accident. Meanwhile, Audrey comes gunning for Stacy, trying to rake up the past. Which seems an odd thing to do rather than let the dust settle. It isn't as though Audrey was involved in the events up at the fountain."

Daphne paused to drink some more water and for some reason, it reminded John of the photos he'd taken of the fountain. He wanted to take a look once they finished talking.

"A couple of times I've felt someone watching me." She said.

"Not that strange, is it? You are new to our association

and have a reputation." Rupert asked. "By reputation, I mean that people know something about you already."

"Daphne has a sixth sense about being watched. I've never known her to be wrong about it—and it bothers me she's felt it here. Can you elaborate, doll?" John was uncomfortable. If she was in any danger he'd lock and barricade them into the suite and stand guard.

"Out near the tennis courts and in the English garden. On the night Stacy was out there. It is the main thing which makes me believe she saw something. That and the notes."

Rupert straightened. "Notes? Plural?"

From her handbag, Daphne took the most recent envelope and the first one she'd found. She handed them to Rupert. "I'm going to confess I found Darren's suite unlocked and let myself in. That is where the second one came from."

All Rupert did was raise his eyebrows as his attention was on the notes. He read one, then the other, and returned to the first. With a heavy sigh, he handed them back. "That is Stacy's handwriting. I'd begged her not to pursue him but she obviously wasn't going to listen to me."

"Age doesn't matter. Only the heart."

"How...Daphne Jones, were you listening to my conversation, my private conversation with Stacy?"

She nodded, biting her bottom lip and her cheeks flushed. She was nothing if not honest but this time she may have gone too far.

Throwing his head back, Rupert laughed long and loudly. Even the staff behind the reception desk looked up in surprise.

"I'm really sorry I did. But I had it wrong, didn't I? I thought the note was for you and she'd accidentally slipped the first note under my door because it is right next to yours. But it was because she mixed up the numbers. Seventy-six instead of sixty-seven."

"I'd say so. She's had a thing for Darren for years and he hasn't helped. Always turning on the charm with her but I doubt it went further than that. I tried to remind her how old he is because I'm his age, but she didn't care." Rupert said. "And even worse was her butting into someone else's marriage, regardless of her believing Audrey didn't love him."

I kind of like you. Good morals.

"Do you think Audrey is capable of...um..." Daphne screwed her face up as she tried to sort her question out.

"Murder?" Rupert asked. "No. Look, I know you've seen the worst of her but I've known her for more than a decade. Ever since Darren married her and I've known him twenty years. She is intense, granted. But one rarely is as successful in business as Audrey without being ruthless."

"But not ruthless enough to kill her husband."

As though the thought shocked him, Rupert shook his head rapidly.

Daphne was watching him, her fingers tapping against her leg. She had her thinking face on. Taking in data and processing it. John couldn't wait to talk to her privately and discover what she really believed.

From past the reception desk the sounds of the gala dinner loudened as the doors were opened. A few people wandered out and one of the staff went to meet them, then led them in the opposite direction.

"They'll be going for a smoke." Rupert said. "Good that the staff are taking this threat seriously because even though I don't believe there's a killer at large, some of the guests do and this gives them some confidence. We work so hard during the year to put this conference together and I hate seeing anyone afraid."

"There's more." Daphne continued. "I overheard Audrey on the phone to someone telling them to solve a problem and she had just mentioned Stacy and the hand. I feel in my gut that there is something sinister at play, but what? She was upset the police are coming up here but why?"

Probably it was time to ask the lady. And the timing was perfect for she had just emerged from the elevator and was briskly covering the distance in their direction. And she looked furious.

ACCUSATIONS AND CONFUSION

"Daph? Audrey at your three o'clock."

John's words chilled her. There was no real reason why because he was here and so was Rupert as well as the hotel staff. But her last interaction with the woman was still fresh in her mind.

I'll keep quiet. Let the others talk.

"Rupert, we need to speak." Audrey planted herself where she could glare at them all. "Privately."

"Let me get you a seat. In fact, I insist."

John beat Rupert to it, probably as concerned as she was about his earlier heart issues. He placed another chair between Rupert and himself with a smile.

"Why?" Audrey demanded.

"I'll tell you in a minute."

With a huff, Audrey perched on the edge on the seat.

"What do you need to talk to me about, Audrey?" Rupert asked. "Would you like some dinner? I can ask Mandy to—"

"No thank you. I want to complain about Daphne and

would have preferred to do so without her listening in. I think you need to rescind her award."

I'm not going to say a word.

Thank goodness she'd only picked at her meal. Her stomach churned.

"This really isn't the time, Audrey."

"Make it the time, Rupert. She called me a criminal."

John leaned forward. "That isn't what happened."

"Of course, you will defend her." Audrey turned to Rupert. "Can't you see these people are here to stir up trouble? They have a track record of interfering wherever they go and look at this! Sitting here with you and no doubt lying about me."

Whatever are you covering up?

Although her heart was pitter-pattering too fast, Daphne was intrigued. Audrey was deflecting attention away from herself by attacking others. She'd done it with Stacy as well. So, what was she deflecting attention away from?

"Okay, Audrey. Time to stop you. I have some news and it isn't good. I don't have all the details yet but there is a report that a car, which is possibly Darren's, is in the river down near the town."

Audrey's mouth dropped open.

"I'm sorry, darling, but there's no information yet about whether he is in the car. Emergency services are on their way there."

"But...how? It doesn't make sense." Audrey grabbed one of Rupert's hands. "He told me he wasn't going to make it here."

Time to say something. "But Col went down to the carpark to wait for him and the chef was still in the kitchen ready to make him a late dinner. Would he have let someone here know? Perhaps he couldn't reach you or wanted to surprise you?" Daphne kept her voice gentle.

A tear dripped down Audrey's face. Her eyes were wide.

"I thought he'd gone home after the wedding he officiated. He wasn't keen to drive up late even though he knew I was counting on it. Said something about his pacemaker feeling a bit off. It was adjusted a week ago and he's complained a few times. You don't think he...that the pacemaker..." Audrey took her hand from Rupert's and covered her face as a sob escaped.

"Hey...we don't know if he's even in the car." Rupert put an arm around Audrey's shoulders. "There should be news soon and in the interim, there's no point imagining the worst." He planted a kiss on the top of her head. "Time to stop being angry at Daphne and blaming Stacy for all manner of things. What if we all go back to the dinner for a while. Both of us have presentations to do and it might help if we show ourselves."

"This is my fault. I made him feel bad about letting me down."

"That is silly. Darren makes his own decisions. How about you go freshen up and meet us back at our table inside? If you don't feel like presenting, I'll do it." Rupert released Audrey. "Okay?"

She nodded.

"I'll tell Mandy where we are if she hears anything new. See you inside?" He got to his feet and Audrey stood.

"I'll be in shortly."

The woman who returned to the elevator was at odds with the one who'd stormed over. She walked with her head down and shoulders drooping. Despite her feelings about

Audrey, Daphne's heart went out to the woman. Discovering her husband might have been in an accident was clearly a genuine shock. The tears were real.

Audrey could not have had anything to do with Darren's accident. If the poor man's pacemaker had failed in some way, it was purely accidental. How terribly sad this would be if it turned out he was in the partly submerged car.

More and more this was looking like no kind of mystery at all.

"And this concludes the awards for the evening. Congratulations to each and every winner and my personal thanks to those who worked tirelessly behind the scenes to make this happen." Rupert paused with a glance in the direction of the table Stacy had sat at. She wasn't there and he continued. "Too many people to name, so please join me in one last round of applause. For us all!"

Daphne touched the glass award with her name etched into it. Shaped like a wedding cake, it was for 'Outstanding Client Satisfaction'. She didn't quite believe it and intended to write to every one of the people who'd nominated her. Once she found out who they all were.

"Please feel free to stay as long as you like and dance the night away. The bar is still open. When you are ready to leave, one of the staff is happy to see you to your room." Rupert made to step down but once again, Jessica stood and waved her arms for his attention. "Yes, Jessica?"

"Oh, for goodness sake. Would somebody put a gag on her." Audrey muttered loud enough for their table to hear as she helped herself to a glass of wine.

Jessica stepped forward onto the edge of the dance floor and for a silly instant, Daphne imagined her asking Rupert for the first dance. Clearly the events of the evening were getting to her and the idea of getting into bed soon was appealing.

"Earlier you stated that the death threat was some kind of joke, yet the staff are happy to escort us to our rooms? Are we being lied to? Is this threat real?"

The atmosphere in the room changed. For the last hour, with awards and speeches, and a yummy dessert, the guests had settled back into enjoying their evening. Or at least not looking over their shoulders. But Jessica's questions had people glancing at each other and an undercurrent of murmurs ran through the room.

"The staff are there to make sure everyone is comfortable and if that includes walking to your room with you and even checking under the bed, then they will." Rupert smiled. "I am joking about the last bit. Nobody is telling lies but the hotel management has taken the poem, such as it is, seriously because it's their job to do so. State Emergency Services are working on clearing the road overnight and many of you will leave in the morning, fit and well."

"Only many? Not all?" Someone called.

Rupert rolled his eyes. "I'm staying until Monday. Probably others too."

"Have you found Stacy?" This was Jessica, now with her hands on her hips.

"Not yet."

The murmurs rose into a cacophony of voices and as one, Gloria and Ted joined Rupert. Audrey stared into her glass. Nobody could blame her for not being up to dealing with upset people when she had so much to worry about.

John leaned closer. "I understand the association wanting the dinner to go ahead but it seems to have divided people and increased their fear, being in here without answers."

"Not that anyone has any."

Gloria and Rupert conferred for a minute with Ted listening in, then it was Ted who took the podium. He held his hands out, a bit like a preacher about to pray, and the room quieted. Jessica stayed put.

"Friends. Can we agree this evening—apart from the ridiculous note—has been enjoyable?" Ted asked. "I know you want to. After all, how often do you get the chance to listen to my dad jokes?"

Half-hearted laughter and a few nods.

"Without doubt this conference has been our most eventful. A storm. Trees down. And someone trying to spoil the awards tonight. How about we enjoy some dancing and make it clear we aren't about to let anyone ruin our special night?"

Ted was an impressive speaker. Confident but not loud, and careful to highlight the good and minimise the bad. As people visibly relaxed it was obvious why Rupert had asked Ted to step in for him. The lights dimmed, a popular seventies dance track came on, and the first keen dancers took to the floor. Jessica didn't move and Gloria made her way through the gyrating bodies to speak with her. It only took a minute and then Jessica returned to her seat and Gloria joined Rupert and Ted as they came back to the table.

"I think I might have that glass of wine now." Rupert slumped in his chair and ran a hand across his forehead. "Thank you, Ted. And Gloria."

"They're frightened." Gloria said. "Same as I was. And

Jessica is egging them on which is annoying. Best thing for us all is to shut things down in an hour and let people lock themselves into their suites. Might give them a sense of control and security."

It all was surreal. Watching people dance and laugh while outside of this room, a tragedy was unfolding. She didn't want to be here anymore, among the tables and music. She wanted some fresh air and quiet and a chance to think.

"Feel like a walk, doll?" John asked.

"Mind reader. Yes, please." She reached for her handbag as John stood and picked up her trophy.

"You're not going?" There was alarm in Rupert's eyes.

"We'll take the trophy back to the room then I might show John the view from the roof. I'm only a message away."

"Okay. Yes, of course. But just...well, take extra care."

Daphne planted a kiss on his cheek. "We will."

He grinned and nodded.

The music changed to a ballad and as they left, Gloria and Ted were heading for the dance floor. Rupert had moved next to Audrey and they were deep in conversation.

John took Daphne's arm as they left the elevator. She'd said nothing since leaving the table when he'd sensed she'd had enough of the artificial environment of forced enjoyment back at the dinner. He certainly had.

"How good is this trophy, doll?"

Finally, a real smile from her.

"And well deserved, Daph."

"I wouldn't go that far." She said. "While it was lovely for people to nominate me, I'm only memorable because of the bad things which happened to, or around them. If those things hadn't happened, nor would this trophy and I'd rather their experience with me had been less exceptional."

"Don't agree. They may still have nominated you, without the peripheral events."

As they neared their suite, Daphne located her key. "I'm beginning to feel as if I attract negative events. This is three terrible occasions in the past few months when people have died or gone missing. No wonder that woman blamed me!" Her voice quivered with emotion and John gently took the key from her.

"Time to get you inside, my sweetheart." He unlocked the door and held it open for her. "I might make us a cup of tea."

"I'll be right...back."

Daphne hightailed it to the bedroom and then the bathroom door clicked shut.

With a sigh, he set the trophy down on the counter and prepared tea. He missed Bluebell at this moment. Their teapot and cups. The quiet of the caravan's interior. What a peculiar weekend this had become.

When Daphne emerged, he had tea ready and was sitting at the table near the window. Her eyes were brighter than normal but she smiled. Knowing her, she'd freshened up and given herself what she referred to as a 'pep talk' by reminding herself of her good points. Of which she had many.

"Sorry about before." She sank into the seat. "All got a bit much for a minute."

"Let's sit for a while and enjoy our tea. I've missed doing this."

"No tea up at the river?"

"Plenty. But no Daphne." He grinned.

"And no Daphne-related problems!" she frowned. "I'm not being down on myself, love, simply stating a fact. There are some problems here and one way or another, I can't be like the other guests and not do something."

"The other guests didn't have a note slipped under their doors."

"True. But I don't know if any of that meant anything."

John didn't understand. "Any of what?"

"The note. Or notes. The fountain. Even Stacy disappearing. I'm wondering if it was all about getting attention. Either to or from something else."

"I'm listening."

IDEAS AND CONCLUSIONS

As it was, they decided to venture onto the roof to talk. The tea was nice but Daphne longed for fresh air and although the balcony would have done, showing John the rest of the hotel was something she'd been looking forward to doing.

The hallways were quiet.

As they waited for the elevator the music from downstairs drifted up.

Out on the roof, she drew in a long breath of the night air. The restaurant was still open and she recognised a small group sitting around a table as members of the association.

"I wonder if they got as tired of all the accusations as we did." She said.

"Or they are planning a coup. Some pretty serious conversation going on."

He was right. There were three couples and one person was taking notes as another waved their hands about during an animated discourse. "Well, if they are good luck to them. Rupert and Gloria are steady at the helm and I wouldn't be voting anyone else in. Some of the others though..."

She led the way to where she'd sat the other night. Was it really only twenty-four hours ago? So much had happened.

No wonder I'm exhausted.

For her body, this was true. But her mind refused to quieten down.

They leaned against the brick balustrade. Here, it was peaceful and the air was warm enough to be comfortable. For a while they gazed out over the grounds and then wandered to the other side where the view, during the day, would be breathtaking. Lights from the local town twinkled a long way down.

"I wonder if they've got the car out of the river." John said. "Terrible thing to happen."

"It might take a while. With the SES trying to clear the road who knows how many spare units there are. For that matter, shouldn't the police have arrived by now?" It had been more than the hour or two expected for them to hike up.

Lightning flashed in the distance.

"I'd love to capture that." John reached for his phone and draw his hand from his pocket with a frown. "Oh. Forgot I had this."

It was a round, flat magnet.

"Where did you find that, love?"

"Housekeeping found it in one of Rupert's pockets when they cleaned his jacket."

"The red one?"

"Yes. Said it was in his top pocket." John said.

"But that would affect his pacemaker. Well, maybe it isn't strong enough but why would he risk such a thing?"

"He didn't. Asked me to hang onto it because he didn't want it near him. He's careful of his phone as well. Keeps it away from his chest."

How odd.

"You take some photos. I'm going back to where I sat last night to see if I can remember some things."

"I'll come with you."

"There are plenty of people up here so take your time. I won't go anywhere." She appreciated his concern but had no intention of prowling around in the dark or going anywhere she shouldn't. Once he nodded, she returned to the table and stared at it.

"Rupert was here. Stacy was there. And me."

She sat in the same seat. From here she'd seen Audrey toast Darren for not finding his way up the mountain so she must have had a call or message from him to say as much.

Stacy had gone in search of another drink and been disappointed. But she'd not been gone long.

Rupert's jacket had been on the back of his chair.

She went to the elevator and looked back. He'd been leaning against the balustrade staring into the night. His jacket was still on his chair when she'd left.

"Daph?"

"I'm here."

They met halfway.

"I was thinking about Rupert's jacket and remembered it was on the back of a chair when I left with Stacy. He'd stood up to look at the grounds below. Audrey and the people she sat with were at their table but almost everyone else was gone. I think the restaurant was pretty much closed as well."

"Are you thinking he accidentally left his jacket here and someone took it?" John still held his phone. "Shall I take some pics of the roof?"

"Could have used you last night." With a smile, she slid her arms around his waist. "I wouldn't worry now."

"Which reminds me...I want to upload the photos from the fountain to the laptop. Too hard to see the details on this screen." He planted a kiss on her lips. "Have I told you how beautiful you are? I love what you do for this dress."

"I love you, John Jones." She kissed him back. "We need to come back here when there isn't a conference."

"Couldn't agree more."

There was a noise...voices. Yelling.

They rushed to the balustrade and peered down. Trudging along the driveway on foot were two figures. One of them struggled beneath the weight of a large bundle in their arms. No, not a bundle. A person.

Staff ran from the front of the hotel, flashlights darting here and there as they covered the distance.

"Are those police?" Her eyesight wasn't what it used to be, but she was certain the figures wore police jackets. And yes, police belts and backpacks. "Who are they carrying?"

John had his camera trained on them, zoomed in as close as possible. "You might want to take a look." He held the phone on the police.

It was a woman, her head against the chest of the officer, who looked utterly exhausted but kept her gripped tight in his arms. One of the staff reached him and they transferred her to his arms. Her face—covered in mud and eyes closed—was there on the screen for an instant. And the glittering of the parts of her clothes without mud confirmed it.

Daphne gasped.

"Am I right?" John asked.

"That is Stacy!"

They took the stairs to the foyer, reaching there as the police officers arrived with the staff. The man with Stacy went to one of the sofas and carefully lay her on it while the officer who'd carried her looked around. He was filthy from head to foot.

Mandy pushed a stool from behind the counter with a quick, "Sit. We'll get you to a bathroom to clean up momentarily."

Daphne dropped to her knees beside Stacy and brushed the muddy hair back. "Stacy, dear. It's Daphne Jones. Can you hear me?"

"She'd been unconscious since just after we found her, ma'am."

The other police offer squatted next to her.

"I'm Constable Leon Finnegan. Leon. Is there a medical officer or the like here?"

Mandy overhead. "On it!" She sprinted away.

"Where did you find her? What happened?"

Leon was young. Early twenties. His partner, who still looked wiped out, wasn't much older.

"Are you related to this lady?" Leon asked.

"No. But I know her. Stacy Chester. Oh, John, would you find Rupert and Gloria?" she took Stacy's hand. "She's icy cold. Can we get a blanket?"

"That would help. We had to cut through dense bush to get around the fallen trees and we heard her calling for help. She had fallen and hurt her ankle. We were almost at the top so came here rather than try to descend with her but the ground was pretty rough."

Mandy returned with blankets and towels. "Someone is coming. We have an ex-nurse on staff. Along with a handful of the staff she went to rest to swap with some of the others later on. With all this chaos and worry..." She handed towels to both police officers. "There's an empty staff room which we'll show you to. I think we can loan you both some dry clothes and get housekeeping to look at yours. But at the least you can go and dry off. Take a shower if you want."

Leon straightened. "Thank you very much. I'll stay here for now but Constable Patterson would appreciate a chance to clean up."

"If you'd like to come with me, then?" Mandy led the way, the other officer casting an eye behind him as his footsteps left a trail of mud.

Daphne got to her feet to cover Stacy with a blanket. Leon's phone rang and he moved away. "Sorry. Haven't had reception until now."

Rupert and Gloria ran across the foyer with Ted and John behind them.

"Oh my goodness, honey, look at you." Gloria tutted. "Poor girl."

"She doesn't seem hurt other than an ankle."

"Then why is she unconscious.?" Rupert pulled up a chair to sit near her and like Daphne had, he took Stacy's hand.

"There's a nurse here who is coming to help." Unsure what else she could say or do, Daphne stepped back. She wasn't part of the close friendship between the three but already cared about them.

What was Stacy doing out in the bush?

Leon returned, his phone still in his hand and his face serious. "Would one of you be able to take me to Audrey Sutton?"

Oh no.

Rupert's head shot up. "Is there news about Darren?"

"Er, there is. But I should speak with her first."

"He's been my close friend for two decades. He was in the car. Wasn't he?"

All eyes were on the young constable. "I'm terribly sorry. A body has been removed from the vehicle matching his description and with his driver's licence on their person. Pending formal identification, it appears Darren Sutton is deceased."

"Nooo!"

Stacy sat bolt upright, her eyes wide as she threw off the blanket and snatched her hand from Rupert's.

Gloria dropped her head.

Rupert slumped back in his seat.

"I'll find Audrey." John said. "I'm sorry to hear this." He hurried away.

"Thank you, Leon." Poor chap. So young to be breaking bad news. Police might be trained to handle these times but they were people as well.

He nodded and made his way to the reception desk.

"It's all a lie. He isn't dead." Stacy clenched her hands into fists. "She killed him."

It can't be both.

"Stacy, you need to rest." Daphne said. "We thought you were unconscious. Hurt."

"I am hurt. My ankle. And my...my, heart!" Stacy burst into tears, threw herself down, and covered her head with the blanket.

With a small grunt, Rupert got to his feet. He glanced at the form of Stacy on the sofa, his lips in a straight line. Then, he hugged Gloria, his eyes meeting Daphne's over her shoulder. Tears filled her own eyes at the pain in his. What a dreadful way to end what was meant to be a celebration of the association he presided over.

Audrey and John arrived at the reception desk and Leon spoke to her. There was barely a sign of grief at the news. She kept her head high. Her shoulders back. Only her hands, which rubbed up and down her crossed arms, showed anything was amiss. John stood close by. Such a caring man to be there even for a person who'd shown herself to be rude and unkind.

"I'd better speak with Audrey." Rupert released Gloria, who wiped her eyes on a handkerchief. "What do we do? About everyone else?"

"Not get them involved. They can find out later." Gloria said. "I'll ask Ted to wind things down. Send them all off to bed and put this...horrible day behind us."

"I'll stay with Stacy."

"Are you sure, Daphne?"

"Go and do what you need, Rupert. And you, Gloria. We're fine."

"Not fine." Stacy's words were muffled.

"I know, dear." Daphne sat where Rupert had. "Why don't you sit up so I can help you clean up a bit."

Rupert and Gloria left while they could. Audrey ran across and threw herself into Rupert's arms.

"How could she?" Stacy had emerged and glared at Audrey. "This is her doing."

"Here's a towel. How bad is your ankle?" Noticing her

voice had a sharp tone to it, she offered a friendly smile. "The police officer said you'd had a fall."

"I did."

"Whatever were you doing out in the dark?"

Seeing as Stacy hadn't moved, Daphne retrieved the towel and began wiping mud off her hair. After a minute Stacy took the towel back and cleaned her face as best she could without a mirror. "I don't know where my glasses are."

"Check your pockets?"

"No. I was wearing them when I slipped down the embankment. And I'm not about to go look for them so I'll need to get my spare pair." Stacy swung her feet onto the floor and winced. "Ouch!"

"The nurse will be able to help. Are your spares in your handbag? Actually, where is your handbag?"

"In my room. I only took my phone and key with me. Here." She pulled a key from her pants pocket. "I'm sure they're in my suitcase still. It's open in my suite."

"I'll only be a few minutes so please stay here. Don't disappear again, Stacy, we were all so worried about you. John will come and sit with you." Not waiting for a response, she headed toward the stairs via a quick chat to John to update him. He'd been reluctant to let her go alone but nobody else was free to watch Stacy and she promised to call if she ran into any problems.

As she stepped onto the first stair she paused, frozen by icy cold fear shooting up her spine to her neck, where the hairs all stood up. To look back would be to give away her knowledge to whoever watched her. Because she had no doubt somebody was.

Somebody with evil intent.

EVIL INTENT

At the top of the stairs Daphne waited for a moment, listening. Was anyone following her? The sensation from before lingered. But who was watching her? Only the police officer was new and it wasn't him. Everyone else she knew, even the staff. It was a mystery.

And there wasn't time to worry about it.

Key in hand, she located Stacy's room. Inside, it was smaller than the suite she and John were in but still had plenty of room with a main living area, a bedroom, and bathroom. No balcony. The room overlooked the single-story buildings belonging to staff.

The room was, to put it mildly, a mess. Clothes were left on the floor in both rooms and shoes were scattered around, not always in pairs. Half a dozen cups, some still containing coffee, were on the counter. And an empty champagne bottle sat upon the bedside table. Itching to do a quick tidy to help Stacy, considering her hurt ankle, she went as far as to pick up a top before stopping herself. Stacy might find it upsetting.

"Okay, let's find those glasses."

The suitcase was on the end of the bed, with a handbag beside it. Both were closed. Hadn't she said the suitcase was already open?

Inside was half a dozen items of neatly folded clothing. It was at odds with the lack of respect shown to the clothes on the floor.

"Hopefully, the room wasn't ransacked." It was only half a joke.

There was a slight lump beneath the bright yellow blouse Stacy had worn to the first dinner and taking care not to unfold the blouse, she slid her hands beneath the fabric and lifted it. The glasses case was underneath and she juggled the blouse onto one hand to put the case onto the bed. A handful of coins slid out of one of the pockets in the blouse.

Except...they weren't coins.

"More magnets?"

First there was one in the jacket of a man with a pacemaker. Who denied it was his. And here were more of the same kind. Tucked away in Stacy's pocket.

"Daffodils and ducks!"

She had to call John.

No. The police officer.

No. Take photos.

She opened the camera app on her phone and took a dozen images of the magnets, the blouse, and the suitcase. Then, she put everything back the way she had found them. Magnets in the pocket. Blouse neatly folded. Suitcase closed.

Careful to lock the door behind herself, Daphne slipped the key into a pocket.

The hallway was darker than she remembered. Maybe

the lights were dimmed for the evening? She wasn't hanging around to check and picked up her pace even as she began to tap John's number into her phone.

As she rounded a corner, eyes on the screen, she ran straight into a chest. A man's chest.

"Whoa...slow down."

"Oh, Col. I'm sorry, dear. Silly me, typing a message instead of watching where I was going. Did I hurt you?"

"Nah. I'm tough. Did you take a wrong turn? I thought your suite was in the far corner."

"It is. I came to get St...something for someone. Are you here to check the lights in the hallway?"

He nodded but for an instant, confusion crossed his face. "Actually, I will check the lights but I'm also fixing a window. Mandy just dumped it on me so I'm going to do that before the guests begin leaving the dinner." He scowled and tapped the keys on his belt.

"Do you normally fix things?"

"I just do whatever Mandy tells me. She's the boss. At least for now." He started off again. "Gotta go. Watch your step around corners."

"Did you see Stacy is back? The police officers found her."

He turned back with a nod. "Good news. Not so much about Mr Sutton."

"Did you know him?"

"Met him a few times at conferences and when he visited with his wife a few weeks ago. I'd better fix this window before Mandy yells at me again."

Can't imagine Mandy yelling at anyone.

Col didn't like Mandy. Hadn't Audrey made some comment about some of the reception staff being difficult to deal with? What a shame to work in an environment you didn't enjoy. She'd been lucky almost her whole life to work side by side with John. Real estate had its moments, but never between the two of them.

"There you are." John was at the bottom of the stairs, his face lined with worry. "Everything go alright?"

"We have much to discuss. But first, would you mind taking these glasses to Stacy." She held out the glasses case.

"What are you going to do?" John took the case.

"Offer my condolences to Audrey."

The other woman sat opposite Constable Patterson who had cleaned up and wore a mix of clothing. Audrey held a steaming cup of coffee. On the other side of the foyer, a staff member inspected Stacy's ankle.

"We'll keep you informed of any developments, Mrs Sutton." The officer said.

"Not that it matters now. It won't bring Darren back." Audrey glanced up as Daphne reached them. "I thought you'd retired for the night."

"Just running an errand. I want to convey our condolences for your loss. John and I are so sorry to hear about the dreadful accident."

Audrey blinked a couple of times in rapid succession. "That is kind of you both. Constable Patterson just told me he might have died before going into the river. There wasn't enough water in the car to have been the cause and there were no signs of braking on the road." She sighed. "His heart. He'd been telling me his pacemaker wasn't quite right and had an appointment with his specialist next week."

Unsure what to say, Daphne patted Audrey's shoulder.

"I'm sorry I said your cookies were awful." Audrey said. "Try adding more butter and a bit less sugar."

Now she really didn't know what to say. But Audrey had turned away to stare at Stacy, who was whimpering as her ankle was bandaged. She'd put her spare pair of glasses on and clutched the blanket like a lifeline.

John waited for her part way and just as she reached him, the doors to the conference room opened and people began to leave. He took her arm. "Shall we go outside while they disperse?"

It was good to leave the hotel, once they promised the staff member at the door that they'd stay in sight of the building and not be long. They walked for a couple of minutes and found a bench, where they sat. There was lightning in the sky again and it looked as if the storm was heading back toward them. After everything that had happened, Daphne couldn't muster up any feelings of fear about it.

"Audrey apologised."

"I beg your pardon?" John said.

"She did. For what she said about my cookies, and she even gave me a hint on how to improve them."

"I see. But they are great already, doll."

With a smile, she put her hands on either side of John's face. "They're not great. I still use my mother's recipe and never once questioned it. But I'm ready to move on and explore new ways to make them nicer. Much nicer."

Poor John. He was so supportive of everything she did and there'd been moments recently when she'd had the feeling he was being polite rather than telling her directly that she wasn't the world's best baker. His eyes gave nothing away so she kissed him.

"Thank you for loving me no matter what."

His face relaxed and he squeezed her in a warm hug. "It goes both ways."

Time to show John what she'd found.

What an amazing woman Daphne was. Always something new to surprise him and the revelation about the cookies was huge. How often he'd come up with a plan of how to raise the subject and then never did for fear of hurting her feelings. He remembered the cookies her mother made and somehow, she'd connected some dots and had made a decision to erase them. Another big step forward.

"I don't know where to start." Daphne nudged him. "Stop staring at the sky. We need to get to the bottom of this."

"Sorry. The bottom of what?"

"Do you still have that magnet?" she asked.

Funny thing to ask about.

But he pulled it from his pocket and held it on his palm for her to see.

"As I thought! You'll never guess what I found in Stacy's suitcase." She tapped on her phone. "First of all, her room looked like it was ransacked with clothes and shoes and coffee cups all over the place. But in her suitcase, where she'd said I'd find her glasses case, it was neat and tidy. She'd folded several items of clothing and when I moved one in order to retrieve the case, these fell out."

He took the phone from her and zoomed on the image. "More magnets."

"Seven or eight of them. They were in the pocket of the

blouse she wore the first night. The night she said she saw the body in the fountain."

Goosebumps rose on his arms.

"Let me get this straight. Housekeeping found a magnet in Rupert's jacket pocket. The jacket you saw in the fountain. And Stacy was there, wearing the blouse you just found more magnets in?"

Daphne nodded.

"Rupert is careful about protecting his pacemaker. I imagine anyone with one would have to avoid certain things which might interfere with its working and it made no sense for there to be a magnet in his jacket pocket. Where are you going with this?"

"I honestly have no idea. I think I need to show this to the police but I'd like to think she has a good explanation."

Daphne was way too kind. Raindrops landed on his head and he got up, extending his hand to her. "Time to go back."

On the way, she told him about seeing Col upstairs and his scathing comment about Mandy.

"Not easy to be in charge of something like this." He gestured to the hotel as they neared it. "All credit to Mandy for how she looks after the guests."

"It is a beautiful place. And would be ideal as a wedding and honeymoon destination but I wonder whether with Darren passing away, Audrey will reconsider her plans."

Her plans? He must have looked confused because she gave him a little smile. "Earlier in the evening she started to say fixing the internet coverage would be one of the first things she'd do when...and then she stopped herself."

"Ah, yes. You asked if she was buying the place and she stormed off. I thought at the time it was a peculiar reaction to an innocent question. But you don't know that is her plan?"

"Not at all. Purely speculation. A gut feeling."

And Daphne's gut feelings were better than most people's careful calculations.

"And what is your gut feeling about Darren's accident?"

"I'm not ready to talk about it yet. I have some thoughts. And feelings."

Daphne was in full sleuth mode and if he planned on keeping up, he needed to pay close attention.

DAPHNE'S GUT

Once again, the foyer was almost empty. A few guests lingered, sympathising with Audrey. The two police officers, now both in mismatched but clean clothes, conferred with Rupert, Mandy, and Col at the reception desk.

"Shall we see if Leon is free?" John asked.

Stacy had pushed the blanket aside and sat with her feet on the ground, holding a glass of wine someone must have brought her. "Daphne, Daphne, you're back. Please sit with me." Stacy's voice wobbled and her eyes were red-rimmed.

"We can see when he's free from over there." Daphne wasn't about to miss the chance to let Stacy talk and when they got to her, she gave them a tiny smile.

"My ankle is okay. Just a bit bruised but it hurts. I hurt all over. And I have scratches down my arms from the bushes I grabbed at." She showed her arms. "This has been the worst night of my life."

And Darren's.

"I'm sure your arms will heal fast and your ankle. Is there anything we can get you?" She sat beside Stacy on the sofa and John took the chair which was still pulled up nearby.

"You've done heaps already. I'm sorry I hid under the blanket but I was so shocked about...Darren. I can't believe he's gone because I always hoped..." Stacy spoke quietly with half an eye on Audrey across the room. "She doesn't even look upset."

"We are very sorry for the loss of your friend. When was the last time you talked to him?"

Stacy tore her gaze away from Audrey. "Oh. The other day." Her hand went to her heart. "He phoned to make sure I was attending the conference. So sweet of him. But before I could answer his phone cut out. He sent a text message to apologise once he went home. His battery had gone flat. Here, I'll read the messages to you." She opened her phone.

About to say it wasn't necessary, Daphne's gut told her otherwise with a small tingle of anticipation. Was she onto something which might help?

"I don't want you-know-who to hear. You read them to yourself." Stacy gave her the phone.

After exchanging a quick glance with John, she read the messages.

Darren: Darn phone battery! Home now and charging up. What days are you there for?

Stacy: Mine does that all the time. You can phone if you want. Arriving Friday and leaving Sunday. Or Monday. Depends. ☺

Darren: Better not phone you. Audrey is here working on the purchase offer for HHCR.

Stacy: You still aren't keen on it.

Darren: She wants me to sell my share portfolio to finance it.

I'm yet to be convinced but am keeping an open mind because I love the place. Can't wait to be back there.

Stacy: You deserve happiness. A lot of happiness. ☺

Stacy. Still there?

Darren: Yes, darl. Gotta go.

Stacy: You busy man, you! See you Friday night?

Darren: See you there.

"See? He cared about me. And was feeling like he was being backed into a corner."

There was another message. One from Audrey.

She knew she shouldn't look. But she did.

Audrey: He doesn't love you. Or want you. He is pretending he's young again. Same as Rupert so stop chasing men old enough to be your father!

There was no reply from Stacy.

"May I have my phone?"

"Of course, dear. I'm such a slow reader. It sounded as though he planned to be here so do you know why he changed his mind?"

It took Stacy a minute to answer as she locked her phone and put it back into a pocket. "He didn't."

John was kind enough to find coffee for all three of them, although Stacy protested that more wine was a better idea.

Daphne glanced at her watch. Close to midnight. Outside, rain fell but there was little in the way of thunder or lightning. Perhaps it was waiting until she needed to go outside again. Her mind was working overtime and her body was wound up like a coil. Coffee was possibly a terrible idea but it helped break up the moment to give her a chance to think.

Audrey wanted to buy the hotel. She was sure of that based on those text messages. And she needed Darren's financial help. It would be a big decision. But what really worried her was the message from Audrey. It was sent an hour or so after Darren's so she'd discovered the conversation going back and forth. What did she mean by her reference to Rupert? Had there been something between him and Stacy after all?

"Here we go. Three coffees and some after dinner mints." John put a tray down. "Stacy? I can ask for a meal for you."

She shook her head and then finished the last of her wine in two gulps.

John's eyebrows went up and down and he handed a coffee to Daphne with a small smile. He might not have read the messages but he knew her well enough to sense she'd found something of interest.

"Stacy, dear. A few minutes ago you said something about Darren. When I asked why he changed his mind about coming here you said he didn't. But he never arrived."

"Are you sure?"

"Not at all. But he was found deceased in his car outside the town down the mountain. And the mountain road has been blocked off since this afternoon. Not to mention nobody even saw him here and Col waited at the carpark to drive him up."

"You can't trust someone who has a reason to cover up a crime." Stacy popped an after-dinner mint in her mouth, her eyes back on Audrey who was on her feet staring back.

"We're getting company." John said quietly.

Rupert and Leon both had serious expressions. Well,

Leon looked the way he'd done all along, but Rupert's face was...odd. Not the earlier grief. Nor worry. Was he angry?

"John, do you happen to still have the item housekeeping found in my jacket?" Rupert asked.

Daphne's heart sank. Something bad was about to happen.

John located the magnet and held it out. Stacy sipped coffee, disinterested.

Leon held a zip lock bag open for John to slide the magnet into.

"Stacy, I have a question and you must be honest with me." Rupert said.

Her eyes shot up to his and she put the coffee cup down. "Anything, Rupe. You know I'd never lie to you."

"Last night you and Daphne left the roof together after we'd sat out there. Is it true you returned to the roof a little later?"

She did?

That would change a lot of things.

"Why does it matter?"

"Did you?" Rupert's eyes were intense and his hands curled up.

Clearly, he didn't want it to be true. This was deeply upsetting to him.

"Yes."

Rupert's mouth opened and closed and he took a few steps away, turning his back on them.

"I only went to see if anyone was still there. Daphne didn't want to share her bottle of champagne or come for a walk so I thought I'd find someone else. But everyone had gone and the restaurant was closed and in darkness. Why?"

Stacy made to stand and flopped back onto the sofa. “Darn ankle.”

Leon pulled up another seat and sat directly in front of Stacy. “I have a couple of questions.”

“I’m very tired. Can’t this wait until tomorrow?” Her voice had a whiny tone. “Daphne, tell them I need to sleep.”

Daphne will do no such thing. She wants to hear the questions.

“When you returned to the roof and found you were alone, did you find Rupert’s red jacket and take it?” Leon asked.

Stacy’s eyes widened. “No! Of course not.”

Out of the corner of her eye, Daphne saw Audrey inching closer as Leon continued.

“Did you place one or more magnets into the top pocket of Rupert’s jacket?”

Rupert turned back around and Stacy gave him a pleading look.

“Miss Chester?” Leon pressed. “Did you?”

“No.” she whispered. “Why would I have magnets?”

“Daphne.” John was thinking what she was thinking. This wasn’t how she’d planned to do this.

“May I interrupt?” she said. “I’m sorry, Stacy. I really am but I can’t sit here and not show what I saw to the officer.” After finding the first photo on her phone, Daphne handed it to Leon. “I intended to speak to you about this immediately but you were busy.”

He looked a bit puzzled but as he went through the photos, his face hardened. “Where were these taken?”

Deciding it was prudent to put a bit of space between herself and Stacy, she moved to stand behind John’s chair and put a hand on his shoulder. His hand came up to cover hers, giving her the courage she needed to continue. "Stacy asked me to go to her room to find her spare set of glasses. I still have the key." She held it out to Leon. "She told me to look in her suitcase, which is where I found them. But they were beneath that blouse and when I moved it, all those magnets fell out."

"What magnets? Which blouse?" Stacy demanded.

Leon turned the camera to show Stacy an image of her blouse and the magnets. "These look the same as this one." He held up the plastic bag. "Found in Rupert's jacket."

Stacy's mouth opened and closed. Twice.

"Just what did you do, Miss Murder-on-her-mind?" Audrey butted in. "Did you try to harm Rupert?"

Head shaking from side to side, Stacy began to cry.

"Miss Chester, can you explain how those magnets got into your suitcase?" Leon handed back the phone.

"They're not—sniff—mine. I'd never hurt—sniff—Rupert. I love him."

Audrey laughed. "Sure, you do. We all know he had to tell you to stop following him around, turning up at his place uninvited, and making a fool of yourself. And that is when you latched onto my husband."

Leon looked at Daphne. "I'd like copies of these. Can you send them to my phone?"

She nodded and he handed her a card. Her hands shook too much and John took the phone and card and did it for her.

"You need to fingerprint my room." Stacy brushed the tears from her eyes. "I'm being set up."

Maybe you are. But by who?

"Daphne had my key."

On the other hand...

"Stop it! That is enough, Stacy." Rupert's face was red and he raised both hands. "Don't blame Daphne. Or Audrey. Or anyone. I thought we'd moved past the unpleasantness last year to a place of friendship and respect so why would you try to kill me?"

"Kill you?

"Magnets, Stacy. You know I have a pacemaker and that I don't even have my phone near my chest. The note under Daphne's door was meant for me, wasn't it? Trying to lure me out to your death trap and when I didn't arrive, you threw my jacket into the fountain and made up lies about a body." He shook his head. "Shame on you."

By now Stacy was sobbing and wringing her hands. She was either a good actor, distraught at being caught out, or innocent.

And I don't know which.

Col pushed a wheelchair over. "Mandy told me to bring this." He parked it and then kept walking, going through the front door.

Audrey moved it closer. "Hop in, Stacy. Makes it easier to wheel you straight to jail."

"Mrs Sutton, that isn't helpful." Leon said.

Rupert obviously agreed for he put an arm around Audrey's shoulders. "Come on. We'll find some brandy and make a toast to Darren."

They left in the direction of the conference room and everyone fell silent. Apart from Stacy's sobs. John took a folded handkerchief from his pocket—he had a habit of always keeping a spare—and gave it to her.

"Miss Chester, my partner and I would like to do a search of your room. We'd like you to be present."

Without protesting, Stacy allowed Leon and Daphne to

help her up and into the wheelchair. “Daphne needs to be there.”

“Why?” Daphne wanted to go somewhere quiet to think. Like their suite. In their four-poster bed. And sleep.

“Please.”

“She’ll need to stay in the hallway.” Leon told Stacy as he took the handles and began pushing the chair.

She twisted her head to cast a beseeching look at Daphne.

“I’ll be right up.” It wasn’t worth the argument.

John gave her a funny glance. “Not going up in the elevator?”

“I have a little job for you first.”

HISTORY AND HYSTERICS

Not at all certain he understood what Daphne's motive was, John left her at the elevator and went in search of intel. That's what Daphne called it.

"We need more information about this hotel, love." She'd said. "Think of it as gathering intel."

"What kind of information? The size of the estate and when it was built kind?"

"Probably more the 'is this place for sale' kind. Better yet. Are the staff all happy?"

Shaking his head, he kissed her cheek. What on earth did she mean? How could he find answers with her vague instructions?

On the wall not far from the reception desk was a large photograph of the hotel taken from the front with a dozen or so people in hotel uniforms posing on the driveway. As good a place as any to begin. Although the photograph was in sepia tones, the faces of some of the staff gave away how recent it was. He recognised Col straight away, who had his arm around the shoulders of a woman about the same age.

She was broad shouldered with cropped hair and although he'd only caught a glimpse of one person of that description, he knew it was Cherry, who he'd seen in one of the 4WDs.

Mandy was at the end of a row but wore a white blouse and skirt, not her manager's uniform.

"I was the office girl."

John hadn't heard Mandy approach.

"And now you manage the retreat?"

She smiled. There were lines of exhaustion around her eyes. Daphne had said Mandy was up most of previous night and he'd seen her every time he'd been in the foyer, so when did she sleep?

"The owners—that's Mr and Mrs Burton in the middle of the front row—had the right idea about developing this property but they weren't hoteliers. After two years they wanted to go back to travelling and promoted me rather than hire a new manager. I was already handling most of the administration and was studying to get my degree in business management."

"And you live here all the time?"

"All of it. Haven't had a real break in almost three years but for the most part I love what I do."

"Not so much when there are strange happenings such as this evening's?"

She laughed shortly. "The last couple of days have had their moments."

What is Daphne trying to figure out? She said about staff being happy.

"From my perspective, as a first-time guest who is planning to return, you run the place beautifully. I imagine you have a tight knit team behind you."

The smile she'd had since coming to talk with him

faded. "Hearthstone has good staff. Maisie is awesome and does a lot more than run the day spa. We have two chefs here and I can't imagine working without them. Housekeeping is brilliant, and so on. So, yes. A good team."

He gestured to the photo. "Col and Cherry? Apart from collecting guests from the carpark, what is their role?"

"Whatever they want, lately." She put her hand over her mouth, eyes wide. "I am so sorry." Her words were muffled until she dropped her hand. "I wouldn't ever normally say something without thinking so please accept my apology."

"Honesty is a good thing and I'm not on anyone's side apart from the truth so say what you feel. Daphne and I worked together in close quarters for decades and the times we had other realtors or assistants working for us, they'd always say how united a team we were."

"Oh, you are! I've watched you together and can only hope to have such a loving relationship myself one day."

This warmed his heart. And made him proud of his wife.

"Very kind of you to say." He tapped the photo right where Col stood. "I imagine having a married couple working for you has its challenges. Sometimes couples fight when they work together."

Bait the hook.

Mandy glanced around. There was nobody at all in the foyer except the two of them and she nodded as though she had just had a debate with herself and made a decision.

"Col and Cherry were here for a year before me. Col used to work for a big hotel chain and managed an island resort for a while. Cherry was in the army when they met and knows her way around any vehicle. Any machine. Anyway, they were here when I was hired to fix a few issues on the administration side of things. Mr Burton had made a bit of a mess." She laughed with real humour this time. "To say the least! Col was the concierge. I know, hard to imagine, but he was good at it. But he wanted the job which I was given."

Mandy bit her lip and again, scanned the room, her eyes widening as they stopped on the front door. John followed her stare. Col was speaking to the staff member stationed out there. He waved his arms around and the other person, a young man, stepped back.

"Does he do that often?"

"Too often. Don't get me wrong. He isn't a bad person. And when I was given the promotion, he and Cherry were fantastic and helped me. But lately..."

"Lately?"

She shrugged. "They aren't happy here anymore. I'd better see how the police officers' uniforms are going. Thank goodness for our lovely housekeeping staff who are so flexible with their hours. Like us all this weekend."

As Mandy walked away, her head down, he wanted to say something. Find a way to reassure her that she was doing an incredible job under trying circumstance. She glanced at him over her shoulder.

"Hey. Thanks for listening."

Col pushed the front door open and spent a minute brushing rain from his hair. His shirt was soaked through and there was water on the floor around him.

"Long day?" Might as well see what Col could add to John's growing collection of information. Intel.

With a scowl, Col kicked off one boot then the other and carried them over, his socks leaving wet prints on the timber. "Mate, you have no idea. And now its bucketing down again so I can't even do my job without getting drenched for what, the fourth or fifth time today?"

"At least Stacy was found safe."

"Yeah. Stupid woman trying to get down the mountain on foot. Through the bush no less. She's been a pain every time she comes here."

"Every time?"

Col stared at him. "Sorry. She a friend?"

"Goodness no. Only met her tonight. Wet and bedraggled."

"Yeah. Well, she's trouble. Speaking out of turn here but I have no idea why a decent association like Audrey's would employ such a loser. This isn't the first night I've spent out looking for her instead of cuddling up to my wife. But at least her behaviour has caught up with her and she's going to end up going away for a long time."

The glee on Col's face was disconcerting. Glee. And something else.

"You don't seem surprised." John said.

With a shrug, Col glanced at the photo on the wall. "Some people just deserve what they get. Might take a while but it comes. And now I'm going to get into dry clothes. Goodnight."

"Goodnight."

John worked out the second emotion on Col's face. It was hatred.

Even if Daphne had not known which room was Stacy's, the continuing sobs would have given her a decent clue. A couple of other doors in the hallway were open a few inches as people peeked out.

The door to the suite was open and the wheelchair was

stationery in the living room. Stacy had a box of tissues on her lap and held a fistful. Both police officers searched the living room, wearing gloves and taking care to replace anything they moved, although there was a growing pile on one chair as the clothes on the floor were inspected. It was the neatest and most ordered search Daphne could imagine.

"I really do need to use the bathroom." Stacy began to get out of the wheelchair and Leon turned around.

"We need to go in there and search before you do."

Stacy's face couldn't get much redder.

"What if you two go there first and I'll stay with Stacy?" Daphne wasn't about to leave the other woman desperate for a bathroom stop. "Either that, or I can take her to my suite and let her use my bathroom?"

"Oh, Daphne, thank you. They won't listen to me."

"We are listening. We just need to do our job." This was Constable Patterson. "And you can't take the suspect anywhere."

"Suspect! But I'm—"

Daphne put a hand on Stacy's shoulder. "Officers, Stacy is a person first and foremost and requires access to a bathroom. I'm going to wheel her to my suite to use mine and then return her. No deviations and apart from the couple of minutes with a closed bathroom door between us, she won't be out of my sight."

The constables exchanged a glance. "Five minutes, Mrs Jones. Miss Chester? No disappearing."

"I promise. I can barely use my ankle anyway."

"Just say thank you." Daphne whispered as she took the handles.

"Thank you."

A moment later they were zooming along the hallway as

fast as Daphne could manage. "Hold on, dear. Only a couple of minutes."

"You are so kind, Daphne. From the first time we met you've been so sweet and nice to me. And understanding. I really, really appreciate you standing up for me."

I'm taking you to a bathroom. Nothing else.

"You need a chance to wash your face and take a breath." Daphne said.

"I need a few more glasses of wine!"

"Are you up to telling me why you were leaving the retreat on foot, at night? We were all so worried."

"Um. I went for a walk to clear my head. The stuff people were saying at the dinner really upset me. Pointing fingers at me. Everyone seems nice but there's a lot of jealousy because I'm paid and I have access to Rupert all the time."

"Rupert? As president, isn't he available to members if they need him?"

"Not the way I was." She blew her nose as Daphne powered through the lounge area. "We've worked closely to optimise the benefits to the members. I did most of my work from my home office, but we met up weekly to go over things. Usually at his houseboat. Not that I like being on the water, but I did like his cats."

"And your relationship with Rupert... Oh, I really don't mean to pry..."

I really do mean to.

"You can ask me anything. We are close friends. Nothing more. And even though he, well, he got upset with me and let Audrey say those nasty things? There never was any issue. Not ever."

"It did surprise me."

"He's in shock. Darren was his friend for something like

twenty years so of course he's distressed. We both are." Another sob.

Enough already. "Almost there!"

With a turn of the key, Daphne had the door open and Stacy took over, using the hand rims on the wheels to get to the door of the bedroom.

"The bathroom is through here." She helped Stacy up and between the two of them, they got her to the bathroom. "Okay on your own?"

"I'll hop."

After closing the door, Daphne went to the French doors. Outside, the rain had eased. She'd have liked to open the doors and let some of the warmish night air into the room but it would have to wait. The bed called to her. Inviting her to climb into the sheets and close her eyes for a while. What a mess this day had been. The last twenty-four hours for that matter. Surely nothing else could go wrong before bedtime?

"Oh no!"

The bathroom door opened and Stacy, who looked much fresher, grinned. "The window is too small to climb out."

Daphne had to laugh and Stacy joined in. But the younger woman's laughter turned back into tears and by the time she flopped into the wheelchair, her cheeks were wet again.

"Here's another box of tissues, dear. You are exhausted and hurt and have had a loss so no wonder you are emotional."

"Why is this happening, Daphne?" Stacy cried. "I would never harm Rupert. Nor anyone."

"Let's get you back to your room before those gentlemen come looking." Daphne pushed the wheelchair out of the suite and locked the door before walking at a much slower pace than the trip over. "You don't tell me what made you try and leave the estate?"

"I heard Col and his team." Stacy blew her nose, getting herself back under control. "They had flashlights and were joking about finding me and throwing me in the fountain to teach me a lesson. Gave me a scare and I took off. Next thing I knew, the ground slipped beneath my feet and I was rolling down a steep embankment."

"I'm so sorry. What a horrible thing for them to say. And earlier you said something else about Col. About not trusting someone with a vested interest? What was that about?"

There was no reply. Just sniffles.

They were almost back at Stacy's room and without doubt, the police would have discovered the magnets for themselves. Whatever happened next, probably there'd be no further chance to ask questions and the opportunity to put the pieces together might be lost. This was about more than the accusations thrown at Stacy. Much more.

"Please, Stacy? I'm on your side."

Stacy looked over her shoulder, her eyes puffy. "Why?"

"I like to find out the truth. And I'm not convinced the police have all the relevant information yet. You need to talk to them about what you know or suspect."

"Col and Cherry? They are involved with—"

"There you are." Constable Patterson came around the last corner. "We need you back in your room please, Miss Chester."

The opportunity to find out who Col and Cherry were involved with was gone as the police officer took the wheelchair from Daphne. Before she could say anything, all three of them were back in Stacy's room.

"In here, please." Leon was in the bedroom.

The suitcase was open on the bed.

"Miss Chester. We have located a number of items in this room which we believe are connected to a possible attempt on the life of Rupert Witherspoon. Once the road is clear you'll accompany us to the local station for further questioning and a team will arrive to process this room."

"Are you...are you arresting me?"

From the grim look on Leon's face that was exactly what they were going to do.

DONE. NOT DUSTED

"Do you mind if I cancel the massages?"

They sat on the balcony where Daphne was nursing a cold cup of coffee. Well, it must be getting cold because she hadn't sipped it in ten minutes or so. John had offered to get a fresh one but she'd just given him a tired smile and said this one was fine.

They'd got back to the suite closer to one than midnight and fallen into bed. He'd have let her sleep in for as long as she needed, but the minute he stirred, so did she.

"Of course, we can cancel. But there's no hurry for us to leave. Mandy said to take our time so I can see if the day spa can push the appointment back a bit." John reached over and rubbed one of her shoulders. "Wouldn't a massage feel good?"

"Maybe. I'll wait a few more minutes before deciding." Her hand found his and squeezed it. "I don't remember feeling so tired and so...flat."

"Last night was hard going. But you can't blame yourself for what happened to Stacy."

"If I hadn't shown those photos to the police. Or given them the notes."

She'd handed those to Leon while the other officer was speaking with Stacy.

He shuffled his seat close, and put an arm around her and she leaned her head on his shoulder with a sigh.

"What choice did you have, Daph? Keep potentially vital information to yourself and risk getting in trouble with the law? Or even worse, let her get away with her plan to harm Rupert?"

"I know. But something isn't sitting right and I'm not convinced she hasn't been set up.

I'm struggling to put the pieces together though and I fear time will run out."

There was a tap on the door and John kissed the top of Daphne's head as he stood. "Be right back."

It was room service.

"Don't think this is for us."

"It was ordered on your behalf, sir."

Not wishing to argue, John thanked the young woman who'd wheeled the small cart up and took it through to the balcony.

"Did you happen to order breakfast?"

"I did."

Rupert stood at his balcony, in his dressing gown. His hair was a mess and he looked even more exhausted than Daphne. But his smile was kind.

"You two were in the thick of things last night and I woke up starving and couldn't bear thinking you both might be as well. There's a selection so I hope it helps."

Daphne blinked rapidly.

Don't cry, doll.

Rupert put both hands on the balustrade and leaned toward them. “Listen, buttercup. It is breakfast not a wake so no waterworks.”

She burst into laughter.

“Better. Now, eat up and when you are ready can the three of us sit down and have a talk about what’s happened? Just text me.”

“Thank you, Rupert. This was thoughtful of you.” John said.

The other man waved and went back inside.

“Remind me to tell him no more calling me buttercup.” Daphne said as she lifted the lid off a plate. “After we eat this of course.”

“He is very generous. I think he respects you a lot, doll.”

“Goes both ways. Oh, are those pancakes under there?”

After what proved to be a delicious and much-needed breakfast, John and Daphne made their way to the roof. Rupert waited at one of the tables, scrolling on his phone until he noticed them approach. He got to his feet, offering his hand to John to shake.

“Thank you both. Please, take a seat. I took the liberty of ordering coffee which will be here shortly.”

Rupert wore jeans and a striped shirt, his hair back in its ponytail and sunglasses pushed up on the top of his head. It was a good look on him. Not that John had enough hair left to grow it long even if he was brave enough to change the style of decades.

“When do you leave?” Rupert asked.

“The original plan was about eleven. Mandy said we can

check out later if we want to." Daphne said. "I'm rather keen to get back to Bluebell and..."

"Go? Leave behind this crazy place you got dragged into?" Rupert nodded to himself. "I feel the same. Except I'm heading back to reporters and chaos."

"Because of Stacy?" John asked.

"Because of Darren."

Coffee arrived and they waited until the server left before resuming the conversation. It was Daphne who had questions and for the first time since they'd returned to their room last night, John saw a glimmer of real interest in her eyes.

"I know Darren is...sorry, was, a member of the association, but why should his car accident put you in that position?" she asked.

He seemed to think about the question, stirring his coffee for a while.

Daphne pressed on. "It *was* an accident?"

Rupert raised his eyes to look at her. "I don't know."

Something changed with Daphne. She straightened and her chin lifted. "So, you believe somebody else was responsible."

"Stacy had no way to cause his car to crash into the river. I've considered every possibility and keep coming up with nothing of any use. Which is why I wanted us to talk. Before the police have further questions."

I have questions.

"My understanding is that Stacy is charged with some kind of intent to harm you, Rupert. Not Darren. Are you of the opinion that she would hurt both of you?" John asked.

"Oh. Great question, love."

"So, here's the thing." Rupert gazed at John, then

Daphne. "Stacy isn't the person the police think. She has her issues...don't we all? But she loves this association with a passion and I can't see her doing anything to damage it. Her job means the world to her and for several years she was the most wonderful person to have on board."

"Until?" Daphne leaned her elbows on the table with the cup aloft between her hands.

"Until she mistook our friendship for something more. My fault. Like Darren, I'm a little flamboyant if you hadn't noticed." He grinned. "Part of my success as a celebrant as I attract couples who enjoy my flair and humour."

"Last night Audrey said Stacy had needed to be told to back off...well, something like that. And you mentioned thinking you'd both moved past some unpleasantness. How bad was it, Rupert?"

"Audrey exaggerated everything. And I was in shock when I heard about the magnets. I'm paranoid about interfering with the pacemaker because, quite frankly, I don't wish to die. Particularly not from something preventable. Stacy was carrying on and all I could think about was poor Darren in the river and her having magnets, one of which ended up in my jacket." He picked up his coffee and drank.

Inside the restaurant, a few tables were occupied but out here, they were the only ones. It made for a private place to talk.

Rupert put his cup down. "Stacy and I had a very quiet and frank chat about keeping our relationship professional. It wasn't broadcasted yet somehow, Audrey found out. The only person I'd said a word to was Darren so you can make up your own mind on that."

"Do you think Stacy held a grudge against Darren for telling his wife?"

"Not in the least. She adored him. And somehow it turned her attention from me to him. And it was right before last year's conference and he did himself, or Stacy, no favours by going out searching for the laptop with her."

Daphne made an odd sound. She turned it into clearing her throat and then busied herself sipping coffee. Something had clicked. Something she didn't want to mention in front of Rupert.

Rupert's phone buzzed. "Audrey is looking for me. Now the road is clear she wants to get down the mountain." He pushed himself to his feet. "I'll see you both before you leave?"

"We'll be here for a while yet." Daphne said.

With his customary wave, Rupert left with the walk of a tired man.

"Did you just say we'll be here for a while?"

"I did. We have a murder to solve."

CLUTCHING AT CLUES

The minute Rupert said the word 'laptop' a whole lot of pieces fell into place. For a minute she mentally kicked herself for overlooking the obvious and forgetting important facts but she pushed that aside. She needed a clear head now.

"We need to go back to our suite, love."

She wasn't waiting around for another minute. John caught up with her at the top of the stairs. "I knew you'd worked something out back there."

"When I kind of gurgled?"

"You covered it well enough to fool Rupert. But not me."

"You know me far too well."

As they reached the lounge area on their floor, Leon came around the corner pushing the wheelchair with Stacy in it. The last Daphne had heard, she'd been given another room for the night and the officers would share shifts outside her door, not that she'd have got far even if she did intend to disappear.

"Daphne! Please don't let them take me." Stacy grabbed

her hand as Leon stopped and pushed the down button on the elevator. “I didn’t do anything wrong.”

There were no more tears. Stacy’s skin was paler than normal and her eyes had dark shadows beneath them. Her foot was newly bandaged and she had her handbag on her lap.

“And you’ll be able to get some legal help, dear. The best way to prove your innocence is to be completely honest and as helpful as possible. Now isn’t the time to hide anything.”

Leon offered a grateful smile as the doors opened. “We have one of the hotel shuttles waiting.”

“Oh. Just so you know, I think Audrey is also waiting for one.”

“No, no! I can’t be in the same one. Please, Leon? Please don’t make me?” Stacy beseeched.

“Mrs Sutton will have to wait for the next one. We need to get you to our patrol car and to the station.” Leon pushed the wheelchair into the elevator and turned it. “No sharing rides.”

As the doors closed, Stacy was smiling widely at the police officer. “You are so kind to me...”

When they reached their suite, they were both still grinning at Stacy’s turn around.

“Wonder if she’s found older men too trying.” John said, holding the door open for Daphne. “Better luck with a younger one.”

“Particularly one who she perceives might help her.”

First point of call was finding her latest notebook and second was sitting on the balcony with it. John got them both a glass of water and then brought his laptop out. “I want to download those photos I took the other day.”

"Good idea, love. I remembered something this morning. About a laptop."

How she'd forgotten was beyond her. Probably being almost caught by Audrey had something to do with it.

"What laptop?" John had his open but his attention was on her.

"Quick version. Audrey did a session which turned out to be more self-promotion than anything."

"For her bridal shops?"

"More for her new wedding hub. The committee gave her permission to showcase it with an offer for association members, but she struggled a bit when people asked hard questions and made a comment about wishing she had the presentation which was on a laptop. And the laptop was with Darren, who was supposed to bring it with him."

Opening the notebook, she quickly wrote 'where is the laptop?'.

"Should we be letting the police know to look out for his laptop in the car?" John asked. "Except, what makes it important now?"

Am I completely off base?

"There's a chance—a very small chance—that the laptop is here. In the hotel."

"And dare I ask why you believe this?"

"Because I saw one where it shouldn't have been."

The expression of defeat on John's face almost made her laugh aloud. Not because it was funny but because it was predictable. He was getting used to this new-found sleuthing of hers and offered less resistance each time.

"I saw it when I was in Darren's room. The one he was meant to have."

"Daphne Jones."

"Sorry. But you knew I was in there. With everything else going on, I had forgotten about the laptop until Rupert mentioned the word and then it came back to me. But I'm probably wrong because I only saw a laptop bag. I didn't look inside it." She said.

"I guess I should be proud of you for restraining yourself."

She giggled and began to list her other observations. John plugged his phone into his laptop to move the photos then began going through them. It was pleasant to sit here in the morning air. Not too warm and shaded until the sun moved around the hotel. Her shoulders untensed a bit as she wrote, reminding her about the day spa. In case Maisie was busy with someone, she sent a quick text message, asking if it was possible to change the time until later in the day.

In seconds there was an affirmative response with a new time.

"Maisie has let me change our appointment to midday."

"Hm mm."

Something had John's interest. Daphne peered around at his screen which was zoomed in on...water? He zoomed out. It was the fountain.

"What were you looking at in there?"

"Not sure. I think there might be a translucent item about the size of a pebble. Probably nothing but a bit of rubbish dropped in by a bird or the wind."

He zoomed in as close as he could but lost clarity.

"There's the barest outline there."

From below the balcony, voices rose and they both looked down. Stacy was in the back seat of one of the hotel's 4WDs, the door closed but window open. Cherry stood near the back watching on while Audrey complained to Leon.

Only bits of the conversation were audible but it was obvious she was cross about being relegated to the next lift down.

"Can you see the other officer?" she asked.

"I imagine he's staying here until the forensics people arrive."

Audrey stomped away from Leon, who climbed in beside Stacy. Cherry followed Audrey, putting a hand on her shoulder, and walking with her for a few feet, their heads close together as they talked.

"They look cosy. I wonder what's being said." Daphne added their names to her list with question marks beside them. "Don't think I've spoken to Cherry at all. I know Col thinks well of Audrey and badly of Stacy."

"That's true. Last night he said Stacy was getting what was coming to her. Said she'd been a pain more than once and he was surprised an association...let me think what he said...ah, an association like Audrey's would employ someone like Stacy."

"Like Audrey's? As though she ran it."

John nodded. "We haven't had a proper chance for me to tell you what I found out last night. Not that it was a lot."

Closing her notebook, she gave him her full attention as he told her about the framed photograph where he and Mandy had spoken about the background of the hotel, its owners, and some of the dynamics of the staff. How she'd excused herself when Col came back inside. And Col's enjoyment of Stacy's situation.

Bit by bit, the pieces fell into place.

"John? Are you up for a short walk?"

It was a short walk. In search of Constable Patterson, they went to Stacy's room which was locked with a 'do not disturb' sign on.

"Either he's having a nap or its to keep housekeeping out." Daphne said. "Reception it is."

Guests were checking out and a line of 4WDs waited outside. Staff ferried luggage out and there was an air of urgency in the area around reception. Three staff worked to process the guests and there were lots of 'goodbyes' and 'see you next time' as people left.

There was no sign of the police officer, nor Mandy. But Col was talking to Audrey just inside the door. They stood close together.

"Daph, look over near the front door." He said quietly. "Tell me there's more than a casual connection between Audrey, Cherry, and Col."

"You're right. There's more to it. I remember Audrey telling Rupert she didn't like the way some of the front desk staff treated her. That was on the first night. I wonder if she means Mandy."

Gloria and Ted finished at the front of the line and came across to say goodbye, with kisses from her and handshakes from him.

"What a shame this weekend had so many unpleasant moments, Daphne. I hope it hasn't put you off our association. We always cover the hotel cost of the recipient of the outstanding client satisfaction award but have never expected to get back so much from one. You caught a killer." Gloria held both of Daphne's hands. "I've enjoyed my time with you very much."

"Not put me off at all. And I feel the same about you."

"Well, I think we need to wait out the front for a driver,

so see you both again." Ted took Gloria's arm and they wound their way through the line.

"Lovely people." John liked Ted and had already arranged a meet up to fish early next year.

"Look."

Mandy headed toward Col and Audrey. She must have been outside and she squinted as she scanned the foyer as John had seen her do more than once. When she reached them, she said something to Audrey then to Col, who folded his arms. Mandy lifted her chin and spoke again and this time he smirked and stalked across to meet Gloria and Ted. When Mandy turned to leave, Audrey grabbed her arm and snapped something at her.

"I know we can't hear from this distance, but do you think we need to rescue Mandy? Audrey is furious."

"Let's try."

Before they were halfway there, Mandy shook herself loose and left Audrey in mid-sentence. Or mid-screech.

"So, start looking for a new job."

They made a beeline for Mandy, who held herself stiffly as if she half expected Audrey to throw something at her. Something more than angry words.

"Are you okay, dear?"

"Um. Yes. Sorry, did you need me?"

"We think you need to stay away from that particular guest. She really isn't very nice, is she?" Daphne said.

Mandy's lips flicked up for a second. "Best I don't answer."

"We get the feeling Mrs Sutton is very friendly with Col and Cherry."

"Quite honestly, yes. It probably doesn't matter what I say anymore because my job here will only last until she finalises her purchase of Hearthstone. The day it happens, I'll be fired and those two will take over." Mandy's eyes glistened. "I love my job and I'll keep doing it the best I can until that happens. Please excuse me." Head down, she disappeared into the office behind the reception desk.

Audrey glared at them across the room. For just a second, John considered asking her why she had a problem with Mandy, let alone with his wife. But the second passed and instead, he found Daphne's hand.

"I think a touch of sunshine is in order."

SPARKLY THINGS

"Of all the nerve!"

Daphne had managed to control her outrage until they walked out of earshot of the guests and staff outside the hotel. Every few minutes a 4WD, packed with guests and luggage, drove off. They'd passed Audrey as they'd left the foyer but it was only John's firm grip of her hand which stopped her having words with the other woman.

"Calm down."

"How dare she tell Mandy, who is so sweet and so capable, to look for a new job. She doesn't own the hotel yet."

"Perhaps she never will."

"Well, I'd like to see her face if she can't buy it. But why wouldn't she be able to?"

They slowed down as the path inclined.

"Expensive things, hotels. Didn't you tell me Darren was going to have to cash in his shares to help finance it?"

She stopped dead. "Audrey needed his money for her project. He was on the fence about it. But what if he'd told her no? What if her desire to buy this place outweighed her love for her husband?"

"I'm not sure I follow where you're heading. The police seem pretty sure Stacy made up the story about seeing a body and it's been pointed out more than once that Darren never arrived. What does Audrey and Darren have to do with Stacy?" John said.

Every time she thought she'd worked this out, logic said otherwise.

"Mrs Jones? Mr Jones?"

Constable Patterson ran toward them from the hotel. He was back in his uniform and carried a phone. When he reached them, he was puffing.

"Everything alright, Constable?" John asked.

"Pat. Please, Pat is good."

Pat Patterson? Or Pat short for Patterson? And why are names so interesting?

He continued. "Do you mind if we have a word?"

"Actually, we had been looking for you earlier, but needed to check something." Daphne said.

"What did you need me for?"

"I may have some helpful information. Or it may not be. But why were you chasing us down?"

"I got a call from Leon. Constable Finnegan. He's arrived at the station and was given an update on Darren Sutton. A rather strange one. A witness came forward to say they'd seen a car matching the description of Mr Sutton's parked between trees not far from where it entered the water. The spot in question is a bushy area between the road and river. Only a few metres wide but pretty dense."

Hidden on purpose?

"It was in the morning, many hours before the car was

found in the river. The witness was jogging and checked the car, worried someone might be unwell. It was empty, apart from a suitcase in the back seat." Pat said. "He forgot about it until news got around town. Sometime between then and when it was found, the car came off the road a hundred or so metres further along, where there's a hill sloping down to the water. No signs of tyre marks. Nothing to indicate braking. And the car was in neutral."

Daphne's heart sped up. There was a tingle in her stomach and the hairs on the back of her arms stood up. This was where it all would come together. The clues. The hints. The speculation. The answers were so close she could almost see them.

John frowned. "Darren's car parked but no Darren, then a few hours later, he's in the car and deceased in the river. How does that work?"

"It doesn't." Pat said.

"He died on Friday night and his body wasn't found until Saturday night. Is that what you are saying?" John asked.

"It is. There is a preliminary time of death as being the early hours of Saturday morning."

"How early?" Daphne almost held her breath.

"Don't know. Before dawn though because of certain indicators. But I'm not the person to ask. And the reason I chased after you both is to ask you, Mrs Jones, if you remembered seeing anything else in or around the fountain."

She glanced at John. What if she had this all wrong? He gave her an encouraging smile and her doubt evaporated.

"Pat? I can only give you my observations and they might help, or hinder, but if you want them, can we keep going? We are heading to the perfect place to discuss this."

"Sorry? Where?"

"The fountain on top of a mountain."

"Do you remember anything more about being out here the other night?" Pat walked around the fountain slowly, gazing into the water.

Still no cascading waterfall. The water barely moved.

"Only what I already told you and Leon earlier, after you searched Stacy's room. My first impression was of something, someone, beneath Rupert's jacket. I thought it was him."

"What changed your mind, Mrs Jones?"

"Please just call me Daphne. I much prefer it." she smiled at the young officer. Having lived her life in small towns, she had little time for formality, certainly about herself. She was Daphne, or Daph, to everyone who knew her.

"Why didn't you check beneath the jacket?" he asked.

"I've asked myself that over and over. Had I done so, then Stacy might not be in the mess she is."

Pat stopped his visual exploration of the bottom of the fountain and looked at her. "There was a fair amount of physical evidence pointing to her having placed a magnet or magnets into Mr Witherspoon's jacket. The notes you provided showed her intent to lure him here. And she has now admitted she wrote both of them."

John cleared his throat. "Only one. The second note is an apology for getting his room number wrong."

"Covering her tracks. Allegedly." Pat shrugged. "You

went for help and brought Rupert back. Earlier, you mentioned he'd been shocked to find his jacket here."

"Annoyed, I think was my word. He has several expensive jackets and thought it was ruined by being in the water. When he and I arrived here, we were alone. No sign of Stacy. He pulled his jacket out and laid it on the grass. She ran over from the corner." She pointed. "For some reason she was convinced the body was taken in that direction."

Pat tapped on his phone. "Terrible coverage. Ah...there we go." He showed them a map of the property, pinching the screen to find the English garden. "Okay. This is interesting." He glanced toward the corner. "If I'm reading this right, about ten metres from the corner there is a track wide enough for a vehicle. It links back to the main driveway..." he moved the map on the screen. "Here. Hm." It was within sight of the hotel.

Her stomach lurched and she reached out a hand to John.

"Daph?"

"I think I know what happened. Or some of it. I should never have left poor Stacy on her own."

"Would you like to sit?"

"No, thank you. I'd like for us to find something. In the bottom of the fountain." She pointed to the water. "I'd like for us to locate a diamond."

He had the world's smartest sleuth as his wife and he couldn't be prouder.

For long minutes, he and Pat stared at the water searching for the tell-tale glint from the photo of the object on his phone. While they did that, Daphne disappeared with a cryptic comment about fishing.

"Does she do this often?" Pat had his hands in the water, gently feeling along the bottom.

"Find connections?"

Pat laughed. "I was going to say does she play amateur sleuth often? But that will do."

"Yes to both. She has a knack of seeing the big picture and then the fine details. Like being really good at jigsaw puzzles."

"Is she?"

"Nope. She's terrible at them."

They both laughed.

The water was cool on John's hands as the sun rose above them. Soon it would be uncomfortably warm and with the rise in humidity, no doubt another storm would brew later today. When it did, he would have Daphne and Bluebell far away from here. She had no commitments for a fortnight and it was about time they went home, at least for a few days. Let her sit on the beach in Rivers End and catch up with their friends.

"Have you found it yet?" Daphne puffed a bit. She must have walked fast to get to the hotel and back in such a short time.

"What have you got there?" Pat asked.

"Never been fishing, young man?" John grinned.

Daphne had one of his fishing nets. The smallest one with the tightest mesh.

Clever, clever cookie.

He kissed her cheek. "Perfect."

"Well, thank you. But I haven't even straightened my hair yet!"

They both laughed as Pat joined them.

"Ready to go diamond fishing?" John asked him.

While the men played with the net in the fountain, Daphne sat on the stone bench from the first day, running through every second of that night in her head.

What had she forgotten?

When she'd walked here looking for Stacy, she'd felt someone watching her. But who? And had that person followed her to the garden?

Or were they a lookout?

Had other people been here when she'd arrived? Hidden against the long and dark hedges, or behind statues? A shiver went down her spine. Stacy might have been in terrible danger if she'd accidentally stumbled upon a fresh murder.

So might you.

It didn't bear considering.

Then there was the matter of the water.

Daphne returned to the fountain. "Any luck yet?"

"Not yet." Pat concentrated on the water as John moved the net along the bottom.

"John has super sharp eyes. Maybe if you change over for a bit?"

"Fair enough." Pat didn't seem offended as he took the net from John.

"How deep do you think the water is?" she asked.

"About a foot. Eighteen inches max. Why's that?" John answered as he watched the slow and steady motion of the net.

She mentally gauged the depth of a human male's torso lying down.

"Deep enough for a normal sized body to be mostly submerged I imagine. And if a jacket was over them, it would float, or at least, the arms would."

"If you are asking if a body could have been in the fountain and covered by this level of water, then I believe it could." Pat said. "Whether it was is another thing."

"I remember Rupert standing in the fountain to retrieve his jacket. The water almost touched the hem of his dressing gown and he is fairly tall. Actually..." she retraced her steps of the other night, going around the fountain flashing the light from her phone into the water searching for the body. "Oh. I'd forgotten."

Both men glanced up.

"I just remembered when Rupert and I were here I found a strip of the bricks which were soaking wet. It was on this side, facing that corner. I think that is why Stacy went there looking because when she couldn't catch up with me to ask me to look for her glasses, she came back here, only to find the body missing. She either saw someone disappearing into the corner, or figured the body was carried away in the same direction."

"Pat...a bit more to your left. Slowly." John's face was as close to the water as it could be without touching it. "Stop for a sec." His hand snaked to the bottom and he gently moved it back and forth. "Now!"

With a sudden flick of the net, Pat scooped fast, lifting the net from the water in one movement.

"Did you get it?" Daphne couldn't see as Pat and John worked together to extricate what they'd found. If she was right...

"Ah. Look at this."

On the palm of his hand, John held a small, multi-faceted diamond. Under the sun it sparkled as droplets of water slid off its surface.

"You are both amazing."

Pat opened a small zip lock bag. "It looks like a diamond, not that I'm any kind of expert, but I don't understand the significance. Is it from a ring?"

"Not a ring. But we're going to have to move fast now." To prove her point, Daphne was already on her way. "We have to stop her leaving with the evidence."

WHEN DIAMONDS AREN'T A GIRL'S BEST FRIEND

Daphne was near the tennis courts by the time they caught up with her. Shoving damp feet into shoes wasn't easy and both men then had to jog.

"Do you know who she means?" Pat puffed.

"Audrey is my guess."

John glanced at his watch. Audrey had wanted Cherry to drive her down the mountain but Cherry had taken Leon and Stacy instead. Col was tied up with Gloria and Ted which meant unless Audrey accepted another driver, she'd wait for Cherry to return.

Daphne slowed to let them catch her. "It will depend on how important it is for her to go with Cherry. Or whether she has any inkling we're onto her."

"Wait a second. I mean, can we stop for a minute to talk please?" Pat looked so confused that Daphne nodded and they came to a halt.

From here, the hotel was in view. A 4WD appeared from the direction of the exit.

"Why do I need to stop Audrey leaving?" Pat asked. He

checked his phone, and grimaced as if seeing no coverage again.

"I can't explain it all. But I think you need to check her luggage for two things. One is an earring, missing a diamond. It went missing between her wearing it to dinner on Friday night and morning tea Saturday. The other item is a laptop computer which according to Audrey, didn't arrive here for a presentation she made because her husband was bringing it with him."

Pat scratched his chin. "Unless I have due cause to search her luggage, I can't touch it. Nor can I stop her leaving."

Daphne's shoulders slumped. "Then she's about to get away with murder."

"Who did she murder, Mrs...sorry, Daphne?"

"Well, her husband of course. Or she helped. But she certainly is behind it."

The 4WD stopped at the front of the hotel and Cherry climbed out and headed into the hotel.

"Constable Patterson. At least ask some questions. Ask if the laptop seen in her husband's room is hers. If she's innocent, why would she object to helping?"

He hesitated.

John started walking and Daphne quickly joined him. "Come on, Pat. You can probably ask the hotel to not transport her. At least not until you have a chance to ask some questions."

"Thank you, love." Daphne whispered.

"I have an idea. And I'm hoping Mandy might assist us."

Daphne had all the clues. Probably all the answers. Oh, please, let there be enough time to persuade the police before it was too late.

John excused himself at the hotel entrance and hurried inside.

There were no other 4WDs around and the foyer looked deserted through the open doors so the guests must have all been transported. Pat, with Daphne right behind him, went straight to the back of the parked vehicle, its door open. It was empty and spotless.

"I wonder if they are always so clean." he said.

"Cherry claimed a guest was carsick and she took the vehicle to town to clean it. But she'd do that if there'd been a wet body in it. I imagine."

Pat shot a look at Daphne and she smiled.

"I'm beginning to see where you are going with this." He said. "This is the same vehicle which got caught in town with the storm?"

"It is. I remember the licence plate. All of them are personalised as HHCR for Hearthstone High Country Retreat, then a number. I saw her drive HHCR03 down the driveway early on Saturday morning."

His phone dinged and he grabbed it out. "Thank goodness. Give me a minute, please."

He dialled and walked a few paces away to speak.

Another 4WD nosed along the driveway. And Audrey was coming her way.

"How sweet. Here to say goodbye?" Audrey oozed confidence and her smile was sickly sweet. "Most of the others left and I'd have thought you'd be with them."

"Not just yet. There's some business to finish first."

Audrey snorted. "What kind of business? Think you've uncovered a crime?"

There was no way Daphne was answering that. She ran her fingers across her lips in a zipping motion. Audrey rolled her eyes and turned her back.

The second 4WD pulled up with Col behind the wheel. He nodded to Audrey and glanced at Daphne before heading into the hotel. A minute later he emerged with some luggage and Cherry behind him, carrying more.

Up close, Cherry was powerfully built. Muscular arms and legs beneath shorts and shirt. She certainly had no issue with the luggage. She gave Daphne an odd look but not so much as a smile or hello.

"Can we get a move on, guys?" Audrey opened the front passenger door and put her handbag in the foot well. "I have so many people to talk to about Darren."

"Mrs Sutton, before you leave, I have a couple of quick questions. If you don't mind?" Pat was back.

"Well, I do mind. Your partner prevented me from leaving earlier and I'm not about to be delayed again. I have a funeral to arrange."

"And I am sorry for your loss. This won't take long."

Cherry slammed the back door and came around to the side. "Hop in. I'll get you back to your car." She put her hand on the door and stared at Pat.

"Cherry? Wait on please." Mandy, with John at her side, hurried to the side of the vehicle.

"What now?" Audrey snarled. "Somebody needs to find Rupert. I want him to see what nonsense you're pulling this time."

Cherry grinned.

"This vehicle is unavailable, sorry. I'll have the keys, thank you." Mandy held out her hand.

"Now listen here—" Cherry began.

"Unavailable, why?" Col demanded.

"I have a valid reason."

"Bull. Come on. We'll take the other car." Col opened the back door as if to get the luggage out.

"No. All hotel vehicles are unavailable. Some insurance issue. Bound to be sorted out very quickly."

Audrey's eyes widened.

"So, you might as well answer my questions, Mrs Sutton." Pat said.

Col uttered an unpleasant word. "Audrey, give me a moment or two. I'll get my personal car and take you down there." He strode away.

"The keys, Cherry." Mandy hadn't moved.

With a similar word to the one her husband used, Cherry took a set of keys from her pocket and threw them on the ground.

Pat scooped them up and handed them to Mandy with a quiet, "Thank you."

Someone has to do something. We can't let Col leave with her.

"I noticed your beautiful diamond earrings the other night." Daphne said. "Pity about them."

"Pity about what?"

"How you lost one of the diamonds."

"I most certainly did not!"

"Oh, but we found the missing piece. That's what Pat was going to speak to you about. If you can identify it then he doesn't have to process it through the station."

Pat disguised the flash of surprise by making his face even sterner than usual, and most importantly, he said nothing although his eyes widened.

"Where did you find it?"

"In the garden. John has very good eyesight and he saw a glint and there it was. A diamond. Lucky, I remembered seeing there was one missing from yours. At least, I think it matches. Or maybe you are better just to take it to the station, Constable Patterson."

"May I see it at least?" Audrey finally stepped away from the car door.

Pat took the plastic bag out and handed it to her.

"Well...it does look like mine. And they have great value to me. Sentimental and monetary wise. Thank you!" She curled her fingers around the bag.

"I can't leave it with you until sighting the earring itself to make sure it belongs in it." Pat said.

"Fine. Then, can I go?" Audrey didn't wait for an answer but moved to the back of the vehicle. "Cherry, please get my largest bag down."

"You shouldn't." Cherry didn't move.

"Let me." John reached in and pulled out a suitcase. "This one?" He lay it down on the driveway.

"Yes. I'd like some privacy while I open it, please. Wouldn't want you to have a shock at my lingerie. If it fell out." She raised an eyebrow and John nodded and wandered away. Audrey unzipped the suitcase and raised the top.

From the far side of the building, where the garage was, a jeep turned the corner.

Heart racing, Daphne edged to where she could see the contents of the suitcase. Once Col got here the chance might disappear.

Audrey dug around, moving clothes to find a jewellery box.

"Here it is." She dropped the top but not before Daphne

saw what she'd hoped for. If she could have fist pumped the air, she would have.

After opening her jewellery box, Audrey lifted one of the earrings she'd worn twice around Daphne. "There is a stone missing. How odd."

"So, you didn't notice this?"

"Well, no. It was there on Friday night. And Saturday."

"Negatory. I noticed the diamond was gone during the lunch break. When you were tearing into Stacy. And me. I almost said something to you then but you were so intent on being angry that it slipped my mind."

Col stopped a few metres away, the motor running, and stepped out. Cherry rushed over and spoke to him. It was a brief, intense conversation which ended with them moving to stand on either side of the jeep.

Audrey turned and looked at them, her head tilted. Then she glanced back at Daphne.

"I'm going to leave now. May I take the diamond, Constable?" She added the bag to the jewellery box and replaced the earring before closing the box. "If you need to speak to me about Darren, you have my contact details already. Col. Cherry. Please transfer my luggage."

As she leaned down to put her jewellery box in her suitcase, Col took a couple of steps forward, his eyes on Pat. Then he stopped again and glanced back at his wife.

"How did you get the laptop, Audrey?" Daphne asked.

Audrey straightened, her suitcase still unzipped. "Okay, I'm done with this interrogation. You are a common woman, Daphne. Not a police officer or even a private detective. A busybody of the highest order is all you are."

"But Constable Patterson is a police officer. Pat, I just

saw that laptop bag in her suitcase. The same one I saw in the suite reserved for Darren."

The other woman's mouth formed an 'O'.

Mandy, who'd stayed back the whole time, nodded. "The head housekeeper confirmed the laptop bag was in Mr Sutton's room on Saturday morning when she went in to check the window. We've had reports of leaks around a few windows and have been progressively improving the seals."

"For goodness sake, this is my laptop. I have two and don't know what you are driving at. When I still expected Darren to arrive, I'd been working in his suite. The balcony has a nicer view than mine. I left it there and then picked it up again once he said he wasn't going to be here." Audrey snapped.

"When did he tell you he wasn't joining you here?" Pat asked.

"Late. I don't know. Col waited at the carpark and he didn't show. I rang him. Or he rang. I can't remember."

"If I search your luggage, I will only find one laptop, then?" Pat asked.

"You have no right to touch my things."

Daphne couldn't help herself. "Have you been up to the fountain recently?"

If looks could kill, Daphne would at the least need an ambulance after the glare from Audrey.

"I haven't been there at all this visit."

"You're certain?" Pat asked in a very even tone.

"You are just as stupid as she is. I said I hadn't been to the fountain or even to that garden on this trip."

"Audrey." Cherry hissed from near the jeep. She was tapping her ear and her head kept making sharp little gestures in the general direction of the path to the English garden.

"What have you done, Audrey?"

Rupert's voice boomed from above and everybody looked up. He was on his balcony, hands on the balustrade and disbelief all over his face.

"Are you responsible for Darren's death? Are you?"

She shrank at the fury in his voice, her eyes darting to Pat, then Daphne, then Col.

"N...no. He died in a car accident."

Pat shook his head. "He died elsewhere and was placed into his car some hours before being found."

Audrey laughed.

Getting hysterical, dear, now the truth is coming out?

"None of this is funny. None of it." Rupert went inside.

"What *is* funny is how you think it remotely possible I had anything to do with my husband's death. I do wish you would explain to me how I managed to get down to the river, kill my husband, somehow get him into his car, then be back here before anyone noticed me missing?" Audrey gestured to her body. "I'm petite. Darren is twice my size. Not physically possible and besides, I was never on my own for the whole of Saturday." She folded her arms with a satisfied smile.

"I'll explain it." Daphne said. She wasn't about to lose this hard-won momentum. Over at the jeep, Col and Cherry had their doors open but were listening. Waiting.

Her legs shook so she braced them further apart. John was too far away for her to feel his encouraging touch but he smiled at her and she drew in a quick breath.

"I believe Darren did arrive at the hotel. Most people were at dinner and most of the reception staff were on their break to take advantage of the quiet time. Darren either came through a back entrance or someone was at the desk who wouldn't say anything."

"Cherry!" Mandy burst out. "Cherry told me I was needed somewhere and she'd watch the front. I was only gone ten minutes."

"Liar." Cherry put a foot into the jeep.

Pat finally seemed to notice the movement around the jeep. He took his phone out and tapped a message.

Rupert strode from the hotel, carrying his red velvet jacket in one hand as Daphne continued.

"For some reason he didn't join Audrey on the roof or make his presence felt. And then later, when almost everyone was asleep, he went to the English garden. Something must have encouraged him to go there after midnight. I heard he didn't sleep well so perhaps he went for a walk. But when he got there, he was murdered."

"Don't look at me!" Audrey said. "I was asleep in bed."

"Stop pretending, Audrey." Rupert held the jacket higher. "This jacket has been a source of many hours of entertainment between Darren and I, and for those who don't understand, it was his originally. I won it from him in a game of poker. He won it back playing blackjack. And so on for years. And I deliberately wore it on Friday night expecting him to turn up and we'd end up gambling over it again. And you knew, Audrey, that although we laughed about it, Darren really wanted it back to keep."

Another piece of the puzzle.

"I wonder if Audrey told him she had the jacket and to meet her at the fountain. Nice and dark and secluded up there." Daphne pondered aloud. "Perhaps with a bottle of champagne to toast the moment, because Col found a full bottle there and Stacy hadn't got one left to take."

Rupert clasped the jacket against his torso. His eyes were bright with unshed tears.

"There was no reason for Stacy to harm Rupert. But you, Audrey? You wanted to buy this hotel and needed Darren's shares to do so. Putting a handful of magnets in the inside top pocket knowing he'd put the jacket on was easy. It didn't require physical strength. Just a bit of deception."

"None of this is true. How would I even have moved his body?" The conviction was gone from Audrey's voice, leaving a waver.

The roar of the jeep's motor startled them all. Col and Cherry were in it as it hurtled past them, wheels on the grass and pebbles flying everywhere as it tore toward the exit.

Pat shaded his eyes to watch its progress.

"Shouldn't we go after it?" John asked.

"Give it a minute."

The jeep had almost reached the gate when the flashing blue and red lights of a 4WD police vehicle blocked their way.

"Please continue, Daphne." Pat grinned.

"It was them! It was *all* them. They arranged to get Darren and keep him busy until late. They put the magnets in the jacket. They killed my husband then put his body into Cherry's 4WD. And she drove down early in the morning once the gate was unlocked and put him into his car and pushed it into the river. I never went near any of it."

"Then why, Audrey, did my husband and this constable fish *your* diamond from *your* earring out of the fountain?"

JUSTICE DONE

"I am so proud of you." John settled into a chair beside Daphne and opposite Rupert around a table in the foyer. "You had all the pieces and put them together."

"Not quite all. Rupert's information about the jacket made a big difference."

Rupert had said little since the arrest of Audrey, Col, and Cherry. He'd given his beloved jacket to Pat, who'd promised to return it to him promptly, but whether Rupert really wanted it back was the question. He'd muttered something about it being a death jacket.

Once Audrey had heard where they'd found her diamond, she gave up. She admitted to having been present at the fountain but claimed all she'd done was ask Darren to go for a walk to ask if he'd decided about the shares. When he'd said he intended to retire, not invest in the hotel, Col and Cherry had taken over. Their original plan, if his answer was not to their liking, was to overpower Darren and hold the magnets against his chest to make it look as though his pacemaker failed. The discovery of the red jacket on the roof had made it much easier as he'd put it on himself and succumbed too quickly to do more than cry out once.

She'd been quick to blame the others, explaining that Col had access to every room and easily planted the magnets in Stacy's suitcase after they'd accidentally left the one in his jacket found by housekeeping. "He even found her key to the awards box and put that death threat in there." Audrey had then demanded a lawyer.

"What about Stacy?" Daphne asked.

"I believe she'll be brought back a little later today. Pat apparently spoke to Leon and they aren't pressing charges against her."

"But everything will change." Rupert said. There was a deep sadness and weariness about the man. "She can't keep her position. Not after so many scandals. And I'm not sure who could take over who would be as passionate about the association as she was."

"Jessica." Daphne suggested. "She asks a lot of questions and her ethics are cast in stone."

"Hmm. Worth considering. I guess you aren't interested, buttercup?"

Daphne took John's hand. "I've worked all my life and now I intend to spend the rest of my days enjoying time with my husband, our caravan, friends, and our family. Being a celebrant is a wonderful add on, but if I need to give something up, it is officiating."

"You won't have to do that for a long time, Daph." John said.

"Rupert? I'm happy to help the association from time to time. I'm happy to help you find a replacement. And I'm happy to call you my friend."

"But?" Rupert smiled as if he already knew what she'd say.

"No more buttercup."

The three of them laughed until Mandy arrived with a tray. She smiled at each one as she placed iced tea onto coasters and a plate of cupcakes in the middle of the table.

"I am so grateful to you Daphne. And John." She said.

"What will happen now? You've lost two staff members." Daphne asked.

"No. I've lost dead weight. In fact, I've gained a lot because those two were undermining me at every turn. The rest of the staff are so happy and I am terribly sorry because I hadn't seen how this was affecting them."

"Will the owners still want to sell? I have a client who is always on the lookout for a special property. One which would be an investment." John said.

"I imagine so. And I'm hopeful I might keep my job after all."

"May I have the owner's details?"

Mandy's smile lit up the room. "You are too kind, Mr Jones. And you, Mrs Jones? You are welcome here any time you want and I'll make sure you always get the best of our suites."

"Oi. If you mean my suite then think again." Rupert grinned.

"I do and there's nothing to think about."

The smile didn't leave her face as she almost danced across the foyer floor.

Rupert picked up the plate and offered it to Daphne to select from. "No calling you buttercup. How about cupcake?"

Daphne stood at the balcony. The humidity and the threat of a storm was gone after a refreshing and unexpected rainfall while they had their massages. Her shoulders were relaxed, if slightly painful, thanks to Maisie's vigorous attention to their tenseness. But her back. Oh my. So amazing. Hot rocks were quite fantastic. Even John, who had been hesitant when they arrived at the day spa, had been glowing in his assessment of the massage.

The property was quiet. There were still police up at the English garden and the guests who remained were either in the pool or playing tennis, or else on the roof.

She loved it here. Despite the terrible events and feeling utterly exhausted, she loved the place. If only things had played out differently. No murderous wives. No evil employees.

"There you are. I got lost on my laptop for a bit, adding some of my river photos to Bluebell's Blessings and when I looked up, you'd gone." John put his arms around her, looking over her shoulder. "Such a beautiful place. I hope my old client buys it and leaves Mandy in charge. We'll come back often."

"I'd like that."

John's presence helped. But she still had questions and still couldn't fathom why anyone would murder their own spouse. She might be good at piecing puzzles together but understanding motives was too hard. Poor Darren.

"We haven't packed yet. I need to get started."

John's arms tightened. "You've done a good thing."

"And I would really, really like to go soon."

"Me too. So, let's go and pack."

Bluebell was probably the best thing Daphne had ever seen. The carpark only had a couple of cars left, including a bright yellow Mustang with the plates 'RUPERTS'.

John did his customary check of the outside and backed the car to hook up Bluebell. Daphne made certain there was nothing loose inside. She'd unpack when they got home. For they were heading home, to Rivers End. They'd stop tonight to have a decent sleep but by this time tomorrow she'd walk into their house. Open their curtains. And be home.

She picked up the one remaining item which needed securing in a cupboard. The snow globe of Rivers End. For a moment she played with it, turning it upside down and watching snowflakes fall upon the town which never had snow. A treasured gift from a treasured friend.

"Ready, Daph?" John stuck his head thought the open door. "We can leave whenever you want."

"That would be now, love." She popped the snow globe into an overheard cupboard. "Let's go home."

ABOUT THE AUTHOR

Phillipa lives just outside a beautiful town in country Victoria, Australia. She also lives in the many worlds of her imagination and stockpiles stories beside her laptop.

Apart from her family, Phillipa's great loves include the ocean, music, reading, the garden, and animals of all kinds.

www.phillipaclark.com

BOOKS BY PHILLIPA NEFRI CLARK

Rivers End Mystery Romances (core books)

The Stationmaster's Cottage

Jasmine Sea

The Secrets of Palmerston House

The Christmas Key

Daphne Jones Mysteries

Till Daph Do Us Part

The Shadow of Daph

Tales of Life and Daph

The Charlotte Dean Mysteries

Deadly Start

Deadly Falls

Deadly Secrets

Deadly Past

The Giving Tree

Doctor Grok's Peculiar Shop Short Story Collection

(A bit of fantasy with a twist of magic)

Last Known Contact

(A gripping standalone crime/romantic suspense

Simple Words for Troubled Times

(Short non-fiction happiness and comfort book)

Prefer Audiobooks?

The Rivers End series

The Charlotte Dean Mysteries

Till Daph Do Us Part

Simple Words for Troubled Times

THREE SERIES IN ONE WORLD

Fourteen books across three series - all connected by characters, themes, and lots of heart...

Rivers End came first. Four main books and two companion stories, revolving around old secrets in a tiny seaside town. It is part historical mystery romance, part contemporary women's fiction, and a whole lot of small town values.

The Charlotte Dean Mysteries are set a few hours away from Rivers End, inland among old forests and striking landscapes. Kingfisher Falls is a town with many secrets and Charlotte -who first appeared in Rivers End - finds herself in the middle of solving them. A mix of traditional and cozy mystery with a gentle romance (or two).

The Daphne Jones Mysteries continue the story of Daphne and John, who were supporting characters in all the Rivers End books and appear in one of Charlotte's. They have retired and travel in their cute caravan, Bluebell, to allow

Daphne to officiate weddings and funerals. With her inner sleuth on high alert there is always something exciting going on. This series is cozy mystery but with a strong sense of family.

Check the **Books by** page or Phillipa's website for the recommended reading order of this world set in the beautiful rural countryside of Victoria, Australia.

Made in the USA
Monee, IL
24 May 2025

18096618R00426